THE TORN CURTAIN

AN INSPECTOR VIGNOLES MYSTERY

British Library Cataloguing in Publication Data:
A catalogue record for this book is available from the British Library
ISBN 978-1-904109-20-4

First published 2009
This edition 2016

The Hastings Press
01424 442142
hastings.press@gmail.com
www.hastingspress.co.uk

Cover design by Bill Citrine. Photos by Stephen Done
Printed in Poland by booksfactory.co.uk

~ Author's Note ~

This is a work of fiction and any similarity to persons living or dead is wholly accidental. However, as real life can always be counted upon to prove stranger than fiction, I have taken the bare bones of reality and fleshed them out with huge chunks of imagination. Three Slovene nuclear scientists really did cross the border into Trieste in 1948 with a suitcase of lira on the orders of Marshal Tito, with the intention of purchasing equipment to start the Jugoslav atom bomb programme. They were captured by the British in Northern Italy and held captive but then, somewhat surprisingly, set free and the money returned. Not long afterwards the Jugoslav atom bomb project was abandoned. The Heroes of Telemark have become justifiably famous, largely because of the film of the same name, and they really did undertake the daring and highly dangerous operation mentioned in this book. The only fiction is the smuggling out of a secret tank of heavy water just prior to the sinking of the MV Hydro.

Women were not allowed to compete in the shooting events at the 1948 Olympiad. In fact they could compete in only thirty-one of the 136 events. Despite the fact that women did shoot in the 1920 Olympics, they did not achieve this right again until 1984. It feels comfortable that Lucy Lansdowne's exploits do not, therefore, compromise the real results of that particular Olympiad. The shooting events were held at Bisley Camp, although spectators were not allowed in for safety reasons.

A lot has been written about the government of Clement Atlee and the far-reaching and innovative programme of nationalisation and social reforms it tried to implement. The National Health Service is the most visible survivor of this fascinating period, whilst our odd mix of private and 'not-for-profit', quasi-nationalised railways are only a qualified success. However, in 1948, virtually everything in the land was under state control.

Locomotives from different parts of the country really did take part in the locomotive exchanges of the summer of 1948, and there were a number of special exhibitions and open days to test various livery experiments. Those described in this book are faithful to those trialled that summer.

The spelling *Jugoslavia* has been chosen over the more common, Anglicised Yugoslavia (the pronunciation is identical) because this makes sense when the word is written in context, and swapping between forms would be confusing.

The town of Opčine is pronounced 'Opcheen-a'. The Italianised version is Villa Opicina (Vee-la Opi-cheena).

A Trieste ove son tristezze molte,
e bellezze di cielo e di contrada ...

In Trieste where there are many sorrows,
and much loveliness of street and sky...

From Tre Vie (Three Streets)
Umberto Saba, 1911

In memory of Glyn Davies
1928–2008

Who was in Trieste

THE TORN CURTAIN

May 1948

The Bay of Trieste was bathed in evening sunlight. The sea was the colour of petrol turning to a silvery-grey and sparkling with a million twinkling reflections as it stretched towards the horizon. Not a breath of wind stirred the lazy drifts of smoke curling from the funnels of the ships anchored far out in the deep, shimmering waters, their hulls indistinct at the transition from metal to Adriatic. To his right, across the bay, stood a fairytale castle that gleamed a bright white, burnished by the warm tones of the late sun, its gardens a verdant feast of green foliage and great tumbles of mauve wisteria against the harsh limestone of its promontory. Below, a tiny rowing boat made ripples on the bay like a surface-skating insect.

Trieste harbour was crowded; the *Molo Audace,* a bare, stony finger of a jetty that extended into the bay, was filled with British warships, all looking spick and span in freshly painted grey-and-black with bold numerals on their hulls, each flying limp Union flags at their sterns and crowded against the limestone walls by rusting tender boats unloading coals and provisions. Fishing boats with their red sails drying in the heat of the late afternoon were jostled against smoky cargo vessels in an untidy profusion of masts, nets, crane jibs and drifting steam within the old harbour, whilst the dusky-black passenger steamer approached the stone jetty of the *Molo Bersaglieri*, returning from Cittanova with its deck populated by Jugoslav soldiers and peasant men and women clutching bags and baskets of produce to sell or barter amidst the bustle and noise of the British Zone. A clanking steam engine pulled a motley collection of wagons along the waterfront, its screeching whistle echoing off the towering bulwarks of the Karst cliffs behind the city.

Private Paul Brierley was looking down from a magnificent vantage point high upon this massive escarpment. He was seated on one of the small, fat stone bollards that ringed the base of a tall obelisk, set within a small clearing of Mediterranean pines and bougainvillea beside the winding road and steeply graded tram line. Before him, the *Scala Santa* fell away in a dizzying drop of worn stone steps, down which an elderly woman, weighed down by bags, was making a slow and painful descent. He wondered why she did not choose to await the return of the little blue tramcar from which he had recently alighted. It would have reached its terminus in Opčine by now, and if she waited just a quarter-of-an-hour it would clank and ring its way back down to the city.

He had chosen to get off here today, rather than continue to the end of the line and walk to the barracks as he normally did. His heart had been thumping the whole way up the tortuous climb, but this was not because of the effects of too much wine the night before. As he sat and looked somewhat disconsolately down upon the city, he was reminded that he had indeed drunk a lot. A tin of NAAFI cigarettes bought you a night on the town without a moment's care for the bill, and he'd certainly indulged his fill and was wondering what he had got himself into.

Another engine puffed along the dock, hustling to collect a fresh cargo of wagons. Rendered so small, it resembled a little toy train. Despite the distance, Brierley could recognise it as the little Italian-built locomotive that leaked and dribbled its way up and down the quays each day, shunting and shuffling the wagons of coffee beans, lemons, newly cut timber and other pungent produce, much as it had been doing for a great many years before he and the Royal Transport Corps had taken over. He'd be on that very engine when he clocked on at 4am the next day. He suddenly felt a stab of something between remorse and longing and wished that he were down there now, shovelling a few rounds of coal in the stifling heat of the cab and joshing and joking with his driver, Curly Lambert, on the footplate.

Why had he agreed to meet those two chaps from the éTergeste? Perhaps he should just continue up the hill to Opčine and retreat to the almost-comforting order and regularity of military life. But maybe that was exactly why he had agreed to stick his neck out and do something on his own initiative. He was sick of the routine, the orders, the bulling of uncomfortable boots and the monotony of army food. He longed for adventure, some real excitement — not just dodging bricks thrown during the frequent riots in the town, but something to make his pulse race. Last night's wine had helped to convince him of that, but its effect had worn off and now he was less sure of his decision. He felt another flutter in his stomach and failed to quell the realisation that it was fear, not excitement, causing it.

Brierley rubbed his temples and squinted into the brilliant sun. This reminded him that his precious Ray-Bans were missing. Pilfered, no doubt, by some light-fingered little bugger in that café last night. He'd been warned that the place was full of thieves, so he should have been more careful. He began to have a sneaking suspicion that one of his two new drinking companions had taken them. Or maybe it had been the lovely Lola. He snorted and gave a little shake of his head. She could have tried harder to come up with a name more original. She was probably called Maria. All the Italian girls seemed to be called that. Still, he'd told her it was a beautiful name and made some other embarrassing comments in the hope of a squeeze. Yeah, it had to have been her, she'd been pretty fresh at one point and he remembered her arm around him and how she pressed herself close in a manner that had been quite racy. It would have been easy enough to lift his sunglasses, and she'd get a good price for them. He laughed bitterly at the irony of probably buying the very same pair back off one of the dodgy stallholders at the *Ponterosso* market.

Resting his elbows on his thighs, he bent almost double and spat into the dry and dusty earth beside his boot, the spittle sending a tiny gecko scuttling away. He lifted his head slightly and watched a young couple stroll in the sun, her head resting on the man's shoulder, her long, dark hair flashing in the sunlight, his hand on her amply-curving hip. He was struck by the girl's sensual figure and how she had a build not unlike the temptress Lola. Now he thought about it, what *had* happened to her at the end of the night? Wasn't he supposed to have had something more out of the evening? He'd bought her enough vino and kept her in cigarettes all night, but somehow she'd slipped away into the narrow side streets of the old town with just a couple of quick, wet kisses, leaving just a lingering scent of cheap perfume and a painful yearning as his only reward.

His new companions, meanwhile, had been slapping his back or trying to hug him — like these foreign types were so eager to do — insistently repeating the time and place of their rendezvous. They had distracted him, and his prize had clattered away on her tottering heels whilst his drunken attempts to call her back had been smothered by dirty laughter, prods to his ribs and heavy arms around his shoulders.

He checked his watch. They'd be here soon. He suddenly felt a wave of agitation and stood up. He pulled the tatty brown manila envelope out of his pocket and weighed it in his hands, brow furrowed. The money was appealing — it was almost a king's ransom — but they'd set him up last night, nicked his glasses and duped him with Lola, so would he actually see any of it? She'd been in on it, for sure. He shook his head slowly in resignation. She'd got him all fired up and excited whilst they'd drunk his wine and talked football. Acted as if they were his friends. Then they'd produced that bottle of grappa and that had really finished him off, and so he'd agreed to their demands, got the permits and passes they needed. But could he trust them?

Brierley paced around the base of the obelisk, barely registering a bearded man pushing a cycle up the last few yards of the steep hill, cap pulled forward against the sun and head lowered with the effort. Brierley stopped and nodded, his head in silent agreement with a decision he'd made. He would leave the envelope tucked under a bush, and that way he could say that he had brought the stuff as agreed, and even dropped it off. He could argue that he'd been called away suddenly and that there had been no time to wait. Yes, that would work. And then, if they went back and found it lying there, they'd still give him the money. If it was missing, well, then that was that. He would owe them nothing.

But he wouldn't do it all again. No way. He'd be out of it.

He glanced around and walked to one side of the steps, where a few orange-flowered oleanders were growing beside a thick, low bush he didn't recognise. The ground was dry and dusty, worn smooth by many feet, but close to the edge some thin grass masked the narrow space beneath the bush. He bent over and parted the dry grass with one hand, and reached forward to place the envelope underneath in the deep shade. He moved it a little, first to one side and then to the other. He wanted it hidden, and yet just visible to someone searching for something they suspected might be there.

Finally he felt satisfied with his work and made to stand up. As he did so, his eye caught a sudden movement, a flash of shadow across the grass. His instinct kicked in and he pulled himself upright whilst trying to twist around and reach out for the arm about to strike him. But he was too late. The cyclist had crept up behind him silently, and the short metal bar smashed into Brierley's forehead, his legs crumpling and head lolling lifelessly in an instant. It was a crude but skilful execution. The man with the shapely girlfriend had swiftly moved in on the act, almost catching his falling body and effortlessly hauling it through the bushes as the assailant lifted Brierley's feet. Less than a half a minute later the cyclist was freewheeling at high speed back into town, the envelope in his jacket pocket, whilst the other man had linked arms once again with his girlfriend. After exchanging amorous looks and a kiss, the courting couple continued their evening promenade along the *Passeggiata Napoleonica*.

CHAPTER ONE

DOWN BY THE STATION

Tommy Dorsey

Detective Inspector Charles Vignoles was enjoying the exceptionally fine weather, relieved he had gambled correctly that morning and chosen to wear a short-sleeved shirt, a pair of old but serviceable cricket whites that Anna had managed to revive. It had been more years than he cared to count since he had taken to the field, if he discounted a shambolic, if spirited, appearance in a Spitfire-fund charity match for the railway police. His navy blazer was slung casually over one shoulder, the usual dark homburg replaced by a newly purchased Panama hat jauntily seated at a slight angle on his head of neatly cropped hair. The ensemble was completed by his ever-present pipe. As it was Saturday and he'd worked only a half-day, he considered this outfit an appropriate alternative to his usual Horne Brothers suit, and a far better one in which to enjoy this gloriously early start to what promised to be a fine summer.

His rectangular, silver-framed spectacles had lately sported a clip-on, fold-down contraption that converted them into sunglasses. Vignoles was pleased he'd splashed out on these, as the pavements were glaringly bright and the windscreens of the passing cars reflected sharp flashes of sunlight. Whenever he looked up, the sun seemed unnaturally intense in the cloudless sky, which was marked only by vapour trails from the four growling engines of an Avro Lancastrian airliner crackling above.

Vignoles was standing outside Leicester's London Road station, beside the cavernous porte-cochère that sheltered the Austin taxis, private motor cars and the horses and gigs coming and going in a noisy bustle and stink of exhaust, manure and road dust. Dappled patterns of sunlight and shadow played over the passengers milling around within the cool interior and emerging from the steep wooden steps from the platforms beneath the wide bridge supporting both this massive structure and the London Road that gave the station its name.

His work for the morning over, he'd spent a pleasant ten minutes or so inspecting the locomotives working this line and noting their numbers in his pocket book. He had been particularly assiduous in his locospotting (accompanied by a gang of well-mannered schoolboys sharing in this new craze that was steadily filling the platform ends of Britain) but his motivation had been driven by something more than just a love of the steam traction engine; he had hoped that this harmless activity would push aside a matter worrying away at his mind like a dog gnawing at a bone.

He could not simply explain away this problem, and the endless churning-over of the meagre facts at his disposal made his head ache, so he was relieved that the Midland engines had provided a temporary distraction. Now, feeling a little more relaxed and with a few minutes to fill until Anna arrived, he was studying the splendid building in front of him.

It was a visual treat, and though encrusted with years of smoke and ingrained muck, the red brick and wide bands of limestone still revealed enough colour to look splendid. No amount of soot could mask the stone balustrading that edged the flat roof-line and the row of stone urns placed at regular intervals, as if along the ha-ha of a great country house. Magnificent wrought iron gates stood open at a pair of tall arches, each with a tiled panel above that read 'Arrival' and 'Departure' in deep maroon letters intertwined with a design of flowers and briers thrown into deep relief by the sun. A short clock tower at one end of the building supported an almost Florentine cupola — Vignoles frowned and wondered if 'Florentine' was correct; perhaps it was 'Italianate', but since he had never visited Italy, let alone Florence, he was unsure. Whatever the style, and despite some of the brickwork having been chipped by wartime shrapnel or frost damage, the old station was a splendid construction.

He had passed it many times, lying as it did on one of the busiest roads into Leicester on the edge of an elegant quarter of the city. However, as he had been a London and North Eastern man until 1st January of that year, Vignoles naturally spent most of his time at the smaller Leicester Central, where he had his office with the newly re-named British Railways Detective Department (Eastern Region, Southern Central Division). In fact, he always tended to hurry past London Road; perhaps it was company loyalty that held him back? If that were so, then there should be no such concerns now, as these railway companies were no more. They had each been consigned to history and were now part of one vast and new organisation: British Railways. He, together with another million or so other railway men and women, were now servants of the British Transport Commission and part of Prime Minister Attlee's bold social experiment to create a fully integrated and nationalised transport system, stretching the length and breadth of Britain.

The Railway Executive ran the newly created British Railways, and hoped everyone would work for the common good. But Vignoles knew that old allegiances took a while to die — if they ever did. Despite his enthusiastic endorsement of their bold plans, Vignoles recognised that he was very much an ex-LNER man and still felt an immense pride in the stylish image-making of the old company, with its thrilling, pre-war streamliners and the speeding *Mallard,* although all had long since fallen victims to wartime cuts and postwar economies.

And it was the rival Midland Railway that had built the impressive structure he was standing outside, and though only a mile or so separated the two stations, they were a world apart in style and substance. They competed for almost the same custom. As a result, the employees of each company formed an intense loyalty to their own line, and with nationalisation just five months into its stride, these divisions looked set to linger. The commissioners and their newly appointed middle managers (to a man, fussy types in bowler hats, issuing endless forms, edicts, operating instructions, laws, bye-laws, rule books and additional workings with goodness knows how many appendices) were all saying and doing the right things and even the railway unions were preaching a gospel of unity and comradely togetherness, optimistically declaring, 'They're our railways now!' But it was going to take more than new matching uniforms and badges and a few licks of paint to smooth over years of entrenched rivalries and attitudes.

As Vignoles chewed this thought over, his eye was drawn to a row of small posters pasted illegally onto one of the outside walls. Their strident message reminded him that there were many who vociferously opposed the nationalisation of Britain. The black and blue ink of the print screamed:

Oppose this attack on free enterprise!
Together we can stop the stranglehold of Nationalisation!

Away from the industrial heartlands, many people were railing against the social changes, apparently caring not a jot for the greater good. Even the doctors were fighting the health minister in a most ungentlemanly manner over his intentions for a National Health Service. Vignoles pulled a face and turned away from the poster; he reflected that it was the spirit of fostering a comradely working relationship between the two stations that had brought him there that morning.

The stationmaster at London Road had telephoned the day before to seek his advice, *proper friendly like, if you take my meaning.* The quietly spoken man had repeated the phrase as though nervous that Vignoles would bite. He had wanted *a bit of a chat — just informal, nothing official, you understand?* To get a few pointers over a matter that had been troubling him.

On the surface, it sounded like a trifling matter and Vignoles was surprised the transport police at London Road had not sorted it out already. However, he appreciated that a hand of friendship was being extended and had willingly agreed to pay a visit. Privately, Vignoles had his own reasons for wanting to leave his office and was glad to seize the opportunity to get out. Following his friendly chat with the London Road boys, he was starting to harbour a suspicion that all was not well on the railway. Perhaps the London Road stationmaster had been right to seek his advice and this was not quite the trivial matter it first appeared. But his reasons for thinking this were indistinct, and quite possibly a direct consequence of the disturbing discovery he'd made yesterday morning. A discovery that had thoroughly upset his equilibrium and left him feeling suspicious about everyone and everything.

All had appeared quite normal yesterday morning when he walked into the detective department offices, exchanged pleasantries with WPC Jane Benson and collected a pile of letters from Mrs Green, who was seated behind her massive Remington typewriter. Moments later, armed with a mug of wishy-washy coffee (accompanied by an apology from Benson for failing to find a bean of coffee anywhere in the city) he had seated himself at his desk, his pipe loaded with tobacco, and begun to open his mail.

As he tilted back his wooden chair with its curved arms and ancient cushion that softened the seat, his attention was repeatedly pulled away from the letter he was attempting to read. He ignored the first feelings of suspicion and tried to concentrate on yet another list of new working instructions from the Railway Executive; however, a seed of doubt had started to grow, and this unsettling sensation repeatedly dragged his attention back to his desk. No, it was nothing. But wait, there *was* something wrong... Finally abandoning the letter, he stared with full concentration at what lay before him.

The hairs on the nape of his neck began to stand on end as a flush of realisation flowed down his body. As he slowly ran his eyes over the mounds of accumulated files, reports, papers, pens and pencil stubs, the ball formed of elastic bands — it was essential to re-use everything these days — and the many odd items that found a place on his perpetually untidy desk, he sensed that all was not as it should be. True, everything appeared to be in place within that illogical jumble that made perfect sense to Vignoles, and yet...

And yet everything was just fractionally tidier, that little bit neater and straighter than he had left it the evening before. He looked across his office at the shelves on the far wall, lined with case-files and some curious items of lost property that seemed to find their own and uninvited way there. Oddly, the little statuette of a pretty and very scantily clad dancing girl was now doing her high kick facing in the opposite direction. Anatomically accurate she may be, but surely that was impossible.

His first thoughts were that his memory was playing tricks. But it was the pencil that confirmed his suspicions. He remembered that it had twice rolled onto the floor just as he was about to leave for home and so, after picking it up for the second time, he had jabbed it, point-first and with some annoyance, between a stack of files, to stop it making another escape attempt. However, it was now protruding from a completely different pile of papers and with the point facing outwards!

If Detective Sergeant John Trinder had retrieved a file and dislodged the pencil, would he have bothered to replace it? No. He would let it fall onto the floor and leave it there. And besides, Trinder had been out all Thursday afternoon, rounding up escaped sheep on the line near Quainton Road and from there had gone straight home at Woodford Halse. It was improbable that Trinder would have made an unexpected night-time visit, and no one else would enter his office, let alone touch anything, without his express permission. Apart from Mrs Green, when she undertook one of her twice-yearly spring cleans; but these assaults were not in the least bit subtle. She turned the place upside down, beat the thin rug on the floor until it cried for mercy; washed and scrubbed the floorboards with foul-smelling disinfectant and made neat, perfectly formed towers of papers upon a desk that sparkled with lavender-scented polish, whilst his wooden desk calendar and telephone would be symmetrically arranged in a manner that suited her eye, with his pens and pencils laid out in neat rows between. After such a profound rearrangement it generally took him about a week to find anything and to get his desk back into a healthy state of chaos.

This was quite different: everything appeared to have been carefully moved and replaced as exactly as possible. It was a skilful job, but, despite the intruder's best efforts, Vignoles was certain his office had been searched. He examined the sash window that opened onto the platform, but the retaining catch was in place, and besides, there were metal bars affixed to the wall outside that would prevent ingress by any intruder larger than a hungry cat. The lock on his door appeared to be in good order and there were no telltale marks around the doorjamb, so it had not been forced.

DC Harry Blencowe had been the night duty officer and was now probably sleeping, but as he had no telephone at home, Vignoles would have to wait before he could question him and see if someone had wheedled their way in on a pretext. There were so many new people wandering around with clipboards and official documents, checking and assessing and listing goodness knows what, that it was just about conceivable that Blencowe had been duped by someone masquerading as being from one or other of the many new ministries.

Vignoles searched the drawers of his desk and amongst the paperwork, but nothing appeared to be missing, though it was possible that a few sheets of notes or a letter could have been removed. He would be hard-pressed to notice. Certainly, this was no opportunistic break-in. The intruder had no interest in taking anything obvious and had been particularly careful and meticulous, all of which suggested an altogether more ominous purpose. But what could that be?

Vignoles glanced at his watch and strolled towards the tram stop opposite the Midland station clock tower, shaking off the memory of his discovery and the return of the unsettling thoughts that accompanied it. He looked down Granby Street for the tram that should bring Anna to their prearranged rendezvous. Newly painted lorries in the cheerful scarlet British Road Services livery, a Leicester corporation bus and private cars roared past the striking Art Deco edifice of the shoe store on the corner, as a solitary drunk staggered from the door of the Barley Mow across the road.

The drunk caused a gaggle of well-dressed young women, wearing the extravagant and much-desired new fashion of longer and very full skirts with cinched waists and tightly fitted jackets, to cast reproachful glances as they stepped onto the road to avoid the almost insensible man on his zigzagging progress. Vignoles half wondered if he should do something about the tottering figure that was moving like a bad parody of Charlie Chaplin from one side of the pavement to the other. The drunk collapsed in an untidy bundle in a shop doorway, immobile and unconscious. Where was the bobby on the beat when you needed him? Vignoles managed an ironic smile, readjusted his Panama and tossed his blazer across the other shoulder to relieve the weight from his left hand.

A tall man with a sharply chiselled face, a Ronald Coleman moustache and a haughty expression, wearing an expensive blazer and a generously Windsor-knotted tie, stepped over the drunk's feet — throwing him a withering glance as he did so — then looked up; his hawk-like gaze met Vignoles's for a fleeting second. At that very moment the jingling bulk of a tram, its metal wheels grinding harshly on the rails, passed between them.

Moments later Anna Vignoles stepped off the rear platform, swinging herself playfully on the polished steel grab-pole like a vision from a fashion magazine, her wide skirt flaring slightly to reveal shapely legs and new Norvic sun sandals. Vignoles smiled and all thoughts of the drunk vanished, replaced by a stab of pleasure at the sight of this wonderful apparition.

From across the road and through the windows of the passing tram, the pale blue eyes observed their rendezvous.

Anna touched her husband's shoulder with her slender fingers and her eyes half closed for a moment as she accepted a kiss on the cheek. He detected a subtle hint of scent on her warm skin. She eagerly linked her arm through his and nestled herself against him. 'Let's take the New Walk and you can tell me all about it.'

He wondered if he should tell her about his office intruder. He had said nothing about it the night before, preferring to hope that an explanation might become obvious after a night's sleep.

They crossed the wide expanse of London Road and took a leafy path of pale gravel, edged with verdant, flowery shrubs and shaded by mature trees. This formed a useful cut between the massive abutments of the railway bridge and cutting that held the running lines and the offices of the Prudential Insurance Company, the end wall of which bore two colourful posters advertising the forthcoming London Olympic games.

'It was about a series of rather petty incidents of vandalism. Bad enough in their way, I suppose, and the destruction of property is especially unforgivable in these straitened times.'

'What sort of things?' Anna smiled up at him, glad that he had not been called to a ghastly accident or a suicide, all too frequent occurrences on the railway.

'One was a curious case of paint being thrown — quite deliberately — over the side of a locomotive. Made all the more annoying because it was just back from a major overhaul.'

Anna pushed her lower lip outwards in an expression of puzzlement. After five years in the goods dispatch office at Leicester Central, she had learnt a lot about the workings of the railway, through a slow process of osmosis rather than deliberate study. 'Aw, that would have ruined its nice new paintwork.'

'Frightful waste. They'd just hand-painted *British Railways* along the tender sides and this was quite ruined. There was no question of the engine being allowed out in that state. They said the shedmaster was absolutely livid.'

'Golly, I can imagine.' Anna winced. At a time when much of Britain looked shabby, with an all-pervading air of being somehow unwashed, dusty and faded, it was sad to hear of something that had received a rare dose of care and attention being so senselessly spoilt.

'The cheeky vandals even wrote their initials in the paint. One BD and a certain TR.'

'That was bold of them.'

'Yes. And then there was the theft of a whole consignment of new timetables, all of which were subsequently found floating down the River Soar.'

'Why on earth would anyone bother to do such a thing?'

'I can't imagine. It would have been a hefty bundle to carry, and to what purpose? Just to throw in the river?' Vignoles shook his head. 'There really is no accounting for people these days. I suppose it was just a bunch of idiotic youths. However, the stationmaster had another take on it. He was concerned that these attacks were presaging something more ominous.'

'Really?'

'I think he's getting in a bit of a flap, but I had to indulge him. You may not remember this, but the IRA bombed London Road back in '39, and it turns out that he was the assistant stationmaster at the time. I think it affected him quite badly and he's awfully jumpy. Rather a nervous sort, if I'm honest.'

'I can understand him. The blitz was terrifying, but at least one knew what to expect. We had warnings, what with the sirens and the aircraft engines, and so we could take cover.'

'That was why Hitler's V2 rockets were so effective, because they were silent and came without warning. Likewise, secretly planted bombs — even if they don't actually hurt or kill — are very frightening things to imagine to be lurking somewhere in your station.'

'But stolen timetables? A tin of paint? Not quite a bomb plot, is it? You can't get too worked up about either.' Anna smiled, but Vignoles sensed a slight tightening of her hand on his arm.

'He's just getting worked up over nothing. However, I'm asking myself if there isn't something more behind it.' He was thinking of the intruder in his office, but still chose to say nothing, sensing that Anna was growing apprehensive.

'It will no doubt prove to be reprobate kids,' he continued. 'Too many of them just don't show any respect for the railways these days. We get so many problems from ill-mannered *teen*agers, or whatever it is we're calling them nowadays. They're always throwing stones at carriage windows and the loco crew.'

'I wonder if perhaps the war did it. All those distressed evacuees thrust into alien families and wrenched away from their homes and security and now brought back to a city and people that has changed from what they left. It must have some ill effects. And so many families have been torn apart by war: losing loved ones, homes, work and having no money to live on. You see so many poor creatures scratching a desperate life on the bomb sites.'

'I wonder why the council can't do something. The government is promising a future without poverty, and fair shares for all, but I'm not sure that we've got far towards that yet.' Vignoles paused. 'Not that I have the answers.'

'So, what advice did you offer your new national railway brothers? Apart from caning the culprits and boxing their ears.' Anna spoke playfully, wanting to keep the tone gentle so as not to darken the sunny afternoon.

'I advised them to be extra vigilant and to lock everything away. Check all passes and tickets and challenge any strangers wandering where they shouldn't.'

'Especially if they have an Irish accent and are carrying a ticking bomb.'

Vignoles appreciated Anna's attempt at a joke. 'I suggested he get the men out of uniform and put them undercover to watch and wait for gangs of youths — who will probably not be Irish — when they descend on the railway to cause mischief, and catch them red-handed.'

'An undercover operation. How thrilling!' She gave his arm a squeeze.

'It sounds better than the reality. We could be undercover right now. Just walking together, but actually watching and tailing a suspect. Not so very exciting.'

'You don't find walking with me on this beautiful day, exciting?' said Anna, pretending to be offended.

He smiled and glanced down at Anna; her tailored blouse hugged her figure to perfection. He silently thanked the Lord for Mrs Trinder's magic with a needle and thread. 'A poor choice of words, my dear.'

'Hmm, I forgive you.' Anna hugged Vignoles closer to her side as they made their way down the pleasantly shaded New Walk past Regency and Victorian houses that appeared untouched by war or austerity, each house smartly turned out with pretty front gardens filled with flowers, despite the continuing demands that everyone 'Dig for Victory' to provide fresh vegetables. Even the trees were tall and healthy; the leaves, where caught by the sun, were bright and translucent like the glass in the windows of St Stephen's church, each glowing in a dazzle of fresh greens and pale yellows. The wide gravel path was swept and raked, crunching beneath the many strolling feet with a crisp sound like repeated bites into a summer apple. Above the trees, the church spire and the shapely chimney pots, the sky was an intense blue, like that on the Olympic posters.

'Oh, Charles, I almost forgot: this letter came. The postman delivered it to the Armitages next door by mistake. Mrs A. handed it me just as I was leaving for town.' Anna disengaged her arm and pulled out a white envelope from her handbag. It had a bold overprint in black letters declaring *British Transport Commission*. It felt stiff, as though it contained something more than a fold of a letter.

Vignoles did not quite miss a stride, but he felt a quick flutter in the pit of his stomach as he took it. It was from head office. Straight from the top and those who could — and would — decide his future. Not that he openly feared for his job; but at times, as nationalisation had drawn closer, and then, as the first changes had started to make themselves felt, he had cause to wonder how his position might fare amidst the reorganisation. And now this letter, coinciding with the curious matter of his office being searched. He began to feel uneasy. His was still a relatively new position and one that had not yet become commonplace across the railways of Britain. Whilst there were a great many uniformed transport police, he and his small team, alongside his peers running the Northern Division around Sheffield, Manchester and Hull, were very rare. He'd had some significant successes in detection over the years, but were they enough to keep him employed? What could be the reason for this unexpected letter being delivered to his private address?

'What are you waiting for? It won't explode!' Anna put a hand to her mouth, 'Oops. Bad choice of words.'

'Oh, I was just wondering...' Vignoles left the sentence hanging and ripped open the envelope, tearing it diagonally across the front. The excessive force prompted Anna to give him an odd look. A thick card and a letter were inside. It was instantly recognisable as an invitation, with a dark blue script printed upon an expensive smooth cream backing. Vignoles quickly scanned it then laughed out loud, not because it contained anything amusing, but in relief that his worries were for the moment stilled.

'Well, I never! It seems that you and I shall be going to London this Friday — the fourth — at the invitation of the board.' Vignoles smiled as he read aloud: '*Sir Eustace Missenden and the Board of the Railway Executive...* blah blah... *have the pleasure of inviting Detective Inspector Vignoles and Mrs Charles Vignoles to attend...* blah blah.' He read the next passage with emphasis, '*to view a grand parade and exhibition of locomotives and passenger stock for the evaluation of several proposed new liveries and colour schemes, on behalf of the BTC.*'

'How nice to get such an invitation!' Anna exclaimed. 'A day out in London, Charles. What a wonderful surprise.'

'There's more.' He read the accompanying letter. 'Hmm, it is partly work and partly play; I need to organise some uniformed officers for security on the day.'

'It wouldn't do to have any paint thrown around.'

Vignoles moved his spectacles to the end of his nose and looked over them whilst very deliberately replying, 'No, that would not do at all.'

Anna giggled and Vignoles returned to the letter. 'A room has been reserved — and paid for — at a hotel on the Marylebone Road. Good heavens!'

They both stopped in their tracks.

As did the tall man with the pale blue eyes, following a few yards behind. He sat on a bench and focussed on a crossword clue in his neatly folded paper.

'We can easily get there and back in a day. Why would they pay for us to stay over?' Anna frowned.

'Yes, that is odd.' Vignoles re-read the invitation in the hope of finding an explanation. He looked at the envelope. 'No stamp. So it was delivered by hand?'

'Curiouser and curiouser. Well, let's not complain too loudly; this means an evening together in the big smoke. When did we last do *that*? Are we staying at the Great Central Hotel?'

'Sadly not. It was taken over as the HQ of the British Transport Commission. I suppose that's why the exhibition will be at Marylebone, so all the bigwigs can just walk across the road to attend.'

'But they'll ruin that lovely place. It seems a scandalous use for such a grand building.'

'Perhaps that's our new classless democracy for you,' mused Vignoles.

Anna glanced at her wristwatch. 'If we get our skates on the Lyons Tea House should still be open. I heard that they've got some real coffee again and serve an almost passable attempt at cream with their scones. We can discuss the shopping trip we'll squeeze in while in London. *Vogue* have finally released some patterns of the latest designs, and I simply *have* to find them.' Vignoles groaned theatrically as they walked quickly, arm in arm.

The crossword man appeared to be going in the same direction.

Chapter Two

Underneath the Arches

Primo Scala

With the weather set fair for Whitsun weekend, those rostered to work were hard-pressed to deal with the many questions and complaints and anxious requests to help locate lost children or mislaid bags and to shorten the long queues at the ticket windows. Since about six-thirty, when the first of the many specials pulled out, the station was filled to bursting with those able to take advantage of both the day off and the special cheap day returns to Skegness, Mablethorpe, Bridlington and other delightful escapes from the daily grind.

Some of the men already had their shirt sleeves rolled up and were loosening ties and collar buttons; many wore summer-weight service uniforms, and there was a great variety of caps and hats pushed back over slickly-Brylcreemed hair, or clutched in sweaty hands. The men appeared relaxed as they stood in groups, smoking, joking, smiling and ignoring their wives, girlfriends and elderly parents, and their children, busily running amok. Their thoughts were already drifting to the promise of a deck chair on the beach and a snooze with the newspaper over their faces; or an escape for a few hours in a pub to chat and play cards with their chums.

The women wore lighter dresses, though a number were also in uniform, and all surrounded by baskets and bags of provisions, extra cardigans, umbrellas, blankets and bottles of pop and other precious provisions specially conserved over the previous weeks in anticipation of the outing. Children in their Sunday best or carefully mended school uniform, some elder ones wearing heavily-pressed cadet uniforms, were running helter-skelter with whoops and yelps of excitement, chasing the many special excursion trains that seemed to arrive by the minute, eager to collect the numbers and gawp at the drivers, whilst drawing disapproving looks as they bumped and tripped their way down the packed platforms. Exasperated mothers were shouting ineffectually above the almost deafening noise of the engines huffing, roaring and whistling and the intense hubbub and chatter of the gathering crowds. The shouts of porters and the rumble of their little metal-wheeled luggage trolleys on the platform surface only added to the confusion.

Despite the noise and hubbub, it was the happy holiday atmosphere that prevailed, and something of this mood seeped into those working the station. The staff found their conversations returning to thoughts of their own week away by the seaside. When time allowed, well-thumbed copies of brochures from the new Butlin's holiday camps were passed around, or they commented on the colourful railway posters on the display boards that promoted the delights of Scarborough, Clacton, Filey and distant Pwllheli, competing with the lure of the London Olympics or Don Bradman's much-anticipated final Test appearance at The Oval for the Australians, and discussing how best to use their railway privilege tickets to escape to one or other of these enticements. Work did not feel quite so arduous and the privations of heavily rationed Britain, with all its many coupons, licences and permissions (all in triplicate and with complex exceptions, clauses and deviations to master), felt a little more bearable with the sun warming one's back and providing a much needed flush of saturated colour to the drab city.

Indeed, if an artist were to paint the cityscape that Whitsun Bank Holiday, his palette would need to be loaded with a succession of browns, fawns and greys of every hue, pale greens and a touch of Venetian red and straw yellow. He would need to capture the sooty reds and smoked blues of brick and the grey of cobblestones and faded shop awnings. The few motor cars would be painted black, deep maroon and bottle green, looking like a collection of beetles on a taxonomist's tray. The completed picture, even with these flashes of colour, would still require a final wash of pale yellowish-brown, a hue that seemed to tint everything when the sun shone. And it was this same sun that was pouring its welcome light deep into the dingy railway offices, penetrating the almost subterranean booking hall with great bands of brilliance slanting through the glass roof, thickened by locomotive and cigarette smoke, and swirling dust motes like the beam from a giant cinema projector, animating the bustle of people at the ticket windows before sending them scuttling up the steps to the platforms.

Charles Vignoles and his sergeant, John Trinder, had carried mugs of agreeably drinkable coffee — Violet Trinder having fortunately slipped a small packet of this precious commodity to her husband that morning as a special holiday treat — to the far end of a platform. They were seated on a four-wheeled trolley usually reserved for hauling parcels and mailbags. Vignoles had declared this outdoor office preferable to their own and, as the last of the day's excursions were shortly to depart, the station would soon fall quiet, giving them time to chew over their present investigations. His motivation for this outdoor meeting was also prompted by a lingering sense of unease at being inside his office, which now felt violated and insecure.

Vignoles, looking preoccupied, was in no hurry to discuss work. He commenced filling his pipe and creating a few rapid puffs of smoke to get it going, rather in the manner of the grimy locomotive that at that very moment was huffing its train into motion. Trinder watched the two in parallel and found the comparison amusing. He lit a Black Cat cigarette to offer his own contribution to the smoke already hanging over the station. Both men watched the heavily laden carriages of departing day-trippers, Trinder softly humming the tune to *Underneath the Arches*.

'Did you succeed in rounding up the sheep?' asked Vignoles at last.

'After about half an hour of chasing the blasted animals. They are maddeningly stupid creatures. I shall write a letter to the farmer ordering that he repairs the gap in his fence.'

'Yes, do. This kind of irritation costs us a lot in time and resources.' Vignoles took another puff on his pipe. 'It's like this vandalism we're suffering. I don't know what things are coming to when people want to break, smash and burn everything around them.'

'I agree. I've just been handed another report of stone throwing this morning.' Trinder shook his head and both fell silent as an immensely long train of wooden-bodied coal wagons clanked towards them, hauled by a pair of extraordinarily filthy locomotives, their almost uniform brownish-grey colour relieved only by the startling brilliance of the cream Gill Sans letters painted on the sides of their tenders, the first of which read *British Railways*, the second, however, already so heavily grimed by coal dust that the newly applied letters were rendered a dirty stain except where some wag had deliberately washed clean the letters B, S and A, and with a wet rag had written in the dirt below; *Made in England*.

The pair exchanged glances and laughed. 'At least they've got a sense of humour. Though I fear it presents a sad image for the new railway.' Vignoles continued to watch the engines, their exhaust beats at times synchronised, at others, a mad arrhythmic jumble creating a kind of mechanical *Rite of Spring* that reverberated from the massive Maxim building that overlooked the station.

'Good engines, those. Robinson O4s, in case you were wondering.'

Trinder grimaced and shrugged. 'They all look the same to me, guv.'

'Philistine!'

They sat in silence for a few moments longer. 'This might be a complete waste of time, John,' said Vignoles, waving his pipe at Trinder, 'but I am going to take another look at these vandal attacks. Take a step back, so as to speak, and see if there is a pattern to these unwelcome attentions.'

Trinder was unexcited. 'What's your thinking, guv?'

'It's nothing more than a hunch, but a number of these apparently unrelated incidents are starting to trouble me. I need more information to work with.'

'You think it's some kind of gang at work?'

Vignoles puffed air out of his cheeks. 'Possibly. The London Road boys have had a few odd incidents.' He hesitated a beat, then ploughed on. 'The stationmaster was at pains to remind me about the Irish Republican Army and their terror attacks.'

'Surely not?'

'No, not at all, but it would still do us no harm to get to the bottom of this and stamp it out. Get DC Blencowe and one of the girls to list all the acts of vandalism along the line over the past, let's say, two months, and get London Road to do the same. I was over there Saturday morning, offering the Midland chaps a few practical words of advice, and they're in the mood to take any assistance we can offer. Try plotting the times, places and dates on a map. The exercise might just throw something up. A pattern or a connection — who knows?'

'Righty-o, I'll get straight on to it.' Trinder was puzzled because the incidents he was aware of seemed far too petty to warrant this level of concern, but he knew better than to ignore the DI's hunches.

'Oh, and sergeant...'

Trinder looked at Vignoles, struck by the sudden formality in the DI's voice.

'Guv?'

'Have you had any reason to visit my office on Thursday evening or early on Friday morning? Perhaps you remembered some important document for a case you are working on.'

'No; I went straight home after the sheep incident and spent the evening with Violet. Why do you ask?'

'Oh, nothing. I've mislaid a file. You know what a frightful mess my desk is.' He chuckled lightly. 'It crossed my mind that maybe you or one of the others had removed it.'

'I can't see anyone doing so without permission. Shall I ask them?'

'No, no, forget it. I don't want to look like a chump when I find the file at the back of a drawer!' They both laughed, but Vignoles wondered why he was not being completely on the level with his trusted sergeant.

CHAPTER THREE

WHY STARS COME OUT AT NIGHT

Carroll Gibbons

A long sliver of cloud edged with silver partially obscured the bright disc of the moon. It cast a cold light, but enough to work with, and they could dispense with torches. Their dark clothing, and the inky pools of black between moonlit highlights, were sufficient to conceal their movements.

The factory complex was shabby and careworn, the result of many years of neglect and strafing by wartime fighter planes that had drilled holes in the concrete walls and corrugated asbestos roofing, leaving scars that were only now softening with accumulated grime. Ragwort and coarse grass grew in abundance between the railway tracks and tangles of razor wire, dark with rust, tumbled in messy festoons along the perimeter wall interlaced with bindweed and dog rose. But these barriers were rendered useless as the pre-cast concrete slabs of the perimeter fence were often fractured or tumbling out of kilter and offering ready access inside. Brambles filled the gap between the wall and the buildings and encroached over the far ends of the storage sidings. This untamed nature offered a more effective barrier than the concrete, though strong shears quickly deployed the evening before had cleared a narrow pathway inside.

The night watchman was snoozing, his hard wooden chair tipped back against the wall of his office, feet resting on his desk and cap pulled over his eyes. He was unlikely to stir, and easily visible through the grimy window. One of the gang was posted as lookout, eyeing the watchman and glancing across the wide expanse of the moonlit railway yard dotted with dark blocks of wagons and delineated by the silvery steel rails running in gentle parallel curves and interlacings, snaking off towards the main line. A lonely chiming hoot, like a heartbroken owl, indicated the distant station and the passage of a train.

The gang of four was composed of experienced men. They avoided speaking unless imperative, using just grunts, nods and light taps upon an arm or a back to communicate. They knew almost nothing of each other — it was safer that way — and what they did know was probably false. Theirs was a secretive collective of deception and counter-deception, and their eyes were dark and impenetrable, nervous and suspicious. The shared feeling of tension was palpable. It was a warm night and their fear and exertions added a scent of fresh sweat to that of unwashed clothes, cheap aftershave, hair oil, bitter cigarettes and garlic that mingled with the smells of the factory and the unique odour of a railway yard.

Their leader was a small, muscular man with a fulsome moustache of a type made popular by Stalin. He wore the obligatory black leather jacket, heavy boots, military trousers and shirt, and he carried a small but evil-looking machine gun that reflected the light in an ominous manner. His peaked cap, with a red star pinned to the front, was pushed back over a thick mass of curly hair that glistened with oil like his gun. He claimed he was Serbian but spoke at least four languages fluently and, like everything else about this odd group, the truth was probably buried beneath layers of lies and subterfuge. Who knew who he really was? One of the men had challenged him about his nationality, claiming that he was Russian — or even German! He'd told the man to stop asking questions and keep his mind on the job. He was just 'Comrade Black' to them.

He chewed slowly and waited for the lookout's nod for the all clear. In a stooping run accompanied by a slight creak of leather and the occasional tinkle of small stones under boot, he darted towards the far end of a partially covered loading bay with two of his comrades following close behind, one lugging a canvas bag, the other brandishing a pistol and carrying a can of oil.

The loading bay had concrete posts at regular intervals supporting an elegant elliptical roof constructed of cast concrete arches that vaulted over the railway line in the bay and continued over the main machine-room like a series of pale ribs. The men ignored the corrugated iron doors that were padlocked shut along the raised walkway on the factory side and made their way beside the railway track, overshadowed by the bulk of a line of tank wagons. They were masked from the view of the night watchman if he were to awaken and step out of his office and look along the loading bay. They reached the end of the line of wagons, each man looking up at the tankers as they passed and eyeing the numbers painted on their sides.

Comrade Black moved more slowly now, stepping carefully over the increasingly litter-strewn surface as he advanced towards the end of the siding that was long abandoned and heavily overgrown. He was trying to avoid snagging his feet in the tough tendrils of the brambles that sprawled everywhere. Despite his heavy boots and thick serge trousers he could still feel raw slashes of thorn drawing blood. He pointed angrily at the ground and the man with the pistol slid it into an inside pocket and set to work with a pair of long-handled secateurs, freeing the worst of the tough, spiky shrubs where they crossed the siding. The other two men forced their way forward until they reached what looked to be a massive hedge of vegetation, but as the moon slid free of the cloud they could see the curves and angles of a long-abandoned tanker lurking beneath the brambles, bindweed and dog rose. Both men set to work, cutting and pulling the wagon free, each wearing heavy work gloves but still wincing in pain as they hurried to pull back the vicious natural defence.

Twenty minutes later the wagon was revealed. It looked a sorry state: rusty and heavily stained with green accretions of moss, but complete nonetheless.

Comrade Black unplugged the oil can and poured some of the liquid onto a piece of rag, then nimbly swung himself up onto the running plate and, with a couple of hefty pulls, ascended the ladder and straddled the tank. First working the oil into the release catch and hinges until shiny with lubrication, he then eased the filler cap open. It was so deeply stained and embedded with old grease that it was mercifully rust-free and opened with just one hefty wrench and a short, sharp complaint that was over in a moment. Everyone stood still and waited to see if the sound had awakened the sleeping guard. Nothing stirred.

He pulled a torch from an inside pocket and pushed it into the opening before switching it on. The light bounced back onto his face with a pale, sickly glow, his eyes rendered bright and glassy like marbles. He gazed down at a level pool of rancid golden-brown oil, the heavy fumes of which, after being trapped for so long in the void, made him recoil and retch. He looked away and gulped some fresh air, then impatiently motioned for one of his comrades to offer him a pole or a stick. They were expecting this command and one of the men had already found a suitable length amongst the detritus littering the yard.

Comrade Black hauled it up and cautiously inserted one end into the tank. Collective breaths were held. The tension was straining at their nerves. Failure now was unthinkable. What if this was not the right tanker? Or worse, what if it had been substituted? The stick went down, further and further into the tank. Surely this was too far? But then it met resistance and with a resonant clunk, stopped dead. Breathing recommenced and glances were exchanged. He made a few more reassuring prods and was satisfied that the gloopy viscous liquid concealed their prize. A slight smile of grim satisfaction played across his face.

An hour later and the forlorn wagon now bore two newly painted identification numbers in brilliant white upon a dark background, the oil boxes for the wheel bearings had been topped up with fresh oil, and a prepared typed transit document was slipped into the wire frame on the side of the running frame. The vehicle was now ready to join the line awaiting collection under the loading bay roof. The brakes were released with the help of crowbars to ease the rusted linkage free.

They waited anxiously. A dog fox barked in a distant field. There was the whistle. Taking this as their cue, all four pushed the tanker forwards, every sinew straining and muscle burning with the effort. A creak, a groan, followed by a teeth-jarring squeal of complaining metal rang out, each man hoping that this was lost amongst the resonant bangs and rumbles of the passing train.

The tanker was reluctant to move at first, but as the newly oiled bearings took effect it rolled more freely and gathered speed. They felt it ease away from their hands and could do nothing but watch in horror as it trundled imperiously towards the awaiting line of wagons and the inevitable, deafening clatter of buffers. But the wagon met with resistance from the debris on the track and, in a move that could not have been executed more perfectly by the most expert of shunters, it came to rest with just the gentlest of sounds. It was in place and ready to make the next stage in its long and tortuous journey across Europe.

Comrade Black nodded, but his eyes betrayed no warmth or humour and his expression was oddly inscrutable, in stark contrast to the evident relief on the faces of the others. Now it was time for each to make his prearranged rendezvous and collect the substantial payment promised. And time for Black to say goodbye to his comrades — forever.

He did not know when or where his fellow night workers were to meet their untimely deaths; he just hoped it would be a professional job. He'd been reassured on this point. It would certainly be awkward if their bodies were discovered too soon and difficult questions were asked. He felt a tingle of fear, mixed with regret, flush across his skin. It was tough that these men were to be so horribly deceived, but his paymaster was a ruthless character who was not going to allow sentiment to stand in the way.

CHAPTER FOUR

COFFEE IN THE MORNING

Billy Cotton and His Band

The *Manchester Guardian* covered the story, though it was just a short column accompanied by a tiny photograph of a young and innocent-looking lad, probably taken when he signed up with his regiment. The death of another poor Tommy in some distant part of Europe was not headline news.

However, the story attracted Vignoles's attention over breakfast, probably because the report about the unfortunate soldier contained three small facts that chimed with him in their own way, and so drew his eye.

Private Brierley was serving in Trieste and, until recently, this port had been part of Italy, his in-laws' homeland. Since his marriage to Anna, anything about Italy interested Vignoles. Secondly, Private Brierley was with the 1st Battalion of the Northamptonshire Regiment, which made him almost a local, and, thirdly, Brierley had been serving as a fireman on the railway. The unexpected death of a railwayman would always draw Vignoles's attention. However, the facts — even allowing for military restrictions — were scant and Vignoles had read the report twice through in the time it took him to take a couple of sips of coffee. But he was intrigued enough by the short, sad tale to draw it to Anna's attention.

'Trieste? Mama was there once and she loved it. She was visiting an elderly aunt who lived somewhere not far from the city. This was before the war, of course. I was terribly jealous that she didn't take me along and I remember I was in a fearful mood for days.' Anna made an apologetic face. 'I was quite beastly about it, but she refused to take me out of school for so long.'

'It would have been a great adventure.'

'Yes, but I was just twelve years old, and besides, I don't think my parents could really afford for me to go. That's why she travelled alone. It was a last chance to see her, not a sightseeing trip. And it proved timely, as poor old auntie was killed in an air raid. But Mama liked Trieste. There's a long, curving promenade facing out onto the Adriatic.' Anna stopped and leaned back in her chair, coffee cup in both hands. 'And then there is Miramare.'

'Miramare? What a romantic name.'

'Yes! A magical fairytale castle set on a little rocky promontory. And with such a tragic, romantic tale attached.' Anna sighed wistfully, but instead of explaining, she suddenly wrinkled her nose as if smelling something unpleasant and sat upright. 'But the crazy politicians are claiming this is no longer Italy's. Of course it is! It's quite nonsensical to think otherwise.'

'So whose is it then?'

'Nobody's. It's a military zone or something silly like that. Papa explained it all to me once, but I was so disgusted I've quite forgotten the details.' Anna spoke softly whilst looking into her coffee, carefully controlling her emotions as she continued to speak. 'Actually, the military zone is run by the British and Americans, and no doubt the French are hanging around somewhere in the background.'

'Ah. Well, that's probably for the good, then.'

'How is that good?'

'Let's face it, darling, the Italians have done a darned good job of messing things up and not exactly setting a great example of efficiency and democracy.' He ducked to avoid the bread roll that Anna threatened to hurl at him. He reckoned that if bread had not been so scarce she would not have held back.

'Charles!'

'I'm only going on what you tell me, dearest. I rely upon you to steer me through the impossibly complicated muddle of Italy and its politics. It was not so very long ago it had a dictator, then a king, and now it's a republic! You can't blame the British for wanting to restore some sort of order to at least one part. And besides, you're British. You were born in Leicester, not Trieste.'

'Hmph.' She threw him a fiery look. 'Actually, if I remember correctly, the troops are there because the Jugoslavians decided they wanted Trieste and moved first, then everyone argued like crazy and couldn't agree what to do. So the solution was to give it to nobody. A complete fudge by the Allies, showing no consideration to the logic that Trieste is a part of Italy. So don't blame the Italians for every mistake in this world.'

'But wasn't Trieste part of the Austro-Hungarian Empire? That was not Italy.' Vignoles winked.

'You are treading on dangerous ground.'

He raised his hands. 'Just stating fact!' He eyed the bread roll that Anna had again laid her hand upon. 'But seriously, the reason I mention Trieste is because of this young lad who's been killed. Curiously, the article mentions that he's the second one killed in the same month. Both in the army, and both worked on the railways.'

'Accidental deaths?'

'No. Murder, in both cases.'

Anna placed down her cup without a sound, as the mantel clock marked a couple of beats.

'The article is frustratingly vague, stating only that they were murdered, and, significantly, that in each case, *robbery is not suspected as the motive*. Intriguing, eh?' Vignoles looked up and their eyes met.

'It's hard to know what to make of that.'

'The second one, Brierley, was from Daventry. He was with the 1st Battalion of the Northamptonshire Regiment.'

Anna considered this a moment. 'Is that not the same one that Mr Saunders's lad joined? I remember you told me about him getting his call-up.'

'Gosh, I do think you're right.' Vignoles looked pensive and let the paper drop to the table. 'You know, I might take a ride down to Woodford today and pay a visit on old Saunders. Not seen him for a while. He might be feeling a bit unsettled by this news. Not that I can do anything to help, of course.'

'Good idea.'

'Paul. That's his son's name,' Anna added. 'He might well have been pals with Brierley.'

CHAPTER FIVE

KOMANDANT STANE

Jugoslav partisan song

The bird perched on one of the concrete fence posts, its beady eyes darting across the bushes, grasses and weeds enveloped in the thin layer of early morning mist that only now was starting to burn away to reveal drops of dew like little jewels on clover leaves and rows of sparkling beads along spider webs. This was a good time to hunt as it was not too hot and the bees and insects were out feeding.

A bumble bee made a drunken flight across the railway yard, purring like a smooth motor. The red-backed shrike darted off its perch in a flash of chestnut and grey, swooping fast and low, expertly capturing the ball of dark fuzz in its sharp beak, one of the bee's gossamer wings crumpled inside, the other flapping violently but helplessly against the hard, shiny pincers. The shrike flew towards a strand of rusting barbed wire that topped the perimeter walls and impaled the helpless insect on an empty spike. The shrike hovered a few moments, inspecting its larder of beetles and bees pinned in a deathly row, before returning to its watching post to await another victim.

As it dipped and bobbed and looked around in short, sharp movements, a locomotive moved gingerly along the weedy track, the driver leaning hard out of his cab window whilst moving his left arm from the massive regulator handle to the engine brake in swift adjustments as he tried to judge the safest speed to negotiate the life-expired factory sidings. His fireman was hanging off the steps on the far side, ready to step down and couple up the engine to the waiting line of tank wagons.

The German-built loco was black all over, its red-painted wheels long hidden beneath layers of caked grime and oil; the raking sunlight picking out a range of hues from black through to greasy brown where scarlet had once gleamed. It was streaked by dribbles of limescale and there was a heavy powdering of soot, whilst unhealthy wheals of orange rust had formed around the smoke-box front like a nasty rash of cold sores. The engine clanked heavily with each slow revolution of the wheels, ghosting steam from somewhere between the exposed frames. It hissed like a kettle about to whistle on a stove, and so, despite the almost complete lack of maintenance and the line of bullet holes in the cab roof, the engine had a healthy head of steam.

A man with a dark moustache and spectacles stood at the end of the loading dock, a cigarette in one hand, a clipboard holding documentation in the other. A range of pencils and pens arrayed in the breast pocket of his long, brown warehouseman's coat gave him an air of businesslike authority, although he appeared more interested in closely observing the burning of his cigarette in between puffs, turning it in his fingers with an expression of profound disappointment upon his face.

As the locomotive tapped against the buffers of the waiting train and sighed to a halt, the dissatisfied smoker met the eye of the driver and grinned. 'Death to fascism!' he called out, holding a clenched fist to his temple in the communist salute, his grin not quite matching the grim gesture and words. The driver did the same whilst perfunctorily offering the correct response of 'Freedom for the people!' The official exchange over, they traded more light-hearted greetings about the fine weather whilst the fireman ducked between the engine and the first tanker to couple them together.

They chatted quietly, the words now indistinct above the hissing of the locomotive and the loud, repetitive alarm-call of a bird in one of the scrubby bushes that edged the yard. The driver leaned out of the cab and scribbled his name along the bottom of the documents. He nodded at something and pointed to where the brakevan was waiting to be collected and attached to the rear of the train, its occupant seated on the steps of his vehicle, reading a paper in the sunshine.

Comrade Black lowered his binoculars to wipe away a bead of sweat before raising them again. This was the critical moment. The *chack chack chack* of the angry bird mirrored his own emotions. The driver had now joined the official on the goods platform and was getting the measure of his train. They were nodding. That was good. He took a sudden, sharp intake of breath; the two men were now walking towards the rear — and towards the tanker that he and his comrades had freed just a few hours earlier.

He trained his vision onto the freshly cut and trampled vegetation behind the rear wagon. It was unmistakable for what it was, and he feared that, if the driver saw this, he might become suspicious. Had the bribe been generous enough? He found himself biting his lower lip.

No, it was all right, they were laughing at something as the fireman joined them, his heavy gloves now removed and wedged between one arm and his flank as he proffered a pack of cigarettes.

Come on! Get moving, he thought. He wanted the wagon out of there and far away. *Damned Czechs: always dragging their heels.* He couldn't risk any of the factory workers enquiring about the unexpected removal of the long-abandoned tanker whilst they were still there. It was easy enough to bribe his man, but to keep everyone sweet was impossible. He looked at his watch. The morning shift would start arriving soon. 'Get a bloody move on!' He spoke aloud to himself and could feel his heart pounding.

Now what? The three men were walking towards the locomotive, laughing and joking and pointing. *Yes, you can laugh. But you've a job to do... and if you fail?* He spat out of the corner of his mouth. *I'll make you pay all right.* He touched the butt of the pistol protruding from his trouser waistband. It would be quieter than the machine gun he had wrapped in cloth inside a canvas bag and strapped to the rear of his motorcycle.

A small bottle of a clear liquid appeared from someone's pocket and was passed around. Short lifts of the bottle taken in turn by each man. The slivowice swigged and the men suitably fortified for the morning's work ahead, there was a slapping of backs, and finally, the two crewmen re-boarded their locomotive.

Get going!

The engine gave a short toot and eased the train into motion, wheels squealing and complaining. He trained his binoculars nervously on the rear wagon, praying that the fresh oil would prevent it from running hot. Five minutes later and the brakevan had been attached to the rear and the train had received the signal to move onto the main line. The alarm call of the bird still continued to sound across the now-empty yard.

Comrade Black fired up his motorbike, pulled his goggles over his eyes and roared along the dry and dusty lane, kicking up a pale cloud behind. The road ran parallel to the railway for some distance and he decided to tag behind and observe his prize until it branched away towards Brno. The train steamed merrily along, rolling and bucking on the ancient track with the wagons clattering behind.

The cool air produced thick clouds of white vapour that streamed into his face and partially obscured his view, his solitary rear-view mirror revealing only a mixture of steam and dust. He either did not see, or was not paying sufficient attention to, the black Tatra car that bounced along the narrow road behind him, its three occupants rising and falling in unison upon the softly-sprung seats with every motion of the car's suspension, each one grim-faced, with eyes focused on his back. A striking-looking woman with dark hair and high cheekbones sat in the passenger seat, a beret slouched at an acute angle over one eye. She made an impatient gesture. The driver of the car nodded in response to something the bearded man in the rear said, and put his foot down.

The shrike, calm again now the disturbance had receded, hovered beside a bush flapping its wings in an agitated manner and, in so doing, flushed its quarry from out of the safety of the foliage, and as the tiny fledgling tried to make its escape on wings still unused to flight, was expertly trapped within the hunter's pincer-like grasp. As the bird made the kill, the air was filled by a distant thump and a metallic crunch and the sound of a motorbike engine racing in an uncontrolled rattle followed by something heavy sliding over gravel.

A car accelerated into the distance just as another victim was impaled upon the barbed wire.

CHAPTER SIX

ON THE ATCHISON, TOPEKA & THE SANTA FÉ

Anne Shelton with Ambrose & His Orchestra

A couple of hours after his breakfast conversation with Anna, Vignoles was sitting on a wonky wooden bench set against the outside wall of the engine shed at Woodford Halse, sipping over-stewed tea from a dented, brown-stained, white enamel mug and talking with Tim Saunders, the shedmaster. The bay windows of the office were open and his grubby radiogram was softly playing a chirpy song about an American railroad. The sun was warm and the music pleasing, as the two men enjoyed a stolen moment away from their duties.

They had known each other for a number of years and a friendship had developed during Vignoles's visits to what was known as 'the loco' in the course of his work. These had transformed into purely social calls. They held quite differing opinions on almost every subject and, in many ways, were like chalk and cheese, but Vignoles liked the man's directness and honesty and their sparring on issues — most often political — never descended into bitterness or argument. In fact, Vignoles enjoyed the way Saunders would challenge his beliefs, a good example of which was their differing approach towards the important subject of steam locomotives.

Saunders was strictly pragmatic, judging each of the many varieties of engine solely upon its reliability and ease of maintenance. This was unsurprising, as it was his job to keep sixty of these sometimes recalcitrant beasts running with insufficient resources, poor quality spares and a workforce still decimated by the needs of the recent war. There was little room for sentiment in his world, but Saunders recognised that Vignoles was an out-and-out enthusiast and a knowledgeable one to boot. He could recognise that the detective inspector was not simply admiring the external appearance of an engine, but understood the workings and the operational quirks of the different classes. Appreciating this, Saunders was not above surprising Vignoles by occasionally pulling something unusual from out of the smoky depths of the shed, or having a particularly fine engine cleaned with just a little extra effort and 'bull' if he knew to expect a visit. Vignoles, for his part, was touched that this sometimes gruff man, who was much given to complaining about the injustices of the world, the government, his awkward relationship with the unions and his overly Bolshie workforce, could take the trouble to think like this. It showed a gentler and more playful side to his nature.

And this morning, although his visit had been unannounced, there was an extra special treat in store for Vignoles. The pair were looking across the dusty yard, with its tangle of railway lines, mounds of ash, clinker and dripping water-columns, at a beautifully pristine visitor, its blackberry-black paint varnished to a glossy shine that would please the most demanding drill-sergeant. The paint was as rich and complex as the back of a raven in the morning sunlight, flashing and sparkling as it slowly backed onto one of the shed roads. Vignoles was grinning with boyish delight.

'She's a good steamer, Charles. Spanking new and arrived here directly from Crewe. I wouldn't say no to having a few of these on shed. I've had good reports of how easy they are to work on.'

Vignoles nodded appreciatively. 'A Stanier Black 5. You can see why they're called that. Though normally they're left to get mucky and horrible. Well, that was good timing on my part.'

'She looks handsome, I'll allow that. This is a sneak preview of what is supposed to be a top secret surprise. So don't go letting the cat out the bag or I'll be for the high jump.' Saunders gave Vignoles a sidelong glance. 'Our chief mechanical engineer, Mr Riddles, ordered it to be specially painted like this ready for that exhibition you've been invited to. He's very fond of black, is Mr Riddles.' Saunders nodded appreciatively. 'Eh, but Charles, you'll see some shocking sights there, though.' Saunders shook his head in disbelief. 'Two of the locos have already passed through.' He laughed and took a swig of tea before continuing. 'None of us could believe our eyes. They must have been dreamed up by a colour-blind monkey!'

'That bad?' Vignoles already felt a twinge of excitement at the thought of the forthcoming trip to Marylebone. However, despite the twin attractions of the engine and his friend's story, his eye was caught by a momentary glimpse of a tall, slim and smartly dressed man as he passed a gap in the long rows of wagons near the coal stacks. He was probably walking along the little pathway that ran from the Byfield Road that cut across the fields bordering the yard. This was a route much used by the men to get to the depot, which was inconveniently situated at the far north end of Woodford Halse village. The clear morning light illuminated the man and it was this that attracted Vignoles's attention. Even at that distance it was obvious he was not footplate crew or a fitter, for no one would wear what looked to be an expensive blazer to work in an engine shed.

And there was something oddly familiar about this figure. Vignoles wondered if he had seen him somewhere before.

He brought himself back to listen to what Saunders was saying. The shedmaster was in full flow. 'And so, if you ask me, black will do just fine. We can patch up black in our repair shops, no bother. These bright colours are all very well, but as everything's so short these days, I can't see how we'll get the supplies. You just can't get paint unless it's black or that depressing dark green stuff the Great Western seem to like. And if you do strike lucky and get an apple green or whatever, the pigments are not stable, so they fade and then the new paint doesn't match up with the old. It's asking for trouble.'

'If you had your way everything would be black. Though, if it looks like this, it's a quite lovely sight and is winning me over.'

'And that is exactly the new CME's way of thinking! After the top brass and all the other nobs have had their fill of these garish new colours, he's going to let this one steam into Marylebone on a regular service train, as if nothing special were happening. Everyone will look at this beauty and say...' Saunders adopted a comically posh voice, '*Oh, goodness me! That looks so much nicer, don't you know? I do declare that black is best after all.*' Saunders creased over in laughter and slapped his thigh. 'Priceless. I'm warming to this Mr Riddles.'

Vignoles joined in, enjoying the joke. Had that official-looking gentleman he had caught a fleeting glimpse of been sent down to keep an eye on this secret weapon?

'Changing the subject, Tim, I wanted to ask how Paul is getting on. He's posted to Italy, I believe?'

'Our Paul? He's doing well, thank you. Not we hear that much, of course, as there's only so much he can put in a letter, what with security and everything.' Vignoles nodded. 'He was sent to Trieste at the start of the year. It's considered a good posting. A pretty easy life, he says. Though, of course, they're there for a reason.'

'Keeping that Marshal Tito fellow from getting too presumptuous?'

'Something like that. Stopping the Jugoslavians, the Italians and the Austrians from getting at each other's throats, from what I can tell. I don't suppose those neighbours are the best of pals!' Saunders laughed again, though it now lacked the same conviction. He gave Vignoles a sideways look as he did so, his face taking on a more serious aspect. His voice was quieter when he continued. 'I presume you read today's paper?'

'I did. It reminded me that Paul was out there. That poor lad was in the same regiment, I think.'

'He was. His name meant nothing to me, though.'

'I suppose it was a pub brawl or something that got out of hand. The paper said very little.'

'Probably. Aye, well. Ever the detective, eh?' Saunders drained his mug of tea and threw the dregs onto the ground, where they formed a small, dark stain in the grey ash. 'They deal mainly with rioting and insurrection, from what I understand. It's not exactly a war zone. But I suppose there's always going to be the odd incident.' Saunders sat more upright and filled his lungs with a long inhalation of air. 'Like you say, it was most likely a stupid argument. I'm not worried. Paul can handle himself.'

'When does he get his discharge?'

'End of the year. Not so long now.' Saunders grinned. 'Maybe he'll come and work on the railway. Though in truth, I rather hope he can find himself something a bit, well, a bit *better*, I suppose. I'd like him to get a white-collar position. He's bright enough to be an office wallah.'

'British Railways is going to need a lot of staff, now everything is so much bigger.'

'You're right enough there. But don't get me started on the blummin' National Railway. Run by a bunch of commies! All as red as you can get.'

'That's a bit strong.'

'Not really. We're no better than the Soviets, the way things are going.' Vignoles gave Saunders an inquiring look and prepared himself for the soapbox speech.

'I know you're all for Mr Attlee and his merry comrades, but it's all around us. Look over there.' Saunders pointed to an Austin van, its tailgate opened so that drums of oil could be unloaded into an adjacent storeroom. 'They deliver our paraffin, light machine oils and the like. Now old Dick Turner's been running that business since the twenties. His son helps out now and they've made a decent family business of it. Survived the war and everything. But now what? They've had British Bloody Road Services painted over the sides and they work for the government! Why have *they* taken it over?'

'The British Transport Commission is operating everything on behalf of the people, all for the common good, Tim.'

'You believe that? Forcibly taken for the good of the chancellor, more like! It's just not proper. It fair makes me want to spit.'

Vignoles nodded thoughtfully.

'And look there, flippin' British Parcels Services.' Saunders pointed to a green-painted van with cream letters on its side motoring along the Byfield Road. 'Is there no end to it?'

'But that's part of our postal service. His Majesty's Post Office, no less. Surely you don't object to that?'

'Not if His Majesty owns it, I don't. But then why does it not say so on the side of the van? Say what you like, the State — and not the king — has taken everything over. The railways, the airports, the docks, the electric, the gas, the water, the mines, the ferries, the roads. Of course, I blame the unions. They're getting far too radical. All they do is agitate and spout off about Marxism, Trotsky, class war and I don't know what else. It's got out of hand, Charles.'

'What about this new National Health Service and free schooling? They're going to be a marvellous improvement for us all. It will help equal things out. Even you must concede that's got to be a good thing.' Vignoles raised an eyebrow and waited for the riposte.

'Aye, well, they sound promising enough, I s'pose. But enough really is enough. I want no more of it. And mark my words, I'm not alone in thinking that way.'

* * * *

Twenty minutes later Vignoles had taken his leave of Tim Saunders and cast a final admiring glance at the raven-black engine. As he crossed the yard he stepped carefully over the rails and discarded fire tubes, side-stepped the heaps of old brake blocks, bent fire-irons and jagged lumps of clinker, and threaded his way through a row of stabled engines, each quietly hissing and dribbling hot water, then headed past the rows of wagons and the great steely-grey mounds of coal and onto the footpath.

With a loud screech, a fat magpie slowly launched its potbelly into flight and flapped lazily towards a stand of trees covering the small hill overlooking the loco yard. Vignoles was not superstitious, but he still scanned the woods and felt oddly reassured when he spotted its mate gliding low over the meadow.

'One for sorrow, two for joy.' He saluted both birds.

'Detective Inspector Charles Vignoles?'

The voice was strong and the accent impeccable King's English, suggesting a public school education, an impression backed up by his Old Harrovian tie in an ostentatious Windsor knot.

Vignoles had not seen the man until he stepped out from a tall buddleia bush at a bend in the path. It was as though he had been waiting there. But what was most startling was the clear expectation that Vignoles would reply in the affirmative. The man knew perfectly well who he was.

'May I have a few words?'

Again, this was offered as a question, but his piercing blue eyes and thin moustache, that lent the man a slippery quality, his height and the perfectly-enunciated vowels turned it into something approximating an order.

Vignoles stopped walking and considered his response for a moment. 'Sorry, I have a train to catch.' He made a show of glancing at his wristwatch, whilst surreptitiously trying to assess his challenger by his poise and bearing. The immediate impression was not promising.

'So do I, actually, so we can walk together. It's perfectly quiet here. A most suitable location.'

'Suitable for what? I do not think we have been introduced.' Vignoles started to walk.

'Just a quiet talk, old chap. It won't take long.' The tall man fell into step and reached into his expensively cut blazer to pull out a pack of Senior Service. 'Smoke?'

'No, thank you.' Vignoles frowned and kept his walking pace slow and steady; inside his trouser pocket his right hand was balled into a fist. He was sizing up his best move, wondering if he could launch a right hook to the man's chin if he proved troublesome. If he was swift enough it just might work, but from what Vignoles had already seen, his interrogator would be a dangerous opponent. The man walked with a balance to his step that suggested a deftness that came from physical training. Vignoles supposed that he had been a good rugby player, able to run the flanks, ride the challenges and change direction with ease. The man was slim, but he looked strong. The hands, now lighting a cigarette, were perfectly manicured and moved confidently, whilst a thick band of gold on his left hand flashed in the sun like a warning.

'The name's Henderson, Captain Henderson.' He stopped and thrust out a hand, throwing back his head and exhaling a stream of smoke from his nostrils whilst looking down his nose. It was a haughty and contemptuous action that immediately riled Vignoles, though he still shook hands, feeling the strong grip. 'From the Information and Research Department.'

'I'm not familiar with the name.'

'You probably won't be, old chap; we're a pretty new set-up and still getting our feet under the table.'

'Part of the Railway Executive?' Vignoles breathed more easily. So the man *was* keeping an eye on the special Black 5.'

'Ah, no.' Another pronounced attack upon the cigarette followed and the captain exhaled as he spoke in little puffs like the station pilot engine. 'Actually we report to the Special Cabinet on Subversive Activities. Let's say that we are a side-step from the FO.'

The Foreign Office? Vignoles was perplexed. 'And you do what, exactly?'

'All pretty hush-hush.' He gave a wink as though he were inviting Vignoles to share a secret. 'We're running a few discreet checks. It's nothing grim, but it's strictly off the record.' He flashed a wide grin, showing impeccable teeth, but his eyes were searching.

'And you wish to speak with me?' Vignoles was puzzled.

'Look, what say we walk on?'

They started again towards Woodford, that lay invitingly ahead in a blue haze of heat and locomotive smoke.

'Were you waiting for me?' asked Vignoles.

'It was a perfectly opportune moment.'

'Why not make an appointment to see me at my office?'

'Discretion. And walls have ears, remember?'

'How did you know that I would be at Woodford loco?' Vignoles frowned and clenched his fist again. 'Have you been following me?' Henderson's face started to jog a slight memory of someone he had seen recently.

'I was aware that you were coming here, so I decided it would be far nicer to be outside on such a grand day, don't you agree?' Another flash of a smile and more smoke in twin streams from his nose.

Vignoles held his breath to try and moderate his accelerating heartbeat. He had only made the snap decision to travel to Woodford after talking with Anna at breakfast. So how could Henderson know he would be there? He would have had to be quick off the mark as Vignoles had been in Woodford for little more than an hour.

'What's so pressing that it requires this level of subterfuge?' Vignoles kept his voice level.

'I think I should ask the questions, if you don't mind.' Henderson took a preparatory drag on his cigarette then launched in. 'Would you consider yourself a socialist?'

'I don't see why I should answer that.' Vignoles looked at the captain angrily. 'But I shall. Like the majority of people in Britain, I would say I am. This country needs some rebalancing away from the rich and the landed and the bankers and the toffs.'

'Indeed? So, do you endorse the views of the Keep Left Group?'

'Holding the position I do, I prefer to not discuss politics.'

'But you *did* vote for our present government.' Henderson held up a placatory hand, the cigarette between his fingers. 'You as good as said so. Will you continue to support the Labour Party at the next general election?'

'This is none of your business, captain.'

'Actually, old chap, your politics *is* my business.' He blew a smoke ring, which hung on the air, twisting and slowly expanding until it faded away, like a lost dream. He raised an eyebrow, smugly pleased with his skill.

'I shall always serve any democratically elected government,' added Vignoles, riled, but also puzzled at this unexpected line of questioning.

'Most commendable, inspector. But perhaps not everyone is as reasonable as you. Things are not going quite as smoothly as the government would wish. These are straitened times and people are starting to question the way things are done; the Empire is taking a bit of pounding; new ideologies are springing up all over the place — rather like a rash.' Henderson's smooth and perfectly enunciated vowels betrayed more than a hint of contempt as he closed the sentence. Vignoles stared ahead, wondering where this was leading. 'And there are some who even think the country is not going far enough to the Left.' Henderson eyed Vignoles as he spoke.

'Look here, I've had quite enough of this.'

Henderson suddenly stopped and turned to face Vignoles, his broad shoulders subtly impeding his way. 'I don't think you understand. I do have the right to ask these questions and I shall get your answers. But don't fly off the handle about it, dear chap, as I already know your opinions on just about everything — though I do prefer to hear them from the horse's mouth, if you will pardon the inelegant expression. So now, do be a good fellow and play along and I can get out of your hair — for now.'

Their eyes met, and both knew that Vignoles was considering landing a punch on Henderson's nose. 'I would not recommend that course of action, inspector. I was top of the class in hand-to-hand combat.'

'Did you search my office?'

'Not me, old chap!'

'One of your accomplices, then. Why?'

Captain Henderson evaded the question. 'Let's get back to the matter in hand. Do you still subscribe to the Left Book Society?'

'What?' Vignoles stopped and swivelled around to stare towards the clump of woodland to his left, drawn by another sharp screech from the magpie, that sounded like a broken clockwork toy.

One for sorrow, two for a meddling busybody. Vignoles adapted the rhyme in his head as he watched the heavy bird land, making the bough bounce and sway with its weight. 'Have you nothing better to think about than a bunch of out-of-date books?' Vignoles confronted Henderson again. 'And besides, Attlee and Cripps both supplied volumes to that series. Hardly a crime to read *their* writings, is it?'

'Of course not. No, I was thinking more along the lines of the deliciously mistitled *Soviet Democracy.* An unpleasantly ironic title, don't you think? Was that more to your liking?'

'I haven't read any of that claptrap in years. I cancelled the subscription in '39.' Vignoles felt his throat turn dry. This was crazy. That book title had suddenly triggered a long-repressed emotion. It was as if Henderson had broken a bad dream. Why had he selected that particular book from the hundreds published by the Left Book Society? Vignoles had once carried it around like a prayer book, slung into a haversack or pushed into a coat pocket, ready to be pulled out and used to help win a heated political argument in a café or a student meeting. But these were the actions of a young man, of someone from a different life and a long-lost age. Vignoles wanted to shut out the memories now re-invading his mind. He regained his composure and realised that Henderson was speaking.

'Or perhaps you prefer George Orwell? Not a communist, at least. Though that is not his real name. I'm always suspicious of a man who wishes to be someone else. I wonder what he has to hide.'

'What on earth are you wittering on about? He's an interesting writer, thought-provoking.' Vignoles stumbled on, mind reeling about other things.

'But thoughts, when provoked, can be roused into action. Rather like your old college comrades, eh? They were roused into action in no uncertain terms.'

Vignoles felt the ground lurch as if there was a minor earth tremor.

'You didn't join the International Brigades — unlike your chums. And your young brother, of course.'

A deathly silence fell.

'Not very comradely, was it? Did you doubt your solidarity with the common man, or did your courage fail you?'

Vignoles set his jaw firm and stared ahead. Willie Shannon and Jimmy Baron. So much had happened since those days sitting in the Leicester and Rutland College bar with his two comrades. He'd tried to bury those memories long ago — along with poor Willie, who'd been killed whilst standing waist deep in sea water at Dunkirk. And what of Jimmy? He'd not spoken with him for years. He'd never forgiven him for what happened, although, truthfully, it was not really his fault. Who knows where Jimmy was now, or if he were even still alive? Vignoles remembered hearing that he'd gone into Europe just as the Hitler war broke out, but he'd never summoned the will to find out more.

The memories were intense, uncovering a raw wound of guilt. Perhaps they had been right and he had failed them. They'd been in the vanguard fighting fascism and perhaps if more had rallied to the fight in Spain they might all have prevented the terrible escalation of war that followed.

But it was not thoughts about the International Brigades and the European war that were tormenting Vignoles. It was the memory of his young brother, foolish, idealistic, Jack Vignoles. Why did he — of all people — have to listen to his college chums and to their chatter? Jack had lapped up every daft idealistic notion that Willie and Jimmy had fed him. Reading those stupid red-covered books stuffed with propaganda and dangerous ideas. Vignoles shook his head to try and clear his mind. Of course, it had been him, the sensible older brother, who had first brought the damned things into the house. He had read them avidly at first, drinking in the thrilling ideologies and bending Jack's ear with his newly-found solutions to the ills of the world; and yet, a while later, he had been able to temper this enthusiasm with pragmatism and a sense of balance.

That was how he had tried to explain it in the years that followed Jack's death. He'd steered a line between the extremes, searching for another answer, but Jack had nailed his red flag firmly to the mast and marched off, joyfully singing *The Internationale* and *Katyusha*, eager to join the fight alongside the unemployed, the Welsh miners, the Tyne and Wear steel men, the union activists and eager undergraduates. Vignoles stood upright, outwardly calm. This was history. It was over.

'Inspector, how do you stand on Britain aligning with the French and the Italians in adopting a more leftist solution to our current troubles?'

Vignoles glared at Henderson.

'Or should we go all-in with the Americans and chase the Yankee dollar? Don't tell me you've not been discussing such matters. Have we not all wondered about the way things are going with grim old Uncle Joe in Moscow?' Another smoke ring in the air. 'Of course, a conversation over a pint is one thing, and at the IRD, we're all for free speech.' Henderson stubbed his cigarette out on the ground by twisting an expensive brogue in the dust with hard, decisive movements. 'But one needs to be careful.'

'I'm no supporter of Soviet communism or any other dictatorship.'

Henderson nodded approvingly. 'Glad to hear it. That wouldn't play out well at all. Of course, we knew that all along.'

Vignoles lowered his voice and spoke with menace. 'I serve the King and Empire — and am proud to do so.' Vignoles warmed to his theme. 'Communism promises equality, promises to eradicate poverty and offer full employment — noble ideas all. The theory I find appealing, and yes, this country needs to think more about the workers and less about the rich. But in practice, communism is an excuse for the vicious, the violent and the uneducated to seize hold of a power they can't control and use it to lash out, hurt and kill those who they determine as better educated, more creative, more bourgeois than they are, whilst lining their own pockets at the expense of the poor and the needy. It's a cruel system.'

But even as he was speaking, Vignoles's thoughts were elsewhere.

* * * *

It must have been the spring of 1937. It had been warm and the French windows were open, allowing an unimpeded view onto the vicarage lawn and the floral borders, tall with new growth and abundant flowers. A light breeze occasionally lifted the white voile curtains that served to protect their father's books, in their neat rows on the floor-to-ceiling shelves, from the sunlight. The steeple of All Saints' church rose magnificently above the spreading trees that formed a bower at the bottom of the garden, a reminder that their heated discussion was soon to be ended by the impending demands of the mid-morning service.

Time was fast running out and their father's measured voice betrayed a hint of emotion; just a slight catch in the throat, but it was enough. His rational arguments were falling on deaf ears, and he was losing the battle.

Vignoles had stared at the floor, uncomfortable and embarrassed. The morning had been filled with such argument, and everyone knew that the family was now sailing into dangerous waters; that nothing would ever be the same again. It had never been the 'done thing' to bring unrestrained passions into the house, and Jack's unfettered emotion was disturbing the equilibrium. No one knew how to react. It was as if they were suddenly trying to live with a prickly and awkward house guest who was making them act oddly and talk across each other in an unfamiliar manner.

Vignoles remembered the sound of quietly murmuring voices and what might have been a repressed sob coming from another room. He had felt annoyed with his brother. He did not voice his thoughts aloud, but Jack knew what he was thinking. *Bugger off and go then! Stop ranting and get on your way. Leave us to get back to some real work.* Jack had countered every argument offered by their father, repeating the same litany of pat phrases he'd been spoon-fed by Willie, Jimmy and others in the International Brigades HQ.

'Look, Father — although I shall not call you that again, as we must abandon such outdated bourgeois identities that serve only to reinforce the corrupt and hierarchical capitalist system, and address each other simply as *comrade*.' Vignoles had snorted in contempt, whilst their father just shook his head, gently and with profound sadness. 'Don't laugh, Charles.' Jack hesitated as he wondered if he should not have addressed him, too, as 'comrade'. 'This is a struggle to the death. A fight between tyranny and democracy; we can't just sit back and leave things be! There's no choice between fascism and liberty. The common man's time has finally come to rise up and fight the class war. Why can't you understand? What's happened to you? You used to be the one eagerly anticipating the revolution, but now look at you — a bloody *policeman*! An instrument of the state to keep the workers in their place!' Jack was leaning against the heavy oak drawing room table, his hair cropped short like his idealised image of a heroic worker from a Soviet poster, though tempering this by holding a cigarette in one hand and slouching in an attitude of carefully studied contempt that bordered on arrogance.

Vignoles chose to say nothing. He'd said his piece the night before, when they'd both drunk too much beer in the Red Lion and spent their last night together in a slanging match of drunken shouts and confused argument. It had ended in a fistfight in the lane on the way back to the vicarage, both too drunk to cause any real bodily harm. But Vignoles wondered if part of his anger had been a mask to his own sense of guilt.

There was a need for change in the country and the rise of the new and ugly fascism was alarming. Each day in Leicester, where Vignoles had recently started working for the railway police, he saw the stinking slums of back-to-back houses and the inescapable poverty that lay within their alleys and sunless courts. He saw the unemployed men in grey huddles of old coats, fag ends and flat caps on the street corners. He knew of the demeaning Means Test and saw the long dole queues. All this sickened and appalled him. Feelings made all the more intense because of the harsh contrast between these downtrodden lives and the gentle tick of the grandfather clock and the safe regularity of church life in the comfortable tied house that came with his father's living at Dunton Bassett.

Each Sunday, when Vignoles returned to the family home, he was struck by the beauty of the fields and trees, the haughty ease of the wealthy landowners with their servants, gamekeepers and gay hunt meetings; at the slow and measured life of the pretty village; and the sleepy railway station at nearby Ashby Magna, with its quietly attentive staff who knew each of them as old friends. It was all too easy to forget the smog and the stench of open sewers and rotten housing fermenting in the city heat.

'I have to join the International Brigades,' Jack continued. 'To sit here in our bourgeois comfort and do nothing is unforgivable. Spain is the front line against Hitler.'

'And violence is not the way to solve disputes,' Charles had answered. 'It will only breed more violence. And are you sure that communism is so much better? We must seek to resolve this conflict through debate and consensus.'

'Appeasement serves no one but those already in power! If the workers don't rise up, then we'll all be next. You should be proud that British workers will defend liberty with their lives!'

It was this line that had riled Charles as they walked from the pub. 'You're going to fight for the rights of the working man, are you? You've never done a day's work in your life!'

'With millions on the dole, how am I supposed to gain work?'

'You don't even live off the dole, Jack. You're happy to take a share of Father's modest stipend, and then you have the nerve to deny his God!'

'That's damned unfair, Charles! Anyway, I've no wish to work for this sick and corrupt system. I'm glad I never paid anything to the bloody Empire.'

'And how have you managed that? By living off Father's handouts. The Spanish workers will string you up from a lamppost along with the Nazis when they find that you live off the alms of a vicar!'

The fists had started to fly soon after.

The church bell rang its solitary note with a pleading tone that Sunday morning. 'I see that your mind is set, Jack.' Their father was speaking, aware that he was already awkwardly late getting to church. 'There is nothing else to be said. I think it best that, if you must go, then you do so quickly. You are causing not inconsiderable distress to your mother and sister. Make your farewells, and God speed and protect you.'

'God? He'll play no part in the new world. It's all finished with that now.'

The flashback had taken but moments, but was still powerfully intense.

* * * * *

'I shall be speaking to your superiors about this intrusion.'

Henderson seemed genuinely amused. 'A word in your ear, old boy. If you don't want to become a real-life Dick Barton, then keep away from any of the more subversive influences. I'm glad you've dumped those silly books, but do watch what you say — those damned ears in the wall, again.' Henderson winked. 'Straighten up, fly right and you'll be fine.'

Vignoles felt an odd flush of dread. An actor called Alex McCrindle had recently been sacked by the BBC from the leading role in a popular detective series on the Home Service. The explanation given to the incredulous listeners was that he was judged to hold communist sympathies.

'Don't look so worried. The IRD quite like you. You have a pretty decent report in your file. They'll come calling before long. Toodle-pip!'

CHAPTER SEVEN

A STRING OF PEARLS

Glenn Miller & His Orchestra

It was the morning of the grand exhibition at Marylebone and Vignoles was seated opposite Anna in a comfortable and tolerably clean compartment, being hauled towards London in a spirited manner by a very pretty locomotive called *Butler Henderson*. Vignoles puffed cheerfully upon his pipe and was gripped with an almost boyish excitement, determined to relax and put aside the curious and disturbing events of the past week and fully enjoy the day ahead.

And not before time, thought Anna as she looked up from a well-thumbed copy of *Woman & Beauty* and the pages of hints on how to recreate, in fabric-rationed Britain, Dior's New Look, that had swept the Paris fashion world the previous autumn. Anna recognised the signs that she had her husband back to something like his normal self and allowed a slight smile to form upon her lips.

This was in stark contrast to the previous few days, which had been spoilt by a mounting tension between them. Vignoles had been almost unbearable, both irritated and irritating in equal measure, made all the worse because she had absolutely no idea why he was acting that way. He had capped it by fabricating a completely foolish argument out of nothing just the evening before.

Vignoles, in turn, was unsure why he had not told Anna about Captain Henderson or the search of his office. This lack of openness did not sit comfortably with him and served only to increase the sense of unease steadily mounting between them. He suspected his silence was motivated by a failure to understand what these events signified. He felt cornered and unable to take control of the situation and was both angry and sore as a result.

However, today he felt more able to push aside these nagging thoughts about this strange affair and observed the encroaching suburbs in their distinctive yellow London brick, enlivened by the morning sun. The vast, grey bulk of the Empire Stadium rolled past the window, flags already fluttering around its perimeter in anticipation of the forthcoming Olympiad. Railway tracks criss-crossed and forked, and the electric lines of the Metropolitan dipped into tunnels, whilst local trains paused at Dollis Hill, Willesden Green and West

Hampstead with their overcrowded carriages from leafy Metroland. Gas holders, smoking chimneys, ugly factory backs, deepening cuttings and vaulting bridges closed in on either side as they slowed for the final approach to Marylebone through St John's Wood tunnel beneath Lord's cricket ground.

Vignoles stood at the carriage window to snatch a hurried glimpse of the waiting steam cavalcade. A fan of rails branched off towards a gloomy corner filled with coal sidings and a turntable, and stabled upon these tracks, awaiting their grand entrance into the station, was an odd assortment of locomotives looking like brilliantly coloured sweets spilled upon a grey pavement.

'What a gay sight.' Anna stood close beside him, a gloved hand resting on his arm. She smiled. 'I bet you can't wait to get out there.'

He smiled. 'Indeed I can't.'

Their view of the waiting engines was almost immediately blocked by a string of coaches in pale white and deep purple-brown stabled in the platform adjacent to the one which their train drew alongside.

'Before I become completely engrossed, let me find a porter to take our luggage to the hotel.'

Twenty minutes later their cases were safely stowed in the rather sad and meanly-appointed Orpheus Hotel, whose only attraction was that it was close to the station. Luckily, they were not actually paying for its Spartan facilities.

Upon returning to Marylebone, Vignoles gave the waiting DC Blencowe, WPC Benson and five other uniformed officers their final instructions for the morning. Having watched them march off to their appointed positions, he and Anna showed their invitation card and passed through a low cordon of white-painted wooden posts, from which thick red cords were suspended to form a barrier from the concourse. They strolled along the platform, taking in the sights.

Bunting strung between lampposts fluttered in the brisk but pleasantly warm breeze, lending a gala feel to the station. A small, open-sided marquee had been erected towards the far end of the platform where the train shed canopy ended, and within this shady sanctuary trestle tables covered with white tablecloths were laden with glasses, bowls of punch, bottles of wine, brown ale and sparkling mineral water. Waiters in waistcoats and bow-ties polished and re-polished and generally fussed and fiddled with the arrangement of plates and platters piled high with tiny sandwiches, rolls, pastries and a magnificent display of seafood. Various tarts, quivering jellies, blancmanges and other exciting confections were being trundled into position on a twin-decked trolley by two young women in black dresses beneath white lace aprons and caps, their actions scrutinised by an anxious man with slicked hair, dainty mannerisms and a high, girlish voice, imploring them to 'Be careful! My blancmanges will collapse if you shake them any more!'

'So much food! Gosh; they've spared no expense — or coupons!' Anna was captivated.

'The Railway Executive obviously wants to make a good impression. I don't suppose rationing means very much when it's a government-sponsored event.' Vignoles raised an eyebrow.

A slim youth, smartly dressed in a morning suit, approached with a thick wad of pamphlets in one hand. 'Good morning! Would you like a catalogue of the exhibits?' Without waiting for a reply, he handed them folded sheets of heavy paper bearing a design that echoed that on their invitation. Inside was a list of the ten locomotives and three sets of carriages they would see that morning, each with a brief description of the relevant colour scheme and a space for comments and marks out of ten to be added by each guest.

'Aha, there *is* a Merchant Navy here. Splendid machines, Anna. Mr Bulleid designed them. They're still under construction and really innovative. They use a unique chain drive system for the —'

'Ooh, don't get all technical with me, Charles. We're supposed to be looking at the colours, not at how many cylinders they have. I do hope all the men have brought their wives, as I am quite certain we shall make a far better job of judging what looks best. Men only want to discuss steam pressures and coupling rods.'

'Valve gear.'

'Exactly my point. Now, look at that beauty. Is that the *Mallard?*' Anna pointed towards the end of the platform, where a sleek engine, elegantly air-smoothed and sculpted into complex curves, was slowly backing towards a line of awaiting carriages. 'What a divine colour. A sort of purplish-blue.'

'She's *Merlin*. It says here she is *dark express blue*.' Vignoles stared at the engine with an odd expression on his face. 'Is that not ultramarine?'

'I think it's more of a purple. A truly imperial colour. The Roman emperors wore cloaks of such a colour. They could call this Empire Blue — though actually it *is* purple.' Anna put her head to one side and smiled. 'A velvet coat by Hartnell in that colour would be quite something.'

'As a coat, and worn by you, I agree, but I'm not so sure on a locomotive.' Vignoles adjusted his hat brim to shade his eyes from the sun now streaming down from over the tall house-backs.   'You old stick-in-the-mud. You just want them painted black or perhaps green, like that one.' Her eyes widened in surprise as she looked over her husband's shoulder.

'Oh, heavens.' They both stared. 'What were they thinking?' Vignoles watched with an expression of exaggerated horror as the engine, brash and garish against the muted tones of the sooty brick surroundings, whooshed quietly to a halt.

Anna was laughing and shaking her head. 'Even the best fashion houses would struggle to make *that* colour work. Would you call it lime green? It will show the dirt dreadfully.'

'The sooner it gets dirty the better. I'm starting to wonder if this is not some elaborate hoax. Just look at what's coming in now.' Vignoles pointed towards another engine slowly reversing off the coal lines. The new arrival was huge and resembled nothing more than an elongated metal box, its sides flat and almost featureless. These great slabs of metal were exaggerated by a coat of intense and almost iridescent blue paint that seemed to shimmer and glow with an optical effect created by twin lines of pinkish-scarlet that ran the length of the engine and played uncomfortable tricks upon the eye. The colours jumped and flashed and left odd lines imprinted on their retinas when they looked away.

'I have looked forward to seeing a Merchant Navy, but not in such a shocking colour.'

'Quite an avant-garde art experiment.' Anna stared as the monster rumbled towards them. She grinned at Vignoles. 'This is just how I imagine a fashion show. Full of outrage, spectacle and utterly useless concoctions. Darling, I do believe that I'm enjoying this far more than I expected.'

'Glad to hear it, Mrs Vignoles.' The voice was curt and crisp, startling them both.

'Ah, good morning, sir.' Vignoles extended a hand to his superior. 'Anna, you remember Chief Superintendent Badger?'

'Of course I do. Good morning!' They shook hands. 'Isn't this fun?' asked Anna.

Badger sniffed and inclined his head backwards so that he could see out from beneath the brim of his dress uniform cap, which he always wore pulled low across his brow. He swivelled his body stiffly from his hips to survey the scene as if for the first time. 'Fun? I think it a waste of valuable time and resources. But we must follow the lead of our new paymasters and if they see fit to engage in such frivolities,' he made a slight cough, as if that excused their folly, 'then we must be on hand to keep things running smoothly.' He tried unsuccessfully to make eye contact with Vignoles, but he was taller, so he deftly tipped his cap back using the tip of his swagger stick and looked him in the eye. 'I trust that I can be reassured that all the necessary security measures are in place. There can be no slip-ups today, inspector.'

'All is as it should be, sir.'

'Good, good.' Badger nodded and looked around. He seemed ill at ease, his eyes continually flitting from one place or person to another as though he were anxiously awaiting someone. And indeed, the first of the guests were now starting to appear, the platform quickly filled with bobbing top hats and morning suits, bowlers, a fox stole or two and elegant dresses flicked by the playful breeze. It was as if a wedding were taking place.

'Important day, Vignoles.' Badger glanced at Anna, speaking in a low and carefully enunciated manner. 'I have it on good authority that Lord Delamere is expected.' He risked a playful rise of an eyebrow and nodded approvingly. The shocking-blue locomotive gave a sudden shriek of its whistle and Anna and Charles allowed this to substitute for the gasp of excitement that this information was supposed to elicit. 'Though, I must say, after appraising myself of the guest list, I regret that the greater part are very much of the, ah, proletariat; an awful lot of engineers, planners, administrators and office-wallahs and, of course, the expected muddle of Labour ministers. It's all very *democratic*.' He gave the word an emphasis that made it sound ominous. 'Y'see, Mrs Vignoles, I feel that an event like this needs the touch of class that only a lord can bring.'

Anna could think of no response and so just smiled politely, before half turning to watch the shimmering engine hiss and sigh beside her like a panting racehorse. As she did so, Badger quickly stepped a pace closer to Vignoles and lowered his voice to an urgent whisper.

'Could do with a little talk. Important. Within the next hour.' He stood upright. 'If Mrs Vignoles will excuse me.' His voice was clipped and perfunctory again. 'I should make my presence known.' He bowed stiffly, spun upon his heel as if on the parade ground, his swagger stick firmly wedged between arm and body, and strutted off.

'What a funny chap. What did he want?' Anna rarely missed a trick.

Vignoles frowned. He was pondering that very question. 'Not sure. Probably a favour for another of his insufferable friends.' He reached for two glasses filled with champagne cocktail being proffered on a silver tray by one of the smartly dressed waiters. 'Ah, now, I don't mind if I do.' He'd had quite enough surprises for one week and considered a fancy drink no more than he deserved.

'I say, we are getting the works.' Anna giggled after taking a couple of sips. 'This might slip down too easily!'

At that moment a roving official photographer stepped forwards, a badge to that effect pinned to the lapel of his tweed jacket. He lifted the camera to his eye as he spoke. 'If you could just stand with your backs to the engine and look straight at the camera.'

Holding up their glasses, they dutifully obeyed, Anna enjoying the sense of occasion. 'And another, but not smiling this time.' It was over in seconds and he moved on to find other victims.

The chatter of voices rose as the numbers swelled and the champagne flowed. Flags of the Empire flapped and waved from flagpoles and roof girders, whilst small puffs of smoke gently billowed between the assembled throng, adding a sulphurous tang to the collective odour of cologne, hot sausage rolls, brilliantine, Odorono deodorant and warm engine oil. Chirpy drivers leaned out of the cabs of shiny engines, smiling and posing for photographs, their newly issued grease-topped caps reflecting the light. The band struck up *God Save the King* as heads craned and eyes followed a party of dignitaries promenading the platform, escorted by a tall and well-spoken man who did much pointing and gesticulating. A crowd of managers in bowlers and round-rimmed spectacles fussed behind, accompanied by lab-coated technicians and tailed by a throng of ill-groomed pressmen and photographers with big silver reflectors mounted upon their cameras.

Vignoles saw the new CME, Mr Riddles, and two celebrated top-link drivers — their working blues unusually well-scrubbed and pressed, caps in hand — being introduced to an elderly gentleman with a massive white moustache and a monocle. Perhaps this was Lord Delamere. Sir Eustace Missenden, whom Vignoles did recognise, was shaking someone's hand vigorously and Vignoles smiled as he observed Badger hovering around the official party hoping to shake the hand of at least one of the titled men; he was tolerated, but never part of the inner circle, and largely ignored by all.

Vignoles turned his attention to the exhibits, though not before stopping a moment to admire Anna, who was standing some way apart, marking her card as she appraised the avant-garde art disaster. She was one of the few ladies present modelling a fashionably long and full skirt with a nipped-in waist. As the breeze moved her dark curls across the sculptured lines of her neck, he noticed that she drew admiring glances, some less discreet than others, as she stood with her weight resting on one leg, presenting a fine curve of hip. Vignoles grinned and started to award points. Ten out of ten for his wife.

However, his newly-found equilibrium was soon to be shattered once again. He was taking time to appreciate the pea-green paint and brightly burnished copper work of an ex-Great Western engine, the sweeping curve of the nameplate identifying it as *Banbury Castle*. The sun was on his back and this, coupled with the warmth radiating from the firebox, was lulling him into a gentle torpor, aided no doubt by a second glass of cocktail. But the cut-glass timbre of the voice and the reflection of the speaker's face in the glossy paint, though distorted as if in a fairground crazy-house mirror, startled him like an unwelcome jolt of static electricity on a department store stair rail.

Vignoles spun around, but instead of the man he expected behind him, he found himself confronting an advancing mass of people as they formed into a semicircle, with all the shuffling, bumping and confusion of a good-natured crowd being organised by a photographer. Vignoles moved impatiently from side to side in an attempt to see between the heads and hats, but was repeatedly foiled.

Where was he? Darn it! It had to have been his voice.

Vignoles placed his hands on a succession of arms as he tried to ease his way between the ever more tightly compacting group.

'I say, steady on!'

'Room for one more. Ease over James, and let the gent in.'

'Could you just let me through?'

'Taller ones at the back. No! Stay there, sir! You're quite okay where you are.' A middle-aged woman with a fur stole that stank of camphor, competing with too much 'Evening in Paris' scent and holding a large tumbler of gin and tonic, linked her arm into his. 'Oooh, you're tall. Gosh, what a crush! I need someone to lean on.' She rolled her eyes and put a hand to her mouth, 'I'm a bit squiffy!'

She giggled and slid her arm through his again. 'You don't mind, do you, dearie?'

Vignoles tried to move away.

'Right as you are! Don't move. Now all say *cheeeeese!*' The photographer was braced with legs apart, knees bent and leaning slightly to one side. 'And another. Stay still, sir! Smile. Perfect!'

Vignoles's sight was temporarily affected, having twice succeeded in staring directly into the flash bulb. He screwed his eyes shut and re-opened them. Despite the strange, swimming shapes moving across his sight, he had no doubt who he had seen just moments before. Whilst Vignoles had been an unwilling participant in a group photograph, he'd had a look of supreme shock on his face, for he had stared over the top of the cameraman as the tall and unmistakable figure of Captain Henderson walked briskly into the shady cover of the train shed.

Vignoles extracted his arm from the tipsy lady, who allowed her hand to touch his back as he pushed forward. He broke into a slow run, side-stepping groups of curious onlookers as their eyes followed him with a mixture of curiosity and mild disapproval.

'Odd fellow, running around like a lunatic.'

'I believe he might be that railway detective. I hear he's making quite a splash.'

'D'you think he's going to make an arrest? How exciting!'

'Steady as you go, sir.'

Henderson was nowhere to be seen. The bars of shadow that sliced across the train shed interior were disorienting, as were the spots of light that still danced in his eyes. There were more people within this part of the station than Vignoles had realised. The usual daily travellers were being herded into snaking lines formed behind a temporary barrier that gave controlled access to platforms 1 and 2, reserved for the regular service trains. Whilst it was not as large a crowd as at many of the London termini, it was still a noisy confusion and Henderson was lost within it.

Vignoles stood beside the RAF band playing *A String of Pearls* in full swing, trying to decide where to look next. He walked deeper into the concourse, past the many square, stone-mullioned windows of the ticket office, towards the slightly gloomy side entrance that was almost devoid of people. As he did so, he spotted a door labelled 'Gentlemen'. It was as good a place to look as any.

He turned the handle smoothly and slipped inside, careful to control the door so that it closed with just a soft click. It was cool inside and smelled of a mixture of urine, harsh disinfectant and cheap soap. From behind an inner door that was slightly ajar, he could hear the sound of a cistern refilling and a tap running. Stepping quietly on the stone flags, he glanced around the doorjamb.

Captain Henderson had his back to him. He was washing his hands at a basin and appeared to be alone. Vignoles took a deep breath and, in two long strides, was behind him, one arm snaking around his throat and another reaching for one of his wrists. He snagged Henderson's head backwards and tried to force his arm around his back, but the captain was strong and lithe, instantly jerking a sharp elbow into Vignoles's solar plexus with expert accuracy, whilst rolling to one side and effectively ducking out of the neck hold. Vignoles drew a gasp of breath, though he still managed to strike out and land a firm punch to the jaw and rock Henderson, but as he tried to make good his assault, the captain freed his wrist and parried the second punch easily, landing another hefty blow to Vignoles's midriff and a sharp karate chop to the back of his neck that had him doubled up, winded and gasping for air, his hat rolling across the tiled floor.

'Rather an unconventional greeting, I must say, inspector.' Henderson took a few short breaths. 'Let's not fight, old boy. After all, you will lose.' He held his hands up in a gesture of mock surrender. 'You have a surprising taste for the melodramatic.' Henderson appeared remarkably relaxed. The strains of the gentle Glenn Miller tune filtered through the walls and created an odd soundtrack to their encounter. Vignoles stood up, a bead of sweat trickling down his face and his breathing coming in short and rapid gulps.

Henderson rubbed his jaw. 'Ouch, quite a punch! Now do let's be civilised.'

'Are you still following me?'

'What an odd way to put it! I was hoping to catch you at some point at today's bash. Oh, by the way, mirrors and polished taps are an absolute nightmare if you're trying to sneak up on someone unawares.' He winked, pulled a silk handkerchief from his blazer pocket and dabbed his brow. 'Good job I realised it was you. Might have snapped your arm otherwise.'

'I'm getting a bad feeling about you, Henderson. I'll be watching you.'

'I thought I'd spotted you,' Henderson continued, as if he had not heard, 'but the next thing, I was caught up in some awful official photograph, and it would never do to get my face in the papers, so I legged it and took a Jimmy Riddle.' He extended a hand. 'No hard feelings, eh?'

Vignoles did not shake hands. He was through with such false pleasantries and glared at Henderson, finding the man's supercilious attitude intensely annoying. He stepped towards him, one finger raised. 'I've got officers all over this station. You tell me exactly what this is about or I'll have you arrested!'

'It'll become clear soon enough.' Henderson raised his hands again in mock surrender. 'I'm sorry, inspector. We'd planned to take things steadier, but events have rather taken a turn and urgency is imperative. We needed you both up in London to get things moving and this jamboree was too good an opportunity to miss.'

Vignoles again felt the ground wobble slightly beneath his feet. 'Get us both here? Do you mean my wife and I? Are you saying that our invitations were fake? Some kind of lure?'

'No, they're genuine, but seeing as you were both going to be in town, we hurried matters along. I really can't explain now. There's a room reserved in the BTC HQ, number 204 — just over the way from here. Be there at 3pm, sharp. Alone.'

'A meeting? With whom?'

'Security. Very hush-hush.' Henderson winked. 'Say anything and it could get tricky. But don't be alarmed, this will be quite an adventure and the FO have authorised it.' He paused to rub his chin. 'Meanwhile your wife has another task to fulfil in the afternoon whilst you are busy — and she'll enjoy it tremendously.'

'You leave my wife out of this!' Vignoles hesitated a beat. 'What task?'

'Urgent preparations for a long journey.'

Vignoles felt a cold finger run down his spine. 'That sounds like a euphemism — the sort of trick Stalin would play.'

'My, what a lurid imagination you have. My guess is that she'll have been contacted by now.' He winked again and tapped the side of his nose. 'Keep mum. Now be a good chap and don't ask your officers to do anything stupid, like sniffing around outside. We have the ways and the means to prevent them.'

Vignoles stared at Henderson, unsure of what to say, reeling at the avalanche of startling information he was confronting.

'Now you really must excuse me. I have some matters to attend before three o'clock. Must dash!'

CHAPTER EIGHT

SINGIN' THE BLUES

Frankie Laine

DS Trinder walked through the half-open door of the detective department offices, cheerfully whistling the latest Frankie Laine that had been playing on his gramophone during breakfast with his wife. It was a surprisingly chipper tune, despite the lyrical content, and he'd been either singing or whistling it ever since he had purchased the precious new platter a few days earlier.

He tipped his hat to Mrs Green, ensconced as usual behind her typewriter, and was about to offer a breezy 'good morning' to anyone within earshot, when he froze in mid-action, slowly lowering his trilby back onto his head as he formed a puzzled expression. Mrs G was apparently acting out a particularly difficult charade; gesticulating wildly and forming silent words in a series of exaggerated expressions with her mouth. Trinder had no idea what she was about, but each time he made to speak, she put a finger to her lips and urged him to remain silent.

After what seemed like an age but was probably no more than a few seconds, Trinder wheeled away in exasperation, seeking help from another quarter. He surveyed the large room and saw the slender figure of WPC Lansdowne seated behind one of the two big wooden desks that filled the greater part of the office. Her delicately-featured face appeared small and fragile as she returned his look without the usual 'hullo'.

'What?' Trinder smiled, guessing that this was a rehearsed office joke at his expense. WPC Lansdowne nodded her head, unambiguously, towards the partially-opened door that led into Detective Inspector Vignoles's office and pulled a face.

'Oh golly!' Trinder realised that the super must have dropped in on one of his unannounced visits. Just his luck, with Vignoles away in London. Trinder also grimaced, but Lucy Lansdowne did not respond, which he found surprising. *She's in a grumpy mood today*, he thought, wondering if Badger was in a particularly foul temper, causing her to keep her head down. Trinder took a deep breath and stepped through into the office.

He instantly pulled up short.

Instead of the lean, wiry and impeccably smart Badger, who was all stiff back, massive cap, kid gloves and a fastidiously military manner, he was taken aback to see a rather shabbily dressed man of great bulk, with greasy hair combed over his skull in four dark strands. He was slouched in Vignoles's chair, tie askew, reading the *Daily Sketch*, which was spread open across the various reports and files on the desk.

'Who the devil are you?'

The man looked up and folded the paper closed. 'You must be Trinder. Detective sergeant, is it? Grab a pew. Oh, but give Mrs Whatsit a shout to brew us up a nice cuppa, eh lad?' The man had a broad Yorkshire accent.

'I'll do no such thing. Now you get out of here immediately. This office is private.'

'Whoa, hold your horses! I can explain.'

'You've got ten seconds — and make it good,' Trinder snapped. He pulled the office door open wide in preparation for evicting the intruder.

A locomotive whistled shrilly outside, followed by the first deep, gruff pants as it started into motion, sounds that seemed to blend into a hearty series of laughs that were now making the man's belly wobble. 'Hohoho, I do like your style, lad. You've got spirit. Reckon as we'll get along grand.' The man fished into his jacket, pulled out a well-used wallet and flipped it open to reveal a warrant card. 'We've never met face to face. Detective Inspector Bernard Minshul, Northern Division. Now sort that tea out, close the door and sit down.'

Trinder took a long breath. He was aware of Vignoles's counterpart in Sheffield, and he now recognised the gruff Yorkshire accent, always on the edge of breaking into a smoker's cough, from past telephone conversations.

'I know: you're wonderin' as to why I'm sitting in the DI's office, all familiar-like?' Trinder nodded, opting to watch and listen as he tried to assimilate this shocking revelation. 'Just a social call today. A bit previous on my behalf, I admit, but I'm intrigued to see how he runs his set-up here.'

Minshul made a point of surveying the room, taking in the untidy stacks of files, the shelves at one end of the room filled with all manner of bizarrely odd items. The statuette of the dancing girl drew Minshul's particular attention. After narrowing his eyes and staring at it for a few moments, he turned to look at a length of rope dangling from a metal arm piercing the matchboarded partition wall. 'Now what I really want to know is, what's this for?'

'That's for the bell. The DI uses it sometimes to attract attention.'

Minshul raised an eyebrow, then suddenly grinned like a naughty schoolboy. Grabbing hold of the bell cord, he yanked it vigorously to start a series of uncontrolled rings that filled the offices. Despite the noise, he continued to pull hard on the cord, as though he had never heard a bell before. 'It works a treat.' Another cheeky grin, which almost instantly turned to comic confusion. 'Oh botheration!' The rope untied itself with his exertions and fell limply onto the floor where it lay, like a snake, one end still in his hand. The bell continued in a series of diminishing sounds.

Mrs Green appeared at the office door, a look of acute disapproval on her face, her lips pressed into a narrow line. She stared at Minshul.

'Vignoles can't have tied it properly. The man doesn't know his knot-work. It's easily fixed.' He tossed the cord onto the linoleum floor beside the desk. 'Well, how about a nice brew, eh, love?'

'It's Mrs Green. I'll do it directly,' and she turned away, casting a look of displeasure at Trinder as she departed.

'DI Vignoles will not be in today. If there's a urgent matter that you require assistance with, then we can go to my desk.'

'He's having a jolly day out in London. All right for some, eh? Take a seat, will yer? I'm gettin' neck ache looking up at you standing there like a spare part. And at ease, lad.' Minshul waved a hand and an unlit cigarette towards the empty chair. Trinder slowly sat down, accepting a pack of cigarettes that Minshul tossed across the desk and retreating behind the act of lighting up and blowing smoke whilst he tried to assess the situation.

Minshul sat upright and leaned forward, elbows resting on Vignoles's desk. 'My style is probably a bit different to what you're used to. Now, my being here is not quite official — yet — so you'll not have had notice.' He drew deeply on his cigarette. 'Monday is my first day, so I've been advised.' Trinder swallowed but remained mute. 'If truth be told, I only got wind of the situation first thing this morning. All a bit rushed, like. However, I reckon as it does no harm to get the lie of the land. I like to see what I've been lumbered with.' He grinned, 'Only joking, sergeant.'

Trinder managed to suppress a choking cough. 'I'm not sure if I understand. You're joining us here?'

'That I am. Don't worry, it's only temporary. Well, that's what I were told, any road. I'll be running north and south divisions as one department until Vignoles is back.'

'But he's only in London until tomorrow.' Trinder frowned and tried to stop his stomach churning. Surely the guv wasn't being transferred — or worse.

Minshul lowered his voice. 'I only know what the super told me on the blower, and that were diddly-squat, to be honest. Just that Vignoles is being put on some kind of "special investigation" for a fortnight or so.' He raised his eyebrows. 'Therefore, I am taking over the whole kit and caboodle.'

'My guv's not said anything to me about it.'

'Maybe he was sworn to secrecy. I got the impression that the super was in a bit of a flap about it all.' Minshul flung himself into the curved back of the chair, his weight and momentum causing it to tip excessively backwards on the rocking mechanism below the seat, lifting his feet from the ground as if he were going right over.

'Bloody hell!' He flailed his arms and leaned forward to bring his feet back into contact with the floor. 'This chair's a death trap.' He flushed and glared angrily at the wooden arms he was gripping. 'It'll have to go, straight off. Heap o' junk.' He composed himself, pulling and tugging at his ill-fitting demob suit to no great effect. 'As of Monday, I'm your new guv'nor, so let's get a few ground rules established, that way we can both get off on the right foot. Now, your DI's a good detective, isn't he?'

'The very best!'

Minshul gave a sly smile. 'I'll forgive the implied insult and put it down t' loyalty — a commendable attribute.'

Trinder did not flinch. He owed this man nothing and didn't like his manner or his pushing into their offices without so much as a by-your-leave, and quite possibly without permission.

'He's got a good service record, I'll give yer that, though his methods are a bit unconventional for some. Now I'll tell you this, sergeant. I like good, solid, down-to-earth policing.' Trinder inwardly groaned. The man was a chip off Badger's block. 'I expect firm and decisive action from my officers and no pussyfooting around. If you collar a felon, you make sure you show him the difference between right and wrong, and don't spare the truncheon or the fist. Slap 'em around a bit and they'll soon understand.'

Trinder was only half listening. He was staring beyond the broad bulk of Minshul, past the strands of his greasy hair and through the office window onto the platform beyond. It looked much the same as it had only quarter-of-an-hour ago; a wonderful bustle of porters and barrows, passengers standing, walking, talking, queuing for tea at the mobile WVS van or buying slim periodicals from the WH Smith stall. Bright posters and enamelled advertising signs added a dash of colour to the walls. Strong shadows cast by the glazing bars of the overhead canopy raked across all below in a bold series of geometric patterns, caressing, in a series of smooth undulations, the shapely form of a big express locomotive as it drew to a halt. Smoke glowed as if illuminated from within and drifted amongst the chattering throng. All looked the same as usual; and yet everything had changed.

A disturbing sense of dislocation crept over Trinder. He'd noticed that Vignoles had been out of sorts for a few days. If he had been concealing a change of job, then that would account for his mood. Had the guv known of this unwelcome turn of events and not even had the grace to warn him? Trinder felt betrayed. He gazed at the station scene as if in a trance. It was as if all that was familiar about the station was now altered in some subtle but compelling way. This was now a looking-glass version of the world that he and Violet had woken up to that morning. And he was not sure that he liked it.

'I'm not boring you, am I?'

'Er, no. Sorry.'

'So what 'ave you got on your plate right now?'

'I'm not sure that I can discuss my investigations with anyone other than DI Vignoles.'

'Aye, well, I'm probably being a bit presumptuous.' Minshul paused and picked up an envelope from Vignoles's desk. 'However, presumptuous or not, you might want to cast your eyes over this.' He handed it to Trinder. 'Some homework for the weekend. It don't make any blasted sense to me, but mebbe your eager detective brain will see otherwise.'

Trinder extracted a folded letter from the opened envelope, noticing that this was addressed to the chief super. There was almost nothing to read, just a short typed statement in capitals:

STOP THE SCARLET TIDE OR BUDE IS NEXT.

'What does that mean?'

'I was hoping you might tell me, sergeant.'

'Bude — but that's in Cornwall. Or is it Devon? Somewhere in the West Country, anyway. Why did the super get sent something about the Western Region?' Or is Bude someone's name?

Minshul shrugged melodramatically. 'Beats me. Some daft prank, I expect.'

'What is the scarlet tide?'

'All I know is that the super received it this morning. So have a think on it and report back Monday morning. Seeing as the super's involved, I suggest we give him a good explanation.'

'I'll do my best.' Trinder was still staring at the note.

Minshul visibly relaxed back into his chair, albeit more cautiously. 'You know something? I'm going to like working here.'

I used to, thought Trinder, tucking the letter into his jacket pocket. He felt depressed and deflated.

CHAPTER NINE

PLEASE DON'T SAY NO

Paul Fenoulhet & the Skyrockets

'Everything all right, sir?' WPC Benson gave her boss a searching look. 'I just wondered if there was a problem.'

'Yes. No. Thank you.' Vignoles barely acknowledged her presence.

His mind was racing. Was Henderson on the level? Was he really working for a part of the Foreign Office, for this mysterious Information and Research Department? He didn't like the man skulking around in a most suspicious manner. Then there were those strange questions about his political beliefs. Oddly, it had been these that had done the most to upset Vignoles's equilibrium. In his line of duty, Vignoles was pretty much inured to cross words and confrontations, the occasional throwing of a punch and even being shot at. But Henderson's prying questions — perhaps inadvertently — had opened a floodgate of memories that he didn't seem able to staunch. No matter how hard he concentrated on the present, the events of eleven or so years ago were affecting him now, as if they were still fresh and raw.

He realised that he was staring intently at Benson's black uniform cap, though his mind was actually far away, lost in thoughts of Jack, remembering the short letter sent home from the front by Willie Shannon, telling of events in Barcelona. Its last words were: 'Comrade Jack died a hero and martyr to the cause.'

Vignoles pulled himself together and addressed the puzzled WPC. 'Anything unusual to report?'

'All quiet, sir.' She cast a discreet glance at his crumpled suit and tie. This was most unusual but, as no explanation was forthcoming, she said nothing.

'Have you seen my wife?'

'Over there, sir. I think she has some lunch for you.' Benson pointed towards a series of small wooden folding tables adjacent to the marquee. Anna was sitting at one, tucking into a well-stocked plate of food, its twin lay on the table. He walked across and, as he drew closer, he noticed that a large envelope on the table was holding her attention so effectively that she did not even notice his approach.

'Hullo! Is the food good?'

'Oh, there you are. Yes, marvellous.' She smiled brightly, though with something in her eyes that suggested puzzlement. 'I brought you some before the vultures eat it all. But I must tell you about... Charles, has something happened? You look an absolute fright!'

He looked down and realised that his shirt was rumpled and partially untucked and his tie was in disarray. He started to straighten himself and remembered that his hat was still on the floor of the gents. 'I had a run-in with someone. It was nothing serious.'

Anna gave him an odd look, but surprised Vignoles by not demanding a fuller and more satisfactory explanation. She seemed impatient to change the subject. 'Sit down, something most extraordinary has just happened.'

'You can say that again,' said Vignoles. He sat and took a long sip from a glass of white wine that Anna indicated was reserved for him.

'There were two WAAFs,' Anna craned her neck, 'I can't see them anywhere now — they've just vanished into thin air. Well, anyway, they approached me here whilst you were gone. Where did you rush off to, by the way? And where's your hat?'

'It can wait. Tell me.'

Anna again gave him an odd look and continued. 'They asked if I were Mrs Charles Vignoles, and when I said that I was, they handed me this envelope and told me that I must go shopping this very afternoon for a few changes of summer clothes for us both. Something suitable for a hotter climate, they said.'

'As if you need any encouragement to go shopping.'

'Do be serious, there's more. Listen, here's the really extraordinary part. Look: two five pound notes and a whole page of clothing coupons — issued in our names!' She handed the envelope to Vignoles, who peered inside cautiously, as if it held a small and deadly spider.

'This has to be a fiddle. Some kind of fraud.' He recalled Henderson's words and began to wonder.

'That's exactly what I said, but they reassured me that it was completely legitimate and that I must waste no time at all in kitting us out. Can you imagine anything so queer?'

'Are you quite sure you can't see those girls anywhere?' Vignoles shaded his eyes and scanned the platforms and the mass of people, a great many in service uniforms. 'They just might be on the level. That encounter I had; it was with some fellow by the name of Captain Henderson, an ex-Guardsman who works for a new department linked with the Foreign Office — though I'm very unclear about its *raison d'être*. He's been lurking about all week in one place or another, pushing his nose into my affairs. When I understand more, I'll give you the full story. Anyway, this Henderson has just called me to an urgent meeting at three o'clock and told me that you had a task to fulfil this afternoon — on orders from the FO.'

'Buying clothes?' Anna frowned. 'Surely these coupons must be counterfeit.'

'Or special government issue? It's hard to know what to make of it all.' He ran his fingers through his hair and sat back in the chair, staring at the banknotes and the pristine ration book. He'd seen plenty of fraudulent ones, but these were either the very best he'd ever handled, or authentic.

'If this captain is a regular fellow, then why did he knock your hat off and crumple your clothes?'

Vignoles gave a wan smile. 'I'm going to try and find those WAAFs. If I'm not back in half an hour then do just as they say — go and spend their blessed money and coupons and we'll rendezvous back at the hotel at six and take stock.' *Sotto voce* he added, 'Damn, I wish Trinder was here.'

With a quick kiss on her cheek, he stood up and pocketed a sandwich wrapped in a paper napkin, in the optimistic hope of having time to eat it later.

'Charles, no, wait — don't go charging off again. Well, really!' Anna shook her head and in so doing caught the eye of WPC Benson, who was standing nearby. The policewoman smiled sympathetically.

'No doubt it will all make sense in the end, Jane, though I am blowed if I have any idea what he's up to.' Anna rolled her eyes skywards. She'd been married to him long enough to be used to his impulsive actions and this was definitely preferable to his ugly mood earlier in the week. She stood up. 'Well then, there's nothing else for it. I think I shall pay the empty shops of the West End a visit.'

* * * *

For the second time that day, Vignoles was searching the crowded station. He sought two women in blue-grey uniforms. A gang of young air cadets stood huddled in the centre of the concourse and their uniforms attracted his attention, but he soon realised they were all young men. He wheeled around in frustration, and in so doing, bumped into Chief Superintendent Badger, whose swagger stick jarred a bruise inflicted earlier in the tussle with Henderson.

'Stupid oaf, mind your step!'

'Sorry, sir.'

'Oh, it's you, inspector. Nothing wrong I hope? You're blundering about like an elephant, man.' Badger narrowed his eyes, but without the customary steely gaze and did not await a reply. Vignoles sensed that the super was also out of sorts. 'I need that talk. We can take a drink in here.' Badger pointed towards the station bar.

'Sorry, I am searching for someone.'

'They can wait.' Badger's voice had an edge that brooked no dissent. They walked into the dark interior and, as the door swung closed behind them, they were enveloped in a soft quietness laced with the stale smell of cigars and old beer. A large clock clunked rhythmically, along with a series of gentle ringing sounds as an elderly bartender placed clean glasses on a wooden shelf in front of the tall mirrors that covered the rear wall.

'D'you have any decent gin? No, hang it, I'll take a pint of bitter.' Badger looked at Vignoles. 'Same?'

'Thank you, sir.'

Vignoles was observing Badger with incredulity. This was a complete surprise. It was VE Day when Badger had last invited him for a pint of bitter. The super usually preferred to sip a pink gin or a whisky and soda, a habit that Vignoles suspected was driven more by affectation than preference.

'Is this good?' Badger sniffed suspiciously at his pint. 'Watered down, I shouldn't wonder.' He glared at the bartender.

'London Pride, a fine beer, sir.'

'More used to the northern stuff, myself. I like a dark mild. We'll take a seat in the corner.'

They walked through a large archway into a grand room dominated by a billiard table with lights suspended above the green baize. A small extension of the bar curved across one corner and groups of leather club chairs were dotted around tables with beaten copper surfaces.

'Something has cropped up, Vignoles, and I've been forced to take drastic action. It's all most irregular.' Badger tossed his cap and kid gloves onto an empty chair in an uncharacteristically casual manner and took a healthy draft of beer. 'Has that awful Henderson fellow been in contact?'

Vignoles was startled. 'Yes, we had an *encounter* a short while ago.' He gave some attention to his suit, brushing a sleeve straight.

'He told you of the meeting?'

'Yes.'

'Now look, I'll come clean with you. I've been pretty much kept in the dark over this whole affair, and quite frankly I think it a pretty poor show.' Badger gave a sniff, followed by a slight cough. The full range of nervous tics was coming into play, observed Vignoles. 'No doubt there will be a full briefing at the meeting. I was expecting to join you, but, ahem, of course I shall be required to remain here and oversee the mopping up operations at the exhibition — in your absence.' He sniffed again and looked uncomfortable. He began to flick at minute specks of coal dust on one of his lapels. 'So I've rather come at this cold, you see?'

'Not really.'

'I've had to make some operational decisions on the fly. You might not like them, but so be it. Now look here, for goodness sake, Vignoles, tell me you won't go flying off the handle and refuse to accept the mission.'

'I can hardly make such a promise when I have no idea what is being offered, nor even what you are talking about.'

'Fair point, I suppose,' Badger scowled.

'Am I being redeployed?'

'Only as a temporary measure. I've arranged for DI Minshul to step into your shoes. He's a rough diamond, for sure, but he's a good copper and he'll hold the fort while you're gone.'

'Minshul? Are you serious?'

'Do I look like I'm joking?' Badger took another deep drink and nearly drained his glass. Vignoles felt inspired to do the same. 'For some damned reason they've taken a shine to you and want your services. I tried to dissuade them, but there you have it.' Badger stared at his glass. He suddenly leaned forward and spoke quietly and earnestly. 'Charles, I really need your help in this. It would do me — do us all — a great service if you make a good showing. The detective department can make some waves in Whitehall and with the Railway Executive. It could open a few doors.' He winked.

Vignoles was not sure what to say so he drained his glass.

'Just play ball and don't go putting your foot in it. Don't let the side down, eh?'

'So, where am I going?'

Badger sat upright. The confessional was over. He narrowed his eyes and stared for a few seconds before answering, and when he did, Vignoles thought he detected something between disapproval and envy flicker across his boss's sharp features. 'They're sending you to Trieste.'

Vignoles stared in disbelief. What a curious coincidence.

Badger emptied the last drop of beer and signalled the bartender for two fresh pints before adding, with a masterful sense of timing, 'All expenses paid.'

'Ah.' Vignoles pondered this revelation as the barman placed the two glasses on the counter. He carried them to their table and sat down.

'You'll be briefed at the meeting, so I shall say no more. There's something else: what do you know about Bude?'

'It's a seaside place, somewhere in the West Country.'

'Any idea why it might be linked to a scarlet tide?'

'Well, Bude faces the Atlantic, and there's not much "scarlet" about that.'

'An odd letter came my way this morning. I've sent it up for DI Minshul to cast his eye over. Can't make head nor tail of it.' Badger described what the short note said.

'A warning of some kind? But I can't imagine what.'

Vignoles appraised Badger of his vague suspicions that someone was starting a campaign to cause disruption on the railway.

'Interesting idea, Vignoles, but Cornwall is a hell of a long way from here. Can't see how they're related.'

'Nor me, but the letter was sent to you — at Marylebone. There has to be a connection to yourself and our railway.'

'Hmm.' Badger was unconvinced. 'Well, it's a problem for Minshul and Trinder now. You have more exotic fish to fry.'

CHAPTER TEN

I'M BEGINNING TO SEE THE LIGHT

Ella Fitzgerald & The Ink Spots

At 3pm Vignoles knocked on the door of room 204 and it was opened immediately. He stepped into what had once been the lounge of a suite. It still retained remnants of the original dark wooden furniture, the walls were covered in gloomy William Morris wallpaper of entwined dog roses and briars, and the heavy velvet drapes were drawn back from the bay window by thick cords. Through an open connecting door to what was once the bedroom, he glimpsed a more modern intrusion in the shape of a utilitarian desk with a telephone and an office chair. A broken shard of sunlight reflected from a set of olive-green filing cabinets and burnished an elongated patch of the tired carpet.

Three men were ranged in a loose semicircle of leather armchairs and a spindly affair that once matched a long-vanished dressing table. A vacant chair faced them. A young stenographer in trim army uniform sat to one side with her hands demurely crossed on her lap, her machine on a small side table before her.

Captain Henderson, the fourth man in the room, closed the door behind them. 'Do come in, DI Vignoles. Take a seat.'

Vignoles walked forwards as a man to his far left stood and extended his hand. The bands of braid upon his uniform sleeve informed Vignoles of his rank. He had a full beard that was thick and immaculately trimmed in the naval tradition. His eyes, like two currants in his broad face, were dark and inscrutable. His skin, where not bearded, was tanned and wrinkled by salty sea air and his hair was short cropped with flecks of grey at the sides. His handshake was bone-crushing.

'Commander Turbayne, Royal Naval Intelligence, GSI.'

'General Staff Intelligence, Allied Forces HQ, Mediterranean,' Captain Henderson added helpfully.

The man seated to the far right was in civvies, a homburg placed beneath his chair and one leg crossed over the other showing a length of black sock. A cigarette was in one hand, that was flopped over his knee. His hair was centre-parted and shiny with oil. He took his time in standing and the handshake was damp and weak.

'Denzil Oxenby. Operations Director, IRD.'

'You've met Captain Henderson. Gave him a good left hook from what I've heard, haha.' The speaker was in his early sixties, still in reasonable shape and wearing an immaculate army dress uniform. An impressive array of ribbons dazzled when he laughed, as did his teeth. He did not stand, however, just waved Vignoles to sit. 'You're slipping, Henderson. Letting a man take you from behind.' He gave another hearty laugh. 'And in a lavatory. Good God, man, anyone would think you're turning into a pansy.' He gave a stage wink towards Commander Turbayne.

Henderson clenched his jaw and darted an accusatory glance at Vignoles before stepping out of the room.

'I find it quite unacceptable that DI Vignoles should assault one of my officers in an unprovoked attack.'

'Oh, do be quiet, Oxenby. Henderson's a pro. He should be more bloody careful.' The speaker looked at Vignoles with a wicked grin. 'Sorry, forgetting my manners. Brigadier Sir Terence Harper-Tarr, Allied Military Government, Trieste. So, niceties over, time to get down to business. You know nothing of why you're here and we intend to keep it like that, as far as possible. A strictly need-to-know basis, and trust me, inspector, that is for the best.'

Vignoles coughed. 'I beg to differ, brigadier. Whatever this is about, it will be a considerable hindrance to my work if I am not made fully aware of the whole situation. Good detective work is often about making connections between apparently insignificant details gleaned from a variety of sources.'

'Quite so, but you will work with what we give you, and nothing more. GSI are walking on eggshells right now and a misplaced word could tip us all into a nasty fix. Is that clear?'

It was not, but Vignoles made an expansive gesture with his hands; he had little choice but to acquiesce.

'The notes of this meeting will remain top secret and you will not divulge anything we discuss here today.' Whilst the brigadier spoke, the stenographer tapped lightly upon her keys.

'You will sign the Official Secrets Act, as will your wife. You can do this on her behalf. I have all the necessary documents.' Oxenby, spots of red flushing his cheeks following the brigadier's words, took a lazy drag upon his cigarette before reaching for a leather attaché case propped against a leg of his chair. He clutched it to his chest in a graceless manner and opened the flap, which he tucked under his chin whilst he rootled inside, carelessly scattering cigarette ash on the carpet.

'Later, later!' The brigadier waved impatiently at Oxenby. 'Do you read the quality dailies, inspector?'

'I try to.'

'Then you may have seen the article about the death of Private Brierley.' Vignoles nodded, his pulse suddenly quickening.

'Well, he's the second in a short space of time and we're growing concerned. Commander, would you care to take over?'

Commander Turbayne fixed his beady eyes on Vignoles. His voice was deep and resonant, a good radio voice, Vignoles thought, oddly evocative of rich loam and Havana cigars.

'The first death, that of Private Lawton of the 1st Ox and Bucks, did not attract much attention over at GSI. It was dismissed as the unfortunate result of a private fracas. The murder of Private Brierley on May 29th did pique our curiosity, however, and we shared our concerns with the chaps over at G2 — that's United States Army General Staff, Division 2, Intelligence — and we've started to hear a few alarm bells ringing. Distant and small bells, admittedly, but in this game you learn to take notice.'

Oxenby nodded slowly, reinforcing the point.

'And what game might this be?' asked Vignoles.

'One that requires great delicacy.' The commander gave him a cold stare, then continued. 'Now, for various reasons I shall not go into, the AMG's got thoroughly twitchy.' Vignoles frowned. 'Sorry, these acronyms are a hazard of the job, but you've a long journey ahead and plenty of time to get up to speed. What I'm saying is, that within the Free Territory of Trieste we're taking action to get to the bottom of what's really going on behind these deaths — because there *is* far more to it.'

Vignoles remained silent.

'And that's where you step in,' added the brigadier.

'But surely the military police are investigating.' Vignoles was puzzled.

Oxenby laughed, though he immediately tried to disguise this with a fit of coughing, the attaché case bouncing upon his chest. The brigadier flicked an irritated glance towards him, but this changed into a more rueful expression before he answered.

'The MPs lack the, er, necessary degree of refinement. Of course, they do a decent job sorting out the drunk and disorderly, fisticuffs, ill-discipline, chaps going AWOL, all that nonsense. But we can't have them blundering around the place on such a delicate matter.'

'What about the local police?'

It was the commander's turn to almost choke. 'Good God, no! The Venezia Giulia Police are little more than a bunch of ex-fascists, gangsters, or indolent layabouts. Or all three rolled together.'

'Don't mince your words, commander.' The brigadier flashed a look at his colleague. 'Though regrettably, I cannot disagree. Despite wearing the British bobby's helmet, they've become a bit of an embarrassment.'

'I see,' lied Vignoles. 'But I'm a railway policeman from Leicester. Why me?'

Commander Turbayne replied. 'These two men worked on the railway as stokers — firemen, I think you call them. Neither had been robbed and both were dispatched professionally. A knife to the heart and a single, well-aimed blow; both were neat and quick. The deaths were not the result of drunken fights or robbery, and the only link we can find between their deaths is the railway.'

Vignoles was intrigued and privately pleased that his instinct had proved correct; there was indeed something fishy about Brierley's death. However, he still asked, 'Could it not be mere coincidence?'

'No such thing, in my book. Two men are swiftly dispatched in cold-blooded killings and not a wallet of lira or sterling taken. Not even a wristwatch. I don't consider that coincidental.'

Vignoles was hooked.

'You have a good record at this sort of thing,' the brigadier chimed in. 'You understand the way railways function, their operational quirks, the railwaymen, how they think and behave and work, so you should be able to sniff out things that we might not immediately pick up.'

Commander Turbayne inclined his head back slightly, narrowing his eyes as if looking to the far horizon of an ocean before speaking. 'And we quite like your style.'

'Though I retain some reservations about your political leanings and your wife remains highly suspect.' Oxenby stubbed his cigarette out and gave him an inscrutable look.

Vignoles was visibly shocked. 'My wife remains *what*?' he blurted.

'Suspect. Don't take it personally — all women are a security risk. Such a classification is standard procedure. I'm sure she's a smashing girl, but we'll need to keep a close monitor on her.'

'I do take offence! She's no security risk, nor is she

something to classify.' Vignoles glared at Oxenby. 'And I'm not having some nosy civil servant breathing down her neck whilst I'm away!'

'I think what Oxenby is trying to say, in his rather gauche manner...' The man's cheeks coloured again at the rebuke from the commander, 'is that we can afford to take no chances with regard to security. Women are more susceptible to the overtures of both fascism and communism, so one must always take more care in regard to their loyalties when placed in areas where such influence is rife. You are already aware of the measures we have taken in respect to you own background.'

'My office searched and those ridiculous questions from Captain Henderson?'

'Quite so, and a hell of a lot more you don't know about. We've not had time to do the same with Mrs Vignoles. Though I am sure that we can rely upon her absolute discretion and loyalty.'

'Of course.' Vignoles was already trying to imagine what reaction the news of his hasty departure was going to have upon Anna. 'But why the need to check on her at all?' he continued. 'She works in a railway parcels office. Hardly a den of insurrection, despite what you might think of the unions.'

Commander Turbayne ignored Vignoles's response and continued where he had left off. 'You've done undercover work and you've made connections and deductions that are a step up from your average railway bobby. We've studied a number of case reports. One of the reasons for rifling through your office files, actually.'

'You only needed to ask.'

'If you'd not cut the mustard we could have quietly backed off and left you none the wiser. Vital in this line of work.' Oxenby gave Vignoles an empty look.

Vignoles puffed air slowly out of his cheeks. 'Except that I noticed my office had been searched.'

'But not why.' Oxenby's voice was steely.

'We needed a softly, softly approach to sound you out,' the brigadier explained.

'And for whom would I be working?' asked Vignoles.

'AMGOT,' Commander Turbayne replied. 'That's the Allied Military Government for Occupied Territories. We're seconded to General Staff Intelligence, but all you really need to know is that Captain Henderson will be your man on the ground, and I'm running the show.' Commander Turbayne's inscrutable, currant-like eyes studied Vignoles.

'Intelligence? You make it sound like spying.'

There was a subtle shifting of weight by the three men in their chairs and a short but pregnant pause. The commander's eye betrayed a slight twitch. The moment was over almost before he could register it, but he was sure the stenographer hesitated momentarily in her keystrokes. It was a flight of fancy, but Vignoles could not help but interpret the shrill whistle of one of the locomotives in the adjacent station as a warning note.

'You've been reading some rather lurid pulp fiction, by the sound of it.' The commander laughed heartily, though his eyes never wavered from boring deep into his. 'You must forgive our military mannerisms and terminology. It does make everything sound a little melodramatic to those not within the service.'

'This will be an undercover *police* investigation — Foreign Office driven, nothing more.' Oxenby's voice was dry and curt. 'Hence our involvement.'

'You appear surprised to be selected, inspector.' The brigadier sat back in his chair, neatly directing the conversation onto new ground. 'Your boss, Badger, he was all for passing you over and recommending some blithering idiot from Sheffield, or Doncaster or whatever God-forsaken place up north.' Knowing glances were exchanged, a slight smile strayed onto the commander's face. 'The man just didn't seem to understand what we needed. But we put him straight, and here you are.'

Vignoles wished he'd been a fly on the wall during that exchange.

'Look, this might all be a wild goose chase,' Commander Turbayne began, 'but we simply cannot take the risk. Perhaps the men did just get themselves in with some undesirables who turned nasty. But the argument against this theory is compelling; they would have been robbed of their money and valuables.'

'And they were not.' The brigadier added, 'In Trieste right now, money is king, especially dollars or sterling. One only passes up a chance to take that kind of money if...' he hesitated, as if inviting Vignoles to answer.

'If you are being paid far more to kill them.' Vignoles nodded slowly as he started to turn over the facts.

'Exactly. But who is paying? And to what end?' The brigadier gave Vignoles an intense look, as if expecting instant answers.

'There's no need for detail, but politically things are a bit tense around the FTT.'

'The Free Territory of Trieste?'

'Spot on, Vignoles. We're right on the Front Line. Stalin's

becoming a real worry to the free world and Tito's a loose cannon. Italy's a hopeless muddle with too many fascists or commies running about for comfort. What with Czechoslovakia being taken over by the commies and now things looking very dicey for Berlin, we need to stay ahead of the game.' Commander Turbayne exchanged a fleeting glance with the brigadier. He pulled a packet of Senior Service from his inside pocket and flipped the box open, shaking the cigarettes so that tips of three were protruding. It was time to put Vignoles at ease.

'Smoke?' He proffered the pack and both the brigadier and Oxenby accepted one. Vignoles declined, but extracted his pipe, trying to order his thoughts as he stuffed the tobacco into the bowl.

'Trieste lies at one end of the so-called Iron Curtain, is that right?' he asked.

'Yes. Churchill knew his stuff and was proved right. The Soviets are becoming more threatening by the day and there's a very real worry of war breaking out again over Berlin any time soon. Trieste is also identified as a possible flash point, and for that reason the FO is backing us to the hilt.' Brigadier Harper-Tarr took a hasty drag on his cigarette in a manner that suggested he was more worried than his genial bearing let on.

'So, you are saying that you think the deaths have a political dimension?' enquired Vignoles, puffing on his pipe.

'I prefer to *think* nothing at all. I like to deal with facts and I need you to get me some to work with — and in double-quick time.' The brigadier spoke with the authority of a man used to getting what he asks for. 'What d'you say? Are you with us?'

'Do I have the option of saying no?'

'Haha! I like your style. Good man!' The brigadier leaned across the table and shook hands. 'You'll be leaving tomorrow. A week or so there should do it, but your stay can be extended if needs be.'

'So soon?'

Oxenby ignored the question. 'We knew you didn't have passports, so we're having some made up as we speak, assuming the prints turned out.'

'Ahh, the photographer at the station.' Vignoles nodded as he realised what had happened.

'Yes, he's a staff agent. Not quite the preferred style for a passport, of course, but with some clever darkroom doctoring, they should suffice.' Oxenby had suddenly become animated. 'They'll be ready tomorrow. Henderson will hand them over when he meets you both at Waterloo. We already have your train tickets and visas.'

Vignoles frowned. 'Both? Who is coming with me?'

'I trust your wife is doing her bit and purchasing some extra clothes for the duration?' Oxenby looked concerned. 'You probably only brought overnight bags, but we calculated that these basics would give her something to build on.'

'Are you saying that Anna will travel with me?'

'Of course! I hope you've taken more notice of everything else we've told you! She's Italian — or as good as. She'll prove useful. It might be a British and American zone, but it's like a blasted foreign country out there. Hardly any of the locals speak English.' The brigadier was almost laughing. 'She can translate when you're in the field, and we will provide staff translators for more formal situations. A bit of the lingo will come in handy. Though you'll struggle with the Serbo-Croat, which is a devil of a language. Man and wife together also works extremely well as a cover.'

The brigadier stubbed out his cigarette. 'Trieste is considered to be a good posting, despite these unfortunate incidents, and so don't worry, Mrs V will be kept well clear of the rougher areas.'

Vignoles was open-mouthed.

'We've given you both temporary diplomatic status,' said Oxenby, shuffling papers in a self-important manner. 'A strictly temporary measure, of course. We shall take these passports back upon your return. There's a daily allowance on top of the thirty-five pound limit on currency abroad. It'll go a long way in Trieste.' His voice remained emotionless and flat as he tidied his many forms on the back of the attaché case across his knees. He then proffered a pen for Vignoles to sign.

'Inspector...' Commander Turbayne leaned forwards in his chair, exhaling smoke as he spoke, '... do you carry a gun?'

CHAPTER ELEVEN

WOE IS ME

Oscar Rabin & His Band

There was a short blast on the whistle and work stopped in a series of sounds of tools striking on metal, shovels pushed into loose gravel and heavy, nailed boots crunching on ballast. A collective sigh of relief filled the stifling air. Someone stretched and yawned.

The track gang had been hard at it all day and the early arrival of summer sun had taken its toll on bodies not yet accustomed to such conditions. It always took at least a few days before they adjusted to the heat on their backs and bouncing off the stone ballast, heavy with the strongly pungent odour of creosote from the sleepers. But whilst it made them sweat and their cap bands dark and sticky, it was also a blessed relief from the worrying, bitter winds of winter that had blown long into spring, forming chilblains on feet and hands to make every lift of a sleeper, every pull on the long-handled spanners, an eye-watering sting of pain.

Annie Carrington stood upright and stretched her back, then retied her headscarf to hold the damp hair away from her face. She looked along the length of line they had worked, now shimmering with heat haze, the sides of the rails burnished a deep orange with rust and the polished rail tops like bright slivers of the azure sky above. Green, yellow and rose coloured fields tumbled on either side of the line as a cloud of lapwing wheeled above a patch of rough ground and a slow drift of smoke curled from a distant locomotive held at a signal. She smiled with satisfaction, and though desperate for a bath and a chance to put her feet up and listen to the radiogram, she was content with another day's work done well.

'Come along, slowcoach, Mr Harley's let us knock off for the day.' Annie gently punched the upper arm of her friend.

'Bliss!' Nellie Hibbert grinned, her face blotched on either cheek with a smudge of grease that made her look like a street urchin from a stage show, an image helped by her blue overalls, chequered shirt and neckerchief. She wore a cap over a head of Shirley Temple curls.

Hefting their heavy tools onto their shoulders and falling into Indian file, they followed the lead set by Ganger Harley as they trudged back towards the little red strip of cloth strung between two metal poles that marked the limit of the line possession, a short distance from Rothley station.

They plodded, almost in silence, for a mile or so, the men smoking and offering occasional comments about the evening's drinking session ahead. Annie and Nellie, as usual, were immediately behind Harley. An uninvited chivalry from the six men who made up the remainder of the gang had demanded that the two 'girls' took this position, so the men could 'protect their backs' and 'look out for them'; but this was just nonsense, as their half of the twin running lines was closed to traffic until Harley told the signalman they'd completed their work and the line could be used again. Both women knew the real reason: the men wanted to watch the swing of their hips and look at what womanly curves were still visible beneath their ill-fitting overalls. They were never going to change the way the men behaved, so it was not worth arguing.

They had worked in the line gang for five years and could tackle the job as well as any man. They had to: any weakness would be seized upon and exploited mercilessly. Even now they had to continually insist that they took their place when the heavy sleepers were lifted into position. This was back-breaking work, but both women were grittily determined to do their fair share. If they didn't demand to do so, they knew that eventually they would be seen as weak, as shirkers and then the griping would start all over again that they 'were taking the places of ex-servicemen on the dole'. No matter how many times they received a friendly greeting in the morning, an offer of a cup of tea or a kindly smile during the hardest work sessions, they were under a scrutiny not imposed upon the men. It was unfair and it was unequal, but that was how the system worked. They could abide by its unspoken and unwritten rules, or they could leave and go back to being housewives, shop assistants or factory workers.

It was therefore no surprise that, as they made their way along the line, Ganger Harley spent the whole time looking down at the track, moving his head from side to side like a snake as he checked the work of the day, paying special attention to the sections the women had covered. They knew he was doing it, and in five years he'd had no cause to question their workmanship. This was his prerogative and, as he was responsible for their work, and if they made a mistake lives could be lost, it was fair.

When Harley held his hand in the air and in a firm voice said just the one word, 'Stop!', it came as a surprise. All the more so, because the women knew that this had been one of their better days of work. The gang stumbled into a ramshackle group behind

Harley, their trained eyes already identifying what had caused him to call halt. Annie felt her stomach drop as if on a big dipper in a fairground and Nellie leaned heavily upon a long-handled wrench and made a low moaning sound.

'No one move a step further. I can hardly believe my eyes.' Ganger Harley removed his cap, revealing a balding head turning tomato red from the sun. He darted a look of anger at the two women.

'Dear me. Such incompetence. I've never seen the like.' His voice remained level, the words spoken with great clarity in a hushed tone. The control was ominous and alarming. He replaced his cap and took a few steps forward, one foot on either side of the rail. He knelt down and peered closely at something on the ground, then cleared his throat and stood up and faced the gang.

'Lads, can you see this? You can be my witnesses. Look! This is shoddy. No, no this is far worse — this could be *lethal*!' He glared first at Nellie then at Annie.

There was a low muttering and murmuring from the men, an embarrassed shuffling of feet and a nervous cough. Someone whispered 'Bloody women.'

Annie stepped forward, her face white, despite the heat and the sun, 'But this is impossible, Mr Harley. We checked every single bolt, every fishplate.'

'Did you, now? Well, look at this! Two nuts completely removed and the bolts pulled right out.' Harley knelt down. 'And the others are all loose.'

'But we checked...' Nellie began, but her voice cracked with emotion and she stopped.

'You were probably busy talking about make-up or clothing coupons.' He looked them up and down, noting their grubby faces, oily hands, work-stained overalls and tatty shirts. 'This could derail a train.' He picked up one of the bolts lying loose on the ballast; everyone knew that it should have been threaded through the fishplate and secured tightly to hold the two ends of adjacent rails together.

'I can't explain it, Mr Harley. You know we always do a good job,' Nellie implored.

He hefted the bolt in one hand, turning it and running a finger along the thread. 'You think that joint is good enough to allow a train across?'

'Of course not!' said Annie, tears welling up.

As if to reinforce the point, a train working 'wrong line' approached on the adjacent track, offering a short toot on its whistle to attract the gang's attention. Although moving slowly through the speed restriction, the ground still dipped and rose as each wheel flexed the rails at the joints, which miraculously sprang back into shape as the train passed.

'There's nothing wrong with these bolts except that they are not in place. They're not corroded, worn or damaged.' Harley glared at the women. 'You are hereby suspended. You will leave the railway premises immediately. The lads will fix this mess and get the line fit for purpose, and I will see you ladies in my office at six o'clock Monday morning.'

'Yes, Mr Harley,' sniffed Nellie, unable to hold back her tears. Annie just nodded. There were grumbles and glances from some of the men; others studiously avoided meeting the women's eyes, unwilling to offer sympathy.

The two women walked the remaining half-mile of line alone, heads hung low, shame burning like the sun on their necks.

'We'd have to be blind to miss two bolts dropped onto the trackbed. That almost never happens anyway, and if it does, it's because of a fracture due to freezing or the track shifting. Not just unscrewed and lying there!'

'I just don't understand. We've never put a foot wrong. Oh, Annie, we're in a terrible fix. We might lose our jobs!'

Annie unlocked the chain that linked their bicycles together and they started to wheel them along the cinder path behind the raggle-taggle collection of huts and grounded coach bodies at the far end of Rothley goods yard. '*We* know we're completely innocent, Nellie, but nobody will take our word against that of Mr Harley, or the men. The evidence was plain as day.'

'I don't know how we'll manage without my wages,' Nellie continued, 'it'll be awfully hard going. Should we go to the union?'

'Hmph, the men won't stand up for us women. The union bosses want rid of those who are still in men's jobs, anyway. Even if a union rep pleaded for our reinstatement, he would ask for us to be given jobs as carriage cleaners, not as track workers. Then we'll be on women's wages — much less than we are getting now.'

'Oh my goodness, what will my Bill say? He'll have a fit over this.' Nellie fished a hankie from a sleeve and blew her nose.

'We didn't do it, so there must be some funny business going on,' Annie said. 'Whoever did it must have had the correct tools. We need those great hulking spanners to work on the track, and they don't grow on trees.'

'Golly, I'd not thought of that. You think someone did it deliberately?'

'You know the effort it takes to unloosen those bolts. That's why we've got biceps like duck eggs.'

'Then it's sabotage. We're innocent victims of someone's awful plot.'

They exchanged worried glances as they pushed their bikes along. Brown wicker baskets, which carried their tea-cans and snap-tins, were strapped to the handlebars, creaked as the ticking wheels bounced over bumps in the ground.

'I think we should go to the railway police, Annie.'

'But we have no proof. We're guilty, as far as the men are concerned. Do you really think the police will be any different?' She let out a contemptuous laugh. 'We need some evidence to back up our side of the story, and need it before Monday.'

'We'll start at the scene of the crime and work backwards.' Nellie had composed herself and was thinking hard. 'The men will have re-tightened the bolts by now, but that is not what I am thinking about. Whoever did this had access to the track at some point nearby, yet were out of sight of us and the signalman.'

'It was on a curve in the track, so that narrows down the location.'

'Chosen for that specific reason, I bet. So maybe he trampled through the hedgerow. And maybe he dropped something. It's worth a punt.'

Annie looked at her friend in despair. 'Come off it.'

'Don't give up so easily. And there's something else...' Nellie flicked angrily at a small fly buzzing around her face. 'If this really was sabotage, then it was done in order to derail a train.' They stopped pushing their cycles and looked at each other with the realisation of what that implied. 'Loosening the rail joints on the outside of a curve, so when the line is re-opened the first train along it cops it.'

'Except that the sabotage has been discovered and the defect repaired.'

'But does the saboteur know that?' Nellie slapped her hand upon the saddle of her bike.

'Perhaps not. The man who did this will want to see if he was successful.'

'He might be there now, watching and waiting.' Nellie shuddered. 'Only one way to find out, though! Come along, we can cycle most of the way, then cut across the meadow to the track.'

'But we're suspended, Nellie, we aren't allowed on the line.'

'Then we'll just have to make jolly sure that Mr Harley doesn't spot us!'

CHAPTER TWELVE

COME OUT, WHEREVER YOU ARE

Frank Sinatra & Axel Stordahl's Orchestra

Insects danced in pale clouds upon the evening air as the rich scent of dampening fields filled their nostrils. It was a heady mixture of wet earth, mushrooms and wild garlic. The trees were loud with birds, and a handful of carrion crows hopped through the long grass whilst a stand of bullocks paused in their chewing to observe the women from the other side of a sturdy fence. Annie and Nellie pulled their bicycles to a halt in front of a five-bar gate, sending the skittish beasts skipping backwards a few feet, just as a heavy farm cart pulled by a large and bony horse driven by two Land Army girls drew towards them. The cart was of an antiquated design, its wooden beams and ribs appeared to have been hewn from immense trees before being pegged and jointed together like an ancient galleon. The faded blue and red paint was in places worn away to reveal wood now weather-bleached to a silvery grey, as if it had been at sea.

One of the two women seated high at the front of the cart made a clucking sound and pulled the horse to a halt in a series of leathery creaks and jingles of horse brasses.

'Halloo down there! Enjoying this glorious evening?' She grinned from beneath her broad-brimmed hat.

'Er, yes, thanks.' Annie forced a smile before turning away.

'Are you all right? You both look a bit in the dumps.' The other woman swung herself down from the wagon in an easy movement, collecting a large canvas bag hanging from one of the protruding ribs of the cart at the same time. 'We'll give Samson his feed now. He's worked hard enough today, poor old thing.'

The railwaywomen watched as she slipped the nosebag over the horse's nodding head; they could hear his teeth grinding greedily upon the contents. Annie was silently cursing. She was sure that this was the right place to access the track closest to where the bolts had been loosened, but now it would be impossible to do so without attracting unwanted suspicion.

'Good idea, Doreen. We can rest here awhile.' The driver grinned, 'I'm Julie — Julie Swale.' She jumped down from the wagon and, without waiting for an introduction in return, pulled a wicker basket into view and lifted the cloth laid over the top. 'Look, we've got a few sandwiches, but better still, we've got some bottles of beer!' She grinned. 'I'm thirsty. Care to join us?'

Nellie was flustered and unsure how to react to these unexpectedly friendly faces. 'Oh, but I could really do with a drink!' She suddenly burst into tears; the stress and shock of the last hour finding sudden release. 'I'm sorry. Oh, it's just all too much!' She extracted a handkerchief from a sleeve and blew her nose. 'I think a beer might help.'

The Hopcroft and Norris's Brackley Ale served to loosen Nellie's tongue, and before long she and Annie had recounted the whole sorry tale. Their new pals, Julie and Doreen, reacted with indignation at the way the women had been treated by their supervisor.

'Men are all the same, when it comes down to it,' Doreen Lee said, shaking her head meaningfully.

'Any excuse to get shot of us,' observed Annie, bitterly.

'Aye, but they're happy enough to have us around when they want their meals on the table.'

'And expect us to be filled with excitement when they paw all over us at the end of a long day!'

'At least they're useful for something!' Nellie grinned cheekily, the beer offering a temporary respite to her woes and restoring some of her spirit.

'Chance would be fine thing. Working on a farm at all hours, stinking of cow muck and wearing these, no one will come anywhere near me!' Doreen pulled a comic face and tugged at her thick, bulky fawn-coloured jodhpurs and heavy green sweater. The effect of the beer and a chance to unburden their cares drew a few smiles and gentle, if ironic, laughter.

The four women soon made a decision: they would observe the railway line in a two-pronged operation. 'We'll do anything we can to help,' said Julie. 'Come on, we'd better hurry along and find you some evidence.' She placed wooden chocks on either side of one of the wheels of the cart and tethered the horse to the gatepost.

'We can split into two parties, one of us with each of you, that way we can act as witnesses if we find anything, to help build a case with the police.'

'Good idea, Doreen.' Nellie nodded in support.

'And if there is anyone waiting there, they can have a taste of these!' Julie stood upon the back of the cart and brandished two vicious-looking hayforks, the tines of which were glinting in the late sun.

It was but a short hike across the meadow, lush and plump with grass and clover, dotted with molehills and cowpats from which clouds of buzzing flies arose in one coordinated swarm when they approached. The raking sunlight accentuated a softly trodden impression, suggesting that someone else had already taken the same route, although the shadow-defined linear depression was not sufficiently formed that one could quite call it a path. The excitable bullocks clearly lacked the discipline to have been responsible as they jostled around in a mixture of curiosity, apprehension and snorted breath. The women exchanged knowing glances. This barely visible path just might be the first clue they were looking for.

There was a natural thinning of the hedgerow ahead, and flashing between the gaps in the foliage and brightly illuminated against the gathering shadows was a slow-moving train of coal wagons. It clanked and banged its way south along the 'wrong line'.

'Good, the restriction is still in force,' Annie was speaking. 'But they must be lifting it anytime now. Lets get into position, but move quietly and look for anything suspicious.'

'And any*one* suspicious,' Julie added, her hand gripping the hayfork a little firmer.

It was time to divide into pairs; Nellie and Julie branching off right to work their way along the hedgerow and seek out another place to break through onto the track, the others stepping into the gloomy depths of the hedgerow. Doreen's Land Army uniform proved its worth, with her jodhpurs tucked into thick socks just below her knees, preventing the worst of the snagging that Annie was experiencing to the lower parts of her flapping trouser legs, as thorny briars almost halted her progress and her blue drill jacket caught on twigs and pulled it open. She cursed silently, wishing that she had a tight-fitting ribbed sweater like her new friend, as she yanked her jacket free of another hitch. However, they had soon stepped over a barbed wire fence that had been previously trodden down to little more than a high step-over, and reached the edge of the railway.

'I knew it! Look at this.' Annie whispered urgently as she brushed aside some dampening grass to reveal a hefty spanner of considerable size and bulk.

'Could that be used on the track?'

'Yes, it's one of ours. The same type of issue, any road.' She did not lift the tool, but carefully bent the grasses back to see if anything else were lying there. 'It might have fingerprints on it. Perhaps we'd better not move it and let the police have a look.'

'Good thinking. Look here: a cigarette packet. And still very fresh.' Doreen's voice was excited.

'Someone has been here — exactly as we thought! Crikey, this really could be sabotage.' Annie looked startled. 'And we've found proof of our innocence.'

'This might not prove anything of the sort,' said Doreen, sounding a note of caution, 'though it is an extraordinary coincidence. But you'll need more that this.' At that moment they heard an owl call.

'An odd bird for this time of day,' observed Annie.

The sound was soft and had a slightly breathy tone. It was repeated, but now with a more urgent note. Doreen knelt on the grass and removed her broad-brimmed hat before cautiously lifting her head above the thick foliage, the better to peer along the line whilst remaining hidden as she did so. Her hand motioned Annie to stay still.

'I know that sound.' She spoke in a whisper. 'Julie is fond of owl impressions. I think she's signalling to us.'

Annie nodded and lay prone on the ground, poking her head around a stand of rustling grasses.

It was immediately apparent to both women why the owl signal had been made. A slightly built older man, dressed in a pale grey suit and matching hat, with a wine-red knitted tank top over his shirt and a matching crocheted tie, was standing at the edge of the six-foot some distance up line, where the curve eased before straightening out. He was bending slightly at the waist as he peered into the viewfinder of a Rolleiflex camera fixed to the splayed wooden legs of a tripod. He appeared so engrossed in composing his picture that he was unaware of being observed.

'A photographer,' Doreen whispered, looking down at her companion.

'That must be him! The saboteur. He's waiting to take a photograph of the train derailing and crashing!'

Annie was sceptical. 'He doesn't really look the type.'

'What *is* the type?'

'Fair point. But isn't he too old? I can't see him hefting that dirty great spanner.'

'Appearances can be deceiving.' Annie furrowed her brow and craned her neck forward to get a better view. 'It is a bit of a coincidence though, him being here, right now.'

'But he's standing exactly where the train was to have crashed. Rather foolish, don't you think, if he knew about it? What should we do now?'

'Sit tight. I can hear a train coming along the same track that he — or someone — sabotaged. Let's see what he does.'

The sound of a rapidly approaching train was unmistakable. It was moving at some speed in a clattering roar of pistons, the exhaust beats so fast they had become a continuous sound more reminiscent of the roll of the belt-driven looms in a northern mill than the breathy panting of a steamer. As it rounded the corner, the locomotive, leaning slightly inwards on the cambered track, was something odd and unexpected.

It was an elongated box, devoid of the usual projections of funnel and dome, encased in air-smoothed metal and resplendent in a freshly applied coat of malachite green with bright yellow lines that ran in parallel along the slab sides, the whole ensemble sparkling like a new penny in the coppery fire of the dipping sun. The engine was also rendered doubly curious in that its tender was black and mismatched, creating an ugly and ungainly appearance, like someone wearing odd socks or a pullover inside out.

There could be no doubt why the photographer had chosen that spot and that moment, as he was able to snap the racing train, brilliantly lit along one flank raised by the curvature of the track with the teak coaches it was hauling glowing in a deep orange patina of varnished wood. Fresh coal was being added to the fire and this created a blue stream of smoke that flowed from the concealed chimney and over the roofs of the carriages. For a few seconds it was a perfect composition.

The express hurried past the watching women, kicking up small twigs and leaves in its wake. A wailing whistle filled the air as the photographer raised a hand in acknowledgement of a hand casually displayed in the cab window.

'Did you see that? They were expecting him to be there. They laid that smoke on especially for his snapshot.' Annie rolled onto her back and eased herself up onto one arm. 'We see this happen a lot with the railway photographers. They make requests for dirty rags and the like to be thrown on the fire to make a good smoke.'

'He must be genuine, then.' Doreen pulled her hat back on. The photographer was now standing straight, a hand rubbing his chin, deep in thought.

'Let's go and speak to him.' Annie stood up and brushed some dead leaves from her overalls.

The other two had made the same decision and the photographer was clearly flustered when he looked around to see four tough-looking women, grubby and work-stained and carrying nasty-looking pitchforks, bearing down on him.

He pulled a handkerchief from his breast pocket and mopped his brow, then snarled, 'I say! D'you mind keeping out of the line of sight? I've only got a few minutes more of this light and there's another along any moment.' He peered back into the camera viewfinder.

Nellie plucked up the courage to challenge him. 'Do you have permission to be track-side, sir?'

The photographer straightened up again and squinted with one eye almost shut, causing the other to open excessively wide. It was an expression of intense disbelief, laced with condescension. 'Yes, young lady, I do. And I am taking a pretty dim view of being challenged by a bunch of...' He transferred his staring eye to the fulsome curves of Julie Swale's green jumper, accentuated by the leather belt around her waist, 'Of land gals!'

'We're not all Land Army,' Annie responded. 'Me and my pal work for British Railways. We're track maintenance and this is our length of line. So we have the right to challenge anyone we find trespassing on it.'

'Ladies still working on the track in 1948? The war's been over for three years. So, is that why you were hiding in the bushes?'

'We weren't hiding, we were, er...' Nellie faltered, unsure what she should confess to.

'We saw you getting ready to take the photograph and didn't want to spoil it by making you jump,' Annie ad-libbed. It seemed to pacify the photographer.

'Good job too! I've waited days to see that particular loco. A very rare bird and in a composition I've been planning for sometime. The light, the tilt of the train, a nice head of steam to set the whole ensemble off.'

'Can I see your photographic permit, please?' Annie held out her hand and gave a sweet smile.

He gave her another withering look, but then seemed to relax and reached into his jacket pocket. 'Here you are, miss. I am sure you have a job to do, so I shouldn't complain. Now, if you will excuse me, there's a train approaching and I must concentrate.'

They left him fiddling with his camera and passed the document between them. Apparently, he was Lieutenant DM

Carruthers RN (retired) and he lived in Loughborough. There was little of obvious interest, but it did confirm that he had permission to photograph.

'Excuse me, sir, have you seen anyone else here?' asked Julie.

He looked over his shoulder, impatience again mounting. 'Anyone *else*? Is it not crowded enough already?' He turned back to looking into the viewfinder as the slow heartbeat of an approaching train became clearly audible. 'It's like Piccadilly Circus as it is.'

'Have you seen anyone acting suspiciously? Hanging around, perhaps in the bushes?'

'That would appear to be your forte, if I may say so? And a pretty poor job you did of it too. Whoever heard an owl at this time of day!'

The heavy goods train was in clear view, hauled by an old Great Central fish engine, clanking rhythmically as some moving part knocked with each revolution of a wheel.

'Did you see anyone tamper with the track?' Nellie blustered on, unused to interrogation and having little idea of what she wanted to achieve other than find some clue that might save her job.

'What d'you mean by "tamper"?'

The heavy goods thundered past, the loco crew looking down at the group with quizzical expressions that turned to appreciative grins as they saw the women and there was a suspicion of a wolf whistle, though this was lost in a tactical blast on the loco whistle.

The photographer's face was red with fury. 'You made me mistime the shot. You quite put me off!'

'So you've not seen anyone?' Annie decided to force the point.

'No, I have not! Well, that's a precious frame of film wasted. So now, with your permission, and if you would oblige by returning my permit, I shall take my leave.'

CHAPTER THIRTEEN

FEUDIN' AND FIGHTIN'

Dorothy Shay

DS Trinder was developing a healthy dislike for his newly-imposed boss. The Yorkshireman was bluff and blustering, unnecessarily loud and altogether a peculiar mixture of aggression and forced jollity. He was continually peppering his speech with bad jokes and silly actions, which were rubbing the sergeant up the wrong way. Perhaps Minshul thought this made him appear tough and yet friendly and approachable. If so, it wasn't working with Trinder.

He was standing before what he still considered to be Vignoles's desk, whilst being questioned about his current investigations, Minshul casually flipping through the pages of Trinder's police notebook. He had not been invited to sit, and so his lanky frame towered above the untidy bulk of the DI.

'It's quite a slack time, guv. Thankfully we're enjoying a lull in serious criminal activity.'

'There's always felons at work, sergeant. They don't stop because the sun's shining and we've all had a nice day at the seaside over the Bank Holiday! Yer just not looking hard enough.'

'Actually, I am looking into a recent spate of vandalism along the line.'

'Why the devil didn't you mention that before?'

'DI Vignoles, before he, er, left, asked that we log all the incidents of petty vandalism, cross-referencing with the Midland chaps over at London Road, to see if there is a trend. They've had a number of similar problems.'

'Good. But there's no such thing as *petty* vandalism in my book. Don't forget that. A crime is a crime, I always say. So, where are you up to?'

'DC Blencowe made a list of incidents over the last two months on our patch. Lucy — WPC Lansdowne, that is — collated the results with those from the London Road boys. It's all in this report.' Trinder pulled a neatly folded sheaf of foolscap notes from the inside pocket of his jacket and handed them across the desk.

'Well presented. You've done a good job.'

'Actually that was Lansdowne. She's a meticulous worker.'

'Now y'see, that's one of the benefits of having lasses working here. They know how to handle a typewriter, by 'eck, and some of 'em look fairly decorative, too.' He winked. 'Quite cheer the place up, eh?'

'Actually, WPC Lansdowne is far more than a typist.'

Minshul ignored the comment and carried on, handing the report back to Trinder as he was speaking. 'Right. What about that damn fool letter the super received?'

'I don't know what to make of it. It was posted in the busy main post office in Leicester, so we don't stand a chance of identifying the sender from that angle. There are no fingerprints — other than yours and the super's. And I can't make head nor tail of the curious message.'

'Does that mean you're stumped?'

Trinder hesitated before answering. 'It might be a long shot, guv, but the DI was worried that—'

'I'm the DI now,' interrupted Minshul.

'DI Vignoles thought there might something a bit...' Trinder tried to find a suitable word, 'bigger going on.'

'Bigger?'

'Yes. He wondered if some of the odder incidents over the last few weeks could add up to something more sinister — a plot or campaign of some kind.' He had Minshul's attention and gained confidence. 'DI Vignoles even mentioned the IRA.'

'What? The Irish? Surely they got what they wanted? But they planted bombs, they didn't send silly notes about seaside towns!'

'I am not sure if he said it was the IRA in as many words, but it got me wondering.'

'You can't be serious, lad.'

'That letter does sound like a warning and, on top, there is the incident reported yesterday.'

'I presume you mean this so-called sabotage attempt? What on earth's that all about? I presume you're treating this with the scepticism it deserves or you wouldn't be tellin' me there's no serious crime about?'

'I'm not sure.'

'Give me your understanding of it.'

Trinder recounted an edited version of the curious meeting that had taken place late yesterday afternoon.

He had been seated at one of the large wooden desks,

dictating from the notes sent over from London Road station, whilst Lansdowne typed the report. All was still within the detective department offices. A pool of light from the glass station canopy that formed their ceiling illuminated the desktop whilst casting much of the office into a deep gloom. This same light was striking the young WPC's blonde hair, and the well-polished buttons and insignia upon her black serge uniform were sharply defined and glinted when she moved. Motes of dust thickened the light into almost solid blocks of pale yellow.

They were working diligently, trying to dismiss the disturbing realisation that their trusted inspector had been unceremoniously shipped off somewhere, without a chance to even say goodbye, let alone explain. Both were hoping to find security and comfort in a job well done, when Mrs Green had tapped upon the office door and informed them that two women were wanting to speak to someone about a serious crime.

The women were ushered in to the office, both smartly dressed and wearing hats and gloves, despite the warm weather. Trinder was struck with the impression they had put on their Sunday best and made a special effort in preparation for this meeting.

After they had taken a seat and introduced themselves as Miss Annie Carrington and Mrs Nellie Hibbert, Trinder started to coax out of them their reason for the visit. It was not an easy process. Both were extremely nervous, speaking far too quickly and cutting across each other, whilst glancing across at WPC Lansdowne, perhaps seeking sisterly support from a female officer.

'We're on the railway, see, on the track, but then after what happened, we got thrown out. This morning. Just like that! Mr Harley was not at all sympathetic. It was on account of what happened on the track. He said something was wrong with what we did, but we didn't do that what he said was wrong, on account of it being someone else who did it.' Annie Carrington blustered on.

'Ladies, can you start from the beginning and take it slow, please?' Trinder was already feeling exasperated. 'Let's start with the time and date.'

'It was Saturday last,' said Annie, '5th June, at about five o'clock in the evening. We were on the way back at the end of our shift.' Eventually the whole story was told with Lansdowne taking notes.

'Someone undid the fishplates and took the bolts out. The track was completely disconnected! And that means someone wanted to wreck a train,' Nellie concluded, folding her arms across her bosom in a deliberate manner.

'That is indeed very serious. Where exactly did this happen?'

'About two miles up-line towards Belgrave and Birstall. We'd worked that section then moved on, round a curve, too, so by late afternoon that part of the track was not within our sight.'

After the trackwomen left, Trinder and Lansdowne shared a pot of tea.

'Do you think they concocted that story to cover up their mistake?'

'They didn't strike me as the sort to tell fibs, sarge.'

'Not even to save their jobs?' They both considered this for a moment. 'Mrs Hibbert has a husband and two children; she can ill afford to lose her wages.'

'Hmm. It sounds like they got a pretty raw deal from the railway. Dismissed on the spot. Gosh, that doesn't seem right.'

Trinder nodded and drank some tea. 'You say that, but if they really did leave the track unsafe, what else could they expect?'

Lansdowne was unwilling to accept this viewpoint and her face showed it. 'What about the land girls? They witnessed the discovery of the spanner.'

'That could just be a coincidence. Lots of tools are left lying about on the p-way. I've tripped over a few myself.' Trinder chewed the matter over. 'I wish the guv'nor was here. I'm worried that I'm going to overlook something important. You know how good he is at spotting the unexpected.'

'Indeed I do.' Lansdowne paused and changed tack. 'May I ask you something, sarge?'

'Go ahead.'

'What did the DI say about his absence the last time you spoke with him?'

'He telephoned from London on Saturday evening, as he had Violet's shop number, thankfully. He couldn't speak freely, or at least, that is how it seemed. He said he was as much in the dark as we were about his special investigation, but reminded me to make that list of incidents and try to — what was the word he used? — "interrogate the findings in the light of that curious letter". He does have his own style.' Trinder grinned and finished his tea.

'Then may I suggest that we take the women seriously. At least test their story.'

'I'm inclined to agree. Let me think. Hmm... an attempt to derail a train. All this talk of the IRA and that odd threatening note sent to Mr Badger. It all fits into place!' He slapped the palm of his hand on the table and gave Lansdowne a determined look.

'You could be right there, sarge. What if the spanner does have fingerprints on it? Surely it's worth us retrieving it and getting it dusted. And how about interviewing the photographer? See what he has to say for himself.'

'I admire your enthusiasm, Lucy, but...' Trinder slowed down, 'I suppose that I should first seek instructions from DI Minshul.' Trinder winced. 'Where is he, anyway?'

'I hope he stays away, if that's not too awful a thing to say?' Lansdowne blushed. 'I've not really taken to him.'

'Me neither.' Trinder found no reason to alter that sentiment as he tried to distil the better parts of the interview with the women gangers and his hastily connected plot theory into something plausible for his new boss.

Minshul, however, was far from receptive and the longer Trinder continued, the more exaggerated became the look of disbelief forming upon his face. Trinder ground to a halt and a silence fell between the two men, soon replaced by the sound of feet on the platform outside and a series of clattering bangs as a long train of loose-coupled vans drew to a halt at a signal.

'So, you believe them?'

'I retain an open mind, sir.'

'Very generous, sergeant. Well, there's a time and place for open minds — and this is not one of them. A bigger load of claptrap I've not heard in weeks. It's quite obvious the two women have failed to do their job and are attempting to blame someone else with this cock-and-bull story.' Minshul sat up in his chair. 'Tell me, where is the crime? Some loosened bolts — now all securely fastened with no harm done. A discarded spanner — discarded by whom? By these girls, I shouldn't wonder! It proves nothing. Where's the suspect? The motive? Or are they suggesting that it was an elderly photographer who served king and country in the navy? I wouldn't bet tuppence for a farthing on this saboteur existing.'

Trinder's cheeks started to burn. 'But there is still the matter of the letter, sir. It's nagging at me and though I don't understand to what it's referring, I do know it is a warning of some kind. And the very next day a sabotage attempt is foiled.'

'An *alleged* sabotage attempt.'

'But you must agree that this is a curious coincidence.'

Minshul gave a deep sigh. 'I'm finding it hard to see how a few stolen timetables, a tin of paint and a broken bog seat or whatever constitutes a new wave of Irish Republican mayhem!' Minshul emphasised the point by making a wide, dismissive gesture with an arm. In so doing, he struck a tower of files and sent them tumbling to the floor.

'Bloody Nora!'

Minshul stared at the confusion of papers as if it were their own fault that they now lay where they did. He looked around the office in contempt. 'What is all this — *junk*? It's like one of them blinkin' Housewives' League bring-and-buy sales my missus is always dragging me to. It's all got to go — the lot of it.' He picked up another stack of files and pointedly dropped them to the floor, sending the contents spilling onto the brown linoleum. 'I want all these filed and all the rubbish removed to the corporation tip! Get that pretty, buxom lass in here to do the job!'

'Do you mean WPC Benson?'

'Not too tall and fills her tunic nicely? Aye, that one.'

Trinder felt his face burn. 'She's an experienced officer.'

'I bet she is.' He gave a lascivious wink. 'Without those glasses and scrubbed up in a nice gown, she'd be quite a honey. Still, she'll cheer me up whilst she gets the place tidied.'

'But I need her.'

'That's an order, sergeant!'

Minshul gave Trinder a hard stare for a moment, then spun the chair around so that he might look out of the window. Neither man said a word as Minshul drummed his short fingers on the armrests.

'All right, I'm going to stick my neck out and take your point that there just might be the faintest glimmer of a possibility you're on to something. And since you've given me nothing to tell the super about his crackpot letter, you'd better go away and make some sense out of it all. If you can't, you'd better go out and stop the *Irish Mail* and arrest as many shady-looking Paddies as you can find. Dismissed!'

CHAPTER FOURTEEN

ALLEIN IN EINER GROSSEN STADT

Marlene Dietrich

They were in Villach, Austria, waiting for a new engine to back onto the train and take them on the last leg south to Trieste. It had been a long and tortuous journey, marked by interminable halts at checkpoints and border crossings, lengthy diversions, speed slacks and ugave a deep si
nexplained periods of sitting for hours surrounded by fields and birdsong.

Their carriage had been hauled by a succession of unfamiliar-looking engines as they had rattled, lurched and bumped through a landscape still outrageously shattered by war; the bomb sites of Leicester or Nottingham had not prepared Charles and Anna Vignoles for the scale of destruction, nor the evident suffering of the people, witnessed from their carriage window. This was a vision of a new Europe still in the early stages of reconstruction, and it became hard to remember each broken town when its individuality had been reduced to a depressing rubble of ruins, rows of army tents or huts, temporary signs, motorcades of drab military vehicles, vast emergency bridges spanning the blasted stumps of once-grand piers and abutments, and hungry people in threadbare clothes seeking food and dignity.

But two cities did burn bright in their memory. Cologne had been an endless series of broken walls and gaping windows surrounded by vast mounds of shattered bricks piled into heaps where buildings had once stood; the fractured roads swept surprisingly clean around these weed-strewn areas in a charade of normality. The great cathedral, encircled by clouds of whistling and chattering starlings, arose smoke-blackened and scarred from this monochromatic landscape to look down upon the skeletal train shed and the vast emergency bridge spanning the wide reaches of the Rhine, the grey waters of which were studded with grubby barges pulled by tugboats with smoking funnels.

Vienna had been an unexpected diversion from their planned route. The innumerable problems and delays had forced the train to take a long detour into the Austrian capital, throwing Henderson into a fury at the enforced extension to their journey.

Neither Charles nor Anna complained, however, at the chance to spend a few hours in this fascinating city.

It was a succession of once-grand but now down-at-heel streets, lined with bomb-blasted buildings, tangled telephone wires and shell holes, and groups of sallow people standing on street corners hawking goods. Tables and handcarts were arrayed with curious assortments of family possessions and scavenged articles: broken porcelain figures and beautifully crafted carriage clocks, framed family photographs, oddments of crockery and chairs in need of mending, all offered for sale at knock-down prices. Elderly women, reduced to skin and bone, pulled handcarts with small wheels like toy baby carriages, filled with scavenged firewood or a precious sack of potatoes, across bumpy tram rails and down cobbled streets. Children begging for chewing gum and sweets picked over barren expanses of pulverised brick and roof tiles in air that smelled of the bitter tang of dust and broken building.

Though Vienna had been heavily bombed and there were areas of considerable destruction, it was still remarkable how much had survived of this famously elegant city, though now everything was dark and dirty, the streets tending easily towards gloom, with so many street lamps broken. The fancy stucco of the overblown baroque churches or the imaginative flights of fancy of the Secession architecture were now encrusted with soot or riddled with bullet holes and blast scars. Windows were plugged with bits of damp cardboard or stuffed with rags, the parks dug into plots of land for vegetables and the skeletons of burnt tram cars rusted quietly with buddleia bushes growing around their wheels along tram routes to nowhere.

The Vignoleses had spent an afternoon and much of a night in Vienna, only too happy to stretch their legs and escape the sour air of the overstuffed train. They were delighted to discover that few of the architectural gems appeared to have been lost. For Vignoles, most pleasing of all was the survival of the suburban railway stations of Otto Wagner. Each like a perfectly-formed pavilion in white, gold and green, and although now scumbled with a soft palette of greys and dirty browns, it was easy to imagine elegantly dressed ladies and gentlemen of the old Austro-Hungarian Empire strolling from one of these lavish stations on their way to taking a coffee and a slice of indulgently rich cake in one of the many coffee houses. Not that the Viennese coffee house had disappeared. There were still many to be found along the streets and squares, though it was obvious that times were tough and patrons scarce, whilst the prices were exorbitant. The service and coffee were appropriately dire.

Sitting in the famous *Café Sacher*, Vignoles and his wife observed the pathetic figures inhabiting the richly decorated interior. Frail but proud old ladies with papery skin dressed in pre-war finery, now heavily darned and exuding an air of mothball, sat with a hot chocolate before them, their sad, dreamy eyes suggesting they were trying to relive the lost days of the salon, the opera and extravagant living, whilst grey-haired military gentlemen, with pince-nez of antiquated design and dress uniforms of a long disbanded army, talked of the tactical mistakes of a war superseded by another, more recent conflict. These throwbacks to a lost age sat incongruously alongside spivs, gigolos and louche women in garish make-up, filling the time with cigarettes and a tiny, bitter coffee, seeking a moment of imagined elegance before facing another long night of exploiting a living from the huge army of Allied soldiers filling the bars and clubs.

The Vignoleses also had their first encounter with Churchill's 'Iron Curtain'. They stood and looked at the fresh barbed wire and newly cast concrete blocks placed across roads, and at the lifting barrier and guardhouse that controlled access to the heavily restricted Russian sector, patrolled by severe men in strange uniforms with red stars on their caps and groups of hard-faced characters in long, leather trench coats.

Similarly threatening figures frequently appeared on board their train whenever it was halted for yet another check of their papers and passports. Gruff military policemen, nervous soldiers with twitchy hands on their guns and more shifty types in the apparently obligatory leather coats, with accompanying sour dispositions, would bang the sliding door of their compartment open and commence another lengthy layover of many hours, with just the sounds of tramping, booted feet, shouted orders, barking dogs and the rhythmic sigh and hiss of the vacuum pump on the engine, marking the slow passage of time.

But now, finally, they were close to journey's end, entering the narrow strip of land that formed a natural corridor leading to the city of Trieste, with the jumbled escarpment of the Karst plateau to their left and the silvery-blue expanse of the Adriatic to their right.

The sun was intense and in the train the temperature was in the low eighties, so they had pulled the broad carriage window down as far as it would go to allow in a welcome draught to move the stifling air in the compartment, though this also tugged the curtains wildly, causing them to repeatedly escape from the tiebacks and flick in their faces. As they were at the head of the train, the noise from the American-built S160 locomotive reverberated harshly and threw filthy smoke into the compartment, covering them in smuts and endangering their eyes, but they were all in agreement that this intensely elemental experience was still preferable to stewing with the window closed.

Anna had a book open on her lap; she was making a desultory effort to brush up her Italian grammar, but closed it when Henderson began to speak.

'So here we are: Zone A. The Brits and the Yanks share control, though you'll find the Yanks take a back seat and pretty much leave us to it. It's a narrow strip, extending from Duino — which we're passing now — at the northernmost edge.' Henderson lit a cigarette as he was talking and they all looked out of the window at a yard filled with sombre wagons, at a faintly Art Deco station building in pale marble and concrete and lines of wrecked locomotives, rusting quietly along a weed-strewn siding. 'And it extends south as far as Muggia, where it borders with the considerably larger Zone B, occupied and managed by the Jugoslav People's Army. Trieste itself sits within Zone A, but is technically a separate entity again, run by AMGOT.'

'The Allied Military Government.'

'Spot on. The Brits, Yanks, Eyeties and Slavs pretend they like each other and attempt to maintain some form of dignified co-existence. However, there are regular demonstrations, riots, shootings and fights — but it's quite a nice place, all the same.'

'You like Trieste?' asked Anna, who was attempting to keep her raven-black hair from becoming hopelessly tangled by the wind, retying it yet again beneath a pale yellow silk headscarf, an 'essential' acquisition seized upon during her boon-time spending spree in London, courtesy of the FO.

'Yes. I've been here twice. The first time was in '45 when I was with the 8th Army.'

'You liberated the city?' asked Vignoles.

'No. The New Zealanders did, and we followed a week later.' Henderson sat back on the seat cushions and took a considered drag upon his cigarette, pointing his chin upwards as he exhaled, a mannerism that Anna was finding annoying. 'Actually, it was all a bit of a confusion, as Tito's lot got in first, quite contrary to the agreement. It caused one hell of a stink.'

'Was there much resistance?' Vignoles was half watching the landscape roll past the window, looking at the brilliant world of poplars, pines and scrubby bushes, at the rust-red coloured earth and the dry river beds, the rocky outcrops and the dazzling shimmer of the sea.

'There was some, but one has to admit the Jugoslav Army soon sorted Jerry out. They got a whole pack of partisans to rise up in the city to meet the advancing army. A right raggle-taggle of workers, peasants, women—'

'Women? Fighting?'

'Oh yes, Mrs V. The partisan women gained a pretty fearsome reputation.'

Anna considered this revelation. 'I suppose we'd have done the same if the invasion had come to Britain.'

'Possibly, though I'm no believer in women on the Front Line, as a rule.'

'They didn't have much choice, if the Front Line was right outside their own front doors,' Anna pointed out.

'There were a couple of thousand or more in the partisan uprising and they met the Slovene 9th and the Jugoslav 4th and had the place under control by the next day. The trouble was it had been agreed in advance that the Kiwis were to be the first in and liberate the city. But Tito reneged on the deal and stole a march on us. Of course, he said that it had all been a misunderstanding. Maybe it was, but what most certainly wasn't, was their impertinence in setting up their own administration — they called it the Trieste City Command of the Liberation Front.' He inspected his cigarette, twisting his hand to alter the view as he spoke. 'Catchy title, don't you think?' He laughed contemptuously. 'Anyway, they started running the place like they owned it — bloody cheek!' He snorted.

'Mind your language, please, Henderson.' Vignoles shot him an admonishing look.

'Sorry, Mrs V.' He smiled contritely at Anna. 'But that's how I feel and that's why I say you can never trust a Red. They're out to take over the world and woe betide anyone who resists them.' He flicked the butt out of the window. 'Of course the Allies dug their heels in and we got control back. We were never going to stand for that kind of nonsense.'

'You don't have much time for the great experiment of socialism, do you?' Vignoles asked, recalling their first meeting and the memories it stirred.

'I've seen these people in action and they're a godless, unsentimental lot, obsessed with edicts, rules, committees and subcommittees and everything controlled by secret police. You'll soon find out for yourselves.'

'Do you think there's a political motive to these murders?' Vignoles glanced down at the two thin crime dossiers that had been handed to him at Vienna, courtesy of Commander Turbayne, who had arranged their delivery.

'You're here to find that out, old chap. Personally, I can't see it, though Commander Turbayne is of that opinion.'

'Is that why you are in on this? Because of the political angle?' asked Vignoles.

'You're here to stop us defecting across the Iron Curtain,' said Anna with a smile.

'I trust that will not be necessary.'

'What exactly *is* your role? You've never quite explained it to us. You're not a detective, are you?' she asked.

'Think of me as someone helping you navigate the muddied waters of the FTT.'

'But you work in London. Why not give us a suitably experienced officer on the ground here?' Vignoles gave Henderson a sly look. 'You're over-qualified to be just our guide.'

'I have other duties. I shall be monitoring the investigation and posting my observations back to Whitehall.'

'You are checking we don't suddenly become communists!' Anna grinned wickedly. She enjoyed trying to rattle him.

'That would prove most awkward.' Henderson locked eyes with her.

'Why, what would you do? Shoot us?' She gave him a bright smile.

Henderson changed tack. 'To my mind, Vignoles, the railway lies behind these murders in some manner or another. But the lines cross so many borders and administrations, I can't really see how it fits into any one political agenda.'

'Could it be part of an attempt to seize control of the railway to start a blockade?' Vignoles responded.

'Hard to see how they — whoever "they" may be — could hope to succeed as the sea is still the most compelling way in and out and is heavily patrolled by both the Royal and US navies. In addition, we have troops all along the hilltops looking down on the city, and there are well-guarded border points on every road and railway line.'

Vignoles nodded. 'Smuggling perhaps? Railways and ports have a long association with the trafficking of contraband.'

'More likely. I suspect money will be at the root of this. The chaps who got themselves bumped off were probably on the make.'

'You think they invited the attacks in some way?' asked Anna.

'Pretty likely. There's no smoke without fire, as they say. No one in Trieste kills a Tommy for kicks. If caught they'd be summarily executed in a matter of hours. Same goes for a whole host of other crimes.' Anna looked horrified. 'There's no room for being soft, Mrs V. We've got to keep a lid on the many warring factions and show them who's boss. No, the locals would only risk the firing squad if they were working some kind of deal with very high stakes indeed. Your smuggling theory holds up, inspector. How d'you want to play it out?'

'I shall keep an open mind on motive, but I want to visit the crime scenes this evening. I can start to get oriented and develop a feel for the situation.'

'Righty-o, sounds like a plan. But that will have to wait, as we're coming into Trieste now.'

CHAPTER FIFTEEN

LE ROSE DE TRIESTE

Lorenzo Pilat

With a squeal of brakes the long train of dull green coaches came to a halt. The platform filled rapidly with hundreds of disembarking people, nearly all of whom were dressed in shades of olive, khaki and desert sand, relieved by occasional naval or air force blue. Steel helmets, guns, kit bags and great boxes of equipment started to gather in mounds as the weary passengers assembled themselves. Those returning to duty and familiar with the drill were already striding towards the dazzling sunlight on the *Viale Miramare,* glimpsed through the many arches and windows that pierced the long flanking walls of the station. Fresh-faced army recruits on their first overseas tour stood in awkward groups, blinking in the sunshine, their pale British skin accentuated by the intense light as they smoked and chattered nervously whilst trying to find their allotted welfare officer amidst the confusion.

Anna was immediately conscious of how she stood out from the crowd in her stylish clothes and bright colours, in acute contrast to the almost unadulterated array of service uniforms surrounding her. Even the few women walking along the shaded platform were dressed in muted colours, the faded simplicity of their clothes blending with the great gangs of military personnel, many of whom glanced her way as she passed.

Captain Henderson was fussing with a porter to have their luggage wheeled on a trolley, speaking odd Italian words that peppered his exaggerated English, barked out in short and unnaturally loud phrases. Vignoles, however, appeared impervious to both the attention paid to his wife and the matter of their luggage arrangements. Since he'd been sent here largely against his will, he decided that he deserved at least a few minutes to savour the experience without paying any heed to more practical matters — there would be time enough for that all too soon.

He drank in the new sights, sounds and smells of the station, taking in the futuristic styling of the lengthy concrete platform awnings, the baroque fussiness of the older station building and the salt-rusted signs declaring it to be *Trieste Südbahn.*

They walked down the platform towards their engine, which sounded as though it were panting for breath as it rested in front of the buffer stop, and he noted its pale blue livery, so different to the black applied to virtually every engine he had seen back home. The white letters on the tender declared it to have been supplied by the United States Army Transportation Corps. One of the crew, a powerfully built black man in US Army coveralls, was leaning on the edge of the cab, taking a long draught from his water bottle. He stopped, wiped his mouth with the back of his hand and, catching sight of Vignoles, grinned.

'Hot work?' Vignoles called up to him.

'Sure is, sir. But you should try it in August. Boy, that's really something.'

'It gets hotter than this?' Anna asked, already feeling a bead of sweat forming on her brow, caused by her proximity to the stifling heat radiating from the firebox.

'It surely does, ma'am. I do believe stoking the fires in hell can't be as bad as up here when it's in the nineties.'

Vignoles shook his head at the thought of working in such heat. 'Is this an S160?'

'Sure, siree. But she's all set to transfer to the Jugo-slavs any day soon.' He gave the word an odd stress. 'They call 'em Jay-zee thirty-sevens. Say, you sure know your stuff! You on the railroads?'

'In a manner of speaking.'

Henderson was agitating them to keep moving. 'Our driver should be waiting outside. We can beat the crush if we get a move on.' He ushered them both forwards into the grand station building, and with a regretful glance over his shoulder, wishing that he could continue the conversation, Vignoles followed inside.

The entrance hall was cool, with a high ceiling copiously ornamented with stone-carved figures of bare-chested gods and goddesses, fluted columns and gilded plasterwork. The floor was of polished white and pale grey marble blocks set in a diamond pattern. Anna gazed around and met her husband's glance, rewarding him with a winning smile.

'This is wonderful, darling! Did you know that Mrs James Joyce spent most of her first day in Trieste in this station?'

'Just outside, actually Mrs V. In the *Piazza della Libertà*. She sat on a bench for hours whilst her dissolute husband went to find them somewhere to live. He got drunk along the way and kept her waiting.' He surprised them both with his knowledge of the Irish author as he gestured towards the open space beyond the entrance doors.

They stepped into the sun-drenched piazza towards a great stand of trees shading a square of grass in the centre, the shadow beneath their boughs made deeper by the brilliance that rebounded from the tall, classical buildings that surrounded the square. The heat shimmered around them, emanating as much from the pavement as from the blazing sun above. To their right, a trolleybus was making quiet electrical ticking noises beside a modern-looking depot, the walls of which were plastered with strident political posters. Anna narrowed her eyes against the light as she read some graffiti in big, red-painted letters, that proclaimed *Tukaj je Jugoslavia*. Someone had scored through the words, though rather ineffectually. A group of traders sat beside wooden barrows and upturned packing cases displaying a selection of food produce, mainly plums, peaches, bunches of herbs and salad leaves and mismatched bottles of interesting liquids, all neatly arranged on white tablecloths. Their skin was olive and wrinkled, their clothes as black as the men's brilliantined hair, the women all in headscarves.

A young woman, probably in her early twenties, briskly stepped forward, trim and smart in her green army skirt and short-sleeved blouse, a beret flopped carefully to one side over hair that shone like burnished copper and which mirrored her freckled nose and cheeks. She saluted neatly. 'Detective Inspector Vignoles?'

'That's me, this is my wife, and this is Captain Henderson.'

She offered her hand to each in turn. 'Staff Sergeant Gretton, but everyone calls me Rose. Commander Turbayne has instructed me to accompany you to your quarters. Inspector, you are to meet him at his office in one hour. I shall escort you there.'

'Is the commander here? I didn't see him on our train.' Vignoles was surprised.

Henderson grinned. 'He flew, dear boy. Same for the brigadier, I shouldn't wonder. Places on these flights are like hen's teeth. Strictly for the top brass, don't you know?' Vignoles was not complaining; the rail journey had been fascinating.

A few minutes later their suitcases were stacked neatly in the back of a Willys MB Jeep. Henderson occupied the front passenger seat and Charles and Anna sat in the back. As the young lady officer accelerated down the wide *Corso Cavour* towards the waterfront, a well-built man in his forties, face and arms sun-bronzed, with a thick and unkempt beard and wearing impenetrable sunglasses, moved out of the shadows of the station frontage and tossed a cigarette butt onto the road. He watched thoughtfully as they drove away, not wavering in his gaze until the little vehicle had disappeared from sight.

Rose drove past the boundary of the docks, formed by a long, ornamented stone wall with grand entrance portals that offered glimpses into a bustling world of loading, unloading, sorting and hauling in handcarts, lorries or railway wagons. A six-coupled shunting loco emerged from beneath a stone archway set between two enormous buttresses; it fell easily into step, parallel with their jeep, hauling a string of wagons laden with freshly cut timber.

The railway was embedded in the road surface and quickly branched into three lines that dominated the road curving gently into the distance, fringed on one side by tall buildings. On their right, the dock walls ended by a series of flat jetties and wharfs filled with Royal Navy vessels, steamships, red-sailed fishing boats and the intense blue of the sea.

'The waterfront here is called the *Riva*. Your quarters are halfway down,' Rose explained, speaking over her shoulder.

The jeep bounced over the embedded rails, but, as road traffic was scarce, there was plenty of room for it to keep a safe distance from the engine puffing quietly beside them. One of the crew was resting his elbows on the cab opening, transfixed by the sight of the two women in the jeep. His glance briefly met that of Vignoles and he quickly looked away, busying himself with jetting steam into the road before the water injector caught hold.

Vignoles closed his eyes and took in the sensual delights of the moment: the warm cocoon of heat, the aroma of burning coal, hot oil and highly scented wood mingled with the salty ozone of the Adriatic, and the not unpleasant bouncing of the jeep's suspension. It was hard to remember that he was here to investigate two violent deaths. He must not allow himself to become too distracted by the glorious weather and surroundings.

As if to make the point, the jeep suddenly slowed and the loco sounded its whistle urgently, accompanied by the squeal of its brakes. An ominous murmuring of muffled cries and shouts assailed them and, as they drew close to a broad opening in the line of buildings to their left, the sounds resolved into a coordinated massed chant filled with menace and anger: '*Libertà! Libertà! Libertà!*'

Vignoles opened his eyes and felt Anna's hand squeeze his arm. Rose Gretton swiftly put the jeep into reverse gear and, looking over her shoulder, accelerated with slick expertise until they reached the tail of the train, where they could see the railway guard anxiously observing the drama.

'Blasted rioters!' Henderson exclaimed. 'Don't worry; the army will soon have them under control. It's one of the hazards of living here, I'm afraid.' Despite his casual manner, he was also looking urgently along the waterfront.

'We'll move into the lee of the train,' Rose replied. 'We've not much further to go. They'll leave us be, but it's best to give them a wide berth to avoid the bricks and stones.' She eased the jeep forward between the wagons and the quayside. Sailors and stevedores were standing and watching the growing crowd of protesters, which was becoming steadily louder. The loco snorted and tugged at its couplings as it regained speed. New sounds joined the angry chanting: whistles were being blown and there was the throaty roar of powerful diesel engines, the deep rumble of heavy tyres and what might be the metallic rattle and squeak of tank tracks on tarmac.

Vignoles peered between the wagons and caught glimpses of a mass of men, dressed in heavy working clothes, brandishing home-made placards, sticks, and lengths of timber, and waving red-and-white flags and banners that fluttered in the sea breeze. He could not discern who the crowd represented, though he was sure that the placards were written in Italian.

The sound of a window being smashed was followed by a short scream and then a roar went up in unison, as though a goal had been scored at a football match. In the momentary lull that followed this unified cry it was possible to hear the sound of a great many booted feet running. Stones clattered onto a wagon beside them.

'Damned fools!' Henderson was looking furious.

'*Liberta! Liberta!*'

The staff sergeant put her foot down and they accelerated towards the locomotive and an area of the quay that was free of rioters.

'Who are they? Why are they protesting?' asked Anna.

'Could be Italian republicans, or a pro-Communist Workers' Federation united against fascists, or a Christian Alliance against communists, or simply workers agitating for better pay. There again, they might be Italo-Slavs wanting independence for Trieste or a bunch of Venezia Giulia peasants wanting to leave Italy and join Slovenia. I could go on...' Henderson spoke with disdain.

'The number of conflicting groups struggling for supremacy is bewildering,' said Rose Gretton. She sounded far calmer, and was handling the jeep expertly.

'Allied intelligence keeps a close eye on developments, ensures that the right message is getting through, and helps maintain law and order,' explained Henderson, who was looking over his shoulder just as the sound of a gunshot filled the space above the bay.

'Oh, heavens above!' exclaimed Anna, looked startled.

'That'll be the Tommies. A warning shot in the air soon quietens them down. They rarely shoot to kill.'

'Thank goodness!' said Anna, with relief as she turned around, trying to observe the fleet of army lorries that were disgorging British troops onto the road. 'I think they're Italians.' Anna was trying to read the words painted on a long banner that was being unfurled.

'Dockers from Monfalcone is my guess.' Henderson had also twisted around in his seat, 'Complaining about pay, the working conditions, lack of food — all the usual gripes.'

The crowd had settled with the arrival of the troops, none foolish enough to tackle armed men. A powerful song now arose, oddly stirring and emotional. A long, red banner was stretched across the front of the group, bearing white letters that declared: '*Viva il Comunismo e la Libertà!*'

'It sounds worse than it really is,' said Rose, as she allowed her jeep to slow so that the train could pull ahead sufficiently for her to swing her vehicle over the track across the road and towards an imposing building that towered above them.

The rioters were now clearly visible, clustered at one corner of a wide and open expanse of piazza formed from pale limestone paving that shimmered with heat-haze. The army lorries had pulled up in front of the demonstrators and a stubby little armoured car was pointing a gun above their heads. Soldiers with rifles held before their chests were standing some distance off.

Rose had brought her vehicle to a stand at the entrance to a cordon formed of concrete blocks that created a narrow compound filled with parked jeeps, a Humber staff car and another armoured car acting as gate-guardian. A military policeman saluted, his white gloves brilliant in the sun, and waved them through with a curious look directed towards Anna in her yellow headscarf.

'Here you are — the *Albergo Savoia Excelsior* — the British officers' quarters and mess. This'll be your base. You did rather well,' Henderson sounded envious, 'they've got a pretty decent room lined up. Damned if I know how they swung that for you. I'd not brag about the fact, if I were you.' He raised an eyebrow. 'No sea view, sadly, because they are strictly for officers — but far better than the Lazzaretto barracks by a long chalk.' Henderson was speaking as they climbed out of their vehicle.

Vignoles hefted their luggage out of the rear, only to have it swiftly taken from him by two smartly uniformed orderlies who had appeared from the shaded recess of the grand entrance.

'This is quite some place,' he observed.

'Yes, the Brits spotted this as a decent location and sequestered it in no time,' Henderson replied.

Rose winked at Anna. 'We did better than the Yanks at the Hotel de la Ville.'

'And a cut above the Orpheus Hotel, I shouldn't wonder.' Vignoles nodded approvingly as they stepped into the expansive entrance foyer, a cool breeze wafting from two fans suspended from the ornate ceiling. Apart from the uniformed men coming and going and the portraits of the King and Churchill hung on the wall, the hotel had changed little since its days as one of the grandest in Trieste.

The Vignoleses were shown to their room on the fourth floor. The massive wooden furniture, whilst in need of a good polish, was serviceable and undamaged. The bed was made up with coarse, army-issue linen and the curtains, dusty and sun-faded, were the originals that had once ensured a good night's rest for rich travellers journeying into the hinterland of the lost empire.

Before long, Vignoles had returned to the foyer, to be whisked off for his meeting with Commander Turbayne. Anna remained in the room, flinging the windows wide, and began to unpack their suitcases whilst anticipating taking a refreshing bath in the regulation four inches of water.

CHAPTER SIXTEEN

JEEP JOCKEY JUMP

Glenn Miller & His Orchestra

His briefing session over, Vignoles was impatient to visit the locations where the victims' bodies had been found. There was more ground to make up in the investigation than he had feared.

Commander Turbayne warned him that the investigation was in many respects 'not as far advanced as one might have hoped', and had been brusque and off-hand, probably a little embarrassed by the poor investigative work undertaken, though Vignoles sensed that the commander appeared distracted; their conversation had twice been interrupted by telephone calls, during which he had grunted and barked 'yes' or 'no' a number of times before ringing off.

'A little thin on basic legwork, I'm afraid, inspector. The MPs prefer to throw men into the cooler rather than collect evidence.'

The thin case files that Vignoles had studied on the journey had confirmed the commander's suspicions; Vignoles knew there was a lot of catching up to do. Precious time had been lost and he was glad to be dismissed with the order to 'get something for the brigadier and myself, pronto.'

Staff Sergeant Gretton had been detailed to continue as his driver, a fact that cheered him, because she was clearly as sensible as she was efficient. He was less happy about the annoying and slightly creepy Captain Henderson tagging along. He wasn't even a policeman. Vignoles decided it was worth risking upsetting the applecart by losing the man, if he could.

Vignoles was seated in the front of the Willys MB. He was feeling mildly pleased with himself, for he had duped Henderson into nipping back into the *Savoia Excelsior* on a trumped-up errand and, in his absence, had urged the young staff sergeant to 'put her foot down' and get them away before he returned. 'I need a bit of thinking space without having him breathing down my neck,' he explained. Anna was also pleased: the captain's absence allowed her to sit crossways in the back of the jeep and stretch her legs out comfortably across the empty bench seat.

'Now, Rose, our first port of call should be the one furthest from here, so we can get there in daylight. It's close to the obelisk. Do you know the way?'

'Of course, sir. The obelisk dates back to 1830. It was erected to mark the visit of the Emperor Franz of Austria and the newly built road to Austria. It's a lovely drive on an evening like this and a splendid view.' She accelerated along the *Riva*, now free of rioters and traffic, past a couple of US service trucks, a short row of railway wagons standing opposite a naval vessel and two horse-drawn wagons clip-clopping slowly towards the port buildings.

They soon turned right and into the city itself, along streets of tall and fine stone buildings, some coloured a soft pale yellow; others built from the fine limestone prevalent in the area, and many embellished by statues and carved ornaments, forming great blocks of dark and light as the low sun skimmed its light over the sea and between gaps in the buildings. The road soon started to rise steeply and Vignoles was interested in the tram line that was at first embedded in the surface of their road, but then veered off along its own grassy route at a startling angle.

'I can hardly believe my eyes. That looks far too steep for adhesion alone. Surely it needs rack and pinion?'

'That's the Opčine tram, sir. You'll see one soon enough. They run past the obelisk and on to Opčine — a small border town high above Trieste. It has a unique system to haul it up the steepest gradient. I have no idea how it functions,' she gave him an apologetic glance, 'but the engineering boys say it's something special.' She dropped down a gear and the engine started to whine as it dug into the incline and the road began to twist and turn.

'Don't encourage him, Rose. He'll talk about trams all day if we let him!' Anna laughed. She was drinking in the new sights assailing her on all sides, full of an almost unbearable pleasure at finally visiting her ancestors' home town. The military occupation was a nagging irritation, but now she was here and watching the city dropping away behind the little open-sided vehicle with the scent of pines in the air, this was easy to ignore.

'Actually the tram is of official police interest. It was the means by which Private Brierley is assumed to have arrived at the obelisk.' Vignoles was glancing at the dossier. 'He was barracked in Opčine.'

'Many of the men are billeted there,' explained Rose. 'Others are at the Lazzaretto barracks in the city centre. They generally use the tram, unless they can arrange transport. You wouldn't want to walk up the steep hill too often!'

The road wound its way through trees and past the verdant private gardens of the elegant villas dotted along the hillside. The tram lines reappeared at times from out of tree-lined cuttings as they passed small way-stations during the ascent, the route marked by the overhead electric cable supported on a series of rusting metal poles. Beyond the twin narrow rails, the hedgerows and bushes, pines and poplars, the city resembled a brightly lit model and the whole curve of the bay was clearly visible, the clusters of ships and cranes animated by the glittering sparkle of water.

'There's the obelisk, sir!' Rose pointed towards the unmistakable shape of a tall stone construction like Cleopatra's needle, set within its own discrete area of grass and edged by squat stone pillars linked by decorative chains.

'Stop here. I want to walk the rest of the way.'

Vignoles was already stepping over the low side of the jeep as she slowed it to a halt. He did not expect to find anything after so much time had passed, but his detective instincts still demanded he approach a crime scene with care and attention. As he was doing so, a squeal of metal wheels announced the arrival of a single blue tramcar from around a sharp curve. It paused for a moment to allow an elderly man to step down onto the dusty road and then, with a ting of a bell, it creaked and rumbled past Vignoles and started its vertiginous descent.

'Private Brierley could have stepped off in much the same place.' Vignoles was thinking aloud, partially for the benefit of Anna, who was now a pace behind him. 'He was found immediately behind the obelisk, beneath some bushes. I presume that means over there.' Vignoles extracted three small black-and-white photos of the body and a locating shot. 'I wonder why he came here.'

'Gosh, but look at that view! It's so perfect!' Anna shaded her eyes. 'Perhaps he stopped to look at this on the way back to the barracks. Even soldiers can be taken by a nice sunset.'

Vignoles stood with his back to the pointed stone structure and followed Anna's gaze. 'It certainly is very impressive.'

'Look! There's Miramare!' Anna pointed towards a tiny white castle on a stubby promontory. She bit her lip. 'Oh, I wish I could go there.'

'The Americans have their headquarters in the castle. Strictly off-limits, Mrs Vignoles,' Rose explained, her voice full of genuine regret. Since her arrival, she had grown extremely fond of the area and was pleased to witness Anna's excitement.

Vignoles turned away and looked around in every direction. 'This is a tram stop close to the main road and this looks like a well-used path.' The elderly tram user was walking the same path, as were a number of locals, out enjoying the evening, some with dogs and a few couples arm-in-arm. Two large women were talking loudly and with considerable animation as they approached.

'It's quite a public place. Whoever attacked him was confident and highly skilled. Almost certainly with an accomplice to ensure his body was swiftly hidden.' Vignoles was filling his pipe and staring at the ground, a puzzled look on his face.

'I suppose the attackers could have arrived by tram, car or even on foot,' pondered Anna.

'Yes. In that respect it's a good choice, but from any other point of view it was audacious, to say the least. His wallet was still on his body when found by a Mr... er, *Vrabec*.' Vignoles consulted the dossier. 'Actually it was his dog, a Scottie called Fiki, who made the discovery.'

'It seems so hard to imagine a murder happening in a lovely spot like this,' Rose observed.

'And with such...' Anna paused a moment, 'professionalism, if that is not a callous word.'

'For some reason Private Brierley incurred the wrath of men who knew how to kill. Maybe he was involved with people whom he double-crossed or in some way disappointed.' Vignoles lit his pipe and pushed his Panama back on his head. 'They had to act swiftly — it was a smack on the head, according to the post mortem — and then quickly lift the body into the bushes.' He took a puff on his pipe. 'I suspect that they came here with the intention to kill.'

'Why do you say that?' asked Anna.

'Whatever connected Brierley and his attackers, it was very serious. I will hazard a guess that they came here expecting a pay-off of some sort, but were suspicious of him not delivering. It feels planned; orchestrated.' He nodded as he warmed to his theme. 'Or, maybe he did deliver, but they still killed him, to silence him.'

He walked around the perimeter of the loose square that the obelisk stood within, staring intently at the gravel path and at the dusty dry grasses that fringed it, then commenced inspecting the thick bushes that lay behind. 'Hello, what have we here?'

A few snapped branches and a suggestion of trampled vegetation indicated where a body might have been pulled through. As he peered closer, a soft wind suddenly gusted and whistled through the pines with a faintly sinister sound that transformed the atmosphere into something less benign, and Anna hugged herself.

'The *bora* is getting up,' Rose observed.

'The infamous wind?'

'Yes, Mrs Vignoles. You'll get used to it. Sometimes it blows like a hurricane.'

Vignoles pushed through the leaves and into a tiny clearing beyond. He realised that he was now virtually invisible to anyone standing on the other side. It was a perfect location to hide a body — for a few hours at least, until a curious dog sniffed it out.

He knelt down and started to explore the ground. There were a few old and faded cigarette butts. He kicked an empty, dusty Coca-Cola bottle, now a tomb for a dead spider. He moved deeper into the stand of trees that occupied a rise in the ground, shadows striating the pine needle-strewn ground in thick bands, whilst more wind-loosened needles fell to earth around him. A coal tit made a series of sharp sounds that pierced the air.

Ah. Now, what was this? A shaft of light glanced off a tiny square of folded paper lying against the trunk of a tree, perhaps tossed there by the same wind that was now blowing ever more forcibly in the branches above his head. Vignoles stood up and unfolded it. It was fresh and new; a page torn from a notebook. Someone had written *VE3BF G4000* in pencil on one side, and *Steller Polar* on the reverse. Vignoles had no idea what it meant, but it looked and felt like his first clue. He would need to cross-check, but his innate bloodhound instinct already sensed that this was either Private Brierley's handwriting or something that he'd been given.

It was time to drop back down into Trieste and see if his good luck would continue at the other crime site.

* * * *

Private Victor Lawton of the 1st Battalion Oxfordshire and Buckinghamshire Regiment had met his death on 25th May. Over two weeks had passed and, after reading the report of the incident, Vignoles sensed that a depressing inertia had soon settled upon the investigation.

A single knife wound to the heart had dispatched Lawton in a deadly and efficient strike. As his wallet and wristwatch were found intact on his body, robbery was ruled out and a jealous argument over the affections of a woman was proposed as an alternative motive.

Certainly Private Lawton had been drinking heavily that evening and was last sighted leaving *La Chiave d'Oro,* on his own, at about 1am. This unsalubrious club of notoriety and ill repute was frequented by many a soldier looking to buy the company of a woman. If Lawton had attempted to evade paying the madam for such services rendered, then he could expect to be pursued by her bullyboys. But this did not explain why his wallet was left intact, unless his assailant was disturbed at the last moment. However, this was the explanation favoured by the military police, who subsequently raided the club.

There had been a bit of trouble and some arrests were made, but ultimately it proved inconclusive and no meaningful leads were found. To further undermine the MPs' theory, Private Lawton had settled his bar tab at *La Chiave d'Oro* and even left a generous tip, did not play cards and had also declined the offer of an hour of paid-for passion in a private room with one of the pretty hostesses. And so the trail seemed to stop dead, rather like poor Vic himself, in a narrow street behind the Roman amphitheatre.

'What was the name of the street, sir?' Rose had pulled the jeep to one side of the road, the engine still running.

Vignoles peered at the map he had been given by Commander Turbayne as part of the case documents, the murder sites helpfully marked with small crosses in red ink.

'*Via Donota*. Behind the ruins.' He indicated the place.

'I know it, just off the *Largo Riborgo*. There's quite a maze of small streets that back onto a big park. Dark and quiet. We've been told not to walk alone there at night.' She exchanged looks with Anna, who shivered again and wrapped a shawl more tightly around her shoulders. The wind was giving a cooler edge to the evening, though the roads and buildings were still radiating heat.

Via Donota was a narrow, cobbled street that curved in parallel with the edge of the Roman theatre that fell away to their right in a series of steeply-tiered ancient stone steps. The stumps of columns and lumps of unidentifiable masonry littered the semicircular floor of the theatre, that was composed of gravel and neatly trimmed grass. Bushes fringed the quietly decaying structure and stands of pines whispered gloomily like the ghosts of Roman citizens gossiping on the street corner. Perhaps it was the knowledge that a man had lost his life there, but it felt a doleful place.

They walked a little further, the ancient houses closing in on either side and shutting off the last rays of evening light, now swiftly dimming. Vignoles was surprised by the absence of the gentle twilight he was used to, all the more so as double summer time had ended but two years earlier in Britain, together with its magical midnight brightness.

The street was in the process of being illuminated by a series of gas lamps bracketed to the walls, each one having to be lit by a thin and crooked man with a burning taper on the end of a long pole. He moved with a strange, shuffling gait, crossing from one lamp to another, first using one end of the pole, that had a small metal hook screwed into it, to pull one of the two chains hanging down from the lamp to open the flow of gas, then offering the taper at the other end to the mantle. His work accomplished, the light cast by each lamp was ineffectual, and was a sickly colour that made their skin look aged. His footsteps echoed as he waddled away around a corner. A black cat darted from a narrow cut between two buildings, throwing a cursory glance as the three stood in the middle of the otherwise empty street.

'It's eerily quiet. Where is everyone?' Anna glanced around, the strangeness of the unfamiliar city beginning to creep over her, aided by hunger and tiredness. 'I don't like it here.'

'Let's get after him — he might have seen something.' Vignoles gently, but firmly, steered Anna forwards after the lamplighter.

'Oh, but Charles.' The realisation struck Anna that she was there for a purpose and this was her first opportunity to try and fulfil it. Her heart sank.

'*Signore!* Please, *uno momento, per favore.*' Vignoles deployed almost the sum total of the scant Italian he had managed to learn on the train journey.

The old man stopped and swivelled around, peering up at Vignoles with a look of puzzlement, but recoiled visibly when he saw Anna close behind. He shook his head vigorously and, with his free hand, made a gesture that took no translating. He wanted nothing to do with them.

'Ask him if he was here on the night of 25th. Did he see anyone about the time the man was killed?' Vignoles was trying to interpret the old man's face and actions, already frustrated by his own linguistic shortcomings.

Anna rolled her eyes and took a deep breath, '*Signore, siamo qui per la sera del 25 Maggio?*' She paused as she searched her memory for a word before continuing in a halting sentence. The old man continued to shake his head, turning away from Anna whilst mumbling a response that sounded fearful.

'His accent is hard to follow. Some of the words are not Italian, perhaps. But he's quite clearly saying no.'

'Tell him we're police. Did he see anyone acting suspiciously?'

'*Signore, noi siamo la polizia,*' Anna smiled reassuringly.

'*Polizia?*' The lamplighter grew agitated and faced Anna, indicating her smart summer clothes and pointing at Vignoles's Panama with gestures of incredulity. He spat on the ground, close enough to make a point without actually hitting her, and cursed. His dark eyes flashed, his greying moustache twitched in agitation. He hobbled away, one hand angrily flapping them away and speaking over his shoulder, '*No, non voglio avere niente a che fare con questo. Io non so niente! Nulla, si sente?*'

'My Italian is poor, but that was pretty unambiguous.'

'I sensed that he didn't like us asking.'

'Probably offended by my Italian,' said Anna, giving a long exhalation of breath. 'But did you see his reaction to me — even before I opened my mouth? I think he was frightened when he saw me.' Anna was puzzled. 'Do you think I reminded him of someone?'

'You certainly could be taken for a local,' remarked Rose.

'Brr, I'm not comfortable in this place.' Anna was looking at the shadows surrounding them.

Vignoles gave Anna's arm a light squeeze, then started to look around. 'Nothing to show that a man died here, not even a stain of blood.' He glanced up at the dark shape of a church looming down upon them from a few streets back, then walked slowly about the street, head bowed as he studied the gloomy shadows. He stopped and spun around. 'I don't think this street will give up its secrets. Better to ask why he walked along this particular road that night.'

Anna was trying to shake off her growing sense of unease by concentrating on the map, which she was now angling so as to catch as much of the pale gaslight as possible. 'Do you suppose he was returning to base?'

'It's assumed so. He was billeted at the Lazzaretto barracks. Rose, can you show us where they are?'

'Let me see…' She pointed to a spot on the map. 'Right *there*. They lie between the *Via Francesco Crispi* and the 20th September Road. Though they write it with Roman numerals. It could make sense to cut along here if he were coming from somewhere central or from the old town.'

'He was coming from near *Piazza Cavana*,' Vignoles replied. 'And one can assume he was a bit worse the wear for drink.'

'So he was meandering his way home and perhaps took this lonely little street by chance,' suggested Anna.

'I think that likely.' Vignoles stood with his chin resting on one hand. They all looked around at the sad little road, now even darker as night rolled in.

'If he was not jumped by robbers in a stroke of profound bad luck, that leaves another, more intriguing, possibility: that he was specifically targeted and then followed until he came to a quiet spot. I need time to think. My head is not clear enough.' Vignoles looked at his watch. 'It's been a long day and I believe we can be back at the *Excelsior* in time to change for dinner.'

As they drew close to the jeep, Anna nudged Vignoles and whispered in his ear. 'There's a man at the far end of the street — under the trees. I think he's been watching us.'

Vignoles pulled his hat brim low and took a surreptitious glance as he took his seat in the jeep. The dark shape blended perfectly into the trunks of the Mediterranean pines, but there was the glow of a cigarette being inhaled, and the soft red tip described an arc as it swung downwards again. As his eyes adjusted, Vignoles could just discern a hat and the soft sheen of a leather jacket. As they drew level he looked across at where the watcher was standing, but he had dissolved into the dark, aided by a clump of thick rhododendrons. Vignoles shrugged, it was probably nothing but a local man having a quiet smoke. However, he made a mental note that, when they returned to the hotel, he would unpack the pistol he'd been issued.

Chapter Seventeen

What a Difference a Day Made

The New Mayfair Dance Orchestra

DS Trinder, DC Blencowe and WPCs Benson and Lansdowne had taken a short walk from Leicester Central, along a road lined on one side with hosiery factories and clothes wholesalers, and the massive bulk of the railway viaduct that carried the railway across the city on the other, to take an after-work drink in the Great Central Hotel.

This was a scruffy, down-at-heel sort of place that would win few awards architecturally and with an interior that had seen better days. However, the beer was good and the landlord hospitable, scoring a few extra points in Trinder's eyes because he was happy to tune in to the Light Programme on his splendid radiogram behind the bar whenever it was broadcasting dance music. So, all things considered, it served as a good place to relax after work.

As Trinder took a deep swig from his pint of Everard's Tiger, he nodded approvingly as the New Mayfair Dance Orchestra struck up a cheerful, and perhaps appropriately titled, tune.

He had suggested they all met outside the office, because if they felt anything like he did, they would all be in need of a drink and a chance to shake off some of the stress and shock of DI Minshul's sudden and unwelcome arrival into their world. Trinder was firmly of the opinion that, whilst a pint of ale might not solve the ills of the world, it went a long way towards making those ills far less unpleasant. He also wanted to seek their opinion, in an informal manner that would not undermine his authority, on what they should do about the possible attempted derailment.

'Look, I'm not exactly used to this sort of thing, so I hope I can count on you all to stick with me and back me up. We need to give this our best shot and jolly well prove a point to the new DI. Let's fly the flag for Vignoles and his trusty team, eh?'

Blencowe raised his glass. 'Hear, hear! You can count on me, sarge.'

WPC Benson had already drained most her half pint and was wondering if it were too soon to order another. 'Give me something to do, anything that will get me out of that man's sight. Send me anywhere you like, sir — but no more sorting files whilst he ogles me.' She shuddered. 'Ugh, he gives me the collywobbles!'

Trinder pulled a sympathetic face. 'Understood. Let's try and look at matters from our perspective and not from DI Minshul's. We need to think how the inspector — *our* inspector, that is — might approach this situation.'

'What's the situation, sarge?' asked Jane Benson. 'I feel like I've been left by the wayside.'

'Not an easy question to answer, but this is how I see things.' Trinder ran a hand through his slicked hair by way of preparation. 'At the risk of being melodramatic, I — actually, Lucy and I — came up with a theory. We have reason to suspect that some kind of...' he hesitated a beat and briefly sought encouragement from the young WPC opposite before continuing, 'some kind of attack is being waged upon the railway. This is aimed at causing disruption to services, inconvenience, wastage and, in one very alarming case, possible destruction and injury.'

There was an expectant hush around the table.

'The last proper conversation I had with DI Vignoles was on Whit Bank Holiday, when he reminded me that the railways had been attacked in such a manner once before, and I got the feeling that he was hinting at the IRA.'

Benson looked shocked, and Blencowe sucked breath through his teeth before breaking the silence. 'I remember that. There was a nasty firebombing incident over at their place.'

'Correct. Yesterday I did a bit of research in the library.' Trinder opened his police notebook and read aloud. 'London Road was bombed on 2nd July 1939, in one of seven explosions across the LMS system on that day. But there was more. It all started on the London Underground, when Tottenham Court Road and Leicester Square were targeted that February. They blew up the left luggage offices at both stations.'

'Golly. How awful.' Benson was leaning forward, hanging on his every word.

'They also had a go at King's Cross, and on that occasion the bomb was placed in the cloakroom; it killed a poor doctor who was walking past. Now, we have not had a bomb go off, of course, but I am wondering.'

'Oh, but hang on!' Lansdowne exclaimed. 'What about an incendiary, sarge? A bomb does not have to mean a big bang. I have the lists of vandalism that we made this week. Let me just find it...'

Lansdowne placed her capacious, utilitarian handbag on the table and commenced rummaging inside as the others looked on, extracting a few sheets of foolscap that she proceeded to study with great enthusiasm, running a finger down the neat lines of type. Her bag remained open, revealing letters, ration book and identity card, a handkerchief, lipstick, gloves, a ball of string and goodness knows what else, in a surprising jumble and confusion. Trinder, though not intending to be nosy and intrigued by the WPC's sudden outburst, was fascinated by the shambolic chaos of her belongings, because it was such a stark contrast to the perfectly presented, neatly uniformed and smartly coiffured young woman seated before him.

Lansdowne caught him looking. 'What is it?'

'Sorry. Awfully rude of me. I couldn't help but notice that your handbag...' His face reddened and he stopped.

Benson laughed heartily. 'You are on dangerous territory, sarge. The mystery of a lady's handbag!'

'I thought we were talking about fire bombs, not handbags.' Blencowe took a sip of beer and rolled his eyes.

Lansdowne reached for her bag. 'Oh dear, I'm terrible for hoarding stuff. I'm like a jackdaw.' As she spoke, a letter fell onto the table and, although she reached for it, she was not quick enough to prevent Benson from reading the bold overprinting on the top left-hand corner.

'The British Olympic Committee. Why are they writing to you, Lucy?'

'Oh, it's nothing.' She shoved it deep into her bag.

'Nothing? The Olympics!' Trinder grinned. 'Come on, girl, spill the beans.'

She looked down. 'I don't like to crow about it.'

'That's because you are a jackdaw,' Blencowe laughed good-naturedly.

'I suppose it is exciting, really, but I don't want a big fuss made about it.'

'About what?' asked Trinder.

'Oh, you'll winkle it out of me in the end so I might as well give up now and tell you: I've been selected to compete for the GB shooting team, in the Free Pistol event. As you know I've always been rather good in that discipline.'

'Crikey! That's marvellous news. And you're not kidding — you've got us out of a fix before now, thanks to your crack shooting.'

Lansdowne took a sip of her port and lemon. 'I passed through the final qualifying rounds last month and this letter is about the final arrangements for the games.'

'My, you're a dark horse.' Benson was giving Lansdowne an admiring look.

'I've handled guns since I was a little girl. Daddy always took me along when he went rabbiting and later to his gun club in Melton Mowbray. It's just something I've always been good at. Please, can we all keep it hush-hush? It's better for my concentration and nerves.'

'We all know now, but we can make sure it goes no further. But gosh, what news!' Trinder supped some more beer as the pub rumbled and shook as a heavy train passed on the viaduct immediately behind the back wall. 'Now, back to business. What was it you wanted to show us?'

Lansdowne, happy to turn the attention away from her Olympic qualification, recommended skimming down her neatly typed list. 'Do you remember the fire in the storeroom at Nottingham Midland?' Trinder and Blencowe nodded, but Benson shook her head. 'It destroyed a lot of newly printed papers and other stock. They dismissed it as either an unexplained accident or mindless vandalism, though I must say the investigation appeared awfully lax, and in the light of what you just said, I'm now wondering if it was not more significant than that.'

'How did it start?' Trinder was interested.

'The best explanation they came up with is that something flammable was set alight outside the door, probably paraffin or lamp oil, and this flowed underneath and set the whole lot ablaze.'

'But they thought it was an accident?' asked Benson.

'Precisely. The investigation seemed to accept that flammable liquid had been inadvertently spilled during the day and a stray cigarette had ignited it. I'm thinking that it might have been some kind of incendiary device.'

'What was in the store?' asked Trinder.

'New operating instructions for the Midland line, due to be issued the following day. Without these, every signalman, driver and guard would be unable to perform their duties.'

Trinder was sitting upright and leaning over to look at the list. 'That was a serious blow to the railway. Do we know what the consequences were?'

'Fortunately it was not the only supply of these instructions, though it did destroy the majority of their stock. More were sent up from St Pancras but this still meant that a great number of staff had to share copies and they were forced to run a restricted service as a precautionary measure for a few days until they were sure that everyone was familiar with the changes.'

Trinder nodded. 'Perhaps not an incendiary bomb, for surely remains of the device would have been found, but a deliberate arson attack, nonetheless. That was good thinking. Anything else on the list?'

'The majority of incidents hardly add up to a serious crime problem. A toilet door lock broken in Ruddington; a light bulb smashed in a ladies' waiting room at Central; some track tools pinched in Rothley — hardly an IRA plot.'

They all managed wry smiles.

Trinder groaned. 'We can discount all these. What else?'

'A few: three incidents in one week of bricks thrown at trains from the waste ground near Western Road, similar events near the Abbey Road sidings and the same again on the Midland line — do you want me to read them all out?'

'No, it's just local youths.' Trinder's spirits were starting to sink in the face of such routine vandalism. He produced a pack of cigarettes and offered one only to Blencowe, as neither woman smoked. He lit them both using a homemade lighter.

Lansdowne turned a page. 'I've extracted five that stand out. Firstly the fire, then some timetables that were stolen and thrown into the river. That involved a bit of planning to both execute and accomplish without detection.'

'But it was pointless,' Benson remarked.

'Why would anyone want to do any of these things?' Lansdowne asked, not expecting a reply. 'Then there was the red paint tipped over a loco in the engine shed.'

'Didn't the idiots leave their initials in the paint?' asked Blencowe.

'Yes, they did. And that gives us a lead. I notice they did the same thing a few days later in another attack at London Road, when three of the summer timetables, freshly pasted on the noticeboards, were daubed with paint and the same initials for all to see.'

Benson nodded. 'So these two painting tearaways have to be top of our wanted list.'

Trinder frowned. 'Red paint. Hmm. That letter sent to Mr Badger, it referred to a "scarlet tide". Could they mean red paint?'

'Poured over an engine? I suppose it could,' Lansdowne answered, but she looked puzzled. 'So, they're threatening more red paint being thrown on railway property unless... unless what?'

Trinder explained about the letter to Blencowe and Benson.

'I can't see where a town in Cornwall fits into all this,' added Benson. 'It's rather a long way from here.'

'Neither can I. Okay, we'll come back to the letter. What was the fifth incident, Lucy?'

'The sabotage attempt. Assuming of course, that one believes the story given by the trackwomen.'

Trinder took a long and thoughtful drag on his cigarette. 'If successful we would be looking at a derailed train, and of course injury, perhaps fatalities. A grim thought.'

Almost on cue, a passing train released a loud whistle.

'Three of these events are of special interest,' said Blencowe. 'A warning letter, a fire and a possible derailment. They sound convincing as part of a campaign of disruption.'

Trinder gave him a long look through the blue cigarette smoke. 'What can we find to link them?'

'All are aimed at disrupting services, for example stealing or defacing timetables, and damaging loco to put them out of service,' said Benson, examining the list on the table, brow furrowed in concentration as she spoke.

'I really need to find these vandals who so conveniently left their initials in the paint,' demanded Trinder. 'We'll retrieve the track spanner for fingerprinting and we must also interview the Land Army girls and that photographer chap.'

Lansdowne had a determined look on her face. 'I want to help those two women to prove themselves innocent.'

'Careful. We must remain objective. That's what DI Vignoles is always saying, so beware of jumping to conclusions. I understand that Minshul is travelling back to his neck of the woods as we speak, and won't return until Monday morning.'

'Hurrah!'

'What say we work our socks off the whole weekend, without his meddling and leering, and see if we can't get a result?'

'I'm in, sergeant.' Lansdowne smiled eagerly.

'Likewise,' added Benson, who saluted ostentatiously to make her point.

'You've got my vote,' said Blencowe, draining his glass.

At that moment, a smartly dressed young man placed two small leaflets on their table without saying a word, before moving on to the next.

'Hullo, what's this?' Trinder picked one up.

'Oh, just something political,' said Lansdowne, wrinkling her nose. 'A debate — more likely a rant, I shouldn't wonder — against the government.'

'Looks like anti-communist stuff.' Trinder sat back on his bench seat the better to finish his beer and cigarette.

'Have you seen the title of the debate? *Better Dead Than Red*. Golly!' Benson raised an eyebrow.

'I'm no lover of Stalin, but that's surely going a bit too far for Leicester,' said Lansdowne.

'I steer clear of politics, myself. And I know you're not one for political debate, are you, Lucy?' Trinder smiled.

'Heavens, no. I find politics terribly disconnected from real people's lives. Just a lot of hot air and bluster from a bunch of stuffed shirts. And I can never follow their arguments.'

'A lot of women struggled, even died, to give us the right to vote, Lucy,' Benson reminded her, giving her an arch look. She glanced at the flyer again, though with no obvious interest.

Lansdowne winced and gave an apologetic half-smile. 'I do like Mr Churchill. I'll vote for his party next time, I promise.'

Trinder yawned. 'I think we should call it a day. Good work, everyone.'

As they stood up to leave, Lansdowne gave the flyer another quizzical glance, picked it up, folded it neatly in half and slipped it into the jumble of her handbag. She noticed Trinder watching her with a look of surprise in his eyes, and said, 'It's the jackdaw in me.'

CHAPTER EIGHTEEN

MOON AT SEA

Ronnie Munro & His Orchestra

Vignoles was awakened by a series of sharp raps on the door.

'Inspector Vignoles! Sir!' The knocking continued.

'Coming!'

He swung out of bed and reached for his dressing gown as Anna stirred, sitting up and resting on one arm. Opening the door a crack, he saw a young orderly, who immediately saluted smartly.

'Awfully sorry, sir. But there's been another. Captain Henderson asked that you join him immediately.'

'Another what?' Vignoles was struggling to get his sleepy mind into action.

'One of the lads, sir. He's been killed. At the docks. We have a jeep waiting for you downstairs.'

'Oh Lord! Give me five minutes.'

The orderly saluted again, turned smartly away and Vignoles closed the door.

'Did you hear that, Anna?'

Anna was already out of bed and choosing her outfit for the day. 'Yes I did, Charles. What dreadful news. We must get ready quickly.'

'I must, but there's no need for you to come.'

'They paid for me to travel out here, darling, so it's high time I earned my bed and board. Besides, you need an interpreter.'

There was no time to argue and so, after splashing cool water on their faces and dressing — Vignoles remembering to pocket his revolver — they were soon downstairs and being saluted by Staff Sergeant Gretton, who somehow managed to look immaculate and efficient, despite a tell-tale shadow beneath her eyes.

The morning air was crisp and chill, though a sea haze gently filtered the yellow light of sunrise. Anna was glad she had taken a shawl and Vignoles buttoned his blazer as they raced along the *Riva*, the jeep's headlamps forming twin shafts of light that sometimes appeared solid as they struck thick pockets of mist, and at other times carving through the deep, navy-blue pre-dawn shadows. The mist formed halos around the lights on the ships moored along the quay and, when the mist shredded apart, tiny strings of lights could sometimes be glimpsed out on the *Golfo di Trieste*. One of the small dock locomotives clanked past them and a bright orange glow emanated from the cab as the fireman shovelled, the metallic sounds muffled and softened.

Rose drove around the stubby peninsula that formed the southern tip of the city, taking a road that ran beside a bewildering tangle of running lines and vast marshalling yards that made up the *Porto Franco Nuovo*. This was a more modern and extensive facility than the older docks they had passed the day before, occupying all of the lower edge of the peninsula and stretching in an unrelieved conglomeration of warehouses and wharves, factories, huge shipyards filled with cranes, jibs and skeletal ships like beached whales, that ran down towards the grubby suburbs of Servola almost to the little fishing village of Muggia.

It was an area defined by the sea and the railway, by heavy industry and warehousing, ships and wagons, factory buildings, service roads, yard lamps and the cacophonous clatter of shunting, loading and the heaving about of great lines of wagons holding coal, timber, coffee, cases of tinned food and scented by lemons and other fruits. Tank wagons glistening with spilt fuel oil contrasted with those containing the powerful local brandy distilled in a complex of buildings surrounded by barbed wire and the aroma of fermentation. The air was also heavy with the tang of seawater and burning coal, roasting coffee, stagnant dock water, kelp and rotting fruit, the sea breeze whipping all these competing smells into their nostrils.

Rose pulled the jeep onto a piece of scrubby land beside a perimeter fence and, after a brief conversation with a very young British soldier and two Italians with generously peaked caps and epaulettes on their shirts, both presumably something to do with the dock authority but certainly far more interested in their game of *Briscola* than checking papers, they were admitted through a rickety wooden pass gate and were soon by the track side.

'That was too easy,' observed Vignoles. 'There's been a murder, for heaven's sake.' He looked around for someone to blame. 'Though I have noticed ever since we arrived at Calais that the continentals generally don't fence their railways off, so I suppose it's pretty remarkable they have one here at all.'

They were on the edge of a vast railway intersection that stretched as far as the mist and poor light would allow, tall yard lamps lending a ghostly feel to the scene. Some distance away, the twin lamps of a vehicle pierced the haze like the malevolent gaze of a hunting cat.

'Those look like torches,' observed Vignoles, indicating where lights were bobbing around in the gloom. 'That must be the place.'

They picked their way across the great tangle of track whilst continually looking from side to side to watch out for the many wagons being loose-shunted or clattered into place by a clutch of grunting and roaring steam engines. A massive freight locomotive, that was all exposed pipe-work, open frames and small wheels, could be seen to their right, blowing off steam whilst held at a signal, a small figure leaning from the cab straining to see what was happening. If the victim had been knocked down by a train or loose wagon in the night it would surprise no one who'd attempted to cross this dangerous place.

As they drew closer, the lights and the shadowy shapes holding them resolved into two military policemen, their white helmets, belts and puttees glowing as if luminescent. They were accompanied by Captain Henderson, an army doctor, and a pair of medical orderlies standing beside an ambulance. Two soldiers with rifles in their hands stood guard some distance away.

'That you, Vignoles?' Henderson called across the misty yard. 'Ah, the whole gang, eh?' He nodded a greeting towards Anna and Rose. He eyed Vignoles oddly, toying with the idea of passing comment on his trick the evening before, but chose not to. 'We have the body of one Corporal Albert Priday, or Albee, as he was known to his chums.'

'Have many people disturbed the area?'

'A few. The man who found him, the two MPs and the doctor.' Henderson indicated a sallow, sunken-cheeked man, who looked in dire need of medical attention himself.

Vignoles nodded and addressed the doctor. 'What can you tell me?'

'I inspected the body. It was immediately clear that he was dead, so I had no cause to disturb him beyond the minimum. I felt for a pulse at his neck, but no more. No need. There was some warmth to the body and no sign of rigor.' He looked and sounded tired, his face sallow and lined.

'When did he die?'

'I prefer to await the result of the post mortem.'

'I know. But hazard a guess, I need something to work with.'

'We-ell, if pushed...' The doctor pulled a pained expression.

'You are.'

'Around 2am, but no later than three.'

'And how did he die?'

'I would much rather wait...' the doctor stopped, seeing Vignoles's look of impatience. He was too tired to argue, so he gave the inspector what he wanted. 'A knife through the heart, delivered from behind with a long blade. This takes a lot of skill, but if done properly — and this was — it is an extremely effective method.'

Vignoles nodded. 'Another deliberate surprise attack,' he muttered to himself. 'Where is the body?' He shot Anna a look that suggested she might prefer to hang back.

'In the cabin.' The doctor indicated with his arm.

'Can I borrow that?' Vignoles asked one of the military policemen, who handed over a hefty, rubber-coated torch. He played it across the ground as he approached the small concrete structure.

'He was a goods overseer, working from this hut,' Henderson explained.

'And what does that entail?' Vignoles asked.

Anna answered. 'He checks the identity of all the wagons arriving and departing; he would have a team of number takers to do this. He assigns wagons to different sidings and spurs and get them sorted.' Vignoles crouched and looked at some heavy boot prints in the soft ash outside the cabin door, nodding as he listened to his wife. Anna continued, 'He ensures that the trains are correctly assembled, identifying which wagons were to be unloaded and where, and which were to be forwarded. He directs the men doing the shunting, planning their operations in forming up the various trains.'

Vignoles stood up, walked to the doorway and shone the torch beam into the cabin. A man in a clean and smartly-pressed British Army summer uniform, with voluminous shorts, thick socks and heavy boots, was lying face down on the floor, a dark stain that appeared almost black covering his back and pooling onto the untidy floor. His forage cap was a short distance away; it looked as though it had fallen off as he hit the ground. The man looked oddly peaceful, lying with one arm thrown above his head, one cheek on the floor and his eyes closed. At first glance, he appeared to be in a deep sleep.

'No sign of a struggle.' Vignoles was thinking aloud.

A single bulb hung on a bare wire from the ceiling; a desk was covered with papers and oil-stained folders stuffed with yet more papers. Three ancient wooden chairs were crammed into the small space around a tiny, pot-bellied stove. This was alight, and various chipped enamelled pots and an assortment of containers sat on a small shelf fixed against the back wall beside the stovepipe chimney. The warmth was surprisingly welcome after the cooling effect of the wind, which occasionally sent small curtains of dust racing across the ground outside before suddenly spinning and eddying into little dust devils. Captain Henderson and Anna were standing on either side of the doorway looking in.

'He was found just after three by one of the shunters. I have the man's name and details. I sent him to get a cup of tea as he looked a bit shaken up.'

'Priday was on duty?' asked Vignoles.

'Now that's the odd thing. He was not. It looks like he came back for some reason. The chap who found him seemed almost as surprised by the fact that Priday was here, at this time, as by his death.'

'So why did he return at such an hour?' Vignoles scanned the jumbled confusion of the little office. He knelt down and heaved the body over onto its side, causing Anna to flinch, although she immediately reappeared at the doorway.

He rootled through the man's clothing, observing that the flaps on his blouson jacket pockets were already unfastened and empty. The lining to one of his trouser pockets was pulled out, as if they had been searched.

'Has anyone gone through his pockets?'

'Not that I am aware of. He was already known to the shunter, so he'd not need to do so.' Henderson called across to the MPs and repeated the question, receiving a negative from both.

Vignoles lowered his face close to the floor and, using his torch, peered beneath the stove. He grunted and, reaching beneath with his fingers, extracted two small, creased photographs of a pretty young woman in a Wren's uniform. 'Could this be his girl back home?' He held them aloft for Henderson to see. 'These look as though they came from a wallet. We need to find that.'

Anna put a hand to her mouth. 'That makes this feel even more tragic.'

Vignoles nodded and hunted around the floor, then exclaimed as he found what he'd expected. He collected up a fold of matches, a half-smoked pack of cigarettes and a clean handkerchief, each item fresh and untainted by the dust and grime that pervaded the office.

'This man was killed for something and they searched him to find it, scattering what they didn't want of his belongings as they did so. They may have found whatever it was and taken it.' He stood upright and surveyed the scene. 'But maybe not. Time might have been tight. We'll need to go through these papers and see if anything jumps out.' Vignoles was looking anxious. 'We should really get the scene photographed, but I'm worried that any further delay might prove fatal.'

He tapped a foot on the ground and made up his mind, walking to the door and speaking to the medical orderlies outside. 'Please take him away. And doctor, we need the post mortem results as a matter of extreme urgency. On Commander Turbayne's orders!' Vignoles ad-libbed and caught Henderson's look of mild surprise, though this was quickly disguised.

The doctor mumbled something that might have been acquiescence and sucked unhappily on a cigarette as the two orderlies shuffled into the cabin and hefted Priday's body onto a stretcher before carrying him to the ambulance.

'I have no idea what we're looking for, but you're the dab hand at this sort of thing, captain.' Vignoles threw him an arch look, then picked up sheaves of forms and started flipping through them. 'They're printed in Italian, but many have been completed in English. That's a blessing at least. Anna, maybe you can help?'

Anna and Henderson stepped into the small space and started opening files and peering into drawers.

'From the description of his duties, Corporal Priday was in a good position to control the entry and exit of merchandise conveyed in railway wagons to and from the port. Could he have been involved in some kind of illegal activity?' Henderson asked.

'A reasonable supposition, captain. I'm thinking Priday was trying to smuggle something valuable in or out. Something so valuable that it was worth risking murder to get hold of it. He could have found himself caught between rival gangs wanting to get their hands on the contraband.'

'Or was he just a pawn in their game? Expendable. You hinted at such a thing with Private Brierley.' Anna was turning papers over as she spoke.

'I certainly think these deaths are related. Anna, you know about goods dispatching — it would take more than one man to alter or fake a goods trans-shipment, wouldn't it?' Vignoles had his unlit pipe between his teeth, a sure sign that he was concentrating.

'I should say so. It would need a team working together. One person could not just make up a bill of lading, for example. There needs to be a suitable wagon available, delivered to the right place at the right time — and surely nobody allows one of their wagons to be sent away somewhere for no clear purpose. The wagon will have to be documented as part of a train consist — whence it's come, what it's carrying, and so on — then it must be unloaded and reloaded and this creates yet more paperwork, perhaps customs controls have to be passed, duties levied, then more transit documents, I can go on and on. This needs men — or women — at every point along the line all working to the same objective.' Anna spoke with authority. She was an expert in this field, albeit in a desk-bound capacity, at Leicester Central.

'First Lawton, then Brierley and now Priday. There just has to be a connection. Could they be part of a bigger operation, and one that now appears to be too hot to handle?' Vignoles was flicking over pages of documents held in a grubby manila folder, trying to see anything that offered a clue as to what was afoot.

'What are we searching for, old chap?' Henderson seemed frustrated.

'I wish I knew.' Vignoles suddenly looked at Henderson. 'I've an idea. Lawton was killed on 25th May. Now if the port and its railway operations really do connect these men, and, knowing that Priday was well-placed to orchestrate the movement of wagons and their contents around the railway, there could be a clue buried somewhere within the train movements made during that period. Gather all files, papers, and documents from that date until now. We can study them later and try to make sense of it all.'

They worked for a few more minutes until Anna spoke up.

'Here you are — the paperwork for the last week.' She held up a thick wad of documents. 'Thankfully, there is some order amidst the confusion because this box-file has all of May's train movements in it — and some of June's.'

'Brava!' Vignoles picked up an empty cardboard box that once held tins of bully beef. Anna dropped the files inside, followed by the few personal effects of the late Corporal Priday. 'This gives us something to start with.'

He stepped outside and addressed one of the military policemen. 'Keep guard and let no one enter until I give the order. It might inconvenience the dock operations, but so be it.'

'Very well, sir.'

'I will not fool myself that word has not already leaked out about this, but I do want to keep the manner of his death quiet. The detail about the knife is not to be mentioned.'

'Understood, sir.'

'But before anything else, I need a strong cup of coffee and something to eat.'

'Our best bet will be back at the *Albergo*. There's still an hour until breakfast, but the cooks will rustle something up, I'm sure.' Henderson's stomach rumbled in agreement.

Vignoles started to walk back the way they had come, stepping over the many rails, point-rods and signal wires, carefully looking at the ground whilst peering around the cardboard box held in front of his chest, his pipe jutting from his lips at a crazy angle.

Anna was regretting her hurried choice of footwear that morning, for, whilst her new sandals were perfect for warm weather and within town, the elevated heel was less than satisfactory when negotiating rail sleepers and lumpy ballast. She scanned the yard, searching for the narrow gate they had entered, so they might make a direct beeline and save her ankles.

In doing so, she noticed two men standing some distance away and watching their progress. There was no reason to think that they were the ones that had been standing beneath the trees near the Roman ruins, but Anna still gave them a long look and watched as they turned away in response, walking behind a row of box vans. She wondered if she should say anything but, as she pondered the idea, she noticed a body of men walking through the gate, many pushing bicycles. The dockers were on their way to work and it would be only natural for two of these to see an ambulance and stop to wonder what was happening. She immediately dismissed her suspicions as foolish.

The port never slept, it just worked at a slightly slower rhythm during the night, and as the first bright glow of sunrise etched the ragged line of the escarpment above the city and the sea mist started to burn away, the noise and activity were already increasing; the squeals of brakes and chattering of buffers filling the air as the engines roared like angry dogs. A ship's hooter sounded a long note full of sadness and longing. The massive freight engine was finally released from the signal to start heaving its load up the steeply graded line, a banking engine pushing eagerly like a little terrier at the rear of the snake of box vans, both locomotives jetting black-and-grey towers of smoke high into the air, only for the gusting *bora* to throw them sideways and smash the dark billows against the warehouses and factories until they were torn to ribbons and vanished.

Amidst such noise it was easy to understand how a man could be knifed here and no one notice.

CHAPTER NINETEEN

FISCHIA IL VENTO

Italian partisan song

The wind picked up as the morning sun warmed the streets and the surface of the Adriatic was flicked into millions of small white crests that sparkled against the deep petrol blue of the water.

The Vignoleses had not only found some good coffee back at the officers' mess, but had made the wise decision to suspend the investigation for another hour to eat breakfast, enthusiastically tucking into a mound of scrambled eggs that had not been reconstituted from a packet of powder shipped over from Canada, and a rasher each of strongly flavoured, locally-cured bacon — both undoubted benefits of billeting in officers' quarters.

A young lieutenant seated at their table advised them that there was no rationing in Trieste, but immediately quashed any mounting sense of excitement at this revelation by explaining that food was simply extremely scarce, a situation made worse by the fact that the British, Americans and Jugoslavs could not agree on a system of regulating the supplies fairly, and so it was just an unseemly fight to buy anything in the markets each morning. It was a depressingly familiar story: most shops were virtually empty. Thankfully, the army was at least sure of its own supplies, having entered into a number of beneficial agreements with sympathetic or astute local traders.

Over breakfast Vignoles planned his next move. He decided to pay a visit to the loco shed at which Lawton and Brierley had been based. He would start interviewing the railwaymen there — thankfully, in his mother tongue — and see if anything revealed itself.

Released from interpreter duties, and as it was still very early, Anna decided to visit the *Ponterosso* market and join the jostling throng that gathered there each morning to test her developing language skills and discover for herself the fresh herbs and vegetables that her parents had so often spoken about — assuming there was anything on offer. She planned to spend the rest of the morning examining the trans-shipment documents whilst sitting at a café with a coffee. Neither she nor her husband had much idea of what they were looking for within the documents, and their initial leaf-through of the many pages over breakfast had not inspired either of them. Anna hoped that perhaps a fresh approach to the task when she was more alert and sustained by food would inspire a breakthrough.

Captain Henderson had joined them for breakfast, but had been approached soon after by a smartly turned out man, whom Vignoles assumed was a private secretary. An anxious exchange followed and Henderson made his excuses soon after and left. No explanation was offered when he returned to their table, but he appeared preoccupied, a sensation not lessened by a palpable feeling of unease and nervous tension. Vignoles put this down to the recent murder — he knew the bush telegraph would be busy chattering and Priday's death would now be common knowledge. Whilst many men had encountered far worse situations a few years back, death in combat was somehow different from a callous murder in the night. However, Vignoles was still surprised by the quickness of step, the hurried fussiness and the barked orders all around.

A while later, Staff Sergeant Gretton drove Vignoles and Henderson along the *Riva*. Fishermen were laying their nets out to dry across a wide swathe of the quayside, stretching for what Vignoles estimated to be about a quarter of a mile. The spiteful wind was sending ripples through the nets, making them appear alive and prompting the fishermen to place blocks of limestone at strategic places to prevent the whole lot lifting bodily into the air, ensnaring the jeep and the other military personnel traversing the *Riva*.

As he sat in the rear seat of the jeep — chosen deliberately — Vignoles turned back from looking at the fishermen to observe the captain, and tried to decide what to make of him.

Vignoles did not feel inclined to trust him, and yet he was a civil servant in the British Government, and well connected to some senior figures in the forces, so surely his credentials were beyond reproach. Perhaps his unwillingness to fully include Henderson in his investigations was prompted more by a personal sense of loss that DS Trinder was stuck back at home and lumbered with DI Minshul. How was poor John getting along? He'd rather left him in the lurch with barely time to pass on his apologies for his impromptu departure. It must have been quite unsettling. On balance, perhaps Captain Henderson, despite his haughty manner, was a better option than that foisted on Trinder. Vignoles decided that he had better try and accept the situation and get on with the job in hand. He finally broke the silence.

'Captain, are you aware of any other such fatal incidents in that area of the docks?'

'None at all.'

'But I suppose there is crime down there. It looks a rough place, as most docks are,' continued Vignoles. 'Food is scarce in the town and there's a lot of it being handled off the boats. It would be a great temptation for criminal types to try and muscle in.'

'I don't doubt some of the local ruffians operate around there. The white helmets will be able to tell you more about that sort of thing. I've not heard of a Tommy ever being targeted, though.'

'How about you, Rose? You've been in Trieste longer than the captain.'

'Thankfully we're normally well off limits to this kind of thing, sir. There are unpleasant incidents that we hear about, of course.' She changed gear and negotiated a set of railway tracks crossing the road. 'Every so often the partisans kill a fascist traitor, and the same is given out in return. But mainly you find this is happening in the countryside now, away from the soldiers. There are people still loyal to Mussolini, can you believe that?' Vignoles nodded as she glanced over her shoulder at him. 'Then there are the regular flare-ups between the Italians and Slavs. Sometimes these can get pretty nasty. But to kill three British? It's very strange and unusual, sir.'

Vignoles did not reply. At that moment a long column of noisy army trucks rumbled past them in the opposite direction. The rear of each wagon had the canvas covers rolled back over the metal supporting framework to reveal groups of young men in pale olive green uniforms and wearing an assortment of forage caps, all bearing a red star with a yellow edge.

This was his first sight of the People's Liberation Army of Jugoslavia. He felt a slight pang of disappointment; he was not sure what he had expected, but they looked just like the British Army boys: fresh-faced, clean-shaven lads, their expressions a mixture of apprehension, incomprehension and innocence. Perhaps this was the same with all young recruits, whatever side they were on.

He was suddenly struck by the realisation that Jack, together with his comrades Willie and Jimmy, must have looked much the same; their faces conveying the same mixture of emotions as they made their way towards Barcelona, rumbling along hot and dusty roads through Catalonia, each young man clinging to his ideals, singing the rallying songs and full of apprehension for what destiny had in store.

His eyes briefly met those of a young soldier in the rearmost truck, who appeared to be staring straight through Vignoles with a faraway gaze. The lad looked down and concentrated on extracting the last, tiny fix of nicotine from a cigarette butt wedged between his fingers. This youth was supposed to be the enemy. The red star on his cap was gleaming in the morning light like a warning light, and yet he looked vulnerable. Would his life also be cut short, like Jack's? Would he be shot dead on a hot June night with a bullet in his back on the edge of a waterfront?

❊ ❊ ❊ ❊

The locomotive shed was close to the *Campo Marzio* station at the southern end of the *Riva*. It was sandwiched between the grand station building, a tightly curved, single-track railway line that gave access to the *Riva*, and an extensive walled yard with an imposing entrance filled with rows of American military vehicles.

Rose explained that this had formerly been a market, but since produce had become short it had been turned into a military depot and the evicted market traders had moved their lightly laden barrows onto the streets outside. As she turned the jeep down a narrow access road, Vignoles looked at the many hand barrows and four-wheeled wagons lined up against the kerb stones and at the thin, anxious faces of the traders and the women milling around with great wicker baskets slung from their arms, all tellingly empty of produce.

Ribbons of black smoke issuing from the chimneys of a clutch of equally black locomotives pulled Vignoles back to the matter in hand and he transferred his attention to the loco depot. Though not a crime scene, it might hold some clue to the fate that befell the victims, so he gave his full concentration to the task, placing his pipe between his teeth as he looked around.

The shed was busy, with at least five engines being prepared for work in the warming sunshine, whilst deep in the gloom of the six-lane building he could see two more under repair. A line of engines in various states of decrepitude lay to one side, quietly rusting in the salty air. Some men were moving about, oiling the engines or breaking coal in the tenders; others were belting out ringing tattoos with hefty hammers upon stubborn bits of metal or fiddling with all manner of odd workings bolted onto the outside of these ungainly machines.

The majority of the men were in British or American army overalls, but he noticed a few slightly older men, dressed in grubby civilian working clothes, whom he felt sure were speaking Italian. He was surprised to see a clutch of partisans seated around a table playing cards, their rifles resting nearby in a neat wigwam-shaped stack.

Two of the fitters gladly ceased beating seven bells out of a piece of massive valve motion to take time to speak with him.

'Brierley? I knew 'im, but he were not one'r me mates. Now let me think, was 'e wiv Curly?'

'Yeah, he's the fella who'd know the most.'

Vignoles made a note in his pocketbook. 'And who's Curly?'

'Curly Lambert, 'is driver. The drivers an' firemen are a team; they stick together. He's called Curly on account of his 'aving no 'air.'

'Where might I find him?'

George scratched his cheek as part of the thinking process. 'I think he went out early this morning.'

George's friend called another man over to join them. 'Dunc, what was Curly on today?'

'Target 24. He won't be back until late this evening.'

'Target?' asked Vignoles.

'Every trip, every movement on the line, is given a target as a way of explaining the task. It's easier than writing it all down in detail each time.'

'So you know the targets by heart?'

'The most common ones. We only 'ave to look up the less frequently used targets, as a rule.'

'And Target 24 is up to Villach, so he'll be gone a while.'

'I see. Do you have a list of these targets?'

'I've got one somewhere.' George walked over to a messy workbench and commenced moving things about in an aimless manner. 'I saw one only yesterday. Oh yeah, I remember, follow me.' He gave a quick but approving glance towards Rose. 'I know there's a few in the locker room.'

Vignoles caught Rose's eye and subtly indicated towards Henderson, who had his back to them, apparently more interested in the soldiers and their card game. Vignoles preferred to work alone and was impressed when she immediately understood his mime. She stepped smartly over towards the captain and drew his attention to something in the far distance.

Vignoles swiftly ducked through an open doorway at the back of the shed and entered a narrow corridor lined on one side by sets of wooden lockers, many of which had doors ajar or hanging loose on their hinges.

'Bit of a dump, sir, but we just use it as somewhere to leave a change of clothes or whatever. As you can see, most of the locks are useless, wrecked by the Germans when they left, so we don't leave valuables and that.' The fitter walked over to a windowsill cluttered with junk and stacks of oil-stained papers and started to rummage once again.

'Does each driver and fireman have his own locker?' Vignoles was reading names inked directly onto wood, often on top of Italian or Slav names; others, which could have been German, were heavily scored out.

'Most do. Ah, here we go, guv'nor.'

Vignoles bent down to read the names on the lower doors: 'Private Handley, Arthur. Private Potts, Harry. I can't read this one; he's smudged the ink. Oh yes, Private Brierley. Bingo!' The locker was empty and the door hung open. Vignoles flipped it closed. However, he noticed that the locker beside this was Private Lawton's. This also had no lock and the door was simply pushed closed. Using his little finger to hook into the hole where the lock should have been, he opened it.

There was little inside, but anything was an improvement on Brierley's. A cap, a smart leather belt, a pair of oily work gloves, a crumpled photograph of Mae West (cut from a magazine) and a small notebook. Vignoles picked it up and flipped the pages. It resembled a log of the targets Lawton had worked, with dates.

'We've not looked in there, sir. Sort of feels all wrong. You know? Dead men's things.' George was still patiently holding the sheet of paper for Vignoles to take.

Vignoles slipped the book in his pocket and closed the door. 'You were right to leave it alone.' He was surprised that the MPs had not thought to check the lockers, another example of how even the most basic police routines had been overlooked.

'Would Corporal Priday have used these lockers?' He took the list from George's hand as he asked the question.

'Oh blimey! So it is true? We 'eard that summat was up.'

'I'm afraid so.'

George shook his head. 'Nah, 'e won't have a locker here on account of 'im being on goods. They've got their own place.'

Vignoles nodded. 'Did you say you knew the men who were killed?'

George looked uncomfortable. 'We all sort of know each other, like to say hello to and whatever, but I can't say I was pals wiv Brierley. As for Priday, well, them goods lads don't come down 'ere that often.'

'But you were friends with Private Lawton?' Vignoles flipped through the sheets of foolscap.

'We used to 'ave a beer or two of an evening, a game of cards.' George's nervousness appeared to increase.

'How did he seem in the last days before he was killed?'

He shrugged, 'I dunno. Much the same, I suppose.' He looked at the floor and left Vignoles feeling unconvinced.

'Did he ever talk about meeting someone?'

'What, you mean people?' George glanced out of the window onto a sunlit yard at the rear of the shed, filled with piles of junk and litter. Was it Vignoles's imagination, or was the man half-expecting someone to be out there in the deep shadows?

'Indeed, there may have been more than one.'

There was a moment of stillness as George realised that he had made a slip of the tongue.

'This is a murder investigation. If you know anything, then you must say so, no matter how insignificant it might appear. Failure to do so will bring the MPs calling. I'm quite sure you would not want that.'

The man stared at Vignoles and chewed the inside of his lip. 'I'm not sure, but...' He glanced around again and lowered his voice. 'I suppose the daft bugger might 'ave got 'imself into some sorta mischief. But there was some geezers hangin' around the place over the last few weeks. Shady birds, lurking around like they was up to no good.'

'Can you describe them?'

'I'm not too clever at this sorta thing, but, well, they was sorta medium height, brown 'air, 'ats, jackets, one 'ad a long coat. Maybe they was dockers. No, p'rhaps a bit better dressed than that.'

'But that could describe almost anyone!'

'What am I s'pposed to say? I didn't 'ave a beer wiv 'em. Actually, one might 'ave 'ad a beard. They've scarpered now. Not seen 'ide nor 'air of 'em for a day or so. But I'd know if I saw 'em again.'

He glanced out of the window, his voice dropping almost to a whisper. 'Not long after they turned up, Lawton started to act a bit different. Kept slippin' off somewhere for an hour, quiet-like, and then he'd be back, lookin' pleased as punch wiv 'imself.'

'You think he might have become involved with these men in some way? Something illegal, maybe involving the docks or the railway?'

'Now I ain't sayin' nuffin' like that. I don't speak ill of the dead.'

'I have to ask these questions and you have to give honest answers.'

'Most likely I'm just talkin' a loada nonsense. If I sez any more it's just speccalation. Get a second opinion.'

'Ah, there you are, Vignoles! For a moment I wondered if you'd done another runner.' Henderson's crisply enunciated vowels rang out through the narrow corridor.

'Don't worry, captain, I was just obtaining this.' Vignoles waved the target list in front of Henderson's nose as they trooped back into the engine shed. Vignoles said nothing for a moment, but then made up his mind, taking Henderson to one side, his conversation rendered inaudible to the others by the many sounds in the shed.

'I need your help. If I'm going to get to the bottom of this I need others sharing the workload. I'm going to chance my arm and instruct the MPs to make a list of everyone who was friends, drinking pals or work colleagues with the three victims. The barracks would be a good place for them to start, then down to the goods department offices. When that's done I can try and interview as many on the list as possible. I'll start now by talking to these here in the shed. However, I shall need your help in following up angles that require a gentler touch, and as you were so adept at sniffing around my office, I reckon you'll be perfect for the job.'

'Look here...'

'I know you did, so let's cut the pussyfooting around.' Vignoles stopped short. He wanted to clear the air and move on. 'But that's history. As a matter of interest, how *did* you get in?'

Henderson took a sharp intake of breath then let it flow out in a gentle sigh. 'All right, it was a pretty low trick, I admit, but I was following orders.'

'Of course. But how did you get in?'

'Skylight. I dressed as a workman fixing the roof and it was a simple job to abseil down. Took a matter of minutes.'

'Dammit, I must be losing my touch. I didn't think of that.' Vignoles made a rueful face. 'Now, we have urgent work to do, and unless we knuckle down someone else might get hurt. So I'm prepared to take a punt on your playing straight with me.'

'Very decent of you, old boy.' Henderson was blowing smoke rings and staring into the distance.

'Are you with me or against me?'

Henderson grinned and offered his hand, 'With. And I'll forget the slug to my jaw. Quits?'

They shook hands.

'Sorry if I seem a bit preoccupied, it's just that…' he lowered his voice and looked swiftly towards the soldiers, 'things have taken a rather peculiar turn and the FO's in a bloody tailspin, not to mention everyone in AMGOT. A lot of top brass — Brits and Yanks — are gathering here as we speak.'

'Why?'

'Tito's walked out on Cominform. Turned his back on Uncle Joe Stalin. He's effectively rejected the Soviet Union. There's a bloody great rent in the Iron Curtain, dear chap.'

'Now that *is* a turn-up for the books. But is that not a good thing?'

'Maybe; maybe not. All last week intelligence had been getting a few tip-offs that there was something big about to blow up — and between you and me that was part of the reason I was sent out here — but we didn't expect this. Trieste might be in a nasty jam, as Uncle Joe will take a dim view of Tito now and who knows, he might even attack.'

'Surely not.'

'He's not exactly noted for his generosity of spirit. On top of that, things are getting worse in Berlin. The Allies will either have to airlift supplies in or fight the Soviets.' Henderson pulled his display handkerchief from his blazer pocket and wiped his brow. 'So we have to dream up a damned good story to sell to the press and radio here to ensure the locals don't use this as an excuse to cause an insurrection. I have to leave for a while. Shall we meet later? Let's say four, at the *Albergo.*'

'Agreed.'

'May I borrow Staff Sergeant Gretton for a lift back to HQ?'

'Be my guest.' Vignoles shrugged and pulled a wry face. No sooner had he decided to trust Henderson than the fellow walks off. Typical.

He'd have to do the legwork himself. It was like being a young sergeant again. He pulled out his notebook and started to speak with each of the men in the shed.

CHAPTER TWENTY

ON THE SUNNY SIDE OF THE STREET

Nat Gonella & His Georgians

DS Trinder and WPC Lansdowne started their day by paying a visit to Lieutenant DM Carruthers RN at his home in Loughborough.

The large, semi-detached property was constructed in a mock-Tudor style that combined brick and timber with red roof tiles and stained glass in the bay windows. It had a mature garden consisting of a neatly clipped lawn, standard roses, and a honeysuckle growing up one side of a detached garage with blue-painted wooden doors. It was the sort of house that would have been advertised as 'executive' in the sales brochures before the war. Trinder and Lansdowne walked through a small gate opening onto a crazy-paved path of pink-and-cream stone that lead to a porch with a semi-circular brick arch opening, an oversized ornamental lantern, a round window with more stained glass, and an oak door designed to evoke images of a manor house in the Cotswolds.

The bell clanged and brought the retired lieutenant hurrying and calling, 'Wait! I'll be right with you!' He opened the door wearing a brown apron smelling of chemicals and holding his wet hands out before him, giving them a shake to speed up the drying process. If he was surprised to find the British Railways police in his porch, he did not show it. The production of warrant cards if anything only served to improve his already cheerful mood. He was a man used to, and comfortable with, authority, and was soon ushering them into the front parlour whilst explaining that his wife was in town shopping.

'Gossiping in a queue, I'm quite sure, in the expectation of exchanging those blessed coupons for some rubbish the shopkeeper deigns to hand over! I don't know how she puts up with it.'

They all smiled politely and sat on immaculate sofas and chairs of a dated style that involved a lot of darkly polished wood and fabric of indeterminate colour, but which served to reinforce the town and country image. A carriage clock ticked gently on the mantelpiece below a reproduction of *Flatford Mill* by Constable.

'I do apologise for the awful smell. I was washing fixative from some photographic prints. My wife doesn't approve of the stink, so I try to grab my chance when she's out and hope the air clears. So, what can I do for you?'

'Are you a keen photographer, lieutenant?'

'Oh yes, I'm a member of the Royal Photographic Society and have been vice-chair of the Loughborough Tripods for a number of years.' He noticed Trinder's expression and explained further. 'The name is a bit of a joke, at our own expense, but when we first set ourselves up, hand-held photography was not really possible — still isn't, on a gloomy day with slow film stock — and also because we're rather old school and prefer using a tripod.' He brightened to his theme. 'I have had two slim volumes of my work published. My latest was out only recently. *Shades of Steam* is the title. I wonder if you are familiar with it?'

Trinder smiled. How Vignoles would have enjoyed interviewing this witness. 'I'm afraid not. Could you please tell us about the evening of Friday 4th June? You were out and about with your camera that evening.'

'Indeed I was. A particularly splendid light that was quite perfect for my needs. You see, I'm most interested in capturing the drama of a passing train and the effect of light upon the exhaust.'

Trinder gave a faint smile.

'I succeeded in snapping at least two or three images that I am most pleased with. Funnily enough, those prints are drying off even as we speak. They have quite lifted my mood; one could well prove a hit at the Loughborough Tripods' annual show.'

'Where were you working?'

'Along the Great Central, a favourite haunt, just south of Rothley. I was trackside as I have an annual line pass. I say, do you wish to see it? Is that why you're here?'

Trinder shook his head.

'Most of the regular crews know me. We often pre-arrange for some fireworks out of the chimney to help get a good shot. Really adds to the drama and, at this time of year when the exhaust is usually too pale, a well-timed oily cloth or two in the fire can make all the difference. It's perhaps a little naughty, but it helps no end. Oh Lord! I haven't got some poor fellow in trouble, have I?' He appeared alarmed.

'No, no, not at all. Were you near the section that was closed for maintenance during that day?' asked Lansdowne.

'Yes I was, miss. Not ideal for my purposes, actually. I was rather mad with myself for not checking the line restrictions before heading out that way. However, with wrong line working one can sometimes get a different angle on a locomotive, though the purist in me is never completely comfortable with the train on the incorrect side.'

'Do you recall seeing a track gang in action?' interjected Trinder.

'Oh yes, sergeant. They even appear in one of my shots. A little human interest in the foreground helps tell the story. The noble worker striving to keep the trains running, or something similarly heroic. *Picture Post* likes that kind of thing.'

'Perhaps we may see it?'

'Of course! Come through to my study.'

'Did you speak with any of the track gang? In particular with two women?' asked Lansdowne.

'Did I have any choice? It was they who spoke to me. There were four of them, to be precise.' He stopped and drew breath as he opened the door to usher them through. 'What a strange group they were! Two were Land Army gals. They were all rather excitable and did a good job of putting me off my work.'

'Why do you say that?' asked Lansdowne.

They were stepping into a modest-sized room lined from floor to ceiling with bookshelves against one wall, the other three displaying framed photographic prints of railway subjects. The pictures were boldly composed and full of drama. Even to Trinder's untrained eye, they looked impressive. A camera supported on a highly varnished wooden tripod stood to one side of a large desk with numerous prints in neat piles laid upon it.

'Come into my den! Now, you were asking about the women. They were hiding in the bushes — at least they thought they were hiding, but you'd have to be deaf and blind not to notice them — quite laughable, really. Oh, and they made ludicrous owl-hoots. It was like something from scout camp. Or should that be guide camp? Haha! They could have at least chosen a more suitable bird to imitate. I say, is that why you're here?'

'Not because of their bad birdcalls.' Trinder could not resist the observation, and drew an admonishing look in return. 'What can you recall about the encounter? I'd like you to think particularly about the time leading up to their appearance.'

'Hmm? I have an excellent memory, even though I might be getting on in years, but don't worry, we shall not have to trust an elderly man's memory, as I always keep a log of my photographic jaunts.'

Trinder and Lansdowne exchanged looks. This was the jackpot.

'Here we are!' The lieutenant had opened one of the drawers of his desk and held aloft a small but thick notebook. In neatly formed white letters he had painted '1948/2' on the dark green cover. 'This is the second book this year. It helps me keep things in order. Most important to have order and discipline in everything one does, do you not agree? Probably my naval training: once ingrained, you never lose it.'

Lansdowne smiled indulgently.

'Yes, here we go.' Carruthers was adjusting his spectacles and reading: 'Time, date, place and a record of each train and its locomotive. These...' he indicated with his finger as Trinder took the book from him, 'are the details of the shutter speed and f-stop of each photograph. So important to keep this information, sergeant, as the fellows in the RPS absolutely insist upon it. And this is the film stock and speed. I prefer Ilford, but that is hard to obtain these days and sometimes one ends up with all kinds of rubbish, though on this occasion I was fortunate to have some fine Agfa. German, of course, but darned good quality. Are you a photographer yourself, sergeant?' Carruthers gave Trinder an intense look.

'No. Just the odd snapshot with my wife's Brownie. We are more interested in the subject matter, actually.'

'Aha! You appreciate the magnificence of a steam locomotive at full speed? It quite moves the soul, doesn't it?' He grinned at Trinder, who opted to not take the bait.

'What's this you've written here?'

'Now let me see. Oh yes. *Bude*. Now she was actually my motivation for going that evening.'

'Bude? But that's what was written in...' Lansdowne began, but stopped herself as Trinder gave a slight shake of his head.

'She's a Bulleid Pacific. A Southern Region engine. On the exchange trials they are running right now. They're swapping the best engines from different parts of the country to see how they perform in comparison with those that normally run in each area. A most fascinating exercise, and I'm trying to record every trip she makes.'

'So you knew when to expect this engine along the line?' asked Trinder.

'Hardly a state secret, if you care to make the correct enquiries. She's giving a good account for herself and made a few cracking runs along the London Extension Line.' He held up a thin periodical as he was speaking. 'The *Railway Magazine* is publishing reports on the trials and they list all the expected runs each week. And of course, I have developed my own contacts among the shedmasters and signalmen, and they will often tip me the wink.'

'So, it would be easy for others to do the same.' Trinder nodded thoughtfully, wondering how he had been so unobservant as to have not noticed that this locomotive was operating along their line.

'Can we see the photograph?' asked Lansdowne, sensing that they had just made a significant breakthrough. Her eyes were bright and eager.

Carruthers gave a slight nod in response. 'Indeed, I have it here, miss. It may still be a little damp.' He unscrewed what appeared to be a large flower press and carefully extracted some prints interleaved with blotting paper. 'Are you particularly interested in Mr Bulleid's locomotives? I think they might come out tops, though mechanically, they are rather experimental, with some notable mechanical peculiarities.'

'We are interested in this particular engine, and specifically, this run it made,' Trinder replied, eagerly leaning over the desk to inspect one of the prints now laid out for them.

The picture was perfectly clear and well defined, full of luminous blacks, whites and infinite shades of grey. It showed a powerful-looking engine producing a volcano of dark smoke in great tumbling cumulus clouds from its chimney as it tilted around a curve in the track. Trinder was impressed by the old man's photographic expertise.

'Is this the engine called *Bude*?'

'I've seen this one, sarge!' exclaimed Lansdowne. 'It's painted a very gay green colour, but with an odd black tender. This makes it look mismatched and badly put-together.' She peered at the print with great interest.

'You're quite right, miss: it is indeed a curiosity. They needed to hitch a different tender behind as its own was not fitted with a water scoop for the long journeys it must make. It does look rather ugly as a result, but no less rare and intriguing.'

'Did you notice anything odd immediately prior to the train passing?' Trinder asked.

'Only these blasted women jumping out of the bushes.'

'What about on the track?' asked Lansdowne. 'Were both lines open when you took this?'

'Yes: there was a speed restriction to let the works tamp down, but the crew put on a show for me so that it appears to be travelling faster than it actually was. Here, use this.' He handed Trinder a magnifying glass. 'I was rather pleased with the print.'

Trinder examined it closely. 'There's a lot of detail. What do you think, Lansdowne? Just there on the bridge.'

She took her turn with the magnifying glass. 'Looks like two figures observing the train.' They exchanged knowing looks. 'But they're awfully small. I can't make out any detail.'

'Thankfully they're not any larger. I was toying with the idea of masking them out to preserve the clean lines of the parapet, but I don't think they spoil the composition too much. What do you think?'

'They are vitally important,' Trinder spoke gravely. 'Do you think you could get a blow-up of them?'

'I could try, but the film grain will cause much of the detail to be lost. Are they the reason you are here?'

'We are following a few lines of enquiry about an incident on the line a while before and leading up to the time this train was passing. This picture might prove useful.'

'Ah, then you'll want to see these.' Carruthers selected two more prints from amongst those he had removed from the press.

'This is the line gang in action. You can see their faces quite clearly. I wondered if one of the periodicals might like to use this, what with the drama of the team working hard, the sun illuminating their faces as they tramp along the line with their tools over their shoulders. And in this one, I have just the two men walking along the line, though now with their backs to the camera. I quite liked the composition. I thought to call it *Work done for the day*. I'm pretty sure that these were the two who later went onto the bridge to watch the train pass. I suppose they were interested in this particular locomotive.'

'I'm quite sure they were,' added Trinder, enigmatically.

'And these two were part of the large group?' Lansdowne was comparing the prints.

'One presumes so.'

'It's just that I can't identify them in the group picture. Look, here are the two women gangers.' Lansdowne was comparing the two prints. 'Do you remember if you got all the gang in this picture?'

'I'm quite sure I did. Yes, they were all hard at it. Including the look-out man — that's him in the far distance. Now I think about it, I got the impression these two men were working slightly apart from the others. Perhaps they had a different task that day. I was not really taking much notice. It must have been around four-thirty, going on five, and I was looking the other way, capturing a few shots of the down trains.'

Trinder asked to borrow the two photographs, promising to take great care of them, and asked Carruthers to make a detail of the two people overlooking the bridge.

'Would you recognise the two men if you saw them again?' he asked.

'Oh dear... they all wear the same overalls, caps, neckerchiefs, and all have similarly grubby faces.' He pulled a pained expression. 'I was thinking only about the composition. I say, are they in some kind of trouble?'

Chapter Twenty-one

Katyusha

Russian Traditional Folk Song

Vignoles and his wife were seated on canvas directors' chairs at a small wooden table outside the *Caffé Rossini* beside the *Canal Grande*, the short stub of a waterway that ended in front of a piazza and a domed church. The *bora* had calmed and the sun was beating down on the cream parasol shading their table. They each had a glass of wonderfully cold and dry white wine, and Vignoles was staring nervously at a bowl of what appeared to be green and black grapes but which had a strange, oily sheen.

'Go on, Charles, they're quite safe to eat.'

'They're pretty enough, but what do they taste like?'

'Heaven. Olives are quite simply the most wonderful things.' She popped one into her mouth. 'Bettered only by this...' She reached into a paper bag, pulled out a bunch of fresh pale green leaves and caressed them gently to release a powerful scent.

Vignoles took a deep sniff. 'Mmm. I really do like that. What is it?'

'Basilico. Basil. I'm quite sure we could grow some in your cold frame. We must try to find some seeds to take home. Now eat those olives before I pinch them all.'

'Can't we order some chips? I'm ravenous.'

'Italians don't eat chips.'

'They do — they claim to have invented fish and chips.'

'That's only in England. I'm sure you can have some in the mess tonight. So do you or don't you want to hear about what I discovered in those documents?'

Vignoles chewed thoughtfully upon an olive and nodded assent.

'I've been quite the little detective this morning,' continued Anna. 'Going at it fresh made things clearer.' She pulled a small collection of papers out of her handbag and unfolded them, putting on her sunglasses against the glare of the sun. 'There is one particular goods movement that seems odd — assuming I am interpreting this correctly. You see this number here...' Vignoles nodded and selected another olive, chewing thoughtfully upon it as Anna spoke. 'I take it to be a wagon number.'

Vignoles peered at the document. 'That seems reasonable.'

'Now, you can see that it has been carefully typed in after all the others. It is fractionally at a different angle.'

'Indicating that the form has been fed into the typewriter on a separate occasion.'

'Spot on, Charles, and the number always appears last in the list, just as it would if added after all the others. On one or two occasions it is even a different typewriter.'

Vignoles was now staring at the number with a very odd expression forming on his face, his cheek bulging with an olive.

'Oh, they're not that bad, darling!'

He shook his head, finished chewing and swallowed. 'No, it's not the olives — I'm developing a taste for them, as it happens — it's that number.' He opened his wallet and took out a folded sheet of notepaper. 'Eureka! The same! VE3BFG4000.' Vignoles sat back in his chair and looked at Anna triumphantly.

'Where did you find that?'

'Near the obelisk, close to where Brierley's body was discovered. But it gets better! The page was torn from a small pocketbook — and I know which one.'

Vignoles extracted Private Lawton's notebook from the inside pocket of his blazer and placed it on the table. He flipped over a few pages until he found the right place. The size, the paper and the rulings, as well as the handwriting, matched perfectly. Vignoles put the torn-out sheet up against the ragged-edge strip and it fitted like two pieces of a jigsaw puzzle.

'This was in Private Lawton's locker at the shed. I made the connection between paper and notebook earlier this morning but I was stumped about that number. Now why would Lawton give this wagon number to Brierley?'

'This is interesting.' Anna was inspecting the little book. 'The conveyance documents were completed and signed by Corporal Priday — so that means we've got all three of them tied together by this wagon.'

'Gosh, yes. Let's see how this might fit together; Priday was able to direct a wagon's movements. He could decide where it was sent and when, while Lawton and Brierley were train crew and therefore involved in moving wagons around the network. All three knew about one specific vehicle. All three have been murdered, and so the inference has to be that this was because of their involvement with the wagon and the goods it was carrying. This is darned good work, Anna. What can you tell me about the wagon?'

'Let me start with the easy bit. It first appears on these records at a small factory near Salzburg on May 25th.'

'Is there a name for the factory?'

'The typewriter ribbon appears to be fading, so it is very indistinct.'

'Unfortunate. Or was that deliberate?'

'Who knows? We have no documents that tell of how it got there or what it is conveying, but it looks like the wagon was taken on a series of short trips over a period of several days. It was a curiously active little thing. Here it is again...' Anna flipped the pages and indicated the place, 'at Monfalcone, in a railway yard with documentation to bring it into Trieste, to those great marshalling yards that Corporal Priday oversaw.'

'And where he was killed.'

'Exactly.'

'Is the wagon there now?'

'I assume so. However, we only have documents up until the day before yesterday.' Anna made a rueful face. 'Yesterday's are missing.'

'Interesting. We might just have overlooked them in his office, but I'm wondering if the removal of these documents could be related to his death.' Vignoles took a sip of wine.

'It means we lose the trail of the wagon in Trieste, along with the man who was arranging for its transportation and who knew its exact location.'

They exchanged glances.

'It's an oddly dangerous wagon, Charles. Knowledge of it appears to result in death.' Anna sipped some more wine as she contemplated this realisation.

'Say nothing to anyone about all this. Not even Henderson. Just a precaution.' Vignoles drummed his fingers on the table. 'I'm wondering if Lawton and Brierley were involved in hauling this wagon on its protracted journey and were they paid for their efforts? If so, where is the money? There was nothing in the reports about either having any excessive sums in their personal effects. Or were they dealing with Quislings, who double-crossed and killed them as payment?'

'It's beginning to look like that. You suggested that from the start.'

'Let's work through Lawton's notebook. He's logged all his working trips — "targets", they call them. Let's see if we can place him with the wagon. This will confirm our theory and might help to give me a picture of how events have unfolded since 25th May.'

'"Targets", did you say?' Anna picked up one of the documents. 'That explains something I was puzzling over. Beside each train movement there is a little box with "Tgt" and a number beside it.'

'That will help no end.'

An hour, a second glass of wine and another bowl of olives later, they had cracked it. On at least two occasions Private Lawton had crewed a train that had included the mysterious wagon. However, as he had been the first of the men to be killed, the trail necessarily stopped on 2nd June.

'Frustrating. We need something similar logging Brierley's movements — but his dossier indicates no such log book amongst his personal effects.'

'So where is it?'

'Good question. I could do to talk with his regular driver.'

'And that raises another question. Where are the drivers in this scheme? More to the point, what about the guards? They have the most involvement with the paperwork associated with trains.'

'True. It's inconsistent.' Vignoles sucked on his pipe a moment. 'Let us imagine that we're trying to effect this complex and secretive movement, for whatever reason. You said yourself that it requires a lot of people working together.'

'Undoubtedly.'

'However, as a gang leader, it makes sense to keep the numbers involved to a minimum; it increases the split of the final reward and minimises risk. So, if I were managing such an operation, I would include the fewest number of people that I could.'

'And if sufficiently callous, I would kill them off after they did their part of the work — both to preserve secrecy and to increase my own profit.'

'It stands to reason, Anna.'

'What an awful way to think.'

'Indeed. Fireman are paid less than drivers, so perhaps they are more susceptible to being bribed. Perhaps these two firemen were offering assistance to the goods guards, who are the ringleaders. Hells bells, what if the drivers are behind this plot?' Vignoles looked perturbed. 'I'm speculating now, but it raises a host of unpleasant questions. I might have to play it carefully with the other crew members. But what on earth is so important about this consignment?'

'Ah, now, that is the hard part: I simply can't work out what this wagon is conveying, or even what it looks like. Not helped by the fact that I'm unfamiliar with the terminology, the numbering systems and everything else they use over here. If this document were British, Charles, I could pretty much tell you everything you want, almost down to the colour.'

'Presumably it arrived in Trieste to deliver something. To which factory or wharf was it sent?'

'That information is missing, or perhaps Priday didn't manage to type it out before he was killed.'

'But you believe this mysterious wagon is sitting somewhere in that great yard at the *Porto Nuovo*?'

Anna grimaced. 'I think so. Though it could be shunted off almost anywhere. I get the impression that there are countless places it could be hidden away.'

'Let me play devil's advocate for a moment. Can we be sure that this vehicle is suspicious? Could it not just be that the owners were very slow at passing on instructions and so Priday had to type the details in at the last minute? Maybe that's why the number is in Lawton's book and Brierley's possession — so they could be sure to not miss out on collecting the wagon?'

'Okay, Charles, this is why I took notice of it. At no point do I get any sense of what *purpose* the wagon is serving, of what it's carrying, of who owns it. Nothing. Everything is vague and fuzzy. Just like the typing. Look how many times Priday has smudged the entry or the ribbon is faded. There really is something fishy about this. If we take any one of these other wagons — for example this one...' Anna indicated, with a well-manicured and varnished nail, a number above the one they were discussing, 'I know that this is carrying coal. I can trace who owns the wagon, who owns the cargo and where it is being off-loaded.'

'I'm convinced. I had better go and find this thing. But where the devil to start looking? Is there nothing to help me?'

Anna shook her head slowly. 'Nothing. And how many wagons does that yard process in a week? One thousand? Two thousand? Three?'

'I'll try and get another meeting with Commander Turbayne and see if he will put some troops onto this. I've already got him trying to chivvy the military police on my behalf. The trouble is, all the top brass are running around in an awful state; they have no time for the likes of me anymore.'

Vignoles recounted what Henderson had said about the sudden split between Jugoslavia and the Soviet Union. When he finished they both fell silent for a moment, considering the implications.

'And how did you get on in the engine shed? Anything useful?'

'A few scraps of information, but I don't feel like I have spoken to enough of the men or anyone sufficiently close to the victims to get a really clear picture. There are reports of odd men lurking around the place and suggestions that they might be somehow involved, but the descriptions are vague.'

Anna wondered about the man in the gloom near the amphitheatre, and the two who had watched them cross the railway yard. However, her descriptions would be equally vague and probably unhelpful. She could feel a sense of apprehension building inside and wanted to push away any thoughts that she and Charles were being watched. She adopted another tack. 'Has Corporal Priday's girlfriend been told?'

'I understand that Brigadier Harper-Tarr is arranging for someone to visit her and his family. A grim task, and one that I'm glad I don't have to do. That reminds me, I ought to get these sent back.'

Vignoles reached for the small khaki shoulder bag he had been issued by the army PX store earlier that morning. He had quickly realised that he could not carry a pistol about his person without it being very obvious in his light summer clothes, so this had been a sensible solution. Opening the flap, he extracted the few items of personal effects he had collected at the crime scene and glanced again at the two photographs of the dead man's girl.

One was clearly an official portrait, expertly lit and composed, and the picture was dominated by the young woman's naval uniform and cap, though softened by a suggestion of hair gathered at the nape of her neck. Her face was slightly triangular and her mouth small. She looked thoughtful and considerate. In the other picture, she was wearing a skirt, blouse and a thin, knitted cardigan. The picture was slightly bleached by a pool of bright sunlight. She was standing in a clearing in a leafy wood, probably called to stop and turn so Priday could capture the moment on film.

He flipped it over but there was nothing written on the reverse. Vignoles noticed that the woman was holding a camera case in one hand. He hoped she would at least have some happy memories of that walk in the woods. 'I don't think these have any bearing on the case.'

Anna took them from him.

Vignoles idly picked up the pack of cigarettes, flipped the lid open and shook free those remaining inside. Each was pristine and untouched. Slipping his fingers between the back and the foil liner he found the cigarette card was still in place and extracted it.

'He was not a collector of football cards.' The small rectangle bore a colour photograph of Albert Stubbins, a forward with Liverpool. Anna smiled feebly, still touched by the images of the young woman.

Vignoles tossed the cigarette pack onto the table and opened the small, fold-over pack that contained cardboard matches. Three had been torn off and used.

'Hullo. But maybe he's a bird watcher?'

'Why do you say that?'

'He's written the name of a bird and a date on the inside. Perhaps he wanted to remind himself of a sighting.' Vignoles showed the little matchbook to Anna and the word 'shrike' written in biro.

'What sort of bird is that? I can't say I've heard of it.'

'Sometimes known as the butcher bird. An attractive little thing, but it likes to impale its prey on sharp spikes and thorns. It creates a food larder in that manner.'

'Ugh! How horrid.'

'You say that, but it's only being practical. We have abattoirs and they're a darned sight worse than what this little bird can do with a few insects.'

'But that can't be right.'

'Oh, it is, I once saw a shrike's larder when I was a boy.'

'No, I mean about Priday sighting the bird and making a note to remind himself. It's today's date that he's written.'

'What?' Vignoles lent across and took the matchbook. 'Good Lord, so it is. Thank goodness you noticed. And of course this is the same date he was killed, in his work place, when he was not expected to be on duty.'

'And important documents are also missing — perhaps taken by his killer.'

'So could this be an aide-mémoire? A code word for a rendezvous?'

'A man called "Shrike"?'

'An oddly chilling choice of name.' Vignoles was sitting bolt upright and brandishing his pipe. 'I'm now convinced these three were involved in a high-level smuggling operation, working with a ruthless character masterminding the operation. Our focus must be on the dockyards and finding this blasted wagon and discovering what it holds. Henderson and I also need to find the men seen lurking around. I'm meeting the captain at four, so we can crack on then. There's also one other clue. This odd name written on the scrap of paper Brierley lost when he was killed. I suppose it could be a woman.'

Vignoles flipped the sheet of notepaper over and showed Anna the scrawled name 'Steller Polar'.

'He means *Stellar*. That's "star" in Italian. He's tried to write something down in Italian, but isn't familiar with the language.'

'I can sympathise with that,' Vignoles added.

Anna was thinking. 'He means to say "Pole star". One normally uses that for finding one's way — at sea.'

Vignoles looked flummoxed. 'I'm not sure what to make of this, but it feels significant, all the same.'

'Could the man in the shadows near the Roman ruins play any part in this?'

'That was probably coincidence, dear. Just someone who was told by his wife to smoke outside.' Vignoles tried to keep his voice light. 'However, I prefer that you don't accompany me around the docks. Not until I'm more certain of what we're up against.'

Anna seemed to be about to argue the point, but stopped, a fact that was not lost on Vignoles. He suspected she was already starting to feel the unsettling influence of the investigation. He was not immune, either, from wondering about what unknown forces were at work.

'Hello, what's going on there?' Anna snapped out of her dark thoughts and pointed across the canal towards the *Piazza del Ponterosso*.

This was a square where market traders set up their stalls of bric-a-brac, second-hand clothes, sunglasses of dubious origin, packets of chewing gum, individual cigarettes laid out on neatly laundered handkerchiefs and other desirable items almost certainly obtained from the US Army stores. A large group of women was streaming into this space from along the *Via Roma*, all walking with a sense of unity and purpose.

'What do you think they are doing?' Anna was shielding her eyes against the glare of the sun.

'They seem to be forming up across the road. I think it might be some kind of protest,' replied Vignoles.

The crowd had swelled to something close to a hundred, massed into a dense huddle, arms folded or hanging at their sides, some of them holding small placards of cardboard with slogans painted on. The women looked determined yet subdued, many with drawn and tired faces. It was as though they were assembling more from a sense of stoic duty than burning passion. There was none of the shouting heard the day before.

A motor coach, its roof rack heavily laden with great bulbous bags of laundry, attempted to cross the bridge spanning the canal that gave the square and market its name, but was forced to halt in front of the female barrier. The driver angrily beeped the horn, gesticulating to the women to step aside. A horse hitched to an ancient wooden cart joined the minor traffic hold-up. The scrawny man leading the horse leaned against one of the wheels of the cart and lit a cigarette. A few passers-by, apparently encouraged by the angry coach driver, started to hurl insults, and one or two of the women answered back.

'What on earth's going on?' Vignoles turned in his seat to get a better view.

Two American soldiers at the next table overheard him. 'It's the Union of Slovene Anti-Fascist Women. They do this most days around this time. They come to stand here in protest at the lack of food.'

'Or their lack of dollars to buy the food on the black market,' added his friend.

'I see.' Vignoles flipped his sunglasses into place against the brilliant light.

'The poor things look half-starved,' observed Anna, 'but very determined.'

'We tend to give 'em about twenty minutes or so, then we step in and move 'em on. The likes of that driver get carried away if their protest drags on longer than that.'

'The Italian male is not noted for his patience or understanding. They blow their tops like a volcano!' The servicemen both laughed heartily, apparently unconcerned by the increasingly ugly confrontation now brewing.

Anna looked as though she was going to respond to this insult, but said nothing, more concerned about the sudden shift in mood. A large group of young men with close-cropped hair visible where not covered by an assortment of caps and hats, and all wearing heavy boots and a strange mixture of faded military fatigues, were advancing towards the women, both along the *Via Bellini* and across the bridge, forming up alongside the coach. The passengers inside the coach all appeared to be washerwomen, and were looking out of the windows in alarm at the noisy throng of jeering youths. The stand-off grew increasingly loud, though neither side engaged in direct assault, but it was unnerving and Anna could feel her pulse racing. The women started to link arms and form a solid chain of thin but stoical figures.

'Unity is strength.' Vignoles said quietly.

The women started to sing a lilting melody that was instantly memorable, and soon their voices combined into a powerful and apparently effortless series of harmonies.

'*Katyusha*. I know this song!' Vignoles felt a stab in his chest as he remembered singing the very same song, but with English words, at an International Brigades meeting. On another occasion, Jack and his comrades had sung it as they drank a toast after signing up for the fight in Spain. But that time Vignoles had refused to join them, and he'd walked away, the infectious melody ringing in his ears.

'It's beautiful.' Anna was captivated.

Policemen started to step out from the back of two vans that had suddenly screeched to a halt at the rear of the aggressive youths on the bridge; whilst others, blowing whistles and brandishing truncheons, were trotting up the *Via Bellini* from the direction of the church. The Venezia Giulia police in their incongruously odd British bobby's helmets were coming to bring order to the situation.

The two GIs finished their drinks and stood up. 'We gotta go. This means trouble.'

'But the police are here.'

'Exactly, sir!'

The youths were chanting something ugly and brutish, fingers pointing and clenched fists raised towards the women. Anna bit her lip and frowned, confused by their aggression. 'Why are the Italians showing such hatred towards those poor women?'

'They must be nationalists, I suppose. They're not representative of the majority, I'm sure.' Vignoles took Anna's hand and gave it a squeeze.

The police waded into the stand-off, pushing the youths aside with their arms, though noticeably not using their truncheons, and the angry men appeared willing to give ground to allow the police direct access to the women. Once they had passed the youths, their truncheons were raised in anger and the police were barking commands in aggressive voices. A number of women were pushed violently backwards. There was a surge forwards as youths and police mingled into a seething mass. Anna saw both fists and truncheons rain down on the defenceless women.

'This is outrageous!' Anna held her hands over her face.

'What the devil? Can you see that?' Vignoles turned to address a British soldier, a lance corporal, who was leading a posse of men along their side of the road towards the mass of shouting and screaming people.

The soldier shrugged. 'It's normal. Happens all the time,' he said, and jogged onwards.

Two small armoured cars, possibly those that had been parked outside their *Albergo*, appeared on either side of the *Canal Grande* and proceeded to make their way along the parallel roads towards the fight, the heads and shoulders of the commanders protruding from the gun turrets of each, one deploying a loudhailer and calling for order.

Suddenly it was all over; the nationalists melted away, with just two or three being roughly manhandled by British or American soldiers, whilst the women were fleeing the scene just as quickly, though some were visibly injured; nursing sore elbows, hips and thighs. One woman held a rag to the side of her head, blood streaming down her pale green and white patterned dress.

The police were adjusting their helmets, straightening their jackets and lighting cigarettes. Some were smiling and sharing a joke.

'I'm shocked. The police have just attacked innocent women — they were worse than those thugs.' Anna looked indignant.

Vignoles was silent. He was also taken aback by the violent attitude of the police. He recalled what Brigadier Harper-Tarr and Commander Turbayne had said about the Allied-funded Venezia Giulia force and made a note to try and avoid them at all costs.

Chapter Twenty-two

Hej Tovariši!

Jugoslav partisan song

The tank wagon stood alone on a short stub of a siding tucked away to one side of the vast *Stock* distillery. This was an infrequently used line as it involved extra shunting moves down a long and sharply curved line, and so train crews preferred to take the easier option and shunt the wagons into the newer section of the complex.

The siding did, however, have the advantage of being partially covered by a rusting corrugated iron roof, supported by wooden legs. This took the edge off the burning sun, which rendered any tankers standing outside scorching hot and unpleasant to clamber upon whilst being serviced. The shade beneath the roof was deep, though the many holes in the rusted covering allowed sun to dapple the wagon with tiny spots of light like daytime stars.

A high wall of brick and crumbling rendering was topped by nasty barbed wire and this boxed in the siding down one side and across the end, where a stop-block of timber was fixed directly to the wall and supported a small warning circle of faded red-and-white painted on metal. The opposite side opened onto a twisting mass of pipes, valves and supporting pillars, feeding into a jumble of tall brick buildings that had seen better days. This was the oldest part of the distillery, which occupied a significant section of the *Porto Nuovo* together with an untidy jumble of factories, warehouses, chandlers' shops, seedy bars and walled compounds served by faintly mysterious and almost derelict railway lines that curved sharply around corners, crossed roads at right angles and squeezed between buildings along litter-infested alleys, accessible to only the smallest of the dock engines and their motley assortment of wagons.

An ancient wooden gate, with peeling paint clinging on to the sun-bleached wood, was drawn across the distillery siding and securely padlocked.

Professor Viktor Ferluga peered through a narrow gap between the gate and the supporting post, squinting to read the number on the side of the wagon. He was sure that this was what they had waited for, but he needed to get closer to be sure. The gate was high and, whilst the walls were old and scarred and offered tempting footholds, the wire on top was uninviting.

He lit another cigarette, his second in just minutes, and tried to calm his nerves. This was frustrating: he should have had a work permit, a staff pass or other documents that would allow him to walk into the distillery in broad daylight and get right up close. He could slip the conveyance documents into place that would see it hauled safely away from the British and American zone.

But something had gone wrong and the man with the documents had not kept their rendezvous.

He pressed his face to the wooden gate and looked again, the faded paintwork was hot to his cheek and exuded a slight aroma of oil and turpentine. It was futile, but he hoped for inspiration. He looked down at the weeds growing tall between the heavily rusted track and the brighter yellow striations along the top of both rails that betrayed the recent movement of the wagon into the siding. A brown-and-orange butterfly fluttered down from over the wall and danced around a clutch of blue chicory flowers. If only it were that simple for him to gain access.

He looked back along the line. It appeared unused. He nodded to himself and admitted that this was a well-chosen location. Everything was in place, just as he had been promised. The problem was, he was becoming increasingly worried, and he had plenty to worry about.

There were the knots of British soldiers walking up and down the marshalling yards that he saw on his way to the distillery. What were they looking for? He had a nagging suspicion that they were seeking the same thing as he. Faintly ludicrous though these soldiers appeared, with their voluminous shorts and pale legs, floppy berets, heavy green socks and oversized boots, they were a battle-experienced army and their appearance was deceptive. They were more than capable of causing him considerable trouble and he could expect little sympathy if caught sniffing around.

The sense that something had gone badly wrong was mounting as each hour passed and the soldiers traversed another row of wagons. His nerves were jangling. It was at moments like this that mistakes were made. He had to trust that they could find a way to deliver their precious cargo back to his institute in Ljubljana.

As the professor smoked and peered once more at the solitary wagon, he had serious doubts if their contact — a shadowy figure known to them only as *Srakoper* — was trustworthy. His worries had only been increased by the lunchtime meeting he'd had with his co-conspirator in the *Caffé Eden*.

* * * *

They had met, as usual, at twelve, choosing to sit in the gloomy interior at the rear of the grubby café upon the insistence of Professor Vrabec, who had arrived in a state of acute nervousness. Professor Ferluga had not been pleased to leave the fresher air outside for the sourness of the back room, but he could see that Vrabec was unhappy. It was probably a sensible choice as the nervous demeanour of Vrabec — fiddling hands, anxious backwards glances and rapid chain-smoking — would almost certainly have attracted unwanted attention.

The *barista* at the café was a weedy looking fellow with a habit of glancing their way whenever he passed by. Although he was used to the Slovenes meeting for a lunchtime drink and would sometimes communicate in an odd Triestine version of Slovene and offer the prescribed reply to their clenched fist greetings of '*Smrt Fascismo!*' — acts that suggested he was more friend than foe — one could never quite tell in this city, where prying eyes and ears were never far away, and the suspicion remained he might betray them. It was safer to keep their voices low.

The carafe of open wine was rough and sour, but it was cheap and helped ease the tension, and Vrabec drained his first glass before he was calm enough to speak. 'The problem is our man in the railway yard. It is worse than we feared. He is dead.' Vrabec refilled his glass, drank some more, and then wiped his heavy moustache.

'Are you sure?' Professor Ferluga asked. 'Perhaps it was someone else who had an accident in the yard. Our man would stay away if he got word. It would be safer.'

'Quite sure. And it was no accident, comrade. He was killed.' They said nothing. The smoke curling above the table between them appeared to be filled with dread, clinging at their clothes, stinging their eyes, cloying at their throats.

Ferluga broke the silence after first taking a deep gulp of wine. 'That does complicate things. But who could be doing this?'

'People who want what we want, and who are closing in on us.' Vrabec opened a packet of Lucky Strike, breaking the US Army seal on the cellophane wrapper with some force. 'And there is more: I overheard two military policemen. I am sure they had just come off duty from guarding the place he was murdered, and they were moaning about a hot new detective from England investigating the

~ 167 ~

deaths of soldiers on the railway. I was able to listen as they probably assumed I knew no English. They talked of our man and how he'd been knifed.'

'So that makes three.' Ferluga was staring at the tablecloth, trying to conceal his growing apprehension. 'Since we started all this, three men have been killed.' He wiped his brow with a handkerchief.

'How so? *Il Piccolo* said that the first two were victims of street robbers.' Vrabec was looking puzzled; an unlit cigarette dangling from his lip bounced as he spoke.

'You said yourself never to believe a word printed by the Allied controlled newspapers! Those stories are just imperialist lies and propaganda written to cover the truth.'

'Oh, *zelo dobro*! Now you're telling me. You're saying all three have been...' he dropped his voice to a whisper, 'murdered because of our project?' Vrabec was fiddling with his lighter and trying to hide his trembling hands.

'Let's look at the facts.' Ferluga was also trying to appear calm and in control. 'Our three contacts have all been killed shortly after we met with them, or just before we were due to do so. That can't be coincidence.'

'Far from it, comrade!' Vrabec spoke bitterly and re-filled his glass. 'And we still don't have the documents to access the *Stock* works, nor do we have the forwarding documents for the wagon. You're right: it looks bad.' Concerned about being overheard he glanced around the café, trying to locate the *barista*. 'If our man was killed early this morning, just before our rendezvous, then the killer has those documents.' Vrabec took a final, deep drag on his cigarette before stubbing it out with force. 'Who are these killers? Who else knows about this?'

'Ourselves, and *Srakope*r. No one else.'

'But what if these careless *Angleski* had been talking before they were killed?' Vrabec gave Ferluga a hard stare. 'Or maybe they were forced to talk.' Ferluga contemplated this awful suggestion, but stayed silent. 'We should get out. It's too dangerous now. It must be only a matter of hours before we are caught by either those doing the killing or the British soldiers. And if we're caught in Zone A with that suitcase of money...' He opened his arms wide in an expansive gesture that encompassed a multitude of imagined horrors.

'Sh! Don't mention this. Do you think the reception back home will be any kinder if we just give up? Eh?' Ferluga stared at his colleague. 'The Socialist People's Republic of Jugoslavia needs us to succeed. The marshal himself demands success in this mission. No one said that this would be easy.'

'Actually, comrade professor, you did.' Vrabec's voice was sarcastic. 'This was to be a simple "shopping trip" across the border, was that not how you put it? "To collect goods delivered, ready and waiting." You told me everything was arranged to perfection.' Vrabec's face looked grey with worry rather than anger.

'Okay.' Ferluga smoothed his hair. 'Perhaps I was a little over optimistic. But *Srakoper* will sort everything out.' He looked at his colleague's hang-dog expression and ploughed on. 'I'll seek further directions. He will know what is best.'

'*Je to tako?* And who *is* this man? We have never once met him, never even seen a photograph. How can we trust him?' Vrabec was lighting yet another cigarette. 'And what's with his stupid name?'

'Sometimes, things are better left unknown.' Ferluga was speaking quickly and urgently. 'Our security services have given him their highest recommendation. All I know is that he served heroically with the partisans. And let's not forget that he's got the goods this far. We have to trust he will find a way around these problems.'

'So make contact and let him tell me how we get out of this alive. We're no experts in this kind of work. I'm a scientist, not a bloody spy!'

'Keep your voice down. It looks like we've made mistakes, I admit. We can't risk another, so I advise caution…' Ferluga tailed off. Neither needed reminding of the danger. He was emptying the carafe of wine between the two glasses.

'Listen, we have reason to think the delivery has arrived here in Trst. I shall check that it is where we expect it to be. Tonight, I'll make a dead-letter drop and seek new directions. Just one last push and we can secure it. We must hold our nerve.'

* * * *

Ferluga snapped out of his recollections of the meeting and quickly pulled back from the gatepost. Two men were approaching from a door in the old distillery building. After taking a few deep breaths he carefully eased himself forward again to peer through the gap and watch as the men approached the wagon. They were talking quietly and he strained to catch what they were saying. He was not sure, as their words broke up and faded before he could fully comprehend them, but they sounded like Russians.

That was a nasty surprise.

His pulse raced as he watched the men stand in front of the tanker. One of them indicated the number on the side. This was even worse. The other nodded then looked around in a manner that showed he was concerned they were not being observed. This man stared straight towards the gates; his eyes appearing to look into the professor's open eye peering through the gap. The professor dared not move, as that would surely betray him. He held his breath. The man frowned as if he sensed something, then looked away. Ferluga pulled back against the wall and breathed. He had to move quickly. If Russians were inspecting the wagon, then this spelled trouble.

Picking his way carefully along each wooden sleeper, taking care not to disturb any stones or rusting bully beef cans, or to scatter the many shards of broken glass littering the track, Ferluga moved away from the distillery, his mind racing.

As he turned a corner he came to a level crossing where a single railway line crossed the road at right angles. A woman was standing on one corner, her hand on a rounded hip and the hot sun creating interesting shadows across her pale blouse.

He glanced up and briefly met her gaze, but quickly averted them again. Her healthy good looks and presentable clothes — a stark contrast to the usual street girls — surprised him. Under other circumstances he would have allowed his eye to linger a little, but he did not want to invite her proposition and was worried about being remembered as walking from the distillery. He needed to get away quickly. Ferluga put his head down and walked towards the main railway yards, trying to look purposeful.

The pretty prostitute watched him pass and, as soon as he was lost to view behind a series of telegraph poles and a scrawny tree, she followed.

Chapter Twenty-three

Time Alone Will Tell

Rita Marlowe with Ambrose & His Orchestra

'Where next, sir?'

Following their fruitful visit to Lieutenant Carruthers, DS Trinder and WPC Lansdowne were walking towards Loughborough GC station.

'I think we should take a turn up line and see if anyone between Quorn and Rothley saw those two bogus gangers.'

'Good idea, sarge.'

'We've made an important step forward this morning and our photographer friend has set my mind racing. I'm inclined to believe his story, though I'd like some corroboration. That's what DI Vignoles would demand.' Trinder exchanged looks with the WPC.

They were both still feeling the loss of their trusted boss and Trinder liked to voice his thinking aloud, to seek reassurance. 'It never ceases to amaze me how he has the knack of sniffing out when something isn't right. He dropped the hint, and now we're really on to something.'

'But what is that something? Are we really dealing with an organisation with deadly intent?'

Trinder blew air from his cheeks in a long, slow exhalation. 'Of that I'm still not sure. But I do want to find the two jokers who wrote their initials in paint, as I have a suspicion they are behind this. They may be the same people who tampered with the track. Let's recap what we know.'

'The letter sent to the super warned us about a threat to that special locomotive, *Bude*.'

'A threat that was attempted, but fortunately foiled.'

'And that means the trackwomen are innocent.' Lansdowne gave a little clench of a fist. 'I knew it!'

'And we have a photograph of the possible culprits — though it is awfully small and blurry, so that won't help secure a conviction or get the women off the charge.'

'I suppose you're right. But we do have the perpetrators' initials written in red paint.'

'I'm puzzled by that. Actually, we don't have them, as the

paint has long been scrubbed away and no one thought to take a photograph.' Lansdowne looked crestfallen.

'But we have the track spanner which, hopefully, will have some fingerprints upon it.'

'But that will only be useful if we have someone to compare them with, sarge.'

'If only we knew who sent that blasted letter!' Trinder grimaced in frustration and lit a cigarette.

'Sarge, there's something nagging me about that. How was it supposed to work, as a warning, I mean? Assuming that someone *had* managed to work out what this "scarlet tide" is that has to be stopped and how it referred to derailing the *Bude* loco, how would they tell the perpetrators that it had in fact been stopped, in order to prevent the crime? There was no means of contact.'

'By golly you're right. There has to be some way to respond to the threat. When I was reading up on the IRA attacks in '39, they were all preceded by a clear warning — so evacuations could take place — and followed up by statements to the press.'

'The intention was to cause fear and disruption, not to kill.'

'There was always insufficient time to defuse the bombs, but enough time to minimise injury, and the IRA followed each incident by declaring their responsibility and threatening more of the same, whilst opening the door for the government to negotiate the Irish situation with their known intermediaries.'

'But in our incident, the warning was like a cryptic crossword clue and there was no means to make contact and presumably there has been no word since.' Lansdowne was thinking hard, staring at the hot pavement.

'Even though the train was not derailed, the fear that it might have been could be the IRA's style — but they would surely want everyone to know. Our warning letter was anything but clear, and the tampering was only foiled by chance.' Trinder spoke more quickly as he followed the train of thought. 'And the other incidents, with the possible exception of the fire, are rather amateurish, don't you think? Throwing paint at trains and dropping timetables off bridges.'

'Could this just be a silly, but rather sick, game, sarge?'

'Maybe. An ill-conceived attempt at a campaign of disruption by amateurs.'

'But no less dangerous for that.'

The gentle hump of the Great Central Road was in front of

them as it rose to span the railway, the booking hall of the station, with its saw-tooth-edged canopy, occupying the centre point. Drifts of smoke broke through the wooden palings of the boundary fence from a locomotive waiting below. A horse was hauling a heavily laden cart with a tarpaulined load into the goods yard that lay to their left. The driver made clucking sounds with his mouth and the horse shook its head in a tinkle of bridle and horse brasses and the wagon creaked under the strain as it turned. As they stood to let them pass, another Better Dead Than Red poster, freshly pasted onto the goods office wall, caught Trinder's eye.

'They get everywhere! Blasted bill-stickers. There's a bye-law specifically to stop this kind of thing.'

He started to unpeel one corner where it had been imperfectly slapped onto the brick and it soon eased free as the paste has not yet set hard and the paper retained some dampness.

'This is for the same talk as that flyer we were given. It's taking place tomorrow evening,' observed Lansdowne.

'Don't tell me you're thinking of going.' Trinder ripped the poster in half then commenced attacking some of the fragments that remained stuck to the brick.

'I don't know what it is, sarge, but I have an odd feeling when I read that rather ridiculous title. Something is niggling at me inside.'

Trinder paused and looked at the ragged fragments in his hands. 'It looks like complete nonsense. Have you no better offer for a Saturday night, Lucy? Mind you...' he gave Lansdowne a light-hearted look, fearing that he had been unnecessarily impolite about the WPC's private life, 'DI Vignoles is always telling us not to ignore hunches.'

'Exactly. And that is why I think I'll attend. If nothing else, I can tick them off about fly-posting on railway property.'

'DI Minshul will be delighted by your dedication.' Trinder screwed the paper into a ball and looked for somewhere to throw it. As they advanced towards the station he noticed piles of unsightly rubbish strewn on the far side of the fencing that bordered railway property.

'Look at all this rubbish. Someone should put a stop to it!'

Lucy Lansdowne laughed. 'You are starting to sound like the new DI!'

'Hmph!'

They stepped into the wooden-panelled booking hall and nodded a greeting to the clerk behind his little window. Dirty grey smoke drifted up the creaky wooden stairs, partially enveloping a family buying something from the bookstall. They could hear coal being shovelled into a firebox, a carriage door slamming shut, a water injector was turned off; all clues indicating that the train was preparing to leave.

'Quick, Lucy, we might just catch it!' shouted Trinder, who then hurried down the steps as fast as he could go, a hand raised to attract the driver's attention.

CHAPTER TWENTY-FOUR

TEMPTATION

Perry Como

Vignoles and Henderson were criss-crossing the marshalling yards, accompanying the handful of soldiers assigned to the task of searching for the mystery wagon. It was like looking for the proverbial needle in a haystack and their resolve was not bolstered by the sight and sound of long trains of wagons being hauled away from the port by massive, Nazi-built *Kriegslok* engines, given to the Jugoslav Railways as reparation for the war.

These trains were destined to travel deep into Jugoslavia, Czechoslovakia, Hungary or perhaps even further behind the Iron Curtain. If the wagon was part of one of these, then it was surely lost forever. Even if it were on a train heading into Allied territory, they still faced the Herculean task of tracking it down. For all Vignoles knew, it was too late and the wagon was long gone.

One thing was for sure: it was hot and dusty work and although it was late afternoon the sun was still fierce and unforgiving, bouncing off the cinders, sleepers and rails and further increasing the temperature. It was time for a cup of tea, and Vignoles had seen a likely place to obtain one.

An ancient, ex-Italian army truck, with an ungainly wooden and metal box-like structure on its back, stood in the sun close to the ramshackle collection of huts used by the many shunters working the yard. The truck had a smoking stovepipe chimney sticking out of the roof and white letters painted on the sides identifying it as a NAAFI tea van. A wide wooden shutter was propped up to create a serving hatch, from which two red-faced, red-haired and unsurprisingly sweaty Scotsmen in khaki kilts and tam o'shanters were serving tea, Bovril and indescribably poor coffee from a decrepit kitchen that exuded intense heat. The bacon sandwiches had long gone, so a sun-dried roll with a sliver of sweated cheese and fatty corned beef had to suffice.

Henderson had wandered off, so Vignoles took his roll and enamel mug of tea and walked the few yards to where a locomotive was steaming gently whilst its crew took refreshment. Standing in the shade cast by the engine, Vignoles took time to look at its unfamiliar shape and design, running his eye over the exposed pipes, ungainly connecting rods, wheezing pumps and a multitude of odd appendages affixed to the boiler with little concern for style and grace. It was clearly designed for ease of maintenance, something his friend Tim Saunders would probably approve of. A metal plate screwed to the cab told him that it had been built in Saronno in 1914 by the Italian State Railway. It had somehow managed to survive two world wars and remain serviceable. The cab was wide and generously proportioned and the front spectacle plate was pierced by two oval windows, hooded by small sun deflectors that gave it a sad, hangdog expression from the front. At the rear there was a short, low-slung tender that offered no protection from the elements.

The fireman ceased rattling a fire-iron, clanged the fire-doors shut and turned on the water injector. He then took a deep draught of tea and sat on the edge of the footplate, resting his feet on the short metal ladder that formed the cab steps.

'Not a bad machine, for her age. Not speedy, but with plenty of grunt. Made to climb hills.'

Vignoles nodded acknowledgement. 'I understand there are some tough gradients around here.'

'I should say. When we leave this place, we tend to head eastwards then make a long, sweeping curve north and then back west and up — climbing right to the top of that escarpment around the back of the city. It's one hell of a slog.'

'You'll need to have a good fire, then. Not much room for mistakes on a haul like that.'

'Too right! Many a new lad has got caught out on that run. We often use bankers on the heaviest trains to give 'em a push and help 'em out of trouble. That's what we've been doing all day. Hence me havin' a mug like a minstrel!' The fireman grinned, lifting his hands wide like Al Jolson and exaggerating his noticeably smoke-blackened features. 'Mam-eee!'

Vignoles laughed, glad to forget his concerns for a moment. 'I suppose you get all the clag off the engine up front?'

'Yep. Double the dirt for your money. Lovely.'

'And not a lot of fun running backwards.' Vignoles was looking at the tender piled high with coal.

'In this dry heat the coal just makes dust to blow into your face. You spend most of the time trying to damp it down with the hose. But you get used to it. Anyway, I'm off here soon and straight down the Blue Lagoon for a dip.'

'Blue Lagoon?'

'The open-air swimming pool. A wonderful place and just a short walk from the *campo*. Most of the lads go after a day on the footplate. It's either that or endure the freezing showers at the barracks — if they have any water, that is. There's often a shortage up there in the summer.'

'Sounds like a good plan.'

'We leave our dirty clothes at a laundry that's next door and pick it up clean after a dip, so we're ready for a night on the town.'

'I wish I had the time to join you.' Vignoles grinned as he felt a trickle of sweat run down his back and the dampness under his arms. They watched as two Jugoslav soldiers walked past, both little more than youths, the red stars on their green forage caps as bright as cherries in an orchard.

'What's the deal with the partisans?' asked Vignoles. 'I've seen them riding on the footplate.'

'They ride shotgun and keep an eye on us when we run through Zone B. We do the same if they have to take a train through Zone A. Most often, we swap crews at the border with Italy and Jugoslavia, though sometimes if it's going straight through — up to Austria, for instance — we can stay on if the partisans ride with us. It's all right. We dislike them, and the feeling's mutual, but luckily we can't speak the lingo, so they just smoke and read the paper and we ignore them.'

Vignoles nodded, having lit up his pipe, observing the chatty fireman through the smoke he was making. 'Tell me, did you know either Private Lawton or Private Brierley?'

'Yeah, I knew them, but only to speak to.' He looked into the distance for a few moments. 'The poor bugger who copped it in the yard this morning was a good mate.' He sipped some tea and when he spoke again, his voice was low and laced with menace. 'I'm on the look-out for whoever done him in. I'd like to find him before you do, if you catch my drift.' He glared accusingly at the backs of the young soldiers, and spat on the ground, perhaps to remove coal dust from his throat.

'Do you have any idea why anyone would kill Corporal Priday?'

'Are you a white helmet?' The warmth had suddenly faded from his voice, along with the mirth from his eyes, like the sudden shutting off of light and warmth during a solar eclipse.

'No, not an MP, but I'm heading the investigation, so any help you can give will be appreciated.' Vignoles showed his warrant card to the fireman. 'Detective Inspector Vignoles.' He extended a hand and, after a short hesitation, the fireman reached down and shook it.

'Lance Corporal Harry Hancock.'

'During the week before Priday died, was anything different? Did he act strangely, or change his habits?'

Hancock blew air slowly out of his cheeks. 'Not that you'd say, as such.'

'I sense you have doubts. The tiniest detail may help.'

'Well, lately he preferred to drink in another bar. But I can't see that that means much.'

'Anything might have a meaning. Can you explain in more detail, please?'

'Like most of the lads, we normally take a turn down to the big piazza.'

'*Piazza Unita*?'

'Yep. We like to drink around there, at the *Tergeste*, the *Specchi*, all the big places where we can get together and have a bit of a laugh. But he was suddenly all for going to this smaller bar a bit out of the way. It was okay, and a bit closer to the loco shed and swimming pool. One or two lads go there and so do a few Yanks, but it's mainly for locals and they don't much like us lot barging in. If something went off, a fight or whatever, we'd be a bit exposed.'

Vignoles remained silent, encouraging the man to keep talking.

'So I didn't feel comfortable there. Mind you, it was cheap! The beer costs almost nothing, but let's make no bones about it, we're all pretty flush here in Trieste, so everywhere's cheap to us. It had a funny name: the *Stella Polaris*.'

Vignoles felt a jolt like electricity. He took a sharp intake of breath but kept his voice even. '*Stella Polaris;* the Pole Star. Why did Corporal Priday like it so much?'

Hancock drained his mug. 'Well, he met a woman there, so that might have had an influence. The local women leave us well alone, and anyway, fraternising with local girls is frowned upon — worse luck! So she was a prossie, but he was smitten with her.'

'Did they initially meet at the bar?'

'I think so — but not when I was there.' He stood up and turned the injector off, the water dribbling from the overflow pipe, followed by tiny wisps of steam.

'Did you ever meet her?'

'Come off it! She wasn't the sort of lady you introduce to your mates. I saw her a couple of times, just briefly, and from a distance. She was quite a looker.'

'When was this?'

'Oh, maybe after the second time we went there, just as we were leaving. He made his excuses and I knew he was up to something, and then I saw her on the street. So I left them to it and went back to barracks.'

'And the second time?'

'Last night.'

Vignoles felt a shiver down his spine. 'He was with her?'

'No. She was alone. I suppose she was touting for business. I dunno; I walked the other way. Perhaps I'm old fashioned, but going with her would seem a bit odd, what with my mate and her...' he tailed off.

Vignoles made a gesture for him to continue.

'Well, that was it. Nothing more.'

'Where was this?'

'Close to the *Stella Polaris*. But now I think about it, one thing was odd. I walked the other way, towards the docks, as I didn't want to go right past her.' Vignoles raised a quizzical eyebrow. 'I dunno why. I get a bit suspicious seeing just one pretty girl on an empty street late at night. It might be a set-up to get rolled. It pays to be careful down by the docks.'

'Very wise.' Vignoles was intrigued.

'It was really quiet on the street and, would you believe it, she was following me! I could hear her heels clicking on the pavement. After I'd gone some way I turned around and there she was, looking my way. A bit eager, I thought. Maybe trade was slow.'

'What does she look like?'

'Medium height with a very nice figure and good legs. She was wearing a pale mackintosh — but open. Brown hair, worn straight and shoulder length under a black beret. Nice cheekbones. Lots of sex-appeal.' He winked.

Vignoles nodded. 'I can see she made an impression. And where was Priday?' He was struck by the unsettling realisation that this man could have been describing Anna. This might explain the reaction of the old lamplighter.

'He'd gone on ahead a while earlier. We'd had a few jars, a few hands of rummy and then, suddenly, he got up and said he remembered something he had to do at the yard. Had to go back as it was urgent. I told him it could wait until morning, but he wasn't having any of it. I offered to keep him company, but he refused and said he'd see me the next day.' Hancock tailed off. 'So I went on home.'

'Did he often go back to work like that?'

'No.'

'And it did not strike you as odd?'

'A bit, but he has an important job and I suppose if he had forgotten something... But all today I've wondered, what if I'd stayed with him? Would he still be alive — or would we both be dead?'

Vignoles declined to speculate. 'Did you have much to do with Priday in your working day?'

'Quite a lot, especially if we're working around the yards. That's how we became mates.'

'So he would give your driver and guard the targets to work?'

'Yeah. Quite often it was him.'

At that moment Henderson strolled over and listened in.

'Did he do so yesterday?' asked Vignoles.

'Yeah, he was on duty all day. That's why I was a bit surprised that he was so eager to rush back.'

'What kind of runs did he give you yesterday?'

'Just the usual stuff. Shunting and doing short local trips around the place; no long haul or banking work.'

Vignoles suddenly felt inspired. 'Did you take or collect wagons from anywhere a bit out of the ordinary?'

Hancock pulled a face for a moment. 'I don't know about unusual. We took a delivery over to *Stock* — but down the old line. A right old ride, that was! Just one wagon, thank goodness, which we had to propel all the way with our guard walking in front with a flag.'

Henderson exchanged a knowing glance with Vignoles.

'Would Priday have given your guard some consignment documents? Listing the wagons and where they were to be taken?' asked Vignoles.

'I suppose he did. Though for these short delivery runs they tend to just clip the paperwork onto each wagon. It's not like we're going any distance. So most of the time we get told to just potter off to wherever, and the paperwork can go hang.'

'Going back to last night, what was he doing immediately before he told you he had to go back to the yard?'

'How do you mean?'

'What prompted him to remember that he had something urgent to do?'

Hancock frowned. 'He was patting his pockets. Looking for ciggies or matches, I suppose. But then he got a bit agitated as he went through all his stuff, stood up and said he had to go, sharpish.'

'He was looking for something significant, that maybe he had left at work,' Henderson mused.

'I suppose he did act like that. But what?'

Vignoles ignored the question. 'Had you both been to the Blue Lagoon?'

'We had. It was a scorcher of a day.'

'And you both collected fresh clothes from the laundry?' Vignoles was biting on his pipe, trying to keep his voice calm.

'Yeah. But...'

'We need the name of the laundry and I need you to show us where it is on this map.'

CHAPTER TWENTY-FIVE

A TREE IN THE MEADOW

Ivy Benson & Her Girl Band

Trinder and Lansdowne were at Quorn & Woodhouse station, questioning the stationmaster, Mr Gentle. It was not an enjoyable experience.

'Oh yes, sergeant, I heard about that pretty little mess. And I'm rather surprised that you have not arrested those two women and charged them.' He placed both thumbs into the tiny pockets on the front of his waistcoat and lifted himself up and down on the balls of his feet, an action that made his patent leather shoes squeak. 'I was never a great advocate of women on the railway, and now look where it's got us!'

Trinder sensed Lansdowne bristle beside him, though she remained silent.

'Why the delay? They should be taken straight to court and we shall see what they have to say for themselves!'

The short and surprisingly rotund man was standing beside his desk and attempting to pull himself up to a commanding height in the face of the tall, lanky frame of Trinder. However, despite the efforts of its owner to stand tall, his glossy top hat, sitting in the middle of his desk, was more effectively dominating the room, rather like a malevolent witch's cat.

Trinder found himself staring at the hat as he answered. 'There are a number of avenues to explore. If you or your staff have seen anything suspicious —'

'I have a busy station to run and I don't have time to go rushing around "exploring avenues". The culprits are known to us, so why waste valuable time looking for two railwaymen who know a darn sight more about how to do things correctly than these irresponsible girls?' He extracted a silver pocket-watch and inspected it ostentatiously. 'Now, why don't you go and report to a senior officer that this is an open and shut case, and get back to whatever it is you normally do.'

His entrenched views and arrogant attitude dampened the spirits of Trinder and Lansdowne, and so, after terminating the unsatisfactory interview they stepped outside into the warm sunlight to consider their next move, Trinder privately tussling with the idea that they repair to the nearby Railway Hotel and sample the Everard's Tiger it was noted for serving to perfection.

Trinder was starting to feel the weight of Minshul's command to get a result by Monday. It was all well and good getting an investigation handed over to him, but he wondered if he really had the experience to drive it forward.

As he wrestled with his worries, a train appeared from under the road bridge and, in a series of hisses and breathy sighs, pulled to a halt beside them. A carriage door slammed and a comically blackened face leaned out of the loco cab, eyes and teeth seeming excessively white. The fireman looked back along the train, awaiting the guard's signal to start.

Everything seemed to stop, as if time itself and the whole heat-soaked station awaited the drop of the green flag. Then, as if releasing breath held excessively long in the lungs, the engine sighed and eased itself into motion, rather as an athlete might find the energy to restart after a pause during a long run.

Trinder tipped his hat back on his head to allow some air against his face, leaned against the small brick building that housed the gents toilets, and lit a cigarette. He flicked his lighter open and shut again in quick, deft movements that made a satisfying click each time. He was sure Bogart would approve. He was thinking.

Lansdowne laughed bitterly. 'By golly that man was prejudiced! We know those women are innocent. It makes my blood boil to hear him speak like that.'

'Remember, he does not have the benefit of the information that we have.' Trinder flicked the lighter open and shut a couple more times and gave a weary sigh. 'Perhaps we need a spot of lunch to help order our thoughts.'

'I certainly could do with a cup of tea.'

'Then the hotel across the way should serve admirably.'

As they started to walk towards the far end of the platform where the covered steps lead up to Woodhouse Road, Lansdowne stopped. 'Look, sarge, there's another one.' She indicated the strident political poster crudely pasted on top of a colourful picture extolling the benefits of *Bright, Breezy Bridlington*.

Trinder groaned and made as if he were going to tear it down, but stopped himself. 'You know something? I'm going to accompany you to this damned talk and give them a piece of my mind.'

Lansdowne was unable to conceal her surprise.

He touched the poster. 'It's still wet. It was pasted very recently... perhaps just an hour ago, if that.' He dropped his voice.

'If that bumptious little man hadn't been preoccupied, running his supposedly "extremely busy" station, he might have caught the little blighters. I wonder where they went.'

'They may still be here.'

Trinder nodded in agreement and turned to survey the station, his curiosity piqued by the realisation that they had been minutes away from catching the perpetrators red-handed.

He stood still and, for a moment, forgot about his thirst. He took in the view: the compact goods yard surrounded by rolling fields; the stands of trees and glimpses of substantial red-brick houses with big chimneys. Everything appeared peaceful, ordered and calm. The little station felt pleasantly sleepy in the hot June sun and even a dripping cistern in the gents sounded more like the trickle of a mountain stream. The timber fence creaked quietly as it warmed. The swallows made small but intense squeaks and peeps as they darted above. A distant telephone started to ring.

Across the main line and opposite where they were standing, a series of metallic rings chimed with that of the telephone bell, followed by the scrape and clang of empty milk churns being unloaded from a wooden stage. Trinder, suddenly feeling weary and lacking the energy to hurry to the hotel, watched two men skilfully roll the tall churns by balancing each on its rim whilst twisting the top with their hands, and then place them on their wagon in neat rows like silver chessmen. The horse nodded its head and flicked flies from its ears. A delivery lorry, with *British Road Services* painted on its side, crossed the road bridge, the driver crashing the gears and honking the horn. As the sound of the van diminished, that of the birdsong seemed to rise and take its place. Lansdowne studied the array of posters on a large noticeboard. Trinder felt a bead of sweat roll down his cheek. The irritating telephone was finally answered.

A porter, who had been trying, none too quickly, to busy himself with a clutch of small parcels handed off the recent train, wheeled an upright trolley along the platform as he nodded an acknowledgement to someone behind Trinder. When he drew level, he spoke. 'The stationmaster wants you, sir. Urgently.'

'Sorry?'

'He's calling you to go to the telephone.' The porter nodded in an action that looked as though he were heading an invisible football.

Trinder pulled himself upright and instinctively straightened his hat when he saw the portly stationmaster in his spats and glistening shoes. Trinder thought he resembled a short, fat penguin, and was surprised that he had put on his top hat just to step outside his office door. He indicated with a hand that he was inviting Trinder to enter his office.

'It would appear that they wish to speak only to yourself,' said the stationmaster, speaking with exaggerated care and emphasis.

Trinder picked up a buffed and fragrantly polished telephone receiver that lay upon an immaculately clean ink blotter. 'DS Trinder speaking. Really? Aha. When was this? I see.' He frowned and listened intently. 'It does sound serious. We shall be there as quickly as we can. Goodbye.' Trinder was looking grim.

'Bad news?'

'Yes. The driver of the train that recently departed has been injured between here and Rothley. Had something thrown at him from a bridge and took a nasty blow to the face.'

'That's a damned outrage!' The stationmaster removed his shiny hat and smoothed his thinning hair. He turned to look out of his office window. 'What is the world coming to?'

'We need to get down to Rothley in double-quick time.'

'Of course, of course.' Gentle took a deep breath and puffed his chest out, happy to have an important task to do. 'I shall telephone Loughborough Central and arrange for the next train to convey you.' He squinted at his silver watch and dialled a four-digit number. 'We're expecting an engineer's train shortly — that will suffice.'

※ ※ ※ ※

A short while later Trinder and Lansdowne were riding in a solitary coach that formed part of an engineer's train of open wagons filled with fresh ballast, two tool vans and a weather-beaten brakevan at the tail end. Trinder was leaning on an open window, feeling the warm breeze on his face and smoking pensively whilst they made the short journey to Rothley.

The countryside was looking especially pretty in the afternoon light. The acres of grassland rolling past the carriage windows in gentle undulations were rendered like sheets of yellow or crimson by an abundance of buttercups and clover, each field fringed by hedgerows punctuated by elms, oaks or beeches, with glimpses of distant church towers and the roofs of barns in between. Teams of horses worked the fields and Trinder watched as a wagon stacked high with newly mown hay was hauled along a narrow and steeply graded lane. Rooks wheeled and spiralled around a particularly tall stand of trees marooned, as if an island, amidst a sea of waving grass and meadow flowers. The shadow of the locomotive's smoke slid smoothly across everything in puffy, dark clouds.

Lansdowne was sitting on a wooden bench that ran along one side of the coach. Trinder was humming the melody of *A Tree in the Meadow*, but paused to remark, 'I like that song, Lucy. It makes me feel good, in a funny sort of way, although the words are sad.'

'A little melancholy never hurt anyone. Everywhere looks so lovely today, and yet all is not as it seems. There's something going on out there that's just not right.'

Trinder narrowed his eyes and looked intently at two figures close to the railway line, turning his head in an attempt to focus on them as the rattling train steamed past. Just a pair of farm hands leaning on a fence and sharing a smoke; surely not the type to hurl things at an engineman?

A cloud of dirty grey smoke suddenly blocked his view, and as this snagged on the branches of a hawthorn hedge he caught a fleeting glimpse of someone running parallel to the train. He strained to catch their features, but the coppice was filled by dappled light that flickered and flashed in greens and yellows, softened by the smoke in the branches, and so he found it hard to focus and keep the figure in view. The hedge appeared to climb the side of a cutting, blocking his line of sight, and the mysterious runner was lost forever.

He had snapped out of the inertia that enveloped him after his dispiriting encounter with Stationmaster Gentle and was on high alert. Was this latest attack the next move by the same pair?

The train started across the twin viaducts spanning Swithland Reservoir, and immediately the world around them was transformed into a silvery sparkle of water and reed beds. A row of one-legged herons stood at intervals along the shoreline, as if carved from wood. As the train rumbled off the viaduct spanning the waters, the abutments of a road bridge passed his nose in a flurry of smoke and a brief increase in noise. Trinder craned his neck in an attempt to look at the bridge, wondering if this had been where the object had been thrown from.

As they slowed on the approach to the station, Trinder noticed they had been transferred to the down line, as the up line was still blocked by the stricken driver's train on the far side of the island platform, an angry tower of steam now roaring from the safety valves, ripping into the air above a small, square toilet block that partially masked their view of the locomotive.

The platform was filled with passengers milling around and gossiping in groups, others forming a crush of fascinated observers in a semicircle near the cab of the locomotive. Trinder knew that this was where the driver would be.

'Why are people always so eager to gawp? Can't they just leave the poor man alone?' He spoke aloud over his shoulder as he pushed his way through a gathering of smartly dressed women and a group of young, loud-talking toffs.

An elderly gent with a fishing rod and bulbous tackle bag blocked their path, observing in a strong, plummy voice, 'This is an intolerable delay.'

Trinder felt a rush of irritation flood through him at the man's insensitivity and pushed the rod aside, impervious to the complaints he drew. He gained his first view of the poor driver, and felt shocked. He heard Lansdowne take a sharp intake of breath.

The man was slumped on a bench with blood flowing profusely in glistening rivulets of burning red. It was pouring down his face, soaking into his shirt and railwayman's blues and staining his hands. His hair was matted in spiked clumps, made increasingly worse as he repeatedly rubbed his forehead with a cloth rendered a bright candyfloss pink with his blood. He was uttering a string of curses followed by mumbled apologies aimed at the staring audience. Trinder could see that one eye was almost closed and his face was already swelling into an impressively ugly lump.

Trinder showed his warrant card and asked what had happened. The fireman was the first to answer. 'He got struck right in the face. Some bastard chucked it off o' the bridge.'

The speaker was a scrawny but muscle-bound man with eyes startlingly grey and clear, the irises ringed by a dark line that gave then an unnerving intensity. His hair was dark, though peppered with touches of grey at the temples and receding. He wore a small moustache on a face browned by a lifetime of leaning from the cab of a locomotive. 'Not as I saw it coming, mind. Though I did see it bounce off the coal — after it'd bounced off 'is head first, of course! Haha!' Strangely, the fireman seemed to be more interested in making fun of his colleague's injury than in finding first-aid supplies.

Lansdowne recoiled at the man's laughter, but experience told her that it was just a reaction to the shock.

'I'll kill the little bugger as done this.' Like his fireman, the driver had a strong Liverpudlian accent. 'I could've lost me bleedin' eye. The little scally bastard! Sorry for the language, miss.' The driver looked sheepishly at Lansdowne, but scowled at the others standing around watching him. He looked up at Trinder with his one good eye. 'It's not so much the pain as the shame of it.' He hung his head and pressed the soaked cloth to his temple. 'Ouch! I mean, look at me! I'm covered in the red stuff.'

Trinder stared at the sea of crimson and started to feel nauseous, not helped by the eye-watering smell of what he took to be paraffin or Swarfega soaked into the driver's handkerchief. The fumes were also doing nothing to ease the man's streaming left eye, which had a deep cut just above the eyebrow. Trinder wondered why nobody had offered a clean handkerchief.

'Lansdowne, fetch the first-aid box and ask the porter for some warm water.'

'Righty-o, sarge.' Lansdowne eased through the onlookers.

'What struck you?'

The driver didn't appear to hear Trinder. 'And it would have to be *red*. Just my flippin' luck!'

'Haha!' The fireman chuckled. 'Eh, I'd not thought of it like tha.' I reckon they must 'a chucked it at you on account of you being a bluenose!'

'Ah, leave off, will yer? Anyway, how the heck are they to know as I'm an Evertonian from up on a bridge?' There was a ripple of laughter from those who understood the joke. The driver wobbled slightly and steadied himself with his free hand.

'Yeah, but they said as you was a red when they chucked it.'

The driver blustered on. 'Oi, Mr Policeman, here's yer first clue to who done it: you're looking for a football hooligan who don't like me choice of team.'

Trinder bent down and with a fingertip lightly touched the surface of a pool of red that glistened on the platform. It was sticky and a brilliant hue. He raised the finger to his nose and sniffed.

The driver watched Trinder's face as he realised that it was red paint. 'If all that were me blood, do you think I'd still be sitting here? I'd be checking in at the pearly bloody gates, like as not.' He shot Trinder a disgusted look.

Trinder nodded and flipped open his notebook. The man looked very pale and was probably concussed. He needed to get the questioning over quickly, then see that he was taken to hospital. Lansdowne returned with the first-aid box and, after hearing that it was paint, immediately turned all her attention to administering to the cuts on the driver's face. As she did so, Trinder asked the man to explain exactly what had happened. But there was not much to tell, and after only a few minutes he had recorded everything he considered useful.

Apart from the crew's names and addresses, he noted that they had worked out of Birkenhead Mollington Street shed that morning on a turn to Banbury. The approximate time of the attack had been about two minutes before they arrived at Rothley station, at which moment a tin of scarlet paint had been tossed from bridge number 352 — which was indeed the same that Trinder had identified on the way in.

He wondered if he should take a trip over there on the signalman's bicycle, but suspected that it would be a futile exercise. It would almost certainly be devoid of clues as to the identity of the paint hurler. That sort of luck only happened in fiction books. But he would delegate someone to walk the line to retrieve the tin of paint, in case there were any fingerprints.

He then inspected the locomotive, noting the explosive splatters of glistening paint on the side of the cab, across the coal and dripping down one side of the tender. It would not take much to clean it up and the locomotive was otherwise unscathed.

Trinder stared at his notes, looking for inspiration. The fireman claimed that the paint hurler had yelled something just before the can struck, though with the noise of the engine and the roar of their passing under the bridge at speed, he could not say what it was with any accuracy. He thought it was something about being 'a red'. Trinder dismissed the fireman's insistence that it was connected to the driver's football team colour, but was intrigued all the same. This was the second locomotive to be hit with red paint. Was this the 'scarlet tide' that had to stop? Why would anyone threaten an even worse incident if the police failed to stop this mindless paint-vandalism? It made no sense.

Trinder flipped his notebook closed and placed the black elasticised cord around the pages. The fireman had the injectors on and, to the huge relief of the crowd, had finally stopped the infernal fizzing of the safety valves. Trinder could feel his pulse quieten and was able to think a little clearer without the dreadful noise.

The driver was considered unfit to continue and a relief man was being sent down from Leicester to drive the train forwards into Central, where a qualified first-aider would be waiting to assess him. The crowd boarded the train in anticipation of the restart, their interest waning now it was clear the man was not about to die and was just 'a foul-mouthed engineman from Birkenhead' as one expensively dressed woman proclaimed to her friends. 'Of course, one feels sorry for the poor chap, but he is probably used to fighting and getting into all manner of scrapes,' she concluded. The strident voice of the tweedy fisherman sounded in agreement: 'Absolutely right. The driver must have been known to the attacker, it stands to reason. He's clearly done something to bring this upon himself.'

Trinder noticed that not many voices argued against this harsh opinion. He shook his head in disbelief, but then wondered if the attack was indeed provoked. He tapped his pencil against the cover of his notebook and looked at the red paint on the locomotive a few moments longer. He felt a sudden flash of inspiration, and returned to the driver, who Lansdowne had rendered far more presentable, though the bruise and cut above his eye were darkening and swollen unpleasantly.

'What was that about the assailant calling you a "red"?'

'Eh? Oh, you'd better ask me mate. I never heard it. Or at least I couldn't understand what they shouted.'

Trinder turned to the fireman, 'Can you repeat what you said earlier — you implied the attack was because he was an Everton supporter.'

'That was me just messing. I weren't serious. But they did shout something like "You're dead 'cos you're a red". The noise on the footplate is pretty bad especially near a bridge and then what with this happening, it's pretty much gone clean out of me 'ead.'

Trinder turned to the driver again, 'Are you a member of the British Communist Party?'

'Eh? I'm not sure as I should answer that.'

'May I remind you that this is a police investigation.'

'All right, no need to get heavy handed. It's no secret around Mollington Street that I'm a fully paid up member of the BCP. I'm also the ASLEF branch secretary. I'm doin' my bit to see the hard-working railwayman is treated right by British Railways. We work all hours an' get precious little for our efforts — not even a hot bath at the end o' the day. It's a flippin' disgrace. It's high time we had a share o' the profits and a say in the way things are run.' He looked away for a moment with bitterness in his eyes. 'But you can't seriously think they attacked me because o' *that*, can yer?'

Trinder fell silent. Lansdowne, who had been listening in eagerly, looked intently at the fireman and asked, 'Does the phrase "Better Dead Than Red" sound familiar?'

He instantly became animated and nodded his head vigorously as he replied, 'Yeah! That's it! That was what they shouted. I'm sure of it. Spot on, girl. But how d'you know?'

Trinder and Lansdowne exchanged looks, but neither of them replied.

CHAPTER TWENTY-SIX

Pesem o Svobodi
Jugoslav partisan song

They acted swiftly. Vignoles opened his map of Trieste and marked with a pencil the two sites mentioned by Lance Corporal Hancock: the laundry and the *Stella Polaris* bar. He was not a moment too soon in doing so, as the driver rejoined his engine, throwing Hancock a disapproving glance that suggested he immediately got back to work, and a cold look at Vignoles and Henderson.

As he muttered something about 'gossiping like housewives', the driver opened the drain cocks in a sequence of irritated movements and the front of the locomotive became enveloped in steam. A loud hissing sound fizzled in the air, the signal dropped and, with a series of breathy sighs, the old engine clanked away towards a long train of box-vans awaiting banking up the escarpment towards Opčine.

'It could be nothing, but I get a feeling we're closing in on our wagon. But I don't want the troops or anyone else charging in. We need to play this delicately.'

'Why the hell not, old boy? Storm the damned place and let's see what's what. I'm not sold on this wagon story of yours, but let's at least give it a go and find out.'

'That kind of approach is probably why I am leading the investigation and you're not.' Henderson grimaced. 'No, captain, this needs a lighter touch. We watch and wait and dig deeper. It really is no use finding a wagon full of contraband whilst frightening off everyone involved. We need to know who is behind it and the nature of their operation. And why three men have died because of it.'

'So what's the plan?'

'For now, I'll place a loose cordon around both sites. We'll keep the men some distance away and out of sight. I want them to keep an eye on who goes in and out, and not challenge anyone or make their presence known. However, we'll stop any wagon movements to and from these two areas for the night. Come on, I need a telephone to get Commander Turbayne to put this into immediate operation.'

They started towards one of the goods offices as they talked. 'A third party of soldiers can continue to make themselves visible by strolling up and down a few lines of trucks The idea is to make it seem that we have no idea where to look. This will buy us a little time.'

'Do you think they've rumbled us?'

'They'd have to be completely blind not to see our presence around the port today. It was always a risk to be so obvious, but perhaps this might force their hand.'

'Are you not overlooking something? Why not have a look-see in at that ghastly *Risiera*, or over at *Stock,* and find out if this blasted wagon is even there?'

'Later. Let night fall first. We have other angles to explore before then.'

Both men looked up at the rapidly darkening sky. The setting sun cast a sickly yellow light from below a ragged and ominously black cloud bearing down upon the disturbed surface of the Adriatic, like a safety curtain slowly descending at the close of a play. The great ships moored along the dock walls were creaking at their chains as though nervous and unsettled. The air was clammy with the threat of a coming storm and the gusts of wind that twanged the telegraph wires and shredded the smoke from the steam offered no respite from the falling air pressure. Vignoles felt his head thump and ache.

'After speaking with the commander, I want to call in on the laundry — then we can take a beer in the *Stella Polaris*.'

'Top hole! I didn't realise this detecting business had fringe benefits. My tongue has almost stuck to the roof of my mouth with thirst.'

'There is a serious reason for doing so — but a beer might cool us down as well.' Vignoles wiped his brow.

* * * *

The Blue Lagoon swimming pool was still open, though the place looked deserted, probably because of the imminent threat of an electrical storm heavy in the air. It was in a pre-war, futurist design of modest size, constructed in cast concrete with metal-framed windows and doors and two bas-relief classical sculptures in pale stone depicting a near-naked man and woman facing each other across a squat tower over the entrance. Both figures were loosely draped with folded material of carved stone that barely preserved their modesty as they scowled their Roman-nosed faces at each other in grim, athletic concentration.

'Fascist architecture.' Henderson shook his head. 'Why do their nudes always look so miserable?'

'You might if you had to sit there on a damp towel day and night.'

'I think it tells you something about their ghastly politics. The commies are just the same: tough-looking men and women frowning into the sunrise, holding shovels and pickaxes.'

'Enough art history, captain, the laundry should be near here somewhere.' Vignoles searched along the road. 'That must be the place. Bother, I should have brought Anna along to help with the language.'

As they approached the laundry, an elderly man with a nut-brown face pushed a massive wooden handcart supporting a grinding wheel along the gutter beside them, one wheel creaking painfully with each revolution from a lack of oil. A group of men in work clothes and neckerchiefs hurried homewards, their heads down and caps low; to the amazement of Vignoles, who felt a drip of sweat ease free of his hat band, they wore heavy jackets and pullovers.

'Do they not feel the heat?' He removed his hat and smoothed his damp hair.

'Apparently not.' Henderson dabbed his brow with a handkerchief as they stepped through a colourless door with a dirty pane of glass in its centre, setting a bell clanging above their heads.

The interior was even hotter and damper, with condensation dribbling down the pale-green walls, rendering them glassy. The air, heavy with the smell of soap, steam, washing blue and ironing, clung at their throats and made them gasp. Vignoles immediately felt his shirt back become wet and swiftly doffed his Panama, hoping that his spectacles would clear of the fog that was blurring his vision.

A tiny woman appeared behind the counter, so thin and pinched that her angular body looked more like that of a half-starved teenager, yet as his vision improved after another wipe with his handkerchief, Vignoles could see that she was in her fifties and had a lined and careworn face, a sour downturn to her mouth and beady eyes that fixed on his and held steady. He got the impression that she was a strong character, more than able to withstand any amount of nonsense from army lads.

'Er, *Buona sera, madam.*' She gave a slight nod by way of reply and immediately pointed to a yellowing sheet of paper that listed the services offered and the prices, in English. She knew instantly from his laughable Italian that he was not a local.

'Er, *non, grazie.* I, er…'

She looked bored and held out her hand as if she expected to receive something from Vignoles. '*Numero?*' Her voice was strong yet lacked any enthusiasm. 'You 'ave number?'

'Er, *non. Noi siamo la police*. English police.' Vignoles pulled out his warrant card and showed it. *'Per favore, signora.'* He paused, 'Oh bother! I need to ask you about Corporal Priday.'

She frowned at him.

Vignoles glanced at Henderson, who surprised him by repeating the question in Italian.

The woman suddenly burst into life. She waved a hand in refusal and spoke angrily. It took no translation to understand that she wanted nothing to do with them. She clearly did not like policemen nosing around her business.

'Tell her we have to see his clothes.'

'I'll do my best, old chap. Schoolboy Latin and pidgin Italian is not equipping me for the task.' Henderson took a sharp intake of breath, then asked something of the laundress, emphasising a point repeatedly, but he was met with folded arms and a defiant expression.

'It would appear that, without his laundry ticket number, we will get nothing from her. It's the rules.'

'Blast the damned rules!' said Vignoles, though he knew she could hardly hand out clothes to anyone. He thought for a moment, then remembered that he had obtained a picture of the dead man from the commander that morning. He dug into his jacket pocket, extracted the official photograph and showed it to her. 'Look at this man. *Molto importante!*' He jabbed his finger on the wooden counter for emphasis.

The woman backed away from the image, watched his finger for a few seconds, then looked back at the picture.

'È morto,' said Henderson.

'Oh, Maria!' She crossed herself twice and a thin hand reached to her throat, where a tiny silver cross was suspended from an even thinner chain.

'Si, Madam. Please? You have his clothes?' Vignoles tried to mime by pulling at this clothes and then pointing at the photograph.

The woman shook her head, and Vignoles thought he detected a look of apprehension in her eyes.

Vignoles again pointed at Priday's face. 'Help this man. Help us.' Vignoles felt they were getting nowhere so mimed that he would walk into the main laundry room and search for himself, pointing into the steamy back room and making as if he was about to enter.

This elicited a reaction, and she held up a hand to stop him and nodded slowly, and with resignation. She drew herself up straight and faced Vignoles, speaking rapidly. When she finished, she turned to a large cash register, pressed a key and, with a tinkle, the drawer flew open. She extracted a leaf from an account book trapped under a wire in one of the wide compartments, and placed it on the counter beside Priday's photograph.

Henderson was stifling a look of surprise. 'She will co-operate, but there is the matter of his outstanding laundry bill. A month of unpaid fees.'

'I don't believe this.' Vignoles took a deep breath. 'How much? *Quanto costo, per favore?*'

The woman turned the invoice around to face Vignoles, tapped a finger at a number on the page and folded her arms.

Vignoles peered at the bill, with its long list of entries under the name 'Priday'. Extracting his wallet he unfolded an unfeasibly large quantity of lire notes. He realised that it converted to a pitiful amount in British pounds and felt a jab of pity for the woman. He could hardly blame her for wanting the bill settled. He tossed an extra note onto the pile and received a mumbled '*Grazie, senor.*'

She disappeared into the back room and about a minute later returned with an immaculate stack of clothes, each item perfectly laundered, pressed and folded. Vignoles had never before seen railwaymen's overalls so well-scrubbed and sweet-smelling. He immediately spoiled the effect by opening up Priday's jacket in order to search the pockets. The laundress raised her eyes to the ceiling and muttered something Vignoles did not understand.

Lying between the work trousers and a crisp white shirt were a number of papers, also neatly folded. She had, of course, already taken the precaution of checking the pockets before washing Priday's clothes and had preserved the contents. Vignoles felt slightly silly for not realising she must do this with every garment entrusted to her. A wave of gratitude flowed through his veins. Gushing '*grazie mille*' to her he took the documents and was surprised to find a large denomination note — clearly forgotten by Priday — amongst the papers. He might have been slow in settling his bills, but he was certainly not short of cash. Vignoles was touched by the laundress's scrupulous honesty.

Intriguing though this discovery was, the documents were even more interesting. Even with a cursory glance, Vignoles knew that they were significant. They were written in Italian, but it was obvious they were identity passes and similar documents, all relating to the *Stock* distillery.

He exchanged a glance with Henderson. 'We need to study these away from here.' He slipped them into his blazer pocket and started to re-fold the dead man's jacket. He pushed the pile of clothes back towards the woman, making it clear that she should keep them.

She shook her head and was understandably reluctant. What did she want with this dead man's clothes? Vignoles handed her the banknote he'd found. At her prices, it was enough to pay for a whole platoon to have their shirts laundered. 'Tell her to keep the clothes and that she never saw us — or the documents!'

'Ah, that is rather tricky. I don't know the right words.' Henderson made a stab at it, and, together with Vignoles imploring her to take the money, she finally relented.

'You did not see us. We were not here.' Vignoles hoped — for her own safety — that she understood.

They left the door clattering closed with the bell jangling and nearly stumbled into a pretty young woman who was just about to enter. Vignoles apologised and lifted his hat, but looked away quickly, as did Henderson. Vignoles did not want his face remembered and hoped they had not just placed the laundress in grave danger.

'You think Priday was killed for these?' asked Henderson.

'Yes. I think he was due to make a rendezvous early in the morning, but when he was in the *Stella Polaris* realised that he did not have the documents on him because he'd changed his clothes and accidentally left them in a pocket of the something he'd handed in for washing. I think he left the bar in a hurry to try and get to the laundry before it shut — and failed.'

'Or perhaps he thought he'd left this stuff back in the cabin?'

'Either way, he could not give what he had promised to those he was meeting, and he paid the price.'

'But why kill him? Surely it would be in their interest to wait. With him dead, they would never get what they wanted.'

'A puzzle indeed.'

A number of homeward-bound workers and a brace of US soldiers were walking along the street, so they stepped into a doorway. The double wooden doors were tall and elongated, each with many small panes of cobwebby glass that revealed a glimpse of a gloomy hallway and heavily worn stairs and a number of closed doors. A lantern glowed above their heads and, now sheltered from the irritating wind, they used its light to inspect the documents in more detail.

Though struggling with their limited Italian, they could interpret the layout and structure of the documents sufficiently to tell that they were an identity card for a distillery worker and some kind of permit.

'This would get someone into the distillery.'

'And this would get a wagon out.' Vignoles felt a frisson of excitement as he held up a rectangle of white card bearing the same wagon number he had found on the page torn from Lawton's notebook. Clipped to this was a typed bill of loading that identified the wagon as originating from within the distillery and filled with intoxicating liquor.

'Bingo! The number is the same.' Vignoles spoke quietly but with excitement in his voice. 'Priday has somehow obtained these passes, and it would be easy for him to make up this conveyance document to get the thing out of Trieste. It would not surprise me if one of the goods clerks or guards has a similar copy ready to place in their records.'

'To where is it being sent? Let me see...' Henderson studied the card. 'Ljubljana? Hell's bells — right into enemy territory! This really puts a nasty slant on things.'

'But why on earth smuggle out a tanker of brandy? It has a value, a tidy one at that, but they can buy the stuff there easily enough. It's not worth the lives of three men.'

Henderson was frowning. 'I don't know. Crooks can get pretty ruthless. Whatever the explanation I shall have to report this to Whitehall and to Commander Turbayne. With everything so tense at the moment this might have serious implications.' Henderson looked grimmer than Vignoles had ever seen him before.

'What might this be about?'

'God knows, Vignoles, but I'm fearful that unless we hurry we might be too late to find out.'

'I take the point, but it's too early to take a look in at *Stock*, as the late shift won't have knocked off yet, so let's get a drink at that bar and take stock — so to speak.'

* * * *

The *Stella Polaris* was set into the end of a tall block of apartments that formed a wedge shape where two roads met, rather like a hunk of cheese set on its side, but constructed from a fine pale limestone. The front door was let into the thinnest edge of the wedge, above which was a small and dusty square window with a painting of a star — presumably the Pole Star of its name — on the glass. Three large white letters spelling BAR projected from the wall on a metal frame. In better times they would have been illuminated, but the electric cable was broken and slapped pitifully against the wall in the steadily increasing gusts of damp wind. Rectangles of marble set high into each of the side walls stated that it lay at the meeting point between the *Via di Calvola* and the *Via Mamiani*. The rear of a large and ugly church with a stumpy campanile and offering little obvious comfort, spiritual or otherwise, could be seen around a turn in the road, though the greater part of the neighbourhood consisted of shabby apartments, ramshackle factories, a garage with one ancient petrol pump, and a printing shop. A bakery with an open door offered a vision of a chubby man in a floury apron making small balls of dough, the ovens filling the street with the warm scent of yeast and flour.

The door of the bar opened onto a small widening of the road filled by two spreading lime trees, the fading flowers of which were now fast falling in the wind. There was a tall metal water pump and a drinking fountain let into an ancient wall beside a bench and an abandoned car missing its wheels, thick with dust and the messy detritus of the limes. Pale blue-and-white striped awnings were pulled low over the side windows of the bar and these flapped like yacht sails, under which small, metal-framed chairs with slatted wooden seats were arranged beside circular tables. At one of these, two elderly men were passing the time of day with small glasses of light beer, whilst under their table an anxious dog rested its chin on both front paws and alternately raised and lowered its hairy eyebrows and rolled its alert eyes from side to side with each snap of the awnings.

Vignoles and Henderson, however, were seated inside, the better to observe the comings and goings.

'So what are you hoping to find?' asked Henderson, placing a half-litre glass of pale, sparkling beer on the table.

'Apart from killing time until we take a look for the wagon, I'm interested in this place. Priday came here frequently, and was particularly eager to do so. Why might that be?'

'To make contact with this group who are up to no good?'

'That's my way of seeing things. The name of the bar is also tied into that note torn from Lawton's notebook. This place binds them all together. On top of that, Priday's girl was loitering around this area. She could have been the point of contact.'

'A honey trap?'

Vignoles had not heard this expression before, but he grasped the meaning. 'Yes, that's one way of putting it. However Priday got in with them, at some point he made a deal to hand over the documents we found.' Vignoles fussed with his pipe, making heavy weather of lighting it and using this as cover so he could run his eye over the people gathered inside.

'Anyone here attract your attention? You're the expert in this kind of thing.' Vignoles slipped Henderson a glance. He'd made a bold move in trusting the captain, but could still not completely forget the subterfuge surrounding their first encounter.

'Not quite my speciality, dear chap. My angle is spinning lines — and perhaps a few half-truths. I fight using words these days.' Henderson paused before surprising Vignoles by opening up. 'My job is making two and two add up to six. Or three, or perhaps even four, should the FO feel like playing a straight bat.'

'A propaganda merchant.'

'Let's just say that I help ensure the facts fit with the official line. But facts have a nasty habit of not always conforming, at least not without a little judicious easing here and there.' Henderson drank some more beer and gave an oddly sheepish look at Vignoles.

'And keeping a watch on everyone to ensure they toe that same line? Report any deviation or straying off the track. I wonder what you've been saying about me.'

'I'm not a spy.'

'Not in the strictest sense, perhaps; but you're the eyes and ears of the department you work for. That's why you're here, isn't it?'

'How do you mean, old boy?' Henderson reverted to his habitual mannerism, head flung back, blowing cigarette smoke through his nose, but Vignoles detected a slight glint of unease behind his steely eyes.

'You're here to keep tabs on Anna and I. Checking we don't become unduly influenced by the wrong set. Remember, you warned me not to go the same way as Dick Barton.'

'You may scoff, but we're sitting on the border with a very dangerous enemy, if truth be told. I'm talking about the reds, of course. Even the Yanks are baulking at the idea of taking them on, hence the reason for flying into Berlin and dropping food for the poor blighters marooned out there.'

'Is it that bad?'

'I'm afraid so. Hundreds of flights a day will be needed. They've no idea if it's even sustainable — but if they fail? I don't want to think of the consequences. No, the reds are on the rise, and now they've proved themselves against Hitler, they have a moral dimension that appeals to the working man, to the masses, to the poor and to the unions. But don't be fooled by their pictures of happy workers and heroic peasant mothers sharing the benefits of a bumper harvest — they're every bit as dangerous and ruthless as the Nazis.'

'Or are you just making two and two equal six? Remember the "Victory Harvest" posters? They had a smiling and suntanned young woman looking thrilled at the joy of bringing the British harvest home. No sign of the real blood, sweat and tears the land girls put in, or the rationing and the going without — but it was hardly sinister, either.'

'That was serving a specific purpose. And a noble one at that.'

'All propaganda though, the only difference being that we approve of the sentiment. I can't see the difference, except that we know less about the Soviets or whoever, and so naturally we're suspicious.'

'No, it is different. There's no fiddling the facts with the Soviet Union. We've had men behind their lines for years and we've assembled information that would make your hair curl. Stuff they don't want the man in the street around here to know about. Millions have been killed on Stalin's direct orders. Schoolteachers, intellectuals, writers, poets, musicians, people with brains and intelligence; anyone who might see through their scramble for power and wealth.'

The radiogram behind the bar was playing a stirring song by a massed choir, and this suddenly crackled unpleasantly as a flash of lightning momentarily filled the bar, followed by a deep roll of thunder like distant guns. The heroic song battled on, though the signal was now full of static, its haunting call to arms rendered more poignant by the dark of the street outside, the rapidly increasing flashes of brilliant light and the ground-shaking rumbles.

Vignoles made no reply. He was surreptitiously observing a man at the far end of the room who was wearing a peaked Jugoslav Army cap pulled low over his face, rendering his features hard to discern in the poor light from the solitary bulb in the centre of the ceiling. His beard was wild and straggly, lending him something of the air of a rakish Rasputin. Vignoles did not much like the look of him. But perhaps everyone looked suspicious if you were in that frame of mind. Vignoles looked away and caught sight of the clock on the wall behind the bar.

'Blast! Look at the time. We've missed mess, and I didn't warn Anna.'

Henderson grinned cheekily, perhaps eager to change the subject. 'Ouch, you'll get it in the neck now.'

'She's used to my unpredictable hours.'

'Better give her a call anyway. I can see there's a telephone at the back. And take a closer look at those two chaps sitting over there as you do so.' Henderson nodded towards two men in dark leather jackets hunched over a table; they were nursing small glasses of a reddish-coloured beer.

'The beard?' Vignoles gave a slight nod to acknowledge the tip-off. 'Yes, I noticed him too.' He stood up, his shadow blasted onto the far wall like that of a towering giant as lightning filled the room, immediately followed by a deafening crash of thunder and the sound of torrential rain hitting the street with a sound like the fizz of so many Alka-Seltzer tablets in water.

The telephone was fixed to the wall at the far end of the bar, and as Vignoles left an apologetic message with a well-mannered concierge at the *Albergo Savoia Excelsior*, he noticed that Rasputin appeared to be observing him, though with his face largely concealed by the brim of his cap. Vignoles sensed that the man did not like him being there. Perhaps he was a disgruntled local. Hancock had indicated that they were not thrilled at having Allied troops take over the place.

Although the concierge had rung off, Vignoles mimed listening and mumbled a few words into the crackling tone of the dead line. He wanted to remain where he was a while longer and observe. As he did so, a woman rushed into the bar, her long, pale summer coat was pulled up over her head as an improvised umbrella and this dripped copious amounts of rainwater onto the wooden floorboards. All the men in the bar turned to look, and after quickly surveying the room, she tottered over towards the leather-jacketed men, readjusting her beret that she wore at a slant over her right eye, patting her hair into shape, and flicking drops of water from her clothes.

Vignoles returned to casually scrutinising his disapproving observer, whilst nodding his head in response to an imaginary question down the line. The two men looked annoyed and one betrayed a flash of anger at the sight of the woman beside them. She was young and pretty, a little bedraggled and in need of some kind words, but an undeniably attractive 'honey trap', as Henderson would put it. But all she got from her companions was a sustained barrage of complaints for her trouble.

She pouted sulkily and made an angry gesture towards heaven, then started to comb her long hair whilst tossing her head in obvious agitation before throwing another line back at the two men. It was not her fault the rain had come down in buckets.

Vignoles hung up and walked back to Henderson, who subtly moved his glass on the way up to his lips. 'They know how to make a lady feel welcome.'

'I think they were unhappy that she made such an obvious entrance,' replied Vignoles.

'Hard to see what else she could do — and looking like she does, she'd attract attention in a graveyard. She's got a mouth that could launch a thousand kisses.' Henderson eyed her over the top of his beer glass.

'Never mind the Philip Marlowe stuff,' Vignoles growled, 'have you made the connection yet? She's the only woman in the bar, she's well dressed and looks good...'

'Dark shoulder length hair and great legs... Crikey, are you thinking what I'm thinking?' Henderson eyes met Vignoles's over the rim of his glass as he finished his beer.

'That she's Priday's girl?' Vignoles was speaking barely above a whisper. 'But you've missed the most startling fact. Unless I am very much mistaken, she entered the laundry just as we left.'

'Bloody hell, you're right!' Henderson glanced at her then turned his face away. 'Have they seen us?'

'The men have, but she hasn't. I have an odd feeling about this group. We could do with seeing where they go, and yet we need to get over to the distillery. We need assistance.' Vignoles looked at Henderson as if seeking a second opinion, though the look in his eyes suggested that he had already made a decision.

'But who could we get here quickly enough?'

'When I called the *Albergo*, the concierge told me they've just finished mess — I just hope Staff Sergeant Gretton is with Anna.'

'Surely not? It could be dangerous!'

'Not if they remain unobserved and don't interfere.'

Vignoles stood up, slanting his hat to throw more shadow

and removing his spectacles, hoping that this might prevent his face from jogging the woman's memory. 'Though perhaps it's lucky I don't have time to debate this decision,' he muttered under his breath.

He walked once again across the room to the telephone as the sound of the rain intensified and the thunder cracked overhead like an air raid.

CHAPTER TWENTY-SEVEN

JUGOSLAVIJO

Slovene partisan song

The jeep, with its canvas roof pulled up and the side-sheets with plastic windows securely fastened, turned down the road with twin headlamps throwing long cones of yellow light through the stair-rods of rain. As instructed by Vignoles, Staff Sergeant Rose Gretton pulled it to a halt close beside the abandoned Citroën and cut the lights and motor. The rain beat a loud tattoo on the fabric and the windscreen soon became a mass of rain droplets diffusing the glow of the street lamps and the inviting light thrown out by the windows of the *Stella Polaris*.

Vignoles could barely discern the shapes of the two occupants and this reassured him that they could remain undetected and unidentified during the task he had lined up for them. Applying his shoulder to the door of the wrecked car in which he and Henderson had been hiding for a quarter-of-an-hour, he forced it open on hinges solid with rust and darted across to the jeep, tapping lightly on the side and peering through the plastic at the pale and rain-distorted face of his wife. The metal poppers holding the sheet in place were hurriedly pulled apart and Anna grinned up at him.

'Oh, you're drenched!'

'The captain assures me that these storms are intense but end just as quickly as they began. And it's hot, so I'll soon dry off.'

'We brought you two umbrellas.' Anna handed them up from out of the front seat well.

'Thanks. Where on earth did you get these?'

'Lost property at our hotel, and just like on the railway they have plenty of them!'

Vignoles quickly described the two men and the woman, continually glancing towards the front door in case they came out onto the street whilst they were talking. 'Follow, and if they split up, go after the woman. Don't let them see you, don't interfere if anything happens and, if you suspect they've rumbled you, get out — and fast. That's an order!'

'Aye aye, captain!' Anna made a salute.

'Understood, sir.' Rose looked serious.

'If you have anything to report, phone the *Albergo* and leave a message. I'll do the same. Otherwise we'll meet there at 7am.'

'So late?' Anna frowned.

'Who knows how long they'll be? Chin up! At least you had some food. And do take great care.' Vignoles gave Anna a squeeze on the shoulder and a worried smile before quickly darting away into the enveloping blackness beneath the spreading boughs of the lime tree, to be met by the shape of Henderson stepping out of the gloom to meet him. Unfurling their umbrellas, they strode purposefully towards the docks and the distillery.

As Henderson had predicted, the rain soon lessened then stopped during their hike, though lightning continued to rip apart the inky night sky in jagged strikes as the thunder mellowed into a series of booms and rumbles that mingled with the noise of the busy marshalling yards on the *Porto Nuovo*.

It took only fifteen minutes of brisk walking from the bar until they could not only smell but see the distillery, and Vignoles felt this proximity added yet more weight to his conviction that the two men and the woman were somehow involved.

'In through the front, or sneak around the back?' asked Henderson.

'We'd need a warrant and we'd never get one, and, besides, I don't want to frighten them off by telegraphing our arrival. We'll take a look around the back, along that siding that Hancock described. We need to keep alert for the sentries the commander has posted.' Vignoles was scanning the dark streets, now becoming humid as the water started to evaporate from the warmed cobbles.

'I thought you said they were not to interfere with anyone coming and going?'

'The proof of the pudding is always in the eating — or the shooting. They *should* just let us pass, if they follow their instructions, but it only needs one to be nervous and twitchy and things could get interesting.'

Henderson nodded and, turning to face the tall perimeter wall, took something that glinted from out of his shoulder bag and made a few quiet metallic clicks as he inspected it. 'I suggest you do the same, old boy. All that rain might have got in the works.' He pushed the pistol back into a pocket of his raincoat.

Vignoles hesitated. He was not comfortable with guns and preferred to handle them as infrequently as he could. It was a pity WPC Lansdowne was not there to take care of such matters.

'Here, let me.' Henderson held out his hand. 'I've had years of practice.'

Not for the first time in his dealings with the captain, Vignoles felt a sudden prickle on the nape of his neck. He became acutely aware of the loneliness of their location, standing as they were beside a brick wall topped with coils of barbed wire; the distillery chimney was towering above their heads, bearing illuminated letters that burned the word STOCK into the night sky. The storm drains were running like torrents beneath their feet, whilst plaintive whistles, the huff and chuff of engines and the clatter of wagons echoed around the deserted street. Vignoles hesitated a moment too long and Henderson reacted.

'What's up, old boy? Unwilling to hand over your weapon? I don't blame you. You'd be at a grave disadvantage — just the two of us.'

There was a moment of silence.

'Damn it, Vignoles, if I were going to kill you I wouldn't wait until you gave me your pistol. I'd sooner run a knife across your throat or snap your neck — swift, deadly and silent.' He mimed the spoken actions and gave a grin that looked almost sadistic.

Vignoles felt his mouth go dry. He had no reason to doubt Henderson's ability in commando tactics. He knew nothing of the captain's service record, but he was sure that his position as a civil servant was not a true reflection of his military training.

'Give it here and don't be a chump. I doubt you've even got the blessed thing loaded.' Henderson laughed quietly, but with warmth, his eyes suddenly losing their edge, or perhaps it had never been there and it had just been a trick of the light.

Vignoles managed to summon a half-smile. 'Sorry. That was a poor show on my part. It takes time to develop trust.'

'But time is exactly what we don't have, old boy. Not if your theory is correct, so let's get in there. I want you watching my back with a gun that works, just as you'll want me to do the same for you.'

A few minutes later they had skirted the edge of the distillery and crossed a fan of railway tracks that formed the more frequently used entrance into the complex, then weaved their way among a series of small and poorly lit streets, populated with warehouses, small businesses and a few blocks of workers' housing. The storm had washed everything clean but failed to lift the air of gentle decay from streets that looked increasingly threatening. They met few people;

the lateness of the hour and the heavy downpour had rendered this a virtual ghost town, but when they did encounter the odd man, they passed each other quickly and with mutual distrust. A thin dog with lips curled back from its yellow teeth trotted past, eyeing them suspiciously. This was not a good area and Vignoles was glad he had company.

They reached a level crossing where a single railway line appeared from a narrow gap between factory walls and the squalid backs of tenement buildings. A few windows had lights burning with many opened to allow the sticky air to circulate. An accordion was playing a lilting melody as a man sang with a strong voice. The words floated across the empty railway track and Vignoles could discern the word *Jugoslavio* repeated often in the refrain. There was the sound of glasses clinking and soft voices murmuring from another darkened ground-floor window, serving to remind Vignoles that many invisible eyes could be watching them.

He started as Henderson touched his shoulder and whispered in his ear, 'Next to the telegraph pole. One of ours?'

The dark shape of a figure was leaning against a wall, partially hidden by the thick, timber pole and a bush. The cigarette gave him away. How many times had Vignoles warned men never to smoke when on surveillance duty! He stared intently and thought he could discern the shape of a Tommy's helmet.

'Could be. Ignore him and turn down the track.'

With the uncomfortable sensation of knowing an armed soldier was probably looking at the small of his back and sizing it up as a target, Vignoles stepped onto the rotten track and their feet crunched, unnaturally loudly, on the ballast. They turned a corner without anything dramatic happening and both found their breathing coming a little easier.

Ahead they could see a wooden gate drawn across the siding and a few yard lamps glowing on tall posts. Drifts of steam issued from a pipe set into the side of one of the distillery buildings. Small noises and a low hum rose from behind the gates, perhaps from a generator deep within. A rat scampered along one of the rails then dived under a bush.

They approached the gate and both men pressed their eyes to the gap between gate and post, just as Professor Ferluga had done earlier that day.

The tank wagon was dark in colour and enveloped in even deeper shadow cast by the roof above, though the yard lamps threw enough light to glint off the curve of the barrel-shaped body and the metal ladders that clung to each side. It was an unremarkable vehicle, and yet Vignoles felt a curious sensation of dread creep over him. He had sometimes visualised a box wagon filled with cases of guns or gold bullion or concealing persons attempting to illegally cross the border, so the idea that this dark cylinder held a dangerous secret was oddly unnerving. What could it contain that was so deadly? It could not be brandy. Vignoles was quite sure there were many ways and means of selling this liquor on the black market without the need to resort to murder. No, there had to be something else inside. As he stared at the dark shape of the vehicle he was struck by how much it reminded him of a sleeping animal. A dangerous dog observed in his kennel, slumbering but liable to be awakened at any moment and spring forward, snarling and baring its teeth.

Henderson was inspecting the heavy padlock and chain but shook his head and turned his attention to the walls, searching for handholds. 'We need something to throw over that wire,' he whispered, 'otherwise, it looks easy enough.' He started to hunt around the piles of household rubbish littering the ground and soon returned with what appeared to be a heap of abandoned overalls. The captain grimaced at the foul smell they were giving off, then thrust them into Vignoles's arms.

'Hand them up to me,' he said, then in a series of swift and well-balanced moves, he was soon perched on the edge of the wall.

Vignoles was only too happy to pass up the foul bundle, closing his eyes instinctively and trying not to breathe. Henderson used his furled umbrella to push the wire down onto the top of the wall and cushioned the steel spines with the fabric, before deftly stepping over and dropping down on the far side with barely a sound. Vignoles found it less easy to climb to the top of the wall, one foot scrabbling for purchase, and he found the manoeuvre with the umbrella and protective cushion hard to manage with the same poise. He tore the bottom of a trouser leg and felt a spike rake one of his forearms and draw blood. However, he finally landed on the ground beside Henderson and straightened himself out. 'I don't fancy doing that when we're in a mad rush. We might need an alternative way out.'

Henderson silently indicated that they should move to the lee of the wagon to be out of sight if anyone were to walk through a door that he indicated with his pistol. Vignoles nodded and they scurried across to stand beside the tanker.

This was quite large when up close and exuded a faint aroma of oil from the wheels. Even in the poor light, Vignoles could see that it was extremely grubby and appeared to be of some vintage. Moss and bands of green algae clung to recesses on the lower sides of the tank. It appeared devoid of markings and the manufacturer's plate was missing from the frames, with just holes where the retaining bolts had been. Henderson pointed to the empty wire frame that should hold a conveyance document. Both men thought that this was an encouraging sign. A replacement had not been procured for the one that Corporal Priday had inadvertently left at the laundry, and so the wagon would not be moving any time soon.

Henderson ducked beneath the brake rigging and started to poke about underneath to see if anything were concealed there, whilst Vignoles hung his canvas shoulder bag and umbrella from a buffer shank, extracted his pistol, pushed this into the waistband of his trousers and then, after a quick look around, hoisted himself up.

The ladder was rusty and showed few signs of recent use. He was getting the impression that the tank wagon had spent a long time in storage. This was unsurprising, as so much railway stock had been destroyed during the war that every half-decent vehicle was being dragged out of forgotten sidings, patched up and put back into service.

Perched high on the ladder, Vignoles started to work the restraining catch free; this held the big central filler cap closed. He noticed that it had recently been oiled and opened easily. He was thankful that it did not make a dreadful noise as he pulled the heavy lip open, though as it came to rest upon the tank top, it made a resonant boom. Henderson's head appeared from under the wagon, prompted by the sound.

Slowly, and with great trepidation, Vignoles lowered his face towards the dark opening. It was so dark inside that he had no idea what he was going to find, and feared the worst. He sniffed. The air was stale and cool, with a faint tang of oily metal underlying the heady and full aroma of brandy. It was intense, though not unpleasant. He cautiously put one of his hands into the opening and dipped his forefinger into the liquid.

His finger did not react adversely, so if he was to be stung by some foreign agent mixed into the liquor, it was a slow-acting one. He withdrew his finger and sniffed in the aroma a few times. Then, very cautiously, he tasted it. It *was* brandy! He cupped his hand and scooped a palmful, which he drank. It warmed his insides pleasantly.

He pulled back and looked down at Henderson and shrugged, his mind racing. Had he really got everything so completely wrong? Was this just a wild goose chase, after all? Henderson was shaking his head and Vignoles took this to mean that there was nothing beneath the wagon either. He suddenly had an idea.

'Psst. The umbrella. Hand it up.'

Henderson unhooked the cane handle from around the wagon buffer and did as he was asked. Vignoles took it and, leaning over the open top, slowly lowered the metal ferrule of the umbrella into the liquid. He went slowly, gently swishing the umbrella from side to side so that he might increase his chance of striking something secreted inside. The liquid sloshed in a gentle lapping sound and the heady waves of intoxicating air started to make his head spin. The umbrella was submerged halfway when it suddenly struck something hard as he tried to swing it across the width of the tank from one side to the other.

Dong! The sound was deep and resonant, like the bell of an abandoned church beneath reservoir waters. The umbrella stopped dead, and as he applied more pressure he felt it ride upwards, describing a gentle arc across a smooth and solid object below, the ferrule making a slight scraping sound.

'Keep the noise down!' hissed Henderson, who now had his pistol drawn and was dividing his attention between looking at Vignoles and the door.

Vignoles started a series of exploratory movements, gently prodding the hard metal thing submerged beneath the brandy. It did not budge an inch and by sliding the ferrule of the umbrella across the surface he decided that it was metal, it was smooth and quite possibly a smaller version of the tank it was concealed within.

Distant thunder still rattled around the *Karst* like the pounding of his pulse in his ears. A secret compartment. But what could it contain? He pulled the umbrella out and hung the handle over the access hole, then pushed one sleeve of his blazer past his elbow and, straining to reach far enough inside, commenced feeling with his hand to see if there was an opening to the hidden tank.

But his work was halted by an urgent sound made by Henderson; it was neither word nor cry, but its tone was enough to warn Vignoles of impending danger. He extracted his hand as if scalded, lifted the cover up and over and placed it back down, only for it to be prevented from closing by his umbrella handle. There was no time to extract it. He could hear the sound of heavy-booted feet and all he could do was duck down low and press his body as hard against the ladder as possible. The approaching boots had metal studs on their soles and crunched on the ground with the measured tread of a security guard.

Vignoles hardly dared breathe, and remained perfectly still except for his left hand that was ever-so-slowly moving towards his waistband and the butt of the pistol. This was a tight spot. But where was Henderson? A relative silence fell, in which Vignoles could hear the sounds of distant humming and whirring from within the distillery and the clatter of trucks in the yard. A motorbike roared down a nearby road. The heavy-booted feet stopped. A match was struck. Vignoles strained to listen and probably imagined he heard the discarded match land on the ground. There was a sound of sucked air as the guard dragged on his cigarette. He was leaning against one of the buffers.

Time passed painfully slowly. How long could one cigarette last?

Vignoles felt sweat roll down his back and his hand was clammy on the gun butt. He could not trust himself to withdraw it from his waistband without it sliding from his grasp.

Suddenly, there was a sound of movement. Just a soft, quick noise, sensed more than heard, of feet padding on concrete, followed by a brief, low grunt, an ugly snapping sound and a sharp exhalation of air. There was a rustle of clothing. Then nothing.

'Quick! Lend a hand.'

Vignoles responded to Henderson's urgent command and gratefully moved from the ladder and dropped to the ground. The captain, standing in his socks, was holding the slumped figure of the security guard under his armpits, the man's head lolling to one side.

Vignoles took a sharp intake of breath, his horror clear to read on his face.

'Damn it, Vignoles! I was crouched behind a wheel, just inches away and risked discovery at any moment. I had to do something. Now help me get rid of him.'

'But when he comes around he'll raise the alarm.'

'Only with St Peter. Now do come on, he's a dead weight!'

'What? You've killed him?'

'Silent and deadly. Like I said, hands are the best way. A quick snap of the neck and he's in the land of dreamless sleep. Now, lift his feet and we'll get him hidden!' Henderson's stage whisper was even more urgent and demanding.

The women sat and waited as instructed. As the rain started to ease, the irritating drumming on the canvas roof fell silent. This was the signal for the three figures to walk onto the street.

'Do you think that's them?' asked Anna.

'They fit the description to a "t",' confirmed Rose.

One of the two leather-jacketed men briskly walked away, leaving the other man and the woman standing on the corner.

'Drat. We've lost one already.'

'I'm not sure. They look like they're waiting for something. Yes: listen!'

'Spot on, Rose.' Anna gave her a winning smile. They had agreed to drop formalities and use first names.

An extremely tired Fiat of pre-war vintage turned into the road and pulled up beside the bar, its exhaust blowing in a deep, throaty roar.

'With a distinctive noise like that we might stand a chance of locating them, even if we lose sight.' Rose prepared to start the jeep, waiting for the Fiat to turn the corner ahead before doing so. She accelerated quickly but coasted around the corner, ready to react to the movements of the little car ahead.

'There are the tail lights — turning right!' Anna pointed.

'Got them! Heading towards the *Riva*, I'd say.'

Rose held back about fifty yards as they skirted a small piazza of gloomy buildings, dripping trees and guttering gas lamps. 'Yes, down this road and out near *Campo Marzo* — this is good news, as a jeep is exactly what anyone would expect to see around here. I can risk drawing closer.'

Anna was furling up the side sheet to gain a better view, allowing the noise of the exhaust and the smell of imperfectly burnt petrol to flow in and make her eyes sting. As she dabbed them with a handkerchief, she saw a line of army trucks formed up on the *Riva*, their big diesel engines ticking over in chesty rattles and the headlamps of the truck at the head of the line casting a long raking light that highlighted the polished rail-tops between the granite setts.

A small American shunting engine, of a type shipped over in the weeks following D-Day, waddled towards them along the waterfront, its oil lamps like bright cat's eyes and traces of pale steam clinging around the wheels and pistons. The Fiat bounced on its bad suspension and was caught in the truck's headlamp beams, and both women could clearly make out the figures inside as the driver decided to cut across the rails at right angles in front of the oncoming train, to proceed along the edge closest to the moored ships and the Adriatic.

Rose continued on the other side of the train, watching the little car's lights flash across the road surface between the wheels of the train. 'Dodging trains is popular around here, especially with the GIs after a night out.' She was concentrating hard and kept her eyes on the road ahead.

Anna instinctively grabbed onto the side of the windscreen in anticipation of sudden braking, as the Fiat veered to the right and darted back across the track once it had cleared the brakevan at the rear of the train. The tyres squealed on the wet road as it swung around a corner and set off on a diagonal course across the *Piazza d'Italia*.

'Ouch, that's clever!' Rose slowed and watched the car crossing the vast open space, skirting the rows of wooden chairs and soggy awnings of the cafés. 'Not allowed. If we give chase, it'll stick out like a sore thumb that we're on to them!' She put her foot down and the jeep surged forwards again. 'Watch over to your side and listen to which way they go. I've got an idea.'

Anna kept her eyes to the right as they raced past the open front edge of the piazza and then, as a narrow street opened between two grand buildings, she caught a fleeting glimpse of the Fiat running in parallel. It was now some distance deeper in the town, but going in the same direction. Two more streets flashed by and she was able to track the car's progress.

'They're still there.'

'Good. They're heading for the *Ponterosso* is my guess.' Rose urged the jeep on and as the *Canal Grande* briefly opened up on either side, she slowed and swung them up a road almost at right angles to the *Riva*, just as the Fiat raced across the bridge near the far end of the short canal. Anna recognised the café where she had sat with Charles.

'The roads are like a grid around here, so we can keep them close, but a street away.'

'Do you think they've seen us?'

'I doubt it, Anna. They're just taking care. But it convinces me they have something to hide.' Rose gritted her teeth. 'Listen out for any change in engine note. A drop in gear means a hill climb.'

'Wilco!'

'They seem to be heading towards *Piazza Oberdan*. I'm going to cut up this street and try to pass them, then swing around and sit on their tail.'

The streets were becoming progressively grander, and the buildings taller, as they approached the most modern district of the city. By day, the merchants banks, marine insurance companies and shipping agents were teeming with customers, but now all was dark and locked shut, except for the occasional bar, outside of which groups of sailors and soldiers laughed and smoked.

Rose suddenly braked and dropped down through the gears as a brightly illuminated tramcar clanged its bell and crossed the end of the street in front of them before slowing to a halt. The roaring crackle of the Fiat that had echoed around the stone and stucco walls now diminished to a bubbling note as it idled somewhere within the large piazza that opened before them.

Easing past the tramcar that was now waiting at the terminus, they turned onto the piazza, skirting a central grassy area punctuated with benches, each one occupied by sad figures nursing bottles and piles of rags. The Fiat had drawn up close to the tram station and they could see one of the men buying tickets as the woman prepared to join a clutch of British servicemen already seated inside the cabin.

'The last journey of the night, and it looks like two of them are taking it.'

'Charles said we must follow the woman. So I suppose we chase the tram.' Anna was watching carefully and saw the woman in question take a seat near the rear.

Rose nodded and turned off the *Piazza*, made a loop, and, with headlamps off, slowly eased to a halt on the corner of an intersecting road in a position that enabled them to observe from a safe distance.

'This could prove tricky. It's easy enough to know where the tram is going as it sticks to its tracks and terminates in Opčine, but the line often runs far away from the road and the stops can be quite hidden. If they get off at one of those, we're stumped.'

'And I wonder where he's off to?' Anna mused as the Fiat roared away, sounding like a racing car at Brooklands.

'Here we go, Anna.'

The little blue tram was now nearly full and the driver had walked to the cab at the opposite end. With a rattle of the bell, he eased it away. The tram started the steep ascent of the *Via Martiri della Libertà*, its engine whining with the effort as the jeep stayed close behind. Rose was unwilling to accelerate and overtake. Hanging on the shirt tails of the tramcar, they had a good view into the polished wooden interior illuminated by electric lights and of the woman, who was busy improving her make-up whilst looking into a compact held in one hand, her elbow steadied by resting it on the open window sill.

'She's not seen us, but I'm not so sure about the man. He's staring in our direction.'

'He's a nasty looking character, Rose. How well can he see us, do you think?' Anna was still feeling the rush of adrenaline, but this lengthier observation of their quarry was starting to bring reality home.

'Not too well, as we're in the dark with the roof up.'

As if to remind them why, a heavy splatter of raindrops cascaded onto the windscreen and roof from the tram wires above the road.

'Gosh, the road is steaming!' Anna pointed forwards at the steeply inclined cobbled road surface, where vapour curled upwards in their headlight beams.

'It's still very warm.'

'Oh no, that's all we need!' Anna pointed as an ancient truck, laden with household junk piled high on the rear deck and lashed down by miles of knotted rope, painfully eased its way out of a side road and into their path, labouring to climb the hill and forcing Rose to slow and drop down into first gear as they stared at the collection of broken chairs, chests of drawers, a bicycle with one wheel and tin baths without bottoms.

'I might be able to use it to our advantage. The tram is stopping now. They have to hitch it onto a strange contraption at this point that rope-hauls it up this extra-steep section. They'll be a few minutes before re-starting. With this awfully slow lorry, we have a good excuse not to motor too far ahead and can let the tram catch us up.'

Anna looked across at Rose. 'Have you done this sort of thing before? You're quite a natural.'

'Never. But thanks. I just don't want to make a hash of it.'

As predicted, they made slow progress up the hill and, before long, the tram, which was moving at quite a pace, overtook the jeep and the noisy tinker's truck that was exhaling thick clouds of foul-smelling exhaust. The three odd vehicles continued their ascent for some distance along an increasingly curving road until the tram veered off to the left along its own dedicated route, at which point Rose put her foot down, overtook the lorry and raced uphill.

'They might get off somewhere along this stretch, but there's nothing to be done about that. All we can do is lie in wait further up line and see if they're still on board.'

'We took this same journey last Wednesday. This can't be coincidence. Could they be heading for Opčine?' asked Anna.

'Quite possibly.'

And so, with the twinkling lights of Trieste dropping away behind and regular flashes of distant lightning filling the black sky above the escarpment, they raced on, occasionally spying glimpses of the little glowing tramcar flashing behind the silhouettes of trees like a glow-worm in the summer night. They overtook a heavy train storming the bank and had to wait at a crossing gate pulled closed by a woman in a peaked cap and railway uniform jacket, who waved an oil lamp to show the way was clear for the advancing train. It passed like a great, dark beast in the night, with fiery plumes of smoke roaring from the chimneys of the two engines, one at the front and the banker at the rear, as their percussive exhaust beats rattled across the hills.

The tram also crossed their path, and as it did, Anna felt sure the man in the leather jacket stared right down at her again. It was a hard, cold stare that sent icy fingers down her spine. However, as they made the final ascent, it was not his unappealing look that sent their hearts jumping; it was the unmistakable sound of the wrecked exhaust of the Fiat on the road behind that caused both to exchange apprehensive looks. It was being thrashed mercilessly, and was gaining on them.

'It's simply not possible that they saw us and got word to the driver — not from the tram!' Despite this impossibility, Rose looked anxious.

'It has to be coincidence. He just did whatever he needed to in town and is now just anxious to join the others. It can't be because of us.'

'I do hope you're right, Anna.'

'Do you have a service pistol?'

'Goodness me, no.' Rose glanced quickly at Anna. 'I'll motor on towards the tram station and we'll see if they're still on board.'

She pushed the jeep onwards until they entered the small town, and as the tram sheds and terminus building both rose on a slight elevation to their left, she turned sharply into a narrow side street and cut the motor.

'Let's get out. They won't be expecting two women, even if they are suspicious of our jeep.'

'You're right!' Anna leaped out, shedding her pale mackintosh to reveal a colourful skirt and brilliant white blouse beneath. 'If he did get a glimpse of me, then it was in that drab coat. He might have assumed I was a man in uniform. No one goes undercover wearing a fuchsia skirt!' Anna forced an apologetic smile, conscious that she was inappropriately dressed, but her husband's telephone call had been urgent and there had been no time to change.

Rose was in army uniform, already standing near the steps leading up to the tram station as a group of slightly inebriated British soldiers in similar uniforms stumbled towards her, some making wolf whistles and eyeing her up, though these turned into a barrage of sound when they caught sight of Anna in her widely flaring ankle-length skirt and tailored blouse. This distraction proved Anna's point, and she was able to observe the two suspects from the tram walk briskly across the street, just as the Fiat drew up beside the kerb.

'There they go.' Anna gently fended off a drunken youth who hardly looked old enough to be in active service, and watched him stumble in slow motion against the wall and slide into a bunch of chicory and rocket growing through a crack in the pavement.

'Behave yourselves. Show some manners or you'll be on a charge!' Rose was surprisingly commanding and the men responded, despite the effects of too much beer. Both women watched as the three figures entered a small courtyard set between a café and a row of shops, and approached a tiny house with a balcony. It was set back from the road as if shy to reveal itself, untouched by the light of the few street lamps and further shaded by a spreading chestnut tree.

The women walked a little further along the street before crossing over and doubling back on themselves.

'Let's have a look around the back to get the lie of the land, then find a good place to sit and wait.' Anna was speaking quietly, her dark eyes glinting with nervous excitement.

They picked their way down a narrow side alley until they came to the back access road. The shops had yard walls with wooden doors set into them, but the rear wall of the little house opened directly onto the road. It had one back door and two windows, the lower of which had metal bars across it and was open, allowing a view into a small kitchen illuminated by a faint glow of light cast through an open door.

The two women stood with their backs pressed against the warm stone of the wall, now almost dry despite the recent torrential rain, and listened. Someone was running a tap very close to the window. This was turned off and there followed a series of small metallic sounds. A match was struck twice before it caught, then the soft whoosh of a gas burner could be heard. Men's voices murmured in a different room. Suddenly one of the men called out, using a language Anna did not recognise, but it was clearly a command urging the woman to hurry up.

The woman replied, her voice strong but with a whining, unhappy note. She was doing her best, be patient. The word *kava* was repeated twice in her reply.

Anna looked at Rose, who silently voiced 'coffee' with her lips. They waited an eternity until they heard the sound of the percolating liquid, followed by the tempting aroma wafting through the open window. Anna wished they could lean in and ask for a cup. It smelled delicious mixed with the night air, now heavy with the scent of pine trees, damp grass and that distinct smell of dust fallen to earth following rain.

A tinkle of china, receding footsteps and they finally drew breath.

'That was tense,' whispered Anna.

They took a few steps away from the window.

'Was that Serbo-Croat?'

'I assumed Slovene, at first.' Rose held her mouth close to Anna's ear and her reply was barely audible. 'I know the word for coffee, but little else. I'm no expert, but the sound of their voices made me think they were Russian.'

'Crikey. What are Russians doing here?'

'I could be wrong. Maybe they are Serbs. But we must telephone the inspector immediately. Russians tend to be bad news.'

'There was a public telephone at the tram station.'

'Okay, let's go, but we'll take a long way around. I don't fancy getting caught.'

As they turned to leave, both women stopped dead in their tracks. Across the way, seated at an open window and calmly observing them, was the grey-haired figure of an old man. His glasses had caught a glint of light from a street lamp and this slight change betrayed his presence.

Anna held her breath. He had probably been there the whole time, and if so, they could have no excuse for their suspicious activity.

If he challenged them now, they risked detection. She gave a limp smile and prayed that neither of them looked threatening.

The man fixed his steady gaze upon them, then without uttering a word, slowly pointed with one finger upwards.

Anna lifted her head, and despite the poor light, could see painted on the side of his house in big and bold, carefully formed letters, a slogan that resembled those on the banners carried by the rioters in town. It was almost certainly political in meaning.

HOCEMO JUGOSLAVIJO!

'What does it say?' Anna whispered.

'We are Jugoslavs — or something to that effect. You see this a lot around here. He's stating what side of the fence he's on.'

'I'm not sure what we do now.'

'Don't greet him in Italian.' Rose gave him a sweet smile. Feeling inspired, she raised a clenched fist. '*Smrt Fascismo!*' she mumbled softly.

The old man gave a toothy smile and responded, mumbling something in response that was barely audible but spoken with steely defiance. Anna made the same gesture, slowly and unsure of what she was agreeing to. He nodded and they considered it safe to walk on.

'Where did you learn that? asked Anna.

'They say it all the time around here. I thought it worth keeping up my sleeve, just in case.'

'Phew. Well done.'

'Most people share that opinion about fascists, and it was worth a try as he wasn't Italian. I think he might be sharing our concerns about his Soviet neighbours.'

CHAPTER TWENTY-EIGHT

PESEM O TITU

Slovene partisan song

It was shortly after 8am, and already a lot had happened. Vignoles was sitting with Anna, Captain Henderson and Staff Sergeant Rose Gretton outside the *Caffé Rino*, beside the busy *Strada per Vienna* in the centre of Opčine. Delicious coffee and some *tramezzini* made from thinly sliced white bread filled with slivers of air-cured *prosciutto*, piquant cheese and basil were going some way towards helping push aside the acute tiredness they were all feeling.

The tables and chairs on the pavement beneath the sun-bleached canvas awning were filled with British servicemen topping up their barrack rations and a few local men in their habitual dark suits, pullovers and hats, all of whom were providing the perfect cover to sit, observe and wait for the noisy Fiat and its owners to stir. There had been no movement since they had gone inside just after midnight. The three suspects had no doubt sensibly opted to get some sleep, an option that Anna was now wishing she had been free to choose.

Anna rolled her head slowly in a circular motion and then rolled her shoulders, having cricked her neck at some point whilst slumped in the uncomfortable passenger seat of the jeep. Despite her tiredness and discomfort, she had managed to spend a quarter of an hour in front of a mirror in the toilets with a comb, compact and lipstick and was looking very presentable, a feat that Vignoles never ceased to find remarkable, though undoubtedly aided by her Mediterranean good looks.

All four had fallen silent, preoccupied by their thoughts and weary of staring at nothing very much happening outside the small, pantiled house set back to one side of the café.

Though Vignoles was exhausted, physically and mentally, even if he had been offered a comfortable bed at that moment he was sure sleep would elude him because his mind was racing. He had been just a few feet away as Captain Henderson killed the security guard in cold blood and he'd subsequently been sucked into complicity by helping conceal the body beneath a pile of empty boxes in a darkened corner of the distillery. Vignoles observed the captain as the memory of the awful act nagged away at his conscience. As ever, Henderson was composed, blowing smoke rings as he sat opposite, inscrutable and aloof.

The two had worked swiftly and efficiently at their grim task and Vignoles was struck with a cold horror at how he had followed Henderson's lead, but also acknowledged their effective teamwork. He was part of the crime now, and it was sickening.

* * * *

They had retreated from the distillery shortly after concealing the body, removing any sign of their presence and, as soon as they were walking back along the lonely siding, they had conducted a furious and yet oddly controlled argument, spat out in low, venomous sentences filled with rage. Vignoles could not understand why murder had been the first option chosen by Henderson to get them out of their predicament. Henderson had repeated that they were in a fix and discovery risked blowing the whole operation.

'He was just one man against two! We could have surprised him.'

'I did, old boy. And he was one man with a gun, don't forget.' Henderson had thrown the guard's pistol into some bushes shortly after they had clambered back over the wall. 'One shot and Anna is a widow. I'd probably have finished him off before he fired a second, but how would that help you — or her?'

'You couldn't know that he would shoot.'

'Exactly the point.'

'You should have just knocked him out!'

'This is real life, Vignoles. Only in films does one swift blow send a man to sleep for a day. In reality it can be bloody hard work. It can take many punches, and he still might fight back before he's fully out.'

'But at least he would still be alive.'

'And then what? Tie him up? Using what? He'd just be a bloody inconvenience, waiting to come round and escape when our backs are turned and raise the alarm. This way we know we've bought ourselves time.'

'And what happens when he doesn't show up?'

'We need to find out who's moving this tank wagon and what's in that secret compartment, not worry about a blasted guard! What if he was one of the gang? They've killed at least three men already. They don't take prisoners — so neither do we.'

'I disagree. If you've just killed a gang member then our work *is* still blown. Admit it, you reacted without pausing to think.'

'Decisive action is needed at crisis moments. It was no time to pussy-foot around!'

'There's going to be hell to pay for this. I won't keep quiet, if that's what you think.'

'I suggest you wait until you see how this shakes down and then make your judgement, old boy. There's work to be done and we can't lose time arguing points of morality.'

Henderson and Vignoles stared at each other across the railway line, both breathing hard like two stags after locking horns.

* * * *

Vignoles brought himself back into the present and took a last sip of coffee, feeling its heat warm his insides. He agreed with Anna's suggestion that they immediately order another.

'Real coffee is just such a treat. And goodness knows we deserve it.' There was assent from the others and Anna confidently passed their order on to the *barista* in Italian.

Vignoles continued to observe the captain. He was affable and charming. He was also undoubtedly able and efficient. But this man did not act or talk like a desk-bound civil servant propaganda merchant. If the Information and Research Department needed this calibre of man, then it was a far more deadly organisation than the captain made it appear. Stranger still, Henderson seemed to have a remarkable insight. He'd been correct that their night-time visit would prove dangerous, and had even demonstrated the neck-snapping move as they had stood near the entrance gates. Was this coincidence?

'So, can you tell us anything of your meeting with the commander? Or anything about these three?' asked Anna.

'Very little.' Vignoles saw Henderson's eagle eyes watching him in a silent reminder of the constraints of the Official Secrets Act. There was so much he wanted to tell and get off his chest, but he was both constrained by the rules and wise enough to appreciate that careless talk really would cost lives with the information he'd been given. 'We left the place in question and made ourselves known to a sentry — who was sleeping on the job, so a fat lot of use he would have proved, if things had turned nasty.' Vignoles felt another shiver as he recalled how nasty things had become, but carried on.

'He took us to his commanding officer and I telephoned in and set up a meeting with the commander. When back at base, we were whisked straight in to see him.'

'Gosh, this must be important. That must have been one or two o'clock in the morning,' observed Rose.

'Indeed. I presented my observations, muddled though they were, then we motored out here to lend a hand. I still think you should have taken the chance to go back and get some sleep when we relieved you.'

'Perhaps we should,' said Anna, stifling a yawn, 'but you might need us if they go separate ways. And I prefer to be here and share the problem.'

'I'd prefer you both to stay out of trouble. I really took a risk last night, getting you involved. But there's sense in what you say about them splitting up. As regards the meeting, the commander gave very little away, but, as Gretton remarked, he took the matter seriously.'

Vignoles fell silent again and ran through in his head the full account of their nocturnal meeting, trying to reassure himself that it had actually happened and that he had not just imagined it all or was hallucinating as a result of his extreme tiredness.

When they had walked into the lobby of the *Albergo*, Vignoles had yet again sensed a frisson of tension in the air. There was more activity than he had expected at that hour; not only were the two armoured cars outside crewed and waiting with their engines idling, but within there were aides walking quietly in rapid steps from one door to another across the carpeted lobby whilst the telephone rang repeatedly. A group of officers, seated in leather club chairs to one side of the lobby, looked up from their tumblers of whisky and gave Vignoles and Henderson expectant stares, as though awaiting the imminent arrival of someone important. Two American officers, weighed down with heavy braiding and their pale uniforms and exuding an aura of cool efficiency, were waiting impatiently beside the reception counter, one beating a rhythmic tattoo with his fingers upon the wooden surface.

When the concierge quietly informed Vignoles and Henderson that Commander Turbayne would see them immediately, the two Americans, who could not help but overhear, reacted by tracking them both across the room with intense interest and more than a suspicion of anger. Vignoles felt sure that they had been knocked back in his favour.

If the commander was annoyed at being woken in the early hours, he did not show it, though doubtless he had at least the benefit of a shower, clean clothes and a shave, all of which Vignoles would dearly like to enjoy. He had been asked to present his observations, and gave an edited version of their visit to *Stock* and his thoughts about how the deaths of the three servicemen were linked to the wagon and its secret compartment.

The commander listened intently, occasionally stopping Vignoles to ask a question and trading inscrutable glances with the three other men in the room, all of whom were not introduced. He was trying to obtain from both Vignoles and Henderson accurate descriptions of the three possible suspects and at the end of this period of cross-examination they looked more puzzled than satisfied. From their uniforms he could tell they were of senior rank in the British Army and from the American Intelligence Corps. The American had a thick neck and a shaven head and stared at him the whole time, before firing a series of questions about the tank wagon, demanding a level of detail and observation that Vignoles struggled to satisfy. Captain Henderson was then asked to leave the room, accompanied by the other three, leaving just the commander and Vignoles alone. Vignoles sensed that something was causing grave concern.

However, it was the private conversation that followed that had set his mind racing, the implications of which were so huge that he was starting to admit that the death of the security guard might be justified.

'Do you know who these three characters are, commander?'

'Can't say at this stage. We monitor a great number of undesirables within Zone A, and far more from without.' Those dark, currant-like eyes were inscrutable.

'I sense you expected us to describe different people.'

'Really? Interesting. Certainly we have a puzzling situation on many levels. So, Vignoles, this is how I want you to play it. Tail the three holed up at Opčine and see what they do. They may not be linked with the tanker, but they sound a fair bet and my guess is that if they are involved they'll make a move today. The wagon awaits transit onward to Ljubljana. We'll maintain a light cordon around the distillery to observe what goes on. But I want the wagon to commence its journey. We'll darned well make sure it gets clearance. Leave the door open for them to step in and get it suitably labelled. So keep your head down and play it by ear. Though I should point out that other, er, agencies are interested in your discovery and now moving in to take over. So you will duck out and leave well alone when I give the order.'

'I see.' Vignoles paused to contemplate this surprising fact. 'When can I meet with these other agencies?'

'You can't. As I said in London, this is a strictly "need to know" situation. However...' The commander opened a pack of cigarettes as he was speaking. 'Join me in a smoke?' His voice softened and Vignoles sensed he was going to be thrown a tit-bit from the captain's table. 'There *is* something I'd like to share with you. Privately and absolutely within these four walls.'

Vignoles gratefully accepted the invitation and filled his pipe.

'Have you heard of Telemark? The Vemork hydro plant?'

'That name rings a bell.' Vignoles paused with his pipe in his mouth and a lighted match above the bowl of tobacco. 'Some Norwegian chaps with the SOE did extraordinary things there to stop the Nazi atom bomb programme.'

'Correct, and absolute heroes to a man.' Turbayne leaned forward across his desk. 'Did you know that they invented a whole new technique for skiing downhill? They could descend hills even the crack Wehrmacht mountain troops declared unski-able. They call it the "Telemark turn". This gave them the advantage of approaching the hydro-electric plant down sheer slopes not being watched because they were considered impassable. Marvellous stuff, eh?'

'But what on earth has this to do with the wagon in Trieste?' Vignoles lit his pipe and stared at the commander through the gently curling smoke. This was all very diverting, but there was work to be discussed.

'Do you know what they were making in the hydro plant?'

'Was it a special type of water that can be used for the atom bomb? Though I can't say I understand the physics behind it.'

Turbayne surprised Vignoles by laughing, 'Nor do I! The only water I understand is the salty stuff that fills the oceans and conceals U-boats.' A faraway look briefly crossed the commander's sea-dog face, with a tautening around the mouth that confirmed he knew perhaps too much about such things.

'They call it deuterium oxide,' he continued, 'or heavy water, though it weighs exactly the same as the normal stuff and smells, tastes and looks the same. You could drink it and not notice anything other than it not tasting very fresh. But it's very valuable and very scarce as it takes considerable effort to create and under quite special circumstances. It's got an extra hydrogen molecule or something, but we don't need to concern ourselves with that.'

Vignoles had forgotten about his pipe. He was starting to make the connection.

'The Vemork plant was the first in the world to make it, and you can get an idea of how scarce it is when you think of the millions of tons of water a year that pass through such a place, and yet the estimate is that in a good year, they might only make twelve tons of the heavy stuff. The Germans invaded in 1940 and continued production, of course. A tank of this special water, if it had been brought across to Berlin, could have seen Hitler have an atom bomb to drop on Britain or the States. Just think about it, Vignoles! As it was, it took these Norwegian commandos the best part of four years to completely stop the plant. Luckily, the production of the water was even slower.' The commander took an extra deep lungful of smoke and the pause grew heavy with implication.

'Did they not have one tank wagon ready to move? I seem to recall it had been placed on a ferry boat.'

'Correct. Fortunately our intelligence boys got wind of it and the Norwegian resistance sank the SF *Hydro*. Sent it to the bottom of the deep and icy waters of Lake Tinnsjø.'

'But?'

'But there have been rumours over the years that the rail tanker sent to the bottom of the lake was actually the *second* consignment taken out of the hydro plant by the Nazis. There was another that went out undetected a short while earlier. This was a smaller quantity, disguised or concealed in some manner, and thereby missed by intelligence. Of course this was dismissed as the kind of shaggy dog story that does the rounds, and makes a good tale in the pub over a pint. We double-checked all the intelligence at the time to make sure, and felt confident there was nothing in this rumour. And besides, the war was over by then; Hitler long dead and the Allies have the bomb for themselves. We pushed these stories aside and concerned ourselves with other, more pressing matters.'

'But they wouldn't go away.'

'No. Every few months or so, this damned silly story would resurface. There were tales of a milk wagon in Sweden, a tar wagon in Germany, an ancient petrol tanker at the back of a factory in Brno. At one time it was allegedly lifted off its wheels and covered in ivy behind a shoe factory near Salzburg. Take your pick.' The commander toyed with his cigarette as if debating whether to continue. 'There is a certain romance to these tales — but nothing more. That was, until a British field officer ran a Soviet agent to ground and we got some interesting information out of him. Moscow had sent him looking for an elusive tanker filled with heavy water. He hinted that he was not alone in this quest. We now have good reasons to suspect that the Jugoslavs are the front runners in the hunt.'

'And you think that there could be heavy water inside that concealed tank?'

'We have to consider the possibility.'

'And what kind of value does it have?'

'A country that gets this water could be well on their way to becoming atomic.'

'So Jugoslavia is trying to build a bomb?' Vignoles was incredulous.

'It was a revelation to us, but we have reason to believe it's true. The project is in its infancy, but we know that a fledgling atomic department has been created by one of their top scientists, and this man has been gathering other rising stars in that field around him. Perhaps more worrying is now that Belgrade and Moscow have fallen out, where might all this lead? The conclusions are uncomfortable. The Cold War could become extremely chilly if Stalin and Tito both build the A-bomb — and continue to argue. Of course, the water might have become hopelessly contaminated.'

'And we can destroy the tanker. Put a few bullet holes in the side, and it becomes worthless. We could have it done within the hour.'

Commander Turbayne raised a hand and made a slowing down gesture. 'If only it were that simple. Logic says we do just as you say, but this has implications far greater than anything the likes of you and I can influence.' He took a long drag on his cigarette; a clock ticked on the wall. 'There are interested parties who want to use it as a lure to get a bead on some of the top agents operating behind the Iron Curtain. So that is why you will continue to work as you have thus far, trying to find who killed those British soldiers. But you will do nothing to prevent this wagon leaving Trieste — and in one piece. That is an order.'

Silence fell. Leicester Central and the irritations of escaped sheep on the line suddenly felt like something from a far distant world.

Chapter Twenty-nine

A Star Fell out of Heaven
Sam Browne

Violet Trinder was making tomato soup for lunch. She had her dressmaking shop to attend to that morning, and needed to spend much of the afternoon standing in queues for further provisions, so finishing breakfast and making lunch blended into one event. She was following a favourite recipe gleaned from *The Kitchen Front*, and was busy stirring the chopped carrots, potatoes, onion and bacon rinds saved from breakfast in a smear of melted dripping in a pan, whilst keeping an eye on the vegetable stock warming on the other gas ring.

Her husband was seated at the table with yesterday's meagre excuse for a newspaper spread out before him, fastidiously polishing his work shoes. He enjoyed this task and liked to take it seriously, ensuring they were buffed and polished until they reflected like mirrors. He found the task oddly therapeutic and was often able to think things through as he worked. As he bent over and put some elbow grease into it, the sunlight from the open back door caught his head and Violet was struck at how his brilliantined hair, jet black and meticulously combed into a perfect line, matched his footwear.

'Lucy telephoned yesterday — did she say anything to you?'

'No, what did she want?'

'She told me all about her appearance in the Olympics. How exciting is that, John? I could hardly take it in. To think we know an Olympian! We will have to get tickets and see her compete. She wanted me to help prepare her outfit. She's fortunate, because for the pistol event they can wear something simple that will not pose many problems, but there's also the opening ceremony. She will be supplied with a dress, but I very much doubt it will fit without some judicious attention from my needle!' Trinder smiled; his wife was a professional dressmaker, and few ready-made clothes met her exacting standards. 'To compete, Lucy will need lightweight trousers in navy blue and a white, short-sleeved blouse, both with the appropriate badges sewn on. I think I have just the material for the trousers. The biggest headache might prove to be the blazer — I just hope it has decent seam allowances so I can unpick it and tailor it properly. We shall meet up soon so I can measure her up.'

'Excellent. I'm pleased she sought your help. She's a good and conscientious policewoman, you know, and has been a real help in this odd case I'm working on.' Trinder was becoming distracted by the delicious smell of the vegetables and bacon rind started to cook. 'Gosh, Vi, that smells good! I'm starving again and I've only just had breakfast.'

'Eat an apple — we've nothing much else, I'm afraid. We've used nearly all our rations for this week.'

Trinder groaned. 'I heard that the Olympians will get enhanced rations. Perhaps I could find a suitable discipline and enter.' They both laughed.

'So, tell me about this odd case, as you call it. Did you find that paint tin yesterday?'

'Yes, it was retrieved by some fellows walking the track and I had it sent straight across to the forensic labs in Leicester. We explained to them how to prevent getting their own dabs on it.'

'Did you get any prints?'

'Two corkers! Should get lovely images from them.'

'That was awfully careless of them.'

'The paint came from a hardware shop in Rugby. We know this because the paper label was conveniently over-printed with the dealer's name. Blencowe and Benson are going over there this morning. Hopefully they'll remember who they sold it to.'

'So the paint throwers could be from Rugby?'

'Rugby or Leicester would be my guess. It narrows things down a little. But I don't expect the lab boys to find a match with a known criminal on their records; the prints probably belong to an innocent shop assistant. However, they could prove useful if they match those we found on that track spanner.'

'Do you think those incidents are linked?' Violet was chopping a mound of freshly picked tomatoes in half as she spoke.

'Yes, but I need to prove it. Clues are starting to come together, like a jigsaw puzzle. I've singled out the acts that caused disruption, dismissing all the obvious, mindless time-wasting events, and there is a trend that intrigues me — the use of red paint to damage an engine; the stealing and defacing of timetables; the fire that damaged a store room, but which actually caused the most harm by ruining the following week's operating instructions.'

'John, these tomatoes are just wonderful. You did so well growing them. It's funny, but Jenny and I could never get them to fruit like this. Sorry, darling, you were saying?'

Trinder stopped polishing to inspect the shine, then addressed a spot that was not up to standard. 'Relocating the cold frame is what's done the trick, nothing more. They get more sun. Now, this is where it gets interesting. That strange note which was sent to Mr Badger in Marylebone. Remember I told you about it?'

'The one that wasn't about the town of Bude.'

'Yes. Prize chump that I am, I hadn't noticed that a most unusual locomotive bearing that very name regularly thunders up and down on the line at the end of our garden!' As if to make the point, a fast express goods train hurtled past the house on the elevated embankment, whistle screaming as it passed Woodford Halse station, setting the teapot and cups rattling.

Violet smiled. 'Inspector Vignoles would not have missed that connection!'

'Indeed he would not. Fortunately, we still made the connection because —'

'Because of the track gang girls!' Violet concluded his sentence with a hint of triumph in her voice.

'You got it! They were dismissed — wrongly, we now think — because a section of track was unbolted after they checked it. As far as their ganger was concerned, they were guilty. However, they're a plucky pair, so they did a little investigation on their own and found not only a suspiciously appropriate looking spanner in the bushes, but a man taking pictures of trains, specifically of *Bude* as she sped over the very length of line that had been tampered with.'

'Wasn't it this photographer who gave you the tip-off about the engine?' Violet was adding the stock to the chopped vegetables and tomatoes, sending a delicious scent into the room in a cloud of steam.

'Yes. And we think he may have photographed the men who undid the bolts, though they're awfully small in the picture.' Trinder gave one last, admiring look at his handiwork then placed the shoes on the quarry-tiled floor and worked his feet into them. 'Now, Vi, this is where it gets intriguing. Another can of red paint is chucked at an engine driver. As it was thrown, the fireman thinks one of them shouted out something along the lines of "You're dead, you red." Now at this point, our dear Olympian Lansdowne made a most extraordinary connection. She has been fixated on this political meeting to be held tonight in Leicester.'

'The one you're both going to?'

'Yes. She's been pointing out posters and flyers for this blasted thing and generally puzzling over them. I must give her credit for having some kind of hunch about it and not letting the matter drop. After hearing what the fireman said, she reminded me about the headline on the posters which declared, "Better Dead Than Red."'

'That's similar to what was shouted from the bridge.'

'There's more. On two occasions when paint was smeared across a locomotive and noticeboards, the initials BD and TR were left in the paint.'

'Aha! I think I've got it, John: not people's initials, but the first letters of *Better Dead Than Red.*'

'Exactly!'

'So the people behind the political meeting must be the same as are doing this?'

'The *implication* is that they are, but we need proof. The fingerprints on the paint tin may prove useful, but we shall need prints from these political activists to compare them with. The photographic evidence will be too vague to stand up in court, so at present we don't have enough to even arrest them, let alone press charges. We have some way to go.'

'But what do these people want? What do they mean about "stopping the scarlet tide"?'

'I thought at first they meant blood. "Stop the blood" as an anti-war message, perhaps, but then I made the connection. Scarlet is red; just like a red flag.'

'They're anti-communists, then.'

'It looks that way from their vitriolic posters. And fanatical about it.' He replaced the lid on the slim, circular tin of boot polish and wrapped it, together with the little wooden brushes, in an old cloth, then stepped into the cool scullery, raising his voice so Violet could still hear. 'They have a funny way of going about their campaign of political fear-mongering, though. It's very amateurish.'

Violet left the soup to simmer and leafed through a much-worn, dog-eared, spiral-bound notebook filled with recipes and ideas that she had carefully clipped from newspapers. 'Not if they intended to kill goodness knows how many by wrecking that train,' she replied. 'What were the odds against their handiwork being undiscovered?'

Trinder rinsed his hands under the cold tap, shook them dry, and then stood at the open door, his shirtsleeves still rolled up, and lit one last cigarette before heading to the office. He looked down the length of the back yard past the junk-filled Anderson shelter, the outside toilet with the tin bath hung on the wall, the mangle standing in the sun and beyond the rows of potatoes and runner beans on their poles to the wooden gate sagging on its hinges at the end of the garden. The grassy embankment of the railway was a backdrop of pale green spotted with buttercups and clover. Telegraph poles strode along the embankment top like tall wooden giants.

'Their warning message was useless, John. I can't see how anyone could interpret it correctly,' added Violet, who was now washing some plums, having gained inspiration from her book of cuttings. 'And besides, what "red tide of communism" were you supposed to stop, and by when, exactly?'

Trinder took a long drag on his cigarette and considered his response. 'The IRA gave very specific warnings; the time, date and place before detonation. They didn't expect a political solution to be found before the bomb went off, but they spread fear most effectively and, in so doing, perhaps caused a change of heart about the Irish problem. But as for this lot, well, so far the public has not even noticed their actions.'

'They're just playing at being terrorists. You should go and listen to these speakers and see what it is they're so worked up about. Surely they don't mean our government? I'm perfectly happy with all their new ideas. It'll remove a huge burden of worry from our shoulders. We can finally get mother some proper medical attention — free of charge, I can get this blessed tooth seen to — again, free.'

Trinder looked over his shoulder and smiled. 'I'd be happy if they dished out a few rump steaks, too!' His attention was drawn to something outside. 'Hullo, look at those.'

The drone of many powerful aero engines crackled and throbbed across the cloudless gentian blue above Woodford as a formation of six large aircraft formed into twin arrowhead shapes of three, glinted in the sun like thin silver cigar cases with huge, outspread wings. They were very high, but by squinting his eyes Trinder could discern their shape.

Intrigued, Violet wiped her hands dry on her apron and stood beside him in the doorway. 'What are they? They're not Lancasters.'

'No. These are far bigger.'

The pulsating throb of the engines was loud and bounced around their yard.

'They're Super Fortresses.' Trinder was shading his eyes as he spoke. 'American bombers. They can fly so high there's no need for camouflage and so they leave the metal shiny. Gosh, these must be the ones they're sending over to be based here. I read about it in the paper under my shoes.' Trinder paused. 'They're carrying the bomb, Vi.'

She watched them glint in the sun as traces of vapour trailed from the engines and wing tips. 'You mean the A-bomb? Oh, how dreadful!' She put a hand to her mouth and frowned. 'To think they are carrying such a monstrous thing, right above us.'

They watched in silence as the bombers slowly disappeared from sight, though the drone of their passing lingered a while longer. Violet slipped her arm around her husband's waist and they stood close together, both gazing up to the heavens, and both remembering the stories of how *Enola Gay* had flown across just such a cloudless summer sky above Hiroshima.

CHAPTER THIRTY

Slow Freight
Glenn Miller & His Band

Vignoles was unable to repeat the astonishing revelations of his private conversation with Commander Turbayne and regretted that he was restricted to sounding vague and evasive as he parried his wife's enquiries. He fiddled with his pipe to mask his uneasiness, turning it over in his hands and enjoying the rich colour of the briarwood as it caught the morning light. It had been a Christmas present from Anna in 1946. He felt a sudden pang of longing to be back in his armchair in their little semi near the golf course at Belgrave and Birstall.

'But what on earth could be in the, um, the thing?' Anna was deliberately circumspect. 'And did it arrive empty or full? The documentation was just too vague.'

'A good question.' Vignoles had to say something.

Henderson nodded in agreement, 'Why not make a substitution? Could we not find a similar one and swap them, then we could have a proper look.' Henderson was being equally careful with his words.

'I like the idea, but it was a pretty ancient beast. Could we find one that looks the same? Then there is the manoeuvre to make the swap. We can hardly conceal an engine going up and down that line. It's a nice idea, but I just can't see how we can manage it.'

'Gretton.' Henderson looked at the young staff sergeant, whose paleness served to heighten the appearance of the freckles scattered across her nose and cheeks. 'You said they spoke Russian. Are you quite sure?'

'I can't be certain, sir. My previous posting was in Berlin. There were a great many Russians, and one gets to recognise the sounds of a language, even if one doesn't understand the words.'

Henderson nodded, partially at the *barista*, who set down four more small cups of cappuccino, and partially in response to her explanation.

'To put it in musical terms,' she elaborated, 'they have a certain timbre to their voice that is quite distinctive. Mind you, as I'm listening to those men over there...' Rose indicated the *Caffé Vatta*, favoured almost exclusively by Jugoslav soldiers and already filled by at least twenty young men and women in their distinctive green uniforms and forage caps, 'then I begin to doubt my judgement. One or two of them have a similar quality to their voice. I might mistake them for Russians.'

The men, and a handful of women, were chatting, smoking, drinking from tiny cups of coffee brewed in the Turkish style and served in small copper vessels with wooden handles, and a number were knocking back shots of *grappa*. They talked loudly, using expressive hand gestures to make their points, apparently talking across each other, and yet there was a sense of sharing jokes and stories in a comradely manner and enjoying a stolen moment in the pleasant morning sun. Vignoles noticed that some of the men were throwing the occasional glance across the road towards them.

'We'll have to take that with a pinch of salt, but it's set me on edge,' said Henderson, who had ceased blowing smoke rings.

'Movement!' Vignoles sat up and replaced his cup on its saucer without having tasted the fresh coffee. 'The two men are leaving. Anna; you and Rose watch for the woman — ad-lib, but for God's sake take care!'

Trying to look unhurried and relaxed, Vignoles and Henderson made a great show of saying goodbye to the women and strolled along the pavement, apparently interested in the flowers outside the *Il Bucaneve Fioreria* next door. Two leather-jacketed men were walking towards them. Remembering they had got a close look at him the evening before, Vignoles flipped his sun visor down over his spectacles, readjusted his hat so that the brim shaded his face, and faked becoming fascinated by a bunch of pale yellow roses.

The two men suddenly changed tack and approached the flower shop, and so Vignoles moved slightly to allow one of them to swiftly pick up a random bunch of flowers from a zinc pail and enter the dark shop interior. There was a very brief, mumbled exchange and the man stepped back out into the light, holding the flowers by their stalks and allowing them to swing carelessly beside his leg as they crossed the road. Neither appeared to have taken the slightest interest in either Vignoles or Henderson.

Vignoles watched their receding reflections in the shop window. 'My money says that's not a romantic gesture. Is there a churchyard near here?'

Henderson glanced up and down the main road. 'I think so, just across the way from the tram station. Why do you ask?'

'And there's the church spire! Come along, they're heading in that direction. A graveside rendezvous to lay flowers — useful cover, I'd say.'

'Good thinking!' Henderson gave Vignoles a sidelong glance as they waited for a car to pass, casually swinging his shoulder bag around and unfastening the cover. Henderson flipped this over so he could reach inside for his pistol if needed.

'Still loaded, in case you were wondering.' Vignoles gave a grin laced with gallows humour and patted his own shoulder bag.

'Glad to hear it, old boy.'

They forced themselves to walk slowly whilst observing the backs of the two men as they headed down a side street and towards the church, which was set close against the road with only small strips of grass surrounding it. This was not their destination. The men turned left down a narrow, unmade road with a high wall of limestone to the left and a bank of trees and a hedge of flowering ivy to the right.

Vignoles was able to peer through thinning gaps in this scented barrier that was loud with bees looping from one pale flower to another. He could see and smell a field of recently mown grass and the unmistakable sight of a locomotive slogging up the final stretch of the climb from Trieste, throwing puffs of dark, coal-laden smoke into the air, its exhaust rhythmically pounding with that of the banking engine behind.

The narrow *Via Doberdo* had a kink to the left about halfway down its length, allowing Vignoles and Henderson to remain out of sight. Above the wall they could glimpse the shapes of carved headstones, a Cleopatra's needle, and some massive, ornamented tombs. As they cautiously turned the bend in the road, they saw that there was a junction a little further ahead where their road met another and, to the left, an impressive entrance gateway formed from great blocks of a pinky-grey sandstone shaped into rectangular pillars and a heavy sculpted lintel topped by a small pantiled roof surmounted by a wire-thin crucifix. One of the two metal gates stood open and beside this was a wooden hut selling flowers and candles.

As Vignoles predicted, the two men had stepped inside the walled graveyard, and, quickly assessing the situation, Vignoles purchased a bunch of white carnations from the old lady with the flower stall. She smiled and seemed eager to pass the time of day, speaking to him in Slovene in a kindly voice, but Vignoles, lacking both understanding and time, simply placed what was probably an excessively large pile of coins in her hand and entered through the gate, conscious of her effusive thanks hanging in the air behind them.

The cemetery was an impressive sight. The light was blindingly bright and little shade was offered from the trees growing on the far side of the road. Great slabs of different-coloured marble or stone, each shaped, carved, decorated and perfectly maintained, marked the graves. It was a hard landscape, devoid of the lush grass, dark yews and the mossy, illegible gravestones of a typical English churchyard. Vignoles was immediately struck by the smartness and the shining newness all around them. There was none of the decay, the mouldering neglect and the careless forgetfulness that he was accustomed to. Here, offerings and fresh flowers lay at every grave, the stones polished and cared for. It came as a jolt to see the faces of the dead looking back at him from small, oval photographs set into brass frames mounted on many of the headstones. Silent, but smiling or pensive; clearly defined or blurred and fuzzy, the faces were oddly captivating.

Vignoles and Henderson walked slowly along one of the paths, reading the names, whilst carefully observing the actions of the two men, who had split up, one standing closer to the entrance gate and partially hidden by a huge monument in liver-red marble, the bearded one apparently lost in his thoughts before a vast, flat rectangle of pale stone. Henderson nudged Vignoles and they watched as a third man entered the graveyard. He was equally unconvincing as a mourner: his eyes continually flicked from side to side and his hands were clenched so tight that his knuckles were white.

Vignoles understood Henderson's signal and both knelt down as he laid the carnations on the grave of Maria Sommariva. As they dipped out of sight, the picture of poor Maria stared back with a puzzled expression that mirrored Vignoles's own feelings.

The new arrival hesitated and surveyed the array of tombs for a moment, then appeared to make a mental connection between one of the men and the grave before him. He walked across, but neither man greeted the other. They stood side by side, looking down, speaking quietly as befitted the location. Their voices were inaudible, not helped by the whistles and reverberations of the slow freight train rumbling beyond the trees.

The new arrival appeared to be asking for something, holding his hand out in anticipation. There was a slight rise in volume, a quick and sharp exchange followed, both men angry and yet forcing themselves to control their tempers so as not to attract attention. Arms gesticulated in staccato movements. Suddenly, the leather-jacketed man jabbed a finger in the chest of the new arrival.

Both were expecting something from the other, and both seemed immovable in their demands. Vignoles noticed that the other half of the pair was slowly approaching from behind with an unpleasant look in his eye.

They did it neatly and, despite observing them throughout, it was still hard to see how they managed it so discreetly. The argumentative one in the leather jacket was pressing a gun into the small of the third man's back, and yet it would be impossible to see it, unless you knew it was there. At the same moment, his colleague stepped to the other side of their prisoner, his face smiling and speaking in louder and friendlier tones. They were just pals meeting beside the grave of those killed in a bombing raid, and now he was suggesting they went for a drink, or perhaps a ride somewhere, his arm around his friend's shoulder in a vice-like grip.

'What language are they speaking?' whispered Vignoles.

'Serbo-Croat. Or Russian.' They stood up to watch as the tightly formed trio walked towards the gateway.

'There's a second exit over at the back. I'll take that.' Henderson already had his hand resting on the open top of his shoulder bag.

Vignoles nodded in response. His mouth was dry.

The three men left the graveyard, turned left towards the road junction and halted, still earnestly discussing something in their tightly-knit group. A minute passed and Vignoles hesitated beside the flower stall, aware of the old lady's puzzled stare. How should he play this? Follow or intervene?

There was the sound of a lorry engine revving noisily, then the unexpected sight of a large British Army vehicle reversing rapidly and quite dangerously across the street, right in front of the trio. A man was gesticulating to the driver and calling out in an appallingly bad Cockney accent whilst stepping backwards and bumping heavily into the man with the gun.

'Sorry, guv, oi didn't see yer there! Bloomin' driver, eh?'

Vignoles realised that Henderson was hamming it up like a revue player and he responded instantly by briskly darting forwards as the lorry crashed its gears and made a lurching movement that smashed its left front wing into the cemetery wall.

'Oi, watch out, mate! Yer nearly killed us!' Henderson waved an arm wildly, crashing it against the bearded man.

Vignoles was only a foot behind the three, who were visibly surprised by the sudden intervention, and he noticed that the gun had been quickly removed from their prisoner's back and concealed inside the open leather jacket.

'What the hell are you doing? Incompetent fool!' Vignoles added to the confusion and caused the trio to break apart as they twisted around, looking this way and that, puzzled by the noise and the shouting from different directions and the alarming movements of the looming truck, which now lurched backwards. Vignoles roughly barged between the prisoner and one of his captors as Henderson made a play of apologising loudly and vociferously to the gunman who, in turn, was desperately trying to fend him off whilst speaking angrily in some indecipherable language.

The diversion worked and the prisoner, who needed no encouragement, quickly slipped between the lorry nose and the wall. Henderson was still trying to speak to his man, but now with an aggrieved tone, as the Russian angrily pushed the captain away with a voice filled with menace. The lorry, driven by a nervous-looking young British soldier, made more unexpected movements, which prevented either Russian from getting past and after their man.

Vignoles skirted the rear of the lorry in pursuit, but the road was empty. He ran forwards, pulling his pistol from his shoulder bag and clasping his Panama to his head. A few steps along the road and he saw another gap in the hedgerow and took a gamble. Without slowing, he plunged through, closing his eyes as he felt the ivy slap his face and sharp twigs snag his clothes and jab into his arms and legs. He stumbled into a field, took a few steps to regain his balance, and stopped. The freshly cut hay was formed into perfect, rounded stacks like old-fashioned beehives, each one five or six feet high and similarly wide at the base.

Vignoles sprinted towards the nearest and stood so he was concealed from the road. He surveyed the scene, trying to guess behind which his quarry was hiding. The shouting from the road was continuing. He guessed the two Russians would have withdrawn from the chase — for now. The scent of cut grass was strong, and the moist air was filled by the buzz of insects. He could feel his nose starting to itch. Would he or the escapee sneeze first? Vignoles pinched his nose to try and avert the reaction to the pollen.

The sound of train movements clattered across from the far edge of the field as another train drew to a halt. Vignoles realised that this would be the obvious escape route. He ran to the next haystack, sneezed, then moved one more time. As he did so he caught a glimpse of the fugitive as he darted over a broken fence and then dropped out of sight onto the railway below. Vignoles gave chase, reaching the top of an embankment that descended about five feet and which was carpeted with flowers and long, yellowing grasses, and through which a clear swathe was flattened where the man had slithered down. The second train, of vans, open wagons and low-slung transporters with British tanks chained to them, was waiting at a signal set at danger.

Vignoles also slid down the embankment and crouched low in the drainage ditch that bordered the track. He peered beneath the wagons into the inky darkness of the strong shadows cast by the unforgiving sun. The shapes of wheels, brakes, pipes and other clutter were stark in contrast to the strongly illuminated tracks beyond, which shimmered with heat-haze. Vignoles saw legs running towards the head of the train some fifteen feet or so away. He made a crouching run — easier said than done — in parallel, stumbling on the small stones that made their presence felt through the soles of his stout shoes whilst trying to keep the man in view.

The train suddenly jolted into motion. It was quickly gathering pace on the incline and he realised it would soon pass them both. There were two options available; they either waited for it to pass and confronted each other, or climbed aboard.

Still bent low, Vignoles watched as the man (no doubt making the same assessment) commenced jogging downhill, pacing the train until his feet lifted out of sight. Vignoles immediately stood up, sprinted and practically rolled onto the low wooden decking of one of the tank transporter wagons. He clung onto one of the securing chains and hauled himself upright, and, after catching his breath a moment, edged towards the front of the wagon, taking support from the securing chains. He peered around the tank.

The man was on the adjacent wagon, having done exactly the same manoeuvre and they looked at each other in surprise, his face pale as it peered around the great steel links of the tank tracks. Neither moved or said anything for a moment, remaining locked into a mutual gaze of curiosity.

'Stay! There's nowhere to go.'

The man frowned. His moustache twitched.

Vignoles showed the man that he had a gun, though he did not point it at him. He dearly hoped that he would not need to use it. The man continued to stare at him.

'Do you speak English?' asked Vignoles.

The man pulled a face and made a gesture with one hand. 'A leetle.'

'Are you Russian?' Vignoles waved the gun vaguely in his direction to encourage a reply.

'*Ne! Ne!*' A passionate stream of what sounded like invective followed and Vignoles guessed that he was no lover of Russians. 'I Slovene. No Soviet.'

'I'm English. I'm police,' said Vignoles, choosing the simplest words and pointing a finger at himself, then at the man. 'I want to talk with you.'

The fugitive looked back at Vignoles, his face perplexed.

'Why were those men holding you?' Vignoles lowered the gun, sensing no immediate threat. The train was now rattling along the Karst escarpment at a fair lick; signal posts, telegraph poles and the rough-hewn stones of shallow cuttings fringed by purple and yellow flowers flashed past Vignoles's shoulder. The noise of the squealing brakes forced him to shout.

The man stepped closer, working himself around to the front of the tank secured to the wagon he was standing on, one arm raised in a gesture of surrender, the other holding on. Vignoles acknowledged this by nodding and wedging his gun into his shoulder bag, slung diagonally across his body.

The Slovene slumped against the tank as if suddenly overtaken by a great weariness. Vignoles took this as an encouraging sign and, as neither was likely to risk jumping off the train in this dangerous section of track, he worked his way around until they stood face to face. He braced himself against one of the chains, which groaned as the dead weight of the tank shifted with the movement of the train as it twisted its way down the line. Between them, the buffers were locked together, their shanks easing in and out like silver concertinas as the track sped past in a blur. The man said nothing for a few moments, appearing to be gathering strength and wrestling with a decision. Vignoles knew it was time to remain silent. When he finally looked up, he met Vignoles's eyes and then started to talk as though unburdening himself of a great weight, his English far better then he gave himself credit for. He repeatedly sought reassurance that Vignoles was neither KGB nor a member of *Il Blocco Triestino* — a group that Vignoles understood to be virulently fascist — but, once he was satisfied on these points, and certain that Vignoles was British, the man seemed anxious to give himself up.

'You wish to defect? You want to come to England?'

'*Ne, ne!* But I heff big problem, my friend and me. We need help. Is too dangerous. We need...' he searched his memory for the word, 'protection.'

'What is too dangerous? Do you mean those two men?'

'*Ja!* They KGB, for sure.'

Vignoles felt a cold finger run down his spine.

'They kill us. Is bad situation. *Prosim*, we must go to, er, Breetish Embassy. That is, er, best, for sure.'

Vignoles was taken aback. 'The embassy? What is this about? Why are the KGB following you?'

'Is not easy to say here.' He gestured at the moving landscape and the billows of smoke wreathing around them. The train lurched violently. 'We heff much money. We must get it. We must find my friend. Then you protect us, *ja*?'

'Which friend?'

'I have colleague here in Trst.' Vignoles noted that he used the Slovene version of the city's name. 'We work on, er, very important plan. Now, is no longer possible. We must, er, surrender. We have money. Much lire!'

Vignoles was stunned. This was the last thing he expected and was unsure what to make of this astonishing revelation. It had been a summer filled with such moments. 'Can we start at the beginning? Who are you?'

'Professor Ferluga, director of department of Atomic Physics, University Ljubljana, People's Republic of Jugoslavia!' He spoke more confidently now. 'My friend, he Professor Vrabec. He ver-ry good scientist. But we ver-ry bad spies.' He rolled his 'r's for emphasis and nodded.

'Two atomic scientists in the British-United States zone? But what are you doing here? You say you are spying?' Vignoles was stunned. 'This does not look good, I must warn you.'

'No, not spying, is better to say we *buying*.'

'You are shopping?' Vignoles was incredulous.

'We have thirty million lire for something we need very much.'

'Jesus!' Vignoles whistled in amazement. 'What is it you want to buy?' Vignoles had already begun to suspect.

'*Ampak to je ze prepozno*! Is too late, the KGB have this.'

'How do you know?'

'I explain at embassy. Those men ver-ry dangerous. They kill three Tommies. They want kill us.' As he spoke, Ferluga was frantically looking behind their train, though it was implausible that anyone was in pursuit.

For his part, Vignoles did not doubt the professor's assessment. He had been right to suspect the three holed up in

Opčine, but with his suspicions confirmed he began to feel more apprehensive. How long had Henderson delayed the two men? Had he met with any resistance? And for all the drama of the descent, the train was probably travelling at less than twenty miles an hour and could be readily chased into the city.

Vignoles continued to question Ferluga. 'We know about the heavy water.'

'*Prosim?* I not know this word.'

'The deuterium oxide. We know. Is this what you wanted to buy?'

'I see you know a lot.'

Vignoles took this as confirmation. 'How do the KGB enter the story?'

'We have a contact. But we no meet him. He called *Srakoper.*' The professor shrugged his shoulders and made a face. 'I know nothing about him.'

'That is his code name?'

'*Prav zares.*'

'Is that his family name?'

'*Ne, ne, ne!* Is name of bird. I no remember English word. Um, is something like, er, shry… shreek.'

'Shrike?' Vignoles's heart leaped. That name had come up before.

'*Ja!* Is shrike.'

'What is he? An agent with the Jugoslav security services?'

'I not know. We follow his, er, instructions, but all go wrong. British man is killed. Then another. And we no get what we need to make the, er, um, arrangements. We worry: another is trying to buy same thing. And now I know who they are.'

'The KGB.'

The professor nodded. '*Ja!* Plan is ruined! Plan was, I meet British man and give money for, er, um, documents to get into *Stock* and put card on the…' he waved a hand in frustration as he searched for the word.

'Tank wagon?

'*Ja*, tank wagon. For allow it travel to Ljubljana. But the man I must meet is suddenly dead.' Ferluga's vocabulary was expanding as the conversation continued.

'Was this man called Priday? Corporal Priday?'

'That him! And today I meet different men. I did not bring money. They did not bring what I want. They put gun in my back.

Now they kill me, for sure.'

Vignoles felt a flush of dread flow over him. The KGB was the stuff of nightmares, but nothing more than a grim rumour that lacked any substance and played no part in his life. He almost doubted its very existence, but now he — and, more alarmingly, Anna — could end up on their hit-list.

The commander was correct, it was time to get off the case and leave this to the 'other agencies' — but, rather like the train he was riding upon, events were gathering momentum and he was not sure if they could just jump off.

CHAPTER THIRTY-ONE

La Vie en Rose
Edith Piaf

Professor Ferluga was somewhere deep inside the British Embassy, as was his colleague, who had been quickly rounded up by the military police. Allied intelligence officers were hard at it, questioning both.

Vignoles was not invited to take part, a decision that did not surprise him, but he was still disappointed and wracked with curiosity. He had but the bare bones of this extraordinary story. Professor Ferluga had, unsurprisingly, refused to give much away whilst standing on the back of a noisy freight train, speaking to an armed man who claimed to be a policeman from England. He would reserve his full confession for someone ranked higher in naval intelligence. But what he had revealed by the time Vignoles delivered him into custody had been enough to stir up the Allies like a stick rammed into a hornets' nest.

However, if Vignoles had felt pleased with his work that morning and anticipated being thanked for bringing two top atomic scientists into Allied hands, he was getting a very rude awakening. He'd been treated as though he were the defecting spy; questioned in a rough and aggressive manner by unpleasant and sinister-looking men, then left alone in a small room with a guard outside, unable to contact the captain, Anna or Rose. And what was happening in Opčine? He was desperate to find out and get them all out of danger.

The discovery of enemy scientists attempting to buy the heavy water was undoubtedly exciting, but surely the pressing matter was the Soviet KGB agents doing a more deadly job of achieving the same goal. Vignoles could not understand why this fact seemed to have escaped everyone's attention, nor why humourless intelligence officers were endlessly questioning him about how he and the captain had known to rescue the professor from the clutches of these enemy agents at that particular moment. It was all too convenient and riddled with coincidence for their liking.

It fell to Brigadier Harper-Tarr to finally break the deadlock and free Vignoles from his virtual captivity. 'You have certainly caused a stir, Vignoles. I demanded results and, by golly, you've done that, eh? Not the neatest piece of work, perhaps. A little too unconventional and messy — but then I'm not Commander Turbayne. He likes everything planned to the last detail. I'm a soldier, and getting my hands dirty and getting the job done is all that matters.' He eyed Vignoles and lit a cigarette. 'Of course, you'll be wondering what the next step is.'

'There's a lot of unfinished business, brigadier.'

'Indeed there is. But this need not concern you now. The scientists are a tremendous haul and will occupy the intelligence boys for weeks, perhaps months. However, the pressing matter is not these boffins but their intriguing counterparts, who seem to have a predilection for killing our boys, don't you agree?'

'Hallelujah! The Soviet agents have to be prime suspects on all counts. They must be arrested and prosecuted.'

'Stopped, certainly. You have succeeded in the task we set you. However, this is an army operation and I'm in command. We've not been idle these last hours, and a plan of action has been drawn up. You will stand down, as shall Captain Henderson — whenever we find him — and let us get on with the mopping-up operation.'

So, that was it, thought Vignoles. He broke the momentary silence. 'May I ask where the three agents are now?'

The brigadier paused for a moment to consider his answer. 'They have slipped off the radar — probably lying low after the encounter they had. However, everything is in place for the wagon to leave on a goods train early this afternoon, and we fully expect them to attempt to join the train along the line.'

Vignoles nodded; it made sense.

The brigadier appeared to be considering something for a moment before continuing. 'These three are KGB foot soldiers. Expendable. The Kremlin won't mind if they come back alive or not. They're of no real interest to us, either. We need their controller — hence our decision to let them put their plan into motion. We must let them think their plan is working. They could lead us into the very heart of the KGB, the Kremlin, deep into the secret service of the Soviet Union. This heavy water is no ordinary haul and it will attract some senior agents, like wasps to a jam pot.'

'And how are you planning to achieve this? Surely someone will need to ride on the train.'

'We have two commandos riding shotgun, replacing the regular Jugoslav soldiers. Both are fluent native speakers and able to fool anyone.'

'How on earth did you get Belgrade to agree to the substitution?'

'We have two of their top scientists in our custody, caught on a very serious spying charge. That's a damned good bargaining tool. They'll offer full co-operation in return for these bumbling fools — when we've finished grilling them. We're forcing the train to take a more circuitous route, up and over a remote mountain line — the Bohinj Railway. This has the advantage of running close to the Italian border for some distance, which may prove useful, whilst giving us more time to think through the endgame. The guard will also be one of ours. He's the best agent in this theatre and fully used to working with the locals. Odd fellow: bit of a loner; prefers to operate under odd code names.' The brigadier raised his eyebrows. 'No accounting for taste.'

'And how do you see this, er, endgame playing out?'

'Classified, inspector.'

'You are prepared to risk them escaping with the heavy water?'

'They won't succeed. The subterfuge only lasted this long because no one took the stories seriously. The cover is blown and we can hole the wagon at any moment to suit our needs. Besides, the Soviets are already building a bomb. A tank of water is not going to change that grim fact — unfortunately.'

Vignoles wanted to ask more, but knew it would be futile. He should be grateful that the brigadier had shared even this much with him. If he was off the case, then so be it, though his detective mind was unsatisfied.

He turned to more pressing, personal matters. 'Is there any news of my wife? I've been unable to get a single message through since I've been holed up here.' He flashed a look of indignation at the brigadier. 'I'm eager that she returns to the safety of the *Albergo*.'

There was a momentary pause before the brigadier replied. 'Ah, now there is a slight complication. Though I'm quite confident it will soon be resolved.'

Vignoles held his breath.

'She seems to have, um, disappeared. Damned nuisance actually, as we're forced to divert valuable resources into looking for her. What the hell were you thinking, Vignoles? Putting two gals on the tail of the bloody KGB! Pity you could not have kept her here, as we advised. And Staff Sergeant Rose Gretton will be put on a charge for this; she had strict orders to keep her nose out of trouble.'

* * * *

Anna watched Vignoles and Henderson cross the road, apparently oblivious to the mounting sense of danger. They remained seated outside the café, finishing the second cup of coffee, intent on monitoring the house and the life on the street, trying to assess what may or may not be significant.

There was the man on his green bicycle with a ladder tied to the crossbar, the horse pulling a cart piled high with watermelons, the postman with his satchel of letters slung across his chest. A British armoured car trundled past with the hatches open and the soldiers seated with their heads in view, each in floppy berets. There was the little ring of the bell as the tram moved away from the terminus building. An army lorry, driven by a fresh-faced lad, turned down a road that looked far too narrow, immediately followed by the sound of crashing gears and revving engine.

'I wonder where Charles is.' Anna was looking worried. 'Perhaps we ought to see if he needs help.'

'Certainly I think we should move. We've remained here too long.' Rose was also looking ill at ease. They stood up and started to saunter along the street, stopping near Rudolf Zerial's bakery to look in at the almost-bare shelves in the window.

'Oh botheration — look!' Anna turned away whilst placing a hand on Rose's uniformed arm and steered her closer towards the virtually empty shop window display. 'Mm... what a lovely smell of bread!'

Rose nodded enthusiastically, but she was looking from under the peak of her cap. 'She's coming our way!'

'Shall we go inside?' Anna added, theatrically.

The woman had exited the courtyard in front of the small house. She stood on the pavement looking up and down the street before turning and walking towards them.

Anna felt the woman's eyes bore into the nape of her neck as she passed. She listened to the agitated tapping of her heels on the pavement, and observed, 'She's not happy about something.'

Rose nodded and watched the woman approach the Fiat. 'Do you think she's rumbled us?'

Anna swished her bright skirt. '*Mea culpa*. I stand out like a hothouse flower. It is possible.'

'She's taking the car. What should we do?'

'We were instructed to follow her, so we'd jolly well better do so — and hang the consequences,' replied Anna.

'It could be dangerous — are you sure?' asked Rose.

'Charles would expect nothing less!' Anna had rediscovered some of her resolve.

The Fiat's exhaust fired up as Anna and Rose reached their jeep. They lost sight of the little car, but the town was small and the Fiat's noise distinctive and so they soon spotted it halfway down the long approach road to the station. It had pulled over beside a low building constructed of limestone blocks, its engine idling and burbling. Rose was able to place the jeep behind a conveniently parked US Army truck and they crouched low on the blind side of this and watched from beneath the high-slung chassis of the vehicle. Rose had a pair of field glasses and was able to identify the building as an office serving the adjacent goods yard. The door was open, so Rose could see that the woman was inside, together with one of her unpleasant-looking compatriots. They were discussing something with a young clerk behind his desk.

'Can you see Charles or the captain?'

'No sign of either.' Rose maintained a running commentary whilst Anna watched their backs and searched for any indication of where her husband might be. 'The clerk looks worried. Shaking his head. They're remonstrating with him. Fingers pointing at a document on the desk. Oh! The man has a gun, and this seems to have changed the mind of the clerk. Papers are being stamped. They're handing over some money. Heads nodding. A deal has been struck. Here they come!'

The man and the woman got in the car and this soon made a swift turn on the pale gravel road and roared past, scattering small stones in its wake.

'They're in a hurry. But what could have happened to Charles?' Anna was biting her lip.

Rose was already swinging the jeep around. 'We can't let them get away. But it's an awful risk; we really should not be doing this.'

'After them, Rose!'

They were soon leaving the town behind and heading east towards the Jugoslav border along a narrow and potholed road that jolted and threw them from side to side. Rose no longer needed to keep the car in sight as the road surface kicked up pale dust that hung in the air in choking clouds and was readily visible above the ragged bushes and dry stone walls of the arid landscape. The air was aloud with the sound of cicadas; a strange, rhythmic, hypnotic noise that came from all sides in waves and dulled the mind and senses.

'I'll hang right back. We don't want to confront them.' As Rose slowed their vehicle, the sound of the insects grew louder.

'Where is this place?' asked Anna, trying to decide how to pronounce the name on a faded enamelled sign that read *Dol pri Vogljah*.

'I'm not sure. We seem to be wandering around all over the place. That's a Slovene name. Have you noticed how the few houses we've passed all have those slogans painted on the walls? I think we're quite near the border.' Rose glanced across at Anna. 'Do you have your passport?'

'I do. But surely we can't cross over?'

Rose puffed out her cheeks. 'I hope not. It could get a bit tricky.'

'Look, we're near the railway.' Anna pointed to a filthy black engine and a straggle of wagons chuffing towards them in a leisurely manner, visible above a border of bushes covered in great, fluffy masses of rose-coloured flowers to their right. Two British soldiers were seated on a crate in an open wagon immediately behind the engine, their arms and legs lobster pink. The train passed close by and waddled away towards Opčine as the now-empty line swung across the road some yards ahead, guarded by a simple red-and-white-painted bar with a counterbalance weight at one end that had been dropped down onto a Y-shaped crutch set into the verge.

Rose was about to comment on the time it was taking for the crossing keeper to lift the barrier, when she realised, too late, that the Fiat was parked at an angle to one side of the road and the Russian man was standing with his back to the barrier in the centre of the road, appearing to shimmer in the heat-haze. The woman was leaning against the side of the car.

'This looks like trouble.'

'Should we turn around?' Anna glanced over her shoulder at the train now disappearing into the distance and the diminishing shapes of the British soldiers, who might have been able to help.

'No room, the lane is narrow.' Rose was slowing the jeep rapidly.

'Halt!' The man stepped forward, his left hand extended in a clear gesture, a pistol in his right. The woman walked over and stood close to where Anna was seated. She had a machine gun slung across one shoulder.

'*Potni list!*' The man's voice was harsh.

'Sorry, I don't understand.' Rose was trying to stall for time.

'Your pass!' There was an ugly scar across one cheek that did nothing to lessen the menace in his voice.

'Is this a border crossing? It does not look like one.' Anna tried smiling innocently, though she felt a stab of dread run through her.

'*Carina. Ja*, is border. Your papers!' The woman looked down at Anna and, as their eyes met, she extended a hand, palm up and too close to Anna's face. The woman was enjoying the power and control. She suddenly laughed and slapped Anna's face. 'Get out!'

Rose had her passport in one hand, but was trying to delay handing it over. 'Why are you not in uniform? Look, I'm an officer with the British Army and Mrs Vignoles has British diplomatic status. Preventing us from continuing on our way will be considered a grave offence and —'

'Silence!' The dark blue passport was wrenched from her hand. Without any pretence at looking at the document, the man slid it into the inside pocket of his suit jacket and pointed the barrel of his gun close to her face. He ordered Rose out of the jeep. Waving his gun he made the two women stand together as his accomplice hopped into their vehicle and smartly reversed it through a narrow opening in a wall, abandoning it out of sight in a farmer's field.

'You can't do this. This is an absolute outrage! Get your hands off me!' Anna flashed her eyes but got a nasty jab in her ribs from the gun, accompanied by a filthy snigger. A palpable sensation of fear was now crawling over her like a fever, and this was not eased by a fleeting glimpse of what were probably the crossing keeper's legs, sticking out from behind his little stone-built cabin in a most unnatural manner.

CHAPTER THIRTY-TWO

Pesem XIV Divizije
Slovene partisan song

Vignoles forced himself to fight the rising sense of panic, knowing that he must call upon all his reserves of courage and remain calm. If he were to have any chance of seeing Anna alive, then he needed to think clearly without the distraction of fear.

He was lying on his back on a hot tarpaulin folded up in the corner of an open wagon, watching the stream of smoke trail its dirty path across the cloudless blue above Trieste. This was coming from the massive *Kriegslok* locomotive as it slogged its way up the escarpment, and he could feel the banking engine jolt and shove the slow-moving train from behind as they retraced the journey he had made only a few hours earlier. Was it so recently? It felt like days ago. A lifetime since he had taken a coffee with Anna and the others.

There was nothing he could do but wait for the train to complete its noisy ascent and cling to the — perhaps vain — hope that he might encounter Anna further along the line. The brigadier had told him the three Soviet agents were missing, but that he thought they would attempt to join the train at a later point. Vignoles had little option but to concur with this reasoning.

Had Anna somehow fallen into Soviet hands? There was a dreadful possibility, and Vignoles was banking on the idea that they would merely use her as protection to allow safe access onto the train. She had diplomatic status, and this carried weight at the highest levels on both sides of any border. He had to hope that these agents were clever enough to appreciate that Anna could be more useful to them alive. There was an alternative, but he could not bear to consider it.

He felt another wave of panic prickle the nape of his neck, and so he breathed the fumes of the steam engine and closed his eyes, trying to savour the evocative scent and sounds and escape for a few moments back to happier times, whilst breathing slowly and deeply. Small bits of clag from the engine dropped in a grey rain on the wooden floor and collected on the tar-smelling sheet. He opened his eyes to watch a wing of Supermarine Seafires wheel in the sky like pale and graceful terns.

But was he doing the right thing? He had so little time to decide. After leaving the brigadier, though under instructions to remain at the *Albergo*, he had instantly decided that this was impossible.

He could not sit around doing nothing, stewing in apprehension, and so had calmly slipped out of the *Albergo* and made his way to the dockyard to observe the special freight train being assembled.

Captain Henderson had appeared, as if by magic, beside him. 'Thought I'd find you here, old boy!'

'You've heard the news about my wife and Rose Gretton?'

'Yes. I feel desperately bad about it. I should never have asked them to follow that woman.'

'No, it was me who asked them. I have that responsibility on my shoulders.' They stood in silence for a moment. 'What do you know of the Soviets?'

'Gone to ground. I had to let them get away from me.' Vignoles looked at the captain, and, for the first time, saw him look beaten. 'I wanted to follow and see what they did, but after showing myself as I did to break up their group, it was hard...' He tailed off.

'And Anna and Rose? Do you think they followed?'

'That's my opinion. We have to assume they are all together and joining the train later. There are troops swarming over Opčine now, but no sign of anyone.'

'I'll take that as a positive sign.' Vignoles stared at the wagons as they clattered together and chewed on the end of his unlit pipe. 'How did you manage to get that lorry to make such a pig's ear of turning the corner?' Vignoles wanted details and facts.

'It worked better than I hoped. I knew I had but a few moments to cause a diversion when this hulking great lorry tried to squeeze down that narrow road. I knew instantly he had a problem, so I hailed him, and gave him some nonsense about being with the SOE and demanded he made a total hash of the job. Full marks to Private Paul Saunders. I shall ensure that his commanding officer mentions him in dispatches and overlooks the dented wing.'

'Saunders? Is he with the 1st Battalion of the Northamptonshire Regiment?'

'He is. Do you know him?'

'I know his father. He'll be pleased that his son helped us out.' Vignoles managed a faint trace of a smile. 'What do you know of the plans for the tanker?'

'Turbayne has advised the Jugoslavs that they must let the train through in exchange for the Allies hushing up the arrest of their scientists, thus sparing their blushes. I suspect they will cut some sort of deal.'

The formation of the wagons over, the shunting engine had trundled off, allowing the powerful freight engine to back up to the head of the lengthy train.

'The brigadier has posted two crack men on board the locomotive,' continued Henderson.

'Commandos?'

'Yes. If the women should be taken aboard, then they're the best you could ask for.'

'I hope so. But I'm going as well.' Vignoles looked directly into the captain's eyes. 'Don't try to stop me, just get me on board.'

Henderson had not argued the point. Perhaps he felt guilty. Whatever his motivation, he had been a great help in assembling two water bottles and some dry biscuits and in pushing a spare clip of bullets into Vignoles's shoulder bag with a promise to 'do what I can'.

The captain distracted the guard long enough for Vignoles to swiftly clamber into an open wagon. This was coupled to the tanker of heavy water on one side and to two old post office wagons, each with a veranda at either end, adjoining the brakevan at the tail of the train, that was similarly equipped with a veranda. With this convenient arrangement he could pass through and contact the guard if needed.

The train drew to a halt for the border control checks to be carried out and Vignoles snapped out of his thoughts, but continued to lay low and fought the urge to peer over the edge of the wagon to observe what was happening.

The air pump on the locomotive wheezed rhythmically. Steam hissed; a dog barked. Boots crunched on gravel, voices shouted. He heard English voices speaking urgently, barking commands and urging haste. There was a heated discussion. He prayed the checks would be as cursory as promised or he would be for the high jump. The open wagon collected the heat from the sun like a furnace and he shrugged off his blazer and rolled up his shirtsleeves, pulling his Panama's brim low over his brow.

A whistle blew and the engine barked once, then, after a short pause, twice in succession, suddenly issuing a roaring series of rapid explosions as the wheels momentarily lost grip and spun. The driver caught the wheel slip and the beats gathered momentum as the long train of wagons jerked and banged. They were soon out of the station and crossing open country, making the dash across the border. As the train picked up speed and a refreshing breeze cooled him, Vignoles eased into a crouching position and looked over the side to assess the situation. The door of the nearest post van looked to be ajar. This would offer greater comfort and shelter from the sun that was burning his skin.

Climbing across the gap between his wagon and the post van was not easy, the train jolting along at a fair lick whilst the wagons were swaying and shunting, first together then apart, the track flashing past at a dizzying speed. Perched with one foot on the coupling hook, the other on the veranda floor, his shoulder bag slung across his chest and blazer tucked through the strap, he pushed himself off from the open wagon and reached for the metal railings, hauling himself to safety just as the train made an especially violent lurch and nearly threw him between the buffers that momentarily parted before slamming together with a heavy clunk. A wrong move and he would have lost his foot in an instant.

Vignoles stepped through the little gate provided in the railings, pushed the door open with his shoulder and stumbled into the comparative darkness of the musty interior, his eyes struggling to adjust after the brightness outside, further hampered by the flip-down shades on his spectacles. As he took a moment to regain his balance and vision, a voice that sounded oddly familiar spoke from the darkness of the far corner.

'Charlie, I was beginning to wonder if you were ever going to join me.'

Vignoles lifted the shades. A man in a railway guard's uniform was seated on a leather bench originally provided for mail sorters. He was leaning back against a counter edging a great many small open compartments in rows along one side of the interior. Vignoles could just make out the names of towns and cities painted in white below each opening. Beside the man's face he could read *Dunaj* and *Maribor* in letters clearer than the man's features.

'I thought it was you when I saw you clamber aboard. You always were more enthusiastic than athletic.' The man laughed.

Vignoles stared and took a step forwards. 'Jimmy? Can it really be you?'

'Of course! Well met, my friend!' The guard stood up, his broad but lean frame blocking out what little light was coming through the narrow slit of filthy glass on the end wall of the wagon. They shook hands, stiffly, unsure of how to react after so much time.

'My God, Jimmy Baron.' Vignoles needed to speak his name aloud to comprehend this unexpected meeting. 'But why are you here?'

'I should ask the same of you, Charlie boy! Aren't you supposed to be keeping the trains safe from Marxist ruffians in that damned Imperialist country of yours?'

'It's your country too.'

'It was. It could be again, one day, when the revolution comes.' He looked wistful. 'But how's your family? Father still preaching the Gospel to the brainwashed?'

Vignoles narrowed his eyes and looked at Baron, the man whom he had once considered his closest friend. He felt a jab of pleasure and was glad that Baron had not become another casualty of war — indeed, he was very much alive and kicking, if rather gaunt. And yet Vignoles also felt an ambiguity at seeing his old drinking partner. Perhaps it was just too much of a surprise; a surprise intensified because of the curious twist of fate that had seen his thoughts so recently forced back into remembrance of Jack's death. He realised he was feeling a confused set of emotions and unadulterated delight was one of the least powerful. 'So what brings you here, of all places, Jimmy?'

'A long and arduous journey, but the struggle was worth it. I've come a long way since Barcelona — and I don't just mean in miles.'

'I can believe that. Who are you working for? The SOE?'

'I prefer not to say.' He winked.

They fell silent a moment, the space filled by the heavy chug-chug of the locomotive.

'Ah, Brigadier Harper-Tarr placed you on board.' Vignoles felt reassured at this realisation.

'You're well informed. That must be why you made detective inspector!'

'How do you know? I've not seen you since... since *that* night. I was just a constable then, and as uncertain and as green as could be.' He laughed nervously. 'After Spain, you just vanished off the face of the earth. Lost somewhere in the confusion of war, I suppose. I heard nothing for years and even then it was little more than a rumour. So how do you know I'm an inspector now?'

'Intelligence. My game is all about knowledge.'

'Did you know I was in Trieste?'

'The appearance of an English detective and his wife is an unusual occurrence and liable to attract attention.'

Vignoles winced. Baron pulled a packet of cigarettes from his breast pocket and offered one to Vignoles, who shook his head, although he extracted his pipe from the folded bundle of his blazer. As the match flared, the yellow light of the flame threw the lines around Baron's eyes into deep relief. Vignoles noticed that his chin and lower cheeks were paler than his nut-brown face.

'It might surprise you, Charlie, but I made the odd, discreet enquiry over the years and found out you were doing all right. I was glad.' Vignoles watched Baron and puffed his pipe into action. 'I kept myself alive during the war by staying informed. Keeping alert. It was the only way when you're living on your wits, deep in occupied territory.'

'In Jugoslavia?'

Baron nodded. 'And other places. But I was with the partisans from '44. Good fighters. Some of the best, and their commitment to the cause was beyond reproach.'

'The cause?'

'Fighting fascism. That was our only objective: to stamp out Hitlerism. It's still there, you know? Like a deadly fungus lying under the leaf mould in a wood, just waiting to reawaken and infect everything around.'

'Are you Shrike?'

Baron laughed. 'I work under many names and identities.'

'But that is you?'

'Ever the detective, eh?'

Vignoles knew he was correct. 'An intriguing choice of name.'

Baron shrugged. 'I couldn't say. I just like the word.'

'So you're the substitute train guard?' If Baron was Shrike, that asked intriguing questions. The Slovene professor had indicated all had gone well in his dealings with his contact — but if the KGB had muscled in, was that so surprising? This man was also a top British agent, working undercover; perhaps trying to work a double-cross with Tito over the heavy water. More importantly, he was a battle-hardened soldier and a good man to have around when in a tight spot.

'I don't know much about being a guard! I'm better at blowing trains up. I became quite an expert and did a lot of it with the partisans. Railways are more your area, I think.' Baron gave a boyish grin that had the effect of shedding the years. 'Are you just as potty about them as you always were?' Vignoles nodded assent, struck by a sudden wave of nostalgia to be back in a time when everything felt less complicated and their friendship knew no barriers. 'Good, you can tell me how to do this correctly.' Baron was opening the far door as he spoke, 'I should return to that van at the rear. I don't want to raise suspicion. Join me. It would be wiser to stay together.'

'So you've been planted on board to do what, exactly?' Vignoles was eager to keep the thread of the conversation going.

'I'm here to ensure that everything goes smoothly. I can't reveal the details — not even to you, Charlie. I didn't survive the war by speaking freely or carelessly. Even to friends,' he narrowed his eyes, 'although your joining us is an unexpected treat. I'm wondering why you smuggled yourself aboard. Why the interest? This won't be an easy ride.'

It was Vignoles's turn to be circumspect. Baron knew that Anna was in Trieste, but was he aware of the recent turn of events? His loyalty was to Anna, and to Rose, for that matter, both of whom he'd dragged into this mess. Any nostalgic warmth faded as he looked at Baron and wondered what secrets the years apart held. What lay behind those eyes that still glinted with a bright intelligence? It might not be wise to disclose everything. 'I have my reasons. I was investigating the deaths of three British soldiers and this train — or at least, the tanker — appears linked in some way. I suppose I just don't like loose ends.' Vignoles tailed off.

Baron nodded from across the divide between the two vans. 'Step across and duck down. I need to wave flags as we pass through Divaca.'

'Where's that?'

'A busy junction, so it would pay to remain unseen and aid us getting a smooth passage through. We're to head north at this point and into the mountains.'

* * * *

The train was slow and time passed with little obvious forward progress. The temperature increased within the brakevan and the water bottles started to run low. Vignoles and Baron alternated between periods of talking and sounding each other out, often retreating to the safety of boyhood reminiscences or choosing silence when the triple subjects of Jack Vignoles, the International Brigades and Baron's recent activities came too close for comfort. At these moments of mutual silence, Vignoles observed the hot Karst countryside slide past in a vision of limestone cottages and walls, little white churches, fig trees, vineyards green against the red soil, and narrow strips of tilled and cultivated land with the occasional horse or dun-coloured cow. He also looked along the long train as it snaked ahead, and his eyes were repeatedly drawn to the curiously ominous bulk of the black tank wagon. Though he knew it contained only water (and quite a lot of brandy) and this water was harmless without complex processes to render it deadly, he could not wholly erase the image of travelling with a ticking atomic bomb a few yards away.

He spent most of the time, however, searching for any sign of the KGB and its hostages. Each time the lengthy train slowed or halted at a signal, he eagerly anticipated a sign of movement. But there had been none. He reassured himself with the knowledge that the train had proceeded so slowly that a car could easily overtake them.

The afternoon shadows lengthened and the hills ahead grew steadily steeper, bringing a welcome cool tang that hinted at fresher mountain air. Far ahead, Vignoles could see towering peaks glowing orange and gold in the late sun. A raging river of milky turquoise water alternately foamed over rapids or ran smooth like poured paint between rocks in a deepening winding gorge. The water looked almost unnatural with the intensity of the colour. The train squealed around a tight curve away from the river and the engine whistled. Vignoles could see they were about to draw to a halt at a tiny wayside station. The stationmaster in a dark uniform and cap held aloft a white lollipop-shaped baton with a red disc at the end, to ensure that they stopped. A porter stood close by, arms behind his back.

'We're close to the Italian border — so close we could almost throw a stone across,' explained Baron. 'The station staff are often nervy in this border country. They might walk the length of the train, so be careful not to let them see you.'

Vignoles nodded and reluctantly hunched down against one of the van walls. Baron stood on the veranda, flag in hand, but not before first unfastening the cover on the black leather holster threaded onto his belt and slipping the safety catch off the revolver held inside.

There were voices talking in the distance, someone shouted, a laugh at a joke and a harsh metallic squeak as something moved.

'We're taking water. They've just swung the crane across.' Baron spoke softly. 'Damn, but they're getting too nosy, poking around the wagons. I'm going to have a word. Stay out of sight!'

Baron gave a commanding stare before hopping off the train.

A maddening quiet descended. Vignoles could hear a few sounds from the engine, but little else. A buzzard mewed like a kitten high in the sky above. Curiosity was getting too much to bear, so he peered cautiously through the grimy ducket window that gave a view forwards along the train and was surprised to see the platform empty. He instantly sensed something was wrong. He stood and walked onto the veranda, keeping out of sight of the platform and stood listening. He removed his hat, crouched low, edged close to the opposite side of the train and peered around.

His heart leaped. Anna was standing just a few yards away!

Her back was to him and Rose was beside her. He swallowed hard and fought the desire to call out. The woman he had seen entering the laundry and in the *Stella Polaris* was pointing a machine gun at both women, her rouged mouth formed into an angry curl. Her beret almost covered one eye and this made her look slightly crazy. The gun wavered menacingly between the two as she invited them, none too nicely, and in broken English, to climb aboard the nearest of the ancient post vans.

Vignoles pulled his head back behind the edge of the wagon and drew breath. This was not the time to be seen. They were now in the next vehicle, almost within touching distance. But what if they walked across into the brakevan? He would be discovered — and then what? He remembered his gun was inside his shoulder bag and, keeping as low as he could, he scuttled back into the brake and retrieved his pistol and the spare clip, then crouched low, weighing up his options.

But where were the British commandos? And where was Jimmy? This was puzzling. Had these crack men missed such a trick? Vignoles guessed that only the woman agent was holding Anna and Rose captive in the nearest van. If that were so, then what had become of the other two? He decided it was fortuitous that the Soviets had evaded the soldiers for the time being, for at least Anna and Rose were alive, looking reasonably well and aboard a train monitored and guarded by British commandos and one of the finest undercover operators — his old chum, Jimmy! Vignoles allowed a knowing half-smile to flicker across his face. Now he had got over the immediate shock of the discovery, he started to think the situation through. It made sense. Baron must have known all along that this was where they were going to make their move — perhaps a tip-off before the train departed? Baron had deliberately walked away — after first giving strict instructions to Vignoles not be seen and to stay in the brake. He pulled a wry face; he'd very nearly blown that through his own stupid curiosity! So what of Baron and the commandos? The story of the station staff being nosy was just an excuse to join the soldiers and the station staff, perhaps in a smoke and a chat and a shot of *grappa* some way from the train, thereby allowing the KGB officers and their hostages unimpeded access. Leave the door partially open, and the enemy will step right in. Might the post vans even have been placed in the train as a deliberate ploy to lure them aboard? The difficult part was going to be getting Anna and Rose to safety.

Baron swung himself up onto the veranda. He looked slightly flushed and darted Vignoles a questioning look. 'Did you keep out of sight?' Baron spoke in a harsh whisper.

'Of course!' Vignoles allowed a glint in his eye so Baron would understand that he knew what had happened.

Baron just stared back, a slight twitch to one cheek his only movement. 'Good. Keep your head down,' he hissed. He spun around and leaned over the side to blow his whistle and wave his green flag furiously.

'Steady on,' said Vignoles, 'we can work together on this.'

The train lurched into motion with many groans and complaints, a wheel squealed unpleasantly in a high-pitched note. Baron closed the door. He stood looking at Vignoles, his face inscrutable. 'Can we? That would be good — for old times' sake.' His eyes were dark and glassy, and his voice had lost some of its warmth. Perhaps he was on edge, but Vignoles sensed a harder, more aggressive note. 'I'll be calling the shots, though. I recall you walked away the last time we needed you and left your comrades to go it alone — and we all know the consequences.' He shrugged. 'Perhaps it's time to make amends?'

CHAPTER THIRTY-THREE

MAD DOGS AND ENGLISHMEN

Noël Coward

'Right, we've heard enough — arrest them!'

DS Trinder looked sideways at DI Minshul and noticed the mischievous gleam in his eye. The man was clearly enjoying himself.

'But guv, there's nothing illegal going on here. We need to collect evidence.' Trinder was trying to keep his voice low. 'Now we know who they are, we could obtain a photograph from their college and start to show their faces around, see if they jog some memories.' Trinder was whispering furtively and urgently, desperate to prevent Minshul from reacting. 'If we could obtain something with their fingerprints on, we can see if they match with those on the spanner and the paint tin. I was thinking of taking the water jug and glasses they have on stage.'

'Evidence? I can't be doing with that.' One of the audience members gathered in the dingy church hall turned in his wooden seat and gave a momentary glance of annoyance at Minshul. 'Get 'em down the station and we'll soon beat all the evidence we need out of 'em! Come on!'

* * * *

The evening was not going anything like Trinder had planned. In fact it was turning into a complete shambles. The problem was quite simple: Detective Inspector Minshul.

The DI was not supposed to have been there at all and there was little doubt in Trinder's mind that if he had stayed away (as he had promised to do) things would have gone more satisfactorily. Unfortunately, the DI had decided that he had been too hard on Trinder the last time they had spoken and taken a train back to Leicester that afternoon and arrived, unannounced, at the detective department offices just as the sergeant was midway through explaining his strategy for the visit that evening to the Better Dead Than Red talk.

'I reckoned as I'd come and see what I can do to help chivvy things along. Lend a hand. If we really do have a gang of mad terrorists stalking the line, then your DI should be standing firm beside you, not at home digging the potatoes!'

'Thank you, guv. Most thoughtful.' Trinder gave a pathetic smile and inwardly groaned.

'Carry on. Fascinating though your plan is, I'm waiting for you to get to the interesting part.'

'What do you mean, guv?'

'You *are* going to be hauling them in at some point in the proceedings, aren't you?' Minshul asked.

'No, the plan was for Lansdowne and I to attend in plain clothes and observe, collect any printed materials that we feel pertain to the case and to talk to the speakers, though in such a manner as to not reveal our true interest in their meeting and organisation. Gently sound them out and see if we can make a connection.'

'Bloody Nora! "Gently sound them out". If what you've got written on that blackboard is correct, then this is no stamp-collecting group.' Minshul waved towards a carefully composed list of events, evidence, clues and neatly interconnecting arrows in coloured chalks — the efforts of DC Blencowe — that made compelling links towards a central statement written in bold, pinkish-red: Better Dead Than Red. 'They're dangerous. They're train wreckers — or as good as. We can't allow them another single day to go around assaulting our men. No, we'll move in and get down to business.'

'But we don't have any evidence of their involvement.'

'We will, sergeant, we will!'

* * * *

Although he had been forewarned that this was going to be Minshul's approach, Trinder still felt his ears burn as he stood up, his chair scraping the floor and causing the speaker to look his way. Together with WPCs Lansdowne and Benson (Benson having been compelled to join them at the very specific request of DI Minshul) he walked towards the low stage down the centre aisle between rows of empty chairs towards the two young and smartly dressed men on the stage, one of whom was in full flow, denouncing the 'dangerous march towards Marxism and the herding of the masses towards the chasm of communist ideology, with its twin perils of a peasant-worker state.'

A hand-painted banner made from an old white bed sheet and red paint hung limply from the rear wall, the letters formed so they appeared to drip with blood whilst ominously declaring;

THE REDS ARE COMING!
STOP THIS EVIL TIDE BEFORE IT'S TOO LATE

The drama of their banner seemed at odds with the well-mannered demeanour of the two young men with foppish fringes, expensively tailored shirts, silk ties and blazers. They spoke well and with perfect Received Pronunciation. These were well-educated chaps and not your average felon.

'I say, you're eager! We're fielding questions afterwards.' The speaker flipped his hair clear of his brow and gave Trinder a look of mild annoyance. His colleague appeared more interested in WPC Lansdowne in her light summer dress. Both policewomen were attracting attention when seen alongside the other members of the threadbare audience, composed as it was of two sour-faced men who looked like shopkeepers, a florid-faced man of considerable girth with double chins and a hipflask resting on his belly, who appeared to be asleep; an elderly lady, who was probably only there for something to do and the promise of a cup of tea; and two young and eager men in the front row who were almost certainly friends of the speakers.

'Aye, you can answer our questions — but you won't be doing that here, but down the station.' DI Minshul stepped past Trinder, who was hesitating at the foot of the three steps leading up to the stage, and bounded up. 'Come along — we're police officers and this is a raid!'

'What? I would have you know that we have permission, in writing, from the parish clerk himself to give this talk!'

'This is quite out of order! How dare you!' The speaker's friend had pulled himself away from admiring Lansdowne's legs as Trinder moved to stand close beside him.

'Show me your warrant card!' The speaker drew himself up as tall as he could and tried to look confident. 'I know my rights!'

WPC Benson gave an apologetic look. 'I think it best if you just come along quietly with us, sir.' She placed one hand on the speaker's upper arm, hoping to urge him to comply.

Trinder was not quite sure of the exact sequence of events that followed, but he was of the opinion that it was her hand being brushed aside — though with no more force than was absolutely necessary — that triggered everything to spiral into a horrible confusion.

Minshul, who had taken an instant aversion to the young man's Rugby School accent, had taken this brushing aside of his favourite WPC's hand as an act of resisting arrest and grabbed the man by the arms. There had been a scuffle, a few shouts and the next thing they knew, a small table had fallen over in a crash of breaking glass as the carafe of water and glasses that it had supported exploded on the wooden floorboards.

The two young men in the audience vaulted onto the stage to join in, and before he was fully aware of what was happening, Trinder felt a rush of air as someone took a swing, narrowly missing his jaw. Bodies collided and tussled, the water made the floor slippery underfoot and Benson lost her footing, though whether pushed or not was unclear, and afterwards she was quite unable to point any blame, despite the DI demanding that she specifically name the speaker as having been responsible. Whatever the reason for her falling, she was on the floor and her hand was cut deeply on the splinters of glass. Like a red rag to a bull, DI Minshul flew into a fury when he saw her nursing a hand dripping blood, and where before it had been a slight fracas that would soon have quietened down, mayhem ensued for what felt like an eternity, but was probably less than a minute. By the end, Minshul had given black eyes to two of the men and had secured the speaker's arms behind his back in handcuffs. Trinder had taken a few blows to the face and body, but had given more effective ones in return and soon had the second speaker pinned to the floor. Lansdowne had felled one of the young men from the audience and in so doing, inadvertently sent him sprawling off the side of the stage and headfirst into the front row of chairs. He was slowly and painfully sitting up, but had lost all interest in the fight. The fourth man had escaped.

The elderly lady clapped her hands slowly. 'Bravo! Bravo! I've not had such an entertaining evening in months.'

'By 'eck, sergeant! That were a bloody good evening's work, I'd say.' Minshul was grinning from ear to ear as he adjusted his collar and tie.

As the two policemen panted and caught their breath, the distant ringing of police bells drew ominously closer. The evening was about to become even more farcical when, a few moments later, the Leicester Constabulary arrived on the scene and charged into the hall, batons drawn, the blue lights from their Black Maria on their backs through the open doors.

Chief Superintendent Badger was not going to be amused.

CHAPTER THIRTY-FOUR

PUNTARSKA

Jugoslav partisan song

The train restarted in a volcano of noise and smoke followed by a noticeable increase in speed. Vignoles shot a glance at Baron, who said, 'I told the driver to get a move on. We're going too slowly.'

'You're expecting something to happen? You know where and when?'

'Soon enough.' Baron checked his wristwatch, something he had been doing with increasing frequency.

'Are you going to share that with me?'

Baron made a noncommittal gesture.

'We at least need a plan to rescue the hostages.'

'Hostages?'

'You know that they boarded the train?' Vignoles started to feel worried.

Baron surprised Vignoles by shaking his head in a contemptuous manner. 'Idiots! How did they think bringing them along would do any good?' He shrugged his shoulders, 'There is no plan — they're not even supposed to be here.'

'But we must do something! We must rescue them.' Vignoles stood up, feeling a horrible lurch in his stomach that was not caused by the motion of the train.

'Keep down!' Baron growled and Vignoles crouched again, aware that he must not prompt the female agent to use her gun. 'I assume one of them is your wife?' asked Baron.

'Yes. The other is a serving member of His Majesty's armed forces. To do nothing is simply not an option.'

'A distressing situation, but we must look at the operation as a whole and not allow sentiment to cloud our judgement.'

'Sentiment? Rescuing them has to be part of any successful operation! Before we left Trieste there was talk of them jumping aboard, so I can't believe they weren't part of your plans.'

'Oh, don't give me all that bourgeois rubbish about honour and doing the "right thing". It's so damned English.' Baron laughed. 'It's almost charming, in a way.' He now had an edge to his voice that was contemptuous.

'The brigadier will put a rescue operation into action — of that I'm sure.'

'Quite right, and it's underway about now!' Baron glanced at this wristwatch again. 'The aircraft will be airborne. I might detest what they stand for, but I admit a respect for the timekeeping and accuracy of the Fleet Air Arm. Damn good pilots; just a shame they're on the wrong side.'

'What do you mean, "the wrong side"?'

Baron waved the question away. 'But unless they're late, this leaves us no time for rescuing hostages. Sorry, Charlie.'

'Aircraft? What are you talking about?' Vignoles felt a cold sweat form on his brow.

'We'll cross the Solkan bridge soon. I'm sure you'll find it fascinating. Did you know it has the longest single stone arch in the world? About an 85-metre span and pretty much the same above the icy waters of the river. The pilots can get a good, low angle of attack along the gorge and that should help minimise damage to the bridge. The train, however, will take a few rounds from the cannon. It'll be a total wreck.' Baron paused as Vignoles's jaw dropped open. 'Of course, there *is* always a remote possibility of survival, but those cannon shells are vicious things; they rip through wood, steel and concrete without noticing.' He pulled a rueful face. 'Ah, but then there are the partisans waiting in the hills to mop up. They know that at least one woman on board is an agent with the hated KGB. No one loves the KGB. Odd that? So I don't suppose they will stop to ask questions before shooting any women they see trying to jump off.'

'They're going to destroy the train? But why?' Vignoles was aghast.

'We must prevent the tank wagon falling into the wrong hands. Ten seconds of cannon fire will shred the train to pieces.'

'But this cannot be right! The brigadier said the idea was for the train to cross Jugoslavia and travel further — leading us to the heart of the Kremlin. Destroying it now makes no sense!' Vignoles was staring at Baron in confusion.

'Oh, but it makes sense on many levels — levels way above concerns about you and your dear wife.'

The brakes snatched at the wheels as the train started to slow, and Vignoles saw a flicker of annoyance cross Baron's brow. Vignoles darted into the ducket and looked along the length of the train. 'A distant signal at danger,' he muttered to himself, his mind racing. He turned back to face Baron. 'I don't believe what you're saying.'

Baron snorted. 'Listen, I spent three years fighting the Germans alongside the partisans. We agreed strategies, we gathered intelligence and we did all we could to plan in meticulous detail, but most important of all we changed everything and anything the moment the situation demanded it — even at the cost of comrades' lives. The only outcome that mattered was stopping the fascists. Our lives meant nothing. The greater good was all. So now the plans are changing to suit the greater good. I weighed up the odds and made a telephone call as we took water. The good brigadier — credulous old buffoon that he is — was waiting for my directions.'

Vignoles licked his lips. His voice was hoarse as he spoke. 'And what did you say?'

'There were no hostages aboard. That the two commandos had been incapacitated by the KGB agents who were now aboard with the tank — oh, don't worry, the commandos' pride is dented but nothing more; it was a simple job to lure them into the station and jump them. They're trussed up like chickens in the toilets.'

'You jumped our own soldiers?' Vignoles was staring at his old friend, the harsh shadows of the sun throwing his face into sharp relief, the guard's cap shading his eyes. Even as he was speaking, Vignoles was suddenly struck by Baron's similarity to someone he had seen only recently. 'Why would you do such a thing?' Vignoles was slowly pacing the floor, his right hand straying towards the pocket that held his pistol, a sickening realisation creeping over him.

'No need to waste more life than absolutely necessary.'

'I don't believe you. Am I supposed to understand that you deliberately lied about Anna and Rose, knowing that by so doing their lives are at risk, but you saved the lives of the soldiers?'

Baron adopted a look of mock innocence. 'I didn't see the girls climb aboard. Listen: I'll share a secret with you; I owe you that much.'

Vignoles slid the safety catch off.

'If the British destroy the tanker along with the Soviet agents, they will do everyone a favour. I am quite sure that the British and the Jugoslavs will cut a deal. The attack will be blamed on *Il Blocco di Trieste* or some other vile Italian fascist organisation.' Baron spat on the floor. 'We're close enough to the border to be plausible. Finding a mutual enemy to play scapegoat will satisfy both sides — publicly. Privately, a combined operation will serve to ease tensions on either side of the border. Any mention of the embarrassingly awkward involvement of the KGB will be conveniently overlooked, to everyone's relief. The two incompetent scientists will be used as a further bargaining tool. My bet is, the British will send Churchill over to talk with Kardelj, or to Tito himself — they seemed to get along famously, after all — and Tito's foolish plans for an A-bomb will be dropped soon after, in exchange for the return of those bumbling idiots.'

Vignoles was staring at Baron in horror. There was a callous logic to what he heard, but he could not believe that he would deliberately lie about the presence of the women. As Vignoles was considering this appalling revelation, the train gathered speed again and, despite the noise of the wagons and the engine attacking the gradient, he thought he heard an odd little sound, rather like the popping of a champagne cork, from the post van at his back. 'I see the reasoning, but the attack can be delayed until we rescue Anna and Rose.'

'Sorry, out of time — they're closing in even as we speak.'

Vignoles suddenly made a connection. He imagined Baron with a long and unkempt beard and the guard's cap replaced by one bearing the red star with the yellow hammer and sickle. 'Did I see you in the *Stella Polaris*? Were you in the churchyard?'

'Too late for such questions — listen!' Baron dropped the window in the side door, allowing in a blast of air upon which hung the unmistakable drone of Merlin engines. 'I'm sorry, Charles, that it was you, of all people, who had to get tangled in our web, and I'm sure your Anna doesn't deserve what follows.' He made a wry smile that appeared genuine, and yet his eyes communicated an unshakeable conviction. 'As an old friend to another, I invite you to jump off the train and face the People's Army, or stay and take your chances with your wife.' He made an expansive gesture, both arms spread wide.

That was his first, and perhaps only, mistake.

As Baron's arms were at their widest, the door from the veranda flew open, knocking Vignoles aside and allowing Captain Henderson a clear view of his target. There was another 'pop', just like the cork Vignoles had heard a moment earlier, and Baron clutched his shoulder, a stain of red instantly flooding over his fingers. Another 'pop' and Baron's legs folded to the floor, an ugly tear in his fatigues across his thigh.

'Don't move! Don't try anything or I'll kill you — so help me God!' Henderson stepped into the van, both hands on his pistol, the barrel of which was lengthened by a silencer. 'Mrs V and Gretton are okay!'

Vignoles exhaled breath in a huge rush of relief and stared at Baron in horror. He could now see that he was indeed one of the men they had tailed. How had he been so remiss as to not make the connection earlier? He shook his head in disbelief and anger.

'The woman agent is dead,' said Henderson, without taking his eyes off Baron, 'the other man's on the train, near the engine.'

'But the air attack? Have you stopped it?'

Henderson flicked his eyes across to Vignoles for a moment, keeping his gun trained on Baron. 'No time, old boy. I had to work like billy-o to get this far. Damn it, we don't have long, though! Get the women in here — at least at the tail we have a better chance.'

Baron started to laugh. 'We can all go together.' He grimaced and clutched his shoulder, his breathing laboured. 'Shot by your own aircraft — I like the irony.'

'Shut up, traitor! I should kill you now!' Baron made as if to stand up, but Henderson placed a bullet in the wooden floor between his knees. 'Gretton!'

'Sir!' The young staff sergeant appeared beside Henderson.

'Get the woman's gun and stand guard. Any funny stuff, just kill him.'

Rose swallowed, made an uncertain salute and rushed back into the post van.

Vignoles had already dashed across the void between the wagons and flung his arms around Anna. 'Thank God we're together.' He took in the warmth of her body and pressed his cheek into her hair for a precious second or two before gently easing back. 'We have little time. The train is going to be attacked from the air as we cross the next bridge. We have the best chance of survival here at the rear.' Anna's eyes were wide, but she made a gallant job of masking any fear and nodded understanding. 'If the attack starts, lie flat on the floor and keep your head down. I'll see if I can detach our wagon from the train.'

He gave what he hoped was a comforting grin to both women and ushered them into the brakevan. He looked into the dark interior of the post van and saw the shape of the dead woman slumped against the wall, a dark spot of red in the centre of her forehead and a small hole in one of the far end windows. It had been a neat piece of shooting.

He swivelled around and looked down at the coupling chains linking the wagons together, now stretched taut by the weight of the train as it attacked the incline. How could he force one of the links over the deeply curved hook whilst under such strain?

Anna stood on the opposite veranda, holding two long poles used by shunters to uncouple wagons. 'These might help.'

'Only if we can relieve the strain on these links. Can you see the bridge ahead? The line should level out as we approach it.'

Vignoles instinctively removed his spectacles and quickly polished them whilst he was thinking. 'If I apply the brakes to these post vans and make them drag their heels, our wagon should then push up close as it will be moving more freely once we hit the level track.' He winced at his logic. He was no physicist. 'If we get very lucky, we could then lift the chain off. It will just have to work!'

Vignoles was already swinging himself over the side and standing on the access steps, his back brushed by stands of rosebay willowherb that lined the verdant bank of the single-track line. He looked up as Henderson called out, 'I'll do the same on the other!'

'Good man!' Vignoles looked down. The ballast was rushing past his feet and the noise was deafening. However, he was more alarmed by the now-constant drone of aircraft engines and, glancing upwards, he caught a fleeting sight of two pale shapes with clipped tips to their elegant elliptical wings as they curved high across the sky.

He swallowed and eased himself forward, placing one foot on the small metal flap covering the oil reservoir on the axlebox, then reached forward to grasp the long brake handle. He was at full stretch, clinging on with all his might with his left hand and reaching with his right. He had to somehow lift this handle then extract the metal peg wedged into one of a series of holes that held it in place. Once the peg was removed and the handle released, the full weight of the brakes would be applied to the wheels.

He clutched at the side of the vehicle and edged further forwards, finding another precarious foothold on the metal brake rigging. He kicked at the metal peg but it wouldn't budge. He cursed, placed both hands on the long lever, steadying himself with his shoulder pressed hard to the van side as it rocked and swayed, and somehow lifted the lever upwards, working the toe of a shoe into the little loop of safety chain attached to the end of the peg by bending his knees. He wrenched his leg away from the wagon whilst pulling himself upright at the same time and it came free. The handle felt like it weighed a ton; he let it drop and, at the same instant, immediately reached out to cling onto any suitable handhold he could find as the brakes started squealing in an ear-splitting noise that made his head spin. He could smell the shoes burning on the wheels as he stepped onto the brake handle to force them to bind harder. More vegetation swished at his legs and across his back and he narrowly missed being clouted by a post supporting a warning sign.

He worked his way back to the steps and Anna gave him a helping hand onto the veranda. His legs were like jelly and he was breathing hard. He heard the brakes start complaining from the forward vehicle. 'See if the captain needs help. I'll set to work here.' Vignoles took one of the shunting poles and attempted to work the metal hook onto the end underneath the heavy coupling link, but there was still no give from the taut chain.

Anna reappeared with Henderson, whose suit was crumpled and dusted with pollen and a confetti of petals and small leaves. He took the other pole, vaulted the veranda railings, and stood with one foot on a buffer shank of the adjacent vehicle, straddling the void in between as he threaded the end of the pole through one of the chain links and attempted to lever it upwards as Vignoles did the same. Both men strained with the effort, faces screwed tight with concentration.

'I can see the bridge,' Anna called out, 'about quarter of a mile ahead.'

'Come — *on!*' Henderson roared in frustration as he threw all his weight onto the pole, which started to bend alarmingly.

'They're closing up!'

The train was slowing, causing the wagons to bunch together and their free-rolling van to press against the dragging post wagons, relieving the pressure. 'One — last — effort!' Vignoles felt the sweat pour from his brow as he gave every ounce of energy into forcing the unwilling link over the backward curved coupling hook.

'Aagh!' exclaimed Henderson, his face red.

As the link sprang free, Vignoles's pole snapped in his hands with a loud 'crack', the sudden release in tension throwing him hard against the veranda railings and winding him. Henderson was thrown backwards and in a flash was gone.

'Captain!' Anna leaned over the side and spotted him, flat on his back in a thick embankment of grass and flowers. He moved an arm and Anna took this as a positive sign. 'I think he's okay.'

Vignoles was clutching his chest. 'Oh!' He sucked air in through his teeth and stayed bent over. 'I... I think I've... ouch, cracked a... rib.' He steadied himself and eased up into a standing position, gulping air like a beached fish and moving like an old man. 'Damn, that's sore!' He tried to look over his shoulder. 'All right in there?'

'I've got him covered!' Rose was leaning against the open door, propping it open, the machine gun steady in her hands, her face pale, but with a circle of red on each cheek.

Vignoles nodded painfully, although he had regained his breath. He rested upon the veranda rail and looked forwards along the line. The brakevan, now detached, was coasting but gradually slowing down. Ahead was the rest of the train, steaming along a straight and level section of elevated line that he could see veering to the left on a sharp curve onto the approaches of what he thought must be the Solkan bridge.

The deep gorge of the river fell away sharply to the left, whilst ahead the graceful pale limestone of the bridge commenced in a series of narrow preparatory arches, that strode away from sheer rock faces before vaulting across the vertiginous gap on one graceful and slender stone arch that looked too fragile to support a train. It appeared almost to hang in the air, the late sun painting it a warm yellow in sharp contrast with the sheer cliffs behind, which were plunged into deep blue shadows as the gorge turned a corner and was shaded by a great promontory of rock and dense woodland on the far side. The river roared over rapids below and Vignoles caught glimpses of the foaming turquoise water. Anna stood beside him, her hand on his shoulder.

'We must stop this brakevan and get off.' Vignoles turned towards the tall column with a metal handle at the top that was set into the floor of the veranda, but winced as he felt his ribs burn with pain. He pulled a face and gave Anna a pleading look. Without hesitating, she took over, releasing the safety chain and spinning the handle around until the brakes started to bite.

'You and Rose jump off. I'll take my chance here with Baron. Ouch, my ribs are burning like fire.'

'Darling, I can't possibly leave you in this state. And Rose has her job to do, as well.' Anna gave her husband a look that brooked no dissent; besides, there was no time to argue.

As they came to a halt just a few yards from the small retaining walls that marked the start of the approach across the void, the train was now almost broadside to them exactly equidistant from each end of the long bridge. There was a crackling roar of a throaty exhaust as a Seafire flew low along the gorge, waggling its wings slightly to adjust the line of fire from the twin cannons protruding from its wings. These burst into life in a deafening rattle of sound that echoed around the gorge, as thin traces of vapour marked the streams of shells flashing through the air. A raking series of explosions riddled the parapet of the bridge, throwing up great clouds of limestone dust like bursting bags of flour, and wooden-bodied vans blew apart in a mass of splinters and chippings. One wagon was lifted clean off the track and flung over the side, instantly transformed into a crumpled mess of metal and firewood. The aircraft's engine rose to a high-pitched note as the pilot lifted its nose sharply and skimmed over the stricken train, soaring upwards whilst twisting in the air like a graceful bird of prey.

The second fighter was now swooping down, adopting a different angle of attack. As it lined up, a man suddenly stood up in the middle of an open wagon immediately behind the locomotive tender and released a burst of machine gun fire towards the diving aircraft, but his target was too fast and twin jets of cannon shells further ripped the train apart, striking the black tank wagon and causing it to explode in a great shower of liquid, rendered golden by the sun. The solitary machine-gunner instantly fell silent. As the aircraft pulled up, pieces of debris, dust and what looked like millions of shreds of paper slowly tumbled towards the river, twisting, turning and falling in slow motion. The graceful shapes of the Seafires dipped behind the Italian hills and an eerie calm fell across the scene.

The footplate crew stood beside their miraculously intact engine, staring in blank horror at the scene, aghast at the twisted frames and shattered, bullet-riddled wreckage strewn across the bridge, a thin, curling skein of smoke from the locomotive mingling with the dust and smoke of burning and lazily drifting down the river gorge.

'Crikey!' Anna was still holding the brake handle.

'That's the end of the heavy water — and good riddance! I presume that was the other Soviet agent with the machine gun? He stood no chance. And neither would we.' Vignoles slowly straightened himself and walked, a little stiffly, into the brakevan. He looked down at Baron, now seated in a pool of red. After a few moments he spoke. 'We need to get that seen to. You've lost a lot of blood.' Vignoles's face was impassive.

'Don't bother.'

'Anna, can you see if there is anything that would serve as a bandage?'

'I told you not to bother.' Baron shifted his weight and sat more upright against the side of the wooden van. 'I'd rather die than be taken your prisoner.' He spat the words out. 'My life counts for nothing; only the triumph of the great struggle for the people!' He started to cough, 'but you'd not understand that. You never did, eh, Charlie? What is one life lost along the great march to socialism?' He stared at Vignoles. 'Jack understood. He died proud.'

'With a bullet in his back on the waterfront in Barcelona? I hardly think so.'

'What would you know?'

'Who do you *really* work for? Not the SOE?'

'Of course not!' Baron started to pull a handkerchief out of his trouser pocket, still spluttering and coughing. 'At least not in the sense you mean.'

'Damn you, Jimmy. You double-crossed us!'

'And not just the British! I fooled all of you. Haha...' He tailed off into a wracking series of coughs, holding the handkerchief to his mouth as his face flushed pink with the exertion. 'That fool Harper-Tarr wanted a way into the heart of the KGB.' He gasped for air, then again pressed the square of grubby cotton to his mouth.

'Do you need some water?'

Baron waved the offer away with his hand. 'I was right here, under your noses all the time... aagh!' He suddenly convulsed, his eyes staring as bubbles of spittle formed at the corners of his mouth. His body twitched once, then twice in spasm, before falling limp, his head lolling to one side.

'Cyanide pill! Hell and damnation, he's taken his secrets with him.' Henderson, looking even more bedraggled, was leaning on the far doorpost and breathing hard.

Vignoles looked down at Baron's dead body, saying nothing for a few moments. 'He was once my closest friend,' he murmured. He paused, and everyone stared at him in amazement at his revelation. 'You think you know someone, but now I wonder if you ever really do. I knew he was a communist, and he was always passionate, idealistic, one could almost say romantic about the idea — but to come to this? To betray his King and Empire?' He shook his head.

'Our problems aren't over yet.' Henderson moved his head to suggest they look outside. Men in leather jackets and caps, carrying pistols and with sour expressions, accompanied by uniformed soldiers all with the red star on their caps, were approaching the brakevan along the track.

'I suggest we put our guns down and wave something white, then pray that diplomacy will get us out of this pickle.'

As they stood on the rear veranda Vignoles fished a big white handkerchief out of his pocket. Anna took it from him and began to wave it, linking her free arm through his. With as much calm and nonchalance as he could muster, Vignoles lit his pipe. 'Stiff upper lip, everyone!'

CHAPTER THIRTY-FIVE

BELLA CIAO

Italian partisan song

Vignoles settled back into the seat cushions, enjoying his pipe. Anna was snoozing, her head against his shoulder, an open book on her lap. His newspaper had slipped to the floor. The sun was pleasantly warm in the compartment, though without the ferocity of the Mediterranean and Vignoles was glad of that. He need not draw the curtains across the window and so hide the view of the lush Kent countryside with its pretty villages, hop fields and oasthouses.

As the pale blue smoke curled from the briarwood bowl into the sunlight, he listened to the exhaust of the rather splendid locomotive that was hauling their boat train towards London. It was an attractive beast that went by the name of *Howard of Effingham* and was still painted in the cheerful bright green of the old Southern Railway with big 'sunshine' letters to that effect along its tender. There was something inescapably summery about the Southern — a far cry from the dour and uniform black of the engines on the Continent.

Vignoles was glad to be back in England and eager to stand on the familiar platforms at Marylebone, filled with boyish anticipation as an old and familiar friend of an engine — perhaps *Grand Parade* or *Butler-Henderson* — backed onto the waiting coaches in readiness to haul them to Leicester, and then home to their semi in Belgrave and Birstall. He knew that Anna shared the same emotions. As they had stepped off the ferry at Dover, she had taken a deep lungful of English air and stated, without irony, 'There's no place like home.'

'You're not sad to leave Italy behind?'

'Of course. I shall miss the blue of the Adriatic, the scent of the herbs, the taste of fresh figs and the hot sun on my back. But I understand now what Dorothy meant in that film.' She paused and looked wistful. 'Though I never did get to see Miramare.'

'It was overrun with military. It might have proved to be just as disappointing as the *Wizard of Oz*. Some things are perhaps better left as just a dream.'

'But we will return one day. When the soldiers have gone and things are more settled. It would be nice to see everywhere under less fraught circumstances.'

'I shall look forward to that day, though I fear it's an awfully long way off.'

Vignoles took another puff on his pipe and readjusted himself, his heavily bandaged ribs still aching. Anna snuggled closer.

Fraught was a word that had characterised the many tedious and sometimes alarming hours that had followed their arrest. They had been bundled into an army truck and driven for what felt like forever until they were manhandled into a stinking, ill-lit concrete blockhouse set into the middle of who-knows-where and separated from one another. Under a bare light bulb, seated on a hard chair in a room that stank of urine, blocked drains, sweat and fear, and with a window that was just a narrow strip of frosted glass encrusted with spiders' webs and dead flies, Vignoles had felt the hours crawl by, losing all track of time — his watch had been broken during his exertions — as his head grew increasingly muddled with tiredness and pain and a raging thirst. Men in the obligatory leather jackets, and others in uniform, questioned him relentlessly, at times cajoling and wheedling and offering bitter cigarettes whilst trying to sound friendly, and at other times they were just plain threatening.

Following what was probably about twenty-four hours of isolation, it finally came to an end, and at least no actual physical harm was done. Both Anna and Staff Sergeant Gretton reported that they had been treated adequately — perhaps their diplomatic passports held some sway, after all. Captain Henderson, however, looked particularly grey and subdued. He appeared to be in pain, but when questioned explained that it was just the after-effects of tumbling from the train.

They were offered soup, bread and delicious Turkish coffee that coursed through their fatigued bodies like a restorative, before being brought back into the blinding light and intense heat of the outside world and driven on another interminable journey to a lonely border crossing, where Jugoslav and British officers faced each other uneasily, the tension only releasing when they had stepped across the invisible divide and through what Henderson had muttered was 'the tear in the Iron Curtain', and so back into the safety of Zone A.

Yet more apparently endless questions and more waiting had inevitably followed, until finally they were allowed to take baths, change their grubby clothes and sit for an evening meal, feeling almost dead with weariness. But Rose did not join them, and soon the disturbing news filtered through that she was under military arrest and serving time in solitary confinement for her role in the incident at the spurious border crossing. Her crime? She had no authority to observe suspects, nor to give chase or to approach a border crossing — real or imagined — and on top of that she had contrived to get herself and her diplomatic charge captured and interrogated by enemy agents. This ugly dose of reality had come as a shock as they disconsolately sat for what Vignoles jokingly called 'their last supper'. The indignation they all felt at Rose's treatment was thrown firmly back in their faces by unsympathetic officers seated at the same table, all of whom freely expressed the opinion that she 'deserved what she got for disregarding orders'.

With what felt like indecent haste, tickets were procured for a train to take the three still at liberty back to England. This was due to depart at 6 o'clock the following morning, and Vignoles sensed that they were all an awkward thorn in the side of the Allied diplomats and top brass, who wished to be rid of them quickly. The feeling was mutual, and Vignoles was not disappointed that he had not been given a chance to speak with either Brigadier Harper-Tarr or Commander Turbayne.

The journey home had been largely uneventful and had allowed all three to catch up on some much-needed sleep. It also gave Vignoles more than enough time to mull over everything that had happened. He was still puzzling over some aspects of the case and had not reached any satisfactory conclusions. There were anomalies and inconsistencies that neither he nor Henderson could explain.

The problem was compounded by the fact that Vignoles was convinced that Captain Henderson's Information and Research Department was nothing less than a front for MI6. Of course the captain had strenuously denied this. Henderson was willing to go only so far in their conversations. He was never going to be free to let Vignoles in on what the IRD really knew about the operation they had become entangled in, and this rankled, but the Official Secrets Act was not to be ignored, as Vignoles had been reminded by the British military in Trieste. If Vignoles felt frustrated by Henderson's lack of candour, he tempered his feelings with the suspicion that the Jugoslav secret police had given the captain an exceptionally hard grilling in the sinister blockhouse. There were strange raw marks on the captain's wrists and he moved as though his legs and back were bruised. He had paid a higher price than any of them.

Vignoles knew he should just let the whole thing drop. He must abandon it to the diplomats, the secret services and the politicians. Leave fact and fiction to mingle and intertwine into whatever story they felt would best serve their purposes. But he was not satisfied. He could not just push the deaths of the three soldiers aside and forget about them. He needed to understand who had done what and why, and he had to understand why his old chum, Jimmy Baron, had deceived his country and ended up dead from a cyanide pill, and why Henderson had known to put a bullet in him.

So finally, when Vignoles walked into his office at Leicester Central, behind his genuine pleasure at seeing his colleagues again and all the handshakes, cheerful greetings and heartfelt smiles, he was still worrying away at these questions, turning them over and over in his head just like the melody of a popular partisan song that Anna had taken to singing, which had become imprinted in his mind and repeated itself until he felt almost maddened by the infectious tune.

Vignoles rested his hands on the familiar, smooth, wooden arms of his old chair (that DC Blencowe had hidden in a cupboard to avoid DI Minshul's cull) and cast his eyes around the impossibly tidy surroundings of what was once his familiar office. It was unrecognisable. Minshul may have his faults, but he was a neat worker, although credit was probably due to WPC Benson, from what Trinder was telling him. Free of the junk and detritus and of the dusty files leaking papers and the unsteady stacks of reports on the floor, the room looked quite presentable and Vignoles wondered if head office would sanction a lick of fresh paint to the walls.

He apologised to DS Trinder: 'Sorry, I can't quite get used to all this.' He idly opened a drawer on his desk and found it to be empty. Where had all the clutter gone? Where were the pencil stubs, the empty gas mask case and the collection of farthings in a tinplate money box? Reassuringly, the dancing girl had survived, though now placed on his desk with her pert bronze breasts pointing straight towards him in disconcertingly close proximity.

Vignoles lit his pipe and forced himself back to his questioning of Trinder. 'Sorry, where were we? Oh yes, so, after the arrest and the associated scuffles, what happened?'

'The local civvies arrived, thinking that we were roughing up the speakers.'

'Were you not?'

'They threw the first punches!' Vignoles refrained from further comment and merely raised an eyebrow, waiting for Trinder to continue. 'But I do accept that it did not look good. After we had sorted out this unfortunate misunderstanding with the constabulary and they went on their way…' Trinder's cheeks were burning, 'we brought the two men back to the station and started to file charges.'

'Who were the suspects?'

'Peter Mackintosh, Percival Doubleday and one of their two chums, a fellow called Smith.'

'Don't tell me, his first name was John?'

'How did you know? Oh yes, I see. We didn't even get the chance to ask him his address, because his legal chap suddenly appeared, throwing his weight around and demanding the immediate release of his clients.'

'How the devil did he arrive so quickly?'

'As we were making the arrests the same person who telephoned the local police also called Mackintosh's father. We assume the caller was the fourth man, guv, the one who escaped.'

'I infer from the tone of your voice that this eminent legal gentleman is someone important.'

'Sir Terence Mackintosh QC. A former director of the London & North Eastern Railway.'

'Ah. Unfortunate.'

'It got worse. Not only was Peter Mackintosh represented by one of the top legal families in the area, but we were soon informed that Chief Superintendent Badger was a personal friend of the Mackintoshes. I understand there was a rather heated exchange on the telephone between DI Minshul and the super. We were told to release all three men immediately, without charge. Things have not improved since. We have been warned off from investigating either Mackintosh or Doubleday, and the DI has been sent packing; mind you, I think your imminent return may have had something to do with that, guv.'

Vignoles puffed on his pipe and for the hundredth time that morning heard the joyful refrain of *bella ciao, bella ciao, bella ciao ciao ciao* circle around inside his head. 'You believe that these two are responsible for the sabotage attempt and the paint-throwing?'

'Yes, guv, I do. Interestingly, Sir Terence vehemently opposed the nationalisation of the railways. He was quite outspoken on the subject and some of his comments were pretty close to the bone. I've been reading up on him in the newspapers at the library. It might explain his son's anger.'

'I vaguely remember. However, Sir Terence knew how far he could go and how to remain on the right side of the law.'

'Indeed, guv, but his dim and hotheaded son clearly does not — at least that's my belief. Young Mackintosh set up this half-baked political campaign with his college chum, Doubleday, at the start of the year. They are unashamedly anti-nationalisation, anti-union, anti-communist and passionately in favour of free enterprise. We have a collection of their handouts and they are clearly advocating "non-democratic means" to stem what they like to call the "Scarlet Tide of Communism".'

'As in the note sent to the Badger.'

'Exactly! But we need to prove they wrote and sent that note and that they unbolted the track. We do have fingerprints recovered from the paint tin that struck the driver, but we came unstuck at this point because we didn't have time to take the prints of Mackintosh and Doubleday before they were released. I'm convinced we would get a match.'

'It will be hard to obtain their prints to compare as things stand now, John.'

'Indeed. We've been warned off in no uncertain terms. But we have no other suspects. If we can't proceed, then it's a miscarriage of justice.'

'The arrest was a bungled affair. It was foolish to wade in like that. I fear you threw them a perfect escape route.'

Trinder's face was burning. 'My original plan was ignored. We needed to gather more evidence before doing anything else.'

'Quite so — and that is what you will continue to do now, just with far more discretion. If these two men really are guilty, then they will have had the fright of their lives, and, whilst I deplore the pulling of rank and the use of familial connections, one should not overlook the fact that the formidable Sir Terence will have torn a strip or two off his son in no uncertain terms. The scandal of his son acting like a terrorist would destroy them both if it were to become public. I don't suppose either man will be taking part in any further immature acts of vandalism or political campaigning.'

'That's all very well, guv, but what about the trackwomen who lost their jobs? If we simply brush the affair under the carpet to protect the good name of a better-connected, better-educated and far better-paid family, they'll continue to live with the humiliation of their dismissal and the reasons for it. They have no chance to clear their names.'

'I have no intention of allowing any such injustice to railway staff, but we must be patient and cautious. My point is, you now have time on your side, as I think we can safely assume that there will be no more attacks, but that is no reason to stop collecting evidence to build a case sufficiently strong that charges will have to be brought — no matter what Badger and this man's father might think as they drink pink gins at the golf club.'

'Glad to hear it!' Trinder brightened up noticeably, happy to have his boss back again. 'But where do I start?'

'I suggest you find a few sheets of paper similar to that used on their note, and locate a number of different typewriters in the building and exactly replicate what they typed. Note the model and location of each typewriter. File these away ready for when we can get warrants to search the Mackintosh and Doubleday houses and do the same on any typewriter they might have access too. It's like fingerprinting with type, as no two are identical. Prove beyond argument that one of their machines originated the note.'

'Or course! What a dunce I am not to have thought of that!'

'You might want to sniff around their student digs. Of course I would never condone the idea that you try to convince the caretaker to allow you inside on whatever spurious reason, but it may prove instructive if someone were to do so. Vignoles grinned. 'You know what these lads look like and if you could lay your hands on a photograph of each man you might ask that helpful photographer to paste their heads on the bodies of two track workers to mock up a picture and start asking discreet questions — someone will have seen them. But take a tip from me. Hound their two friends Mr Smith and Mr Jones, or whatever their names are. They'll be the foot soldiers and may well have done the dirty work. If I'm not mistaken you haven't been stopped from investigating those two.'

'Indeed not!' Trinder grinned. 'Righty-o!'

'And another thing — find out which of the suspects has connections with Birkenhead. Someone knew about that driver's affiliations and was sufficiently worked up about them to cover him in paint. The crew lodge overnight at Woodford Halse, so perhaps the driver had been bending people's ears in the local pubs? You'll get your men. Just learn to be patient and never give up.' Vignoles stopped and gave his pipe some attention. He caught himself tapping the fingers of one hand lightly upon the chair arm, beating out the rhythm of that damned infectious song.

He looked at Trinder and it was obvious that his sergeant was burning with curiosity about the mysterious mission that had sent his boss to Italy, but was politely restraining himself from asking. But why should Trinder remain in the dark? Vignoles had missed having him to bounce ideas off. The Official Secrets Act could go hang! No one else was playing him a straight bat, so why not take decisive action for a change and talk to someone he could trust?

After requesting fresh cups of coffee from Mrs Green and telling her that they were not to be disturbed, Vignoles did his best to explain the goings-on of the past few weeks, speaking quietly and avoiding using family names, but otherwise doing his best to explain what he thought had happened. Trinder listened attentively throughout, only occasionally intervening to ask a question to clarify a point.

'I'd appreciate your observations, John.'

'The case doesn't feel closed.'

Vignoles sat back in his chair, already reassured that his sergeant was thinking like him. 'What questions do you want answered?'

'When did this "Shrike" fellow first became involved in locating and securing the tank of heavy water for the Soviets.'

'Why?'

'Because it will shed light, not so much on his motives — we know he was the very worst kind of traitor working ultimately for the Soviet Union — but upon the thinking of those who were controlling him on our side.'

Vignoles grinned at Trinder through his pipe smoke. 'Exactly! Carry on.'

'Shrike was supposedly brought in at the last minute by the British Army to oversee the train and look after the hastily-agreed joint objectives of the Allies and the Jugoslavs. But was not Shrike also the contact man for the two scientists?'

'Yes. One of the professors told me he was — and we can only assume that MI6 was playing him as a double-cross agent against Tito, to reveal his atomic intentions.'

'Agreed.'

'However, Shrike was at the churchyard when he and one of his accomplices put a gun in the back of the same scientist. At that point he was acting for the Soviets.'

'So he was already part of the set-up that wanted to foil the plan to secure the heavy water for Tito at least the day *before* the attempt to remove the tanker from Trieste. But surely he was involved far earlier? When did he make the switch? From Tito to Stalin — if I can put it in simple terms.'

'I very much doubt he did so halfway through obtaining the wagon for Tito, whilst working as an Allied agent. I can confirm that Shrike was in the *Stella Polaris* and associating with the other man and the woman there.'

'And the other two in the bar were definitely KGB agents. So Shrike was involved about the time the third British soldier was killed. And the woman is suspected to have been the soldier's girlfriend, luring him into trouble. So we tie Shrike into that man's death.'

'I believe we can.'

'But it's more than probable that Shrike was involved from at least the time of the death of the first British soldier — possibly earlier. Now, if that is so and he was technically a British agent, one of our best and most trusted, allegedly...' Trinder took a long drag on his cigarette and exhaled, speaking very quietly through the smoke, 'then that raises some very awkward questions.'

They fell silent for a moment.

Vignoles spoke first, almost whispering, feeling his way forwards. 'He could have been acting out on a limb. A wild card deep undercover and out of sight of his Allied controllers.'

'I suppose that's possible.'

'If that were so, they would not be aware of his involvement in the deaths, and are absolved of collusion. But he played out a complex and clever game that neatly provided a solution to an awful political situation that could easily have spilled over into conflict.'

'That needed input at the highest level. But would an Allied security service allow three British soldiers to be killed, and four British personnel plus two commandos to be placed in deadly peril — for political game playing? Or were the stakes so high they thought it worth the cost?' Trinder looked shocked.

'My God, it sounds even worse when put into words.' Vignoles grimaced. 'Give me your thoughts about the captain and the IRD.'

'He's a spy, an agent, call him what you like. He was reporting all you discovered straight back to this so-called Information and Research Department. But you said the captain intervened and saved your lives.'

'He did, and I would probably not be here now without his actions.'

'Was he sent out to kill Shrike? Could MI6 have sent out another agent to stop the rot?'

'He was unwavering in his decision to shoot, but not to kill. I think he wanted him alive and was frustrated when the cyanide pill did its work. He called Shrike a traitor, he knew of the plans to place hostages aboard and at what station, he also knew about the air attack.'

'But if he knew so much, then why such a risky strategy? Why not move in earlier?' Trinder had pulled apart his empty carton of cigarettes and as they were talking was scribbling a few words on the inside of the flattened carton, drawing little arrows to make links between them.

Vignoles pointed the stem of his pipe towards Trinder. 'What are you thinking?'

'We don't have enough detail about the men involved and their real motives. So I was thinking about what these different sets of people might gain from all this.'

'Go on.'

'Jugoslavia wanted the heavy water to start an atomic project and so sent two of their top scientists to buy the tanker and bring it back. They worked with a trusted agent — Shrike — a man who had fought alongside the partisans during the war and who had won their trust. He was probably the man who got wind of the existence of the tank wagon and even suggested the plan.'

'Sounds convincing.'

'But unbeknown to them, Shrike's true loyalty was to the Soviet Union. Stalin saw a chance to wrong-foot Tito over his bomb project and in so doing keep him in his place — and used Shrike to this end.'

Vignoles nodded in agreement. 'The Soviets wanted the plan to appear to fail — but in such a manner that Tito's atomic plans were revealed and dashed at the same time. Tito is compromised by having his top scientists in Allied hands and being questioned, and Tito will have to cut a deal to have any chance of getting them back. Stalin has the perfect opportunity to make Tito squirm, compounded by the fact that these men were happy to hand over an awful lot of hard currency for the heavy water. Trading with the decadent and capitalist West will not sound good in the corridors of the Kremlin! Stalin has a neat bargaining tool to make Tito keep his head down and not act so bullish.'

'But Shrike seems to have been even more clever.' Trinder had made a few more arrows on his little diagram. 'He arranged for the train to be destroyed in circumstances that made it imperative that Tito and the Allies have reasons to conceal the inconvenient truth that the KGB infiltrated deep into both sides of the Iron Curtain.'

'You're quite right. It would be too humiliating to admit that the KGB had run circles around MI6. It suits everyone to jointly concoct a face-saving solution. And remember, Jugoslavia is a valuable bulwark against the mightier and more frightening USSR.'

'But how will the army explain the deaths of its men?' Trinder looked puzzled.

'Their families will be told that they were murdered by a ruthless group of fascists. Special mention will go to one of SOE's finest — "whose name must remain secret for reasons of national security, but who lost his life whilst attempting to prevent these renegades making their escape. It was a successful joint operation, serving to thaw international relations".' Vignoles's voice was bitter.

'I would like to know who controlled Shrike on the British side, and how much they knew.'

The safety valves lifted on an engine outside the window and, amidst the escape of steam, Vignoles ventured to speak, knowing that no prying ears would catch a word of what he said. 'Agreed. I can't believe he acted independently. Someone knew what he was doing and allowed him to kill, or at least be part of the gang that killed. I think he and his controller had in their sights the endgame we have just discussed — a victory for the Soviets.' Vignoles put his pipe on the desk and leaned forward, taking the flattened cigarette box from Trinder. He carefully placed a lighted match to one corner, turned the burning card in his fingers and then dropped it into the ashtray, prodding the ash and ensuring it was fully consumed. 'I want you to make me a promise, John.'

Trinder narrowed his eyes.

'Never mention what we have discussed to anyone. No matter what the circumstances. Not even to me, unless I first raise the issue. Understood?'

'Scout's honour!' said Trinder, giving the three-fingered salute. But, despite his attempt at levity, he looked worried.

* * * *

After Trinder had left the office Vignoles sat for a long while looking out of the window and watching the trains arrive and depart, the people hustling and bustling to and fro. He enjoyed observing how some stood and waited patiently whilst others were agitated and relentlessly pacing about. There were those who stood and stared into the far distance, hands in pockets, whistling, whilst others bought tea from the mobile Women's Voluntary Service cart. Some read books or newspapers, like the man with the light mackintosh slung over his arm, doggedly reading every line of the thin, four-sheet paper. He must be onto the obituaries by now. A big express from London pulled to a stop and the faces were refreshed by a new set of people. And yet the reading man was still there.

Vignoles dialled a number and spoke to a female voice at the other end. After a short exchange she agreed to put his call through.

'Captain Henderson?'

'Inspector, what an unexpected pleasure, old chap. How is Mrs V bearing up after her hair-raising adventure?' His voice was breezy, but guarded.

'I need to ask you a few questions.'

'Oh, I see. I cannot promise to answer, but fire away.'

'There's something nagging at me about these, er, recent events. I want to know how those agents knew to pull that stunt on the girls so quickly.'

'A little bird put them up to it. A little bird that knew rather too much for everyone's comfort — as you are aware. I imagine that the two agents realised they were expendable and banked on a brace of British women to provide an insurance policy against attack.'

'I accept your reasoning for why they took them, but don't try and give me the whitewash that the bird simply knew everything. We were working out on a limb at the time, ad-libbing, and the intelligence boys knew nothing of what we were up to. So unless this bird and his two accomplices were tapping directly into our conversations, he could not have known where they were driving.'

A silence fell for a moment. 'What are you suggesting?'

'How often did you report back?'

'Often enough.'

'After I followed the professor on the train into town, you advised the girls to give chase to the female. Did you then make contact with your, um, controller? Is that the correct title? Did you advise him what they were doing?'

The line clicked and crackled but the captain remained silent.

'So was this a cyphered communication or was it by telephone?'

'You cannot seriously suggest I was responsible for a security breach?'

'Somebody was. Or did that little bird intercept your messages?'

'Impossible. The codes we use are better than Jerry's ever were. Nobody will crack them.'

'Tell me about your controller.'

'Classified, old boy!'

'We're talking about the same gentleman I met in the Great Central Hotel, I believe?'

'Don't speak any more of this! It is not wise.' Vignoles heard another tiny click and, for a brief moment, a hollow resonance. 'I think that is the end of the questions, old boy. Take my advice and consider it a job well done and go back to policing the railway. It would be safer for us all. And don't take this badly — but it would be better not to have any further contact with me. It was nice knowing you, inspector. Farewell.'

The line went dead. Vignoles looked up and noticed that the newspaper reader had gone, as well.

CHAPTER THIRTY-SIX

WE MUST ALL STICK TOGETHER

Geraldo & His Orchestra

The little tank locomotive was of an antiquated design that seemed to capture the very essence of the Victorian age. Its paintwork was rich and deep with the patina of both age and the glossy translucence that comes with the application of much paraffin and light engine oil, further enhanced by a slick varnish of torrential rain sluicing over the curves of the tall dome and chimney. The legend *British Railways* was emblazoned along the tank sides in the startling yellow of the former Southern Railway, bringing a welcome splash of colour to the scene.

The cleaners had no doubt given special attention to this particular locomotive as it was to work for the duration of the Olympiad, shuttling three antiquated coaches down the hastily re-opened branch line to Bisley for the benefit of competitors and those spectators brave enough to witness the shooting events at the National Rifle Association's headquarters, just outside the small Surrey town of the same name. In honour of its important role, two little flags hung damp and limp in front of the smoke-box, one with the five Olympic rings hand-stitched onto a scrap of white cotton, the other the Union Jack, both looking rather pathetic on this typically British August day.

Vignoles was wearing an almost-ankle-length Royal Navy oilskin cape and a huge sou'wester hat that was channelling the rain in a great river down his back. He was braving the weather away from the shelter of the platform canopy in order to take a better look at the engine. It was an M7 class — a type he had rarely seen, and not to be missed. He was also showing comradely empathy with the poor fireman, who had been busy filling the engine from the water crane at the platform end, but was now standing, hunched and miserable, his collar turned up and cap pulled tightly down on his head, attempting to smoke a damp cigarette whilst the thick leather bag twitched with the water gushing into the side tanks.

'May as well just leave the bloomin' filler caps open an' she'll fill up on her own!' the fireman observed bitterly.

'It is awful weather.'

'What 'appened to it, that's what I wanna know? It was bloomin' perfect these few days past. They was faintin' and gettin' sunburnt and Lord knows what at the opening cerem'ny.'

'It was one of the hottest days ever known. I was with my wife in the Empire Stadium for the opening, so I can confirm that. Actually, it was quite the perfect day — though almost too hot in that suntrap of a stadium. Perhaps everyone complained about the heat and this is our reward for being such a bunch of moaning minnies.'

'Yeah, no one's ever satisfied, are they? Too hot, too cold, too dry, too wet!' The fireman took a final, doleful drag on his spluttering cigarette and flung it beneath the wheels of his engine. 'You off down Bisley way for the shootin'?'

'Yes, myself and a group of work colleagues.' Vignoles inclined his head towards the carriages to indicate that the others were already seated in the dry and not getting wet looking at old tank engines. Moving his head sent a torrent of water from out of the brim of his sou'wester over his ankle and into his shoe. 'Ugh! Dratted rain! We're going to watch a friend compete in the Free Pistol event.'

'Best of luck! Hope he gets a medal.'

'She, actually.'

'Blimey.' The fireman looked impressed as he turned the wheel at the side of the water crane to stop the flow. 'Man or woman, we could do wiv' a few more medals, that's for sure!'

'Charles! Do come out of the rain! You'll catch your death out there!' Anna was holding the carriage door open with one hand, an umbrella above her head in the other.

'You'll soon dry off in that nice, warm cab. Cheerio!' With a quick wave, Vignoles dashed along the platform to join Anna, John and Vi Trinder, Harry Blencowe and Jane Benson in the narrow compartment. As they removed sodden oilskins, dripping furled umbrellas and settled down into a damp huddle, water pooling on the threadbare carpet, the guard blew his whistle and the train started to move.

'Gosh, this is a relic from the old London, Brighton & South Coast,' observed Vignoles.

'It's filthy,' observed Anna, looking at the layers of grime encrusted around the steamed-up windows.

'The seat springs aren't up to much,' said Vi, bouncing up and down to illustrate, causing her husband and Harry Blencowe to move as if they were on a boat in choppy waters.

'Trust you to notice the railway company, guv! But then you have the advantage over us; you actually *know* what a London & Brighton coach looks like.' Trinder smiled good-naturedly.

'Observation, John. Always keep in practice, ready for more serious matters. I know almost nothing of the line, nor its coaching stock, but this small, enamel sign screwed to the window sill...' he pointed with the stem of his unlit pipe, 'asking us to *Refrain From Spitting Inside The Carriage* bears the initials of the original railway company.'

'I'm glad they warned me!' Trinder chuckled.

'Do you think Lucy's nervous?' asked Vi.

'I don't know how she can even face standing up there with everyone watching, let alone keep her hand steady,' Anna replied.

'It's a skill-and-a-half, that's for certain. Lucy has real ability, y'know? I can hardly even hit the blessed target,' remarked Vignoles, toying with his unlit pipe. He sighed as he noticed another sign, this one issued by the Southern Railway, advising that it was a no smoking compartment.

'Did you alter her outfits?' Anna asked Vi.

'Oh yes. I needed to do a little bit of nip-and-tuck to get the all-in-one frock to fit. It buttons down the front, you see, and so was rather prone to gaping or pulling. I'll let you into a secret, it was supplied by Bourne & Hollingsworth, who are outfitters for domestic servants and kitchen staff.' Violet winced. 'I can only wonder at what shape they expect these poor women to be to fit such a frock without alteration!'

'Ah, but she was in safe hands with you!' Anna smiled.

'It looks really most fetching, though the blazer isn't the most flattering design, to my mind, as it's blue serge, but lacking a collar. But when you put the whole ensemble together she does look awfully smart and professional.'

'Not too professional, I hope — she'd be barred from competing if that were so.' Jane Benson looked mildly alarmed.

'Actually, that is a bit of a concern, because she has used a firearm on duty, as you all know,' said Vignoles. 'I discussed it with the Badger and he agreed to throw a veil of secrecy over her firearms exploits and to deny any knowledge of her involvement, if such an accusation were to be made. Jolly decent of him.'

'Well, let's all jolly well keep hush-hush about it,' whispered Vi, 'there could be a rival competitor or an official in the very next compartment.'

Vignoles looked at his watch. 'We should be there in about ten minutes or so. It's no great distance, but the line was closed until recently and I don't suppose the track is in tip-top condition.'

'Will the shooting range be under cover?' asked Anna.

'The competitors will be covered and the actual targets for the shorter range competitions should be, but I can't see how they can cover the rifle ranges.' Vignoles was looking at a rather damp programme for the day's events that he had extracted from a pocket.

Jane groaned. 'I think it might be a rather trying day, sir.'

'Not at all. Apart from our very own Lucy, I was rather hoping to see the modern pentathlon shooting event. The Swedish competitor is expected to win gold and has to be worth seeing. He has a most splendid name: Captain Willy Oscar Guernsey Grut!'

'I think he sounds quite dashing,' observed Anna.

* * * *

Denzil Oxenby touched his moustache yet again, pressing it onto his lip more firmly. The rain was trickling down his face and he feared the Cow Gum would not hold up. He was also not used to wearing spectacles and, worse, they were spotted with raindrops and blurring his vision. He would have to lift these out of the way when it came to pulling the trigger.

However, rain also had benefits. Everyone was cloaked in waterproofs, rain macs, military greatcoats or oilskins and wearing hats or holding umbrellas to shield their faces. It was remarkable how one's individuality was suppressed by rainwear. The austerity fashions of the past eight years ensured that the limited palette of muted colours and the simple cut and design of each coat were virtually identical. It was well-nigh impossible to distinguish a competitor, an official, a policeman or a spectator. Even the boy scouts in their capes looked just like slightly shortened versions of everyone else. Oxenby had adopted the popular choice of a voluminous naval cape that was perfect for keeping his precision rifle dry in its long, slim box, plus he would blend into the crowd.

He was sure that his disguise was good enough (assuming that his moustache did not fall off at an inopportune moment). In fact, that morning he had been quite taken aback as he'd admired his handiwork in the black-spotted mirror in his dreary rented room. He was now sporting a newly-shaved and rather shiny bald head, with just a straggling fringe of reddish-brown dyed hair above his ears, a glued-on moustache of (almost) the same colour and an ostentatious pair of spectacles he had acquired on the Continent. They had yellow-tinged lenses, their design very different from the styles favoured in Britain. All in all, he looked quite an oddity. Suitably alien to English eyes.

He smiled to himself. Yes, he would pass muster as Veikko Savolainen, a Finnish competitor in the 300m Free Rifle event. He was sure that no one could pronounce his name, let alone question his credentials. Two days of observing the controlled chaos of the games had left him convinced that a nicely 'foreign' name coupled with a handful of impressive-looking letters written in Finnish and a well-forged passport would do the trick, and he had called upon the best in the business — his own staff in MI6 — to provide all of these.

He felt the balance of the gun case in his hand once more, then gave a quick glance around before stepping forward to join the queue to enter the camp. He watched the wet back of the man in front as the line snaked towards the small, concrete guardhouse that overlooked a red-and-white painted barrier blocking the road into the fenced enclosure. A caped policeman and a soldier in a sodden greatcoat were taking advantage of what little shelter was afforded by a thin mountain ash growing just inside the high perimeter fence, both men occasionally stepping forward to lift the barrier and allow a black car or a half-timbered Austin Tilly van to motor inside; neither man the least bit interested in delaying the process by doing more than passing the most cursory of glances over the documents being shown. A young army cadet was better protected in the guardhouse, and he was saluting a greeting to all, but although he was looking at passes and tickets he appeared sympathetic to the plight of those standing in the rain and was hurrying things along as quickly as he could.

Oxenby felt his pulse quicken as he stepped forward, proffering his Olympic Committee competitor's pass and a rain-streaked letter from the Finnish Embassy.

'Mr Sa...er, Savo...Savo*leen*. Welcome!' The cadet saluted for probably the three-hundredth time that morning.

Oxenby gave a stiff bow, 'Savolainen. The name is Veikko Sa-vo-lai-nen' He spoke in a heavy accent and gave a thin-lipped smile.

The cadet squinted at his pass. 'Apologies, sir. That your rifle, sir?' He nodded towards the long, black leatherette-finished case.

'Yes, officer, eet is so. I heff my full documentations ent my sports gun licence, if you require.' Oxenby spoke slowly, and with a clearly enunciated accent.

'That's quite all right, sir. Good luck!' Another smart salute and the cadet passed his attentions to the next in line. 'Good morning, sir.'

Oxenby breathed more easily and walked into the compound, following the little white-painted wooden signs on short posts that directed him towards the competitors' registration desk inside a series of huge olive green canvas marquees tethered by a veritable forest of ropes and wooden pegs to one side of the grandiose pavilion that was reserved for *VIP Guests Only*.

A clutch of army vehicles was parked in a row before the tents, whilst others were manoeuvring in front of the nearest marquee. Each was driven by a woman, all of whom were young, pretty and wearing bottle green Royal Voluntary Service uniforms. Oxenby curled a lip into a sneer as he watched officials and VIPs in well-tailored morning suits and top hats step out of the chauffeur-driven vehicles close to the entrance to the pavilion. What better example of the decadence and outrageous inequalities of the imperialist west? It was quite correct for the Soviet Union to refuse to have anything to do with this blatant excuse for capitalist propaganda.

People were running to and fro with their heads down against the rain. Oxenby was probably one of the few not cursing the weather. Dipping his own head, he veered off to one side of the marquee entrance between two parked vans, following a WVS girl walking with an older gent, in a black Olympic blazer, white trousers with a watermark forming above his turn-ups, and a broad-brimmed fedora. He was attempting to gallantly hold an umbrella over the head of his young guide. Oxenby tagged close behind, trying to walk with purpose, maintaining a fixed look of concentration on his face. He knew that few people noticed, let alone challenged, someone who appeared fixated on important business.

The three approached an entrance to a neighbouring marquee, guarded by yet another cadet. A soggy sign pinned to the canvas indicated that this was reserved *For Officials Only*. The cadet saluted the gent, but his eyes were on the girl. Oxenby gave a stern and officious nod of his head and an ambiguous signal with his free hand, whilst stepping briskly inside, all actions completed before the cadet could form a question on his lips.

Quickly assessing the situation, he mingled with a group huddled around a trestle table manned by two elderly, white-haired men, busy checking names on typed lists. The table was arrayed with cardboard name badges, boxes of pins, armbands, and numbers stitched onto squares of white cotton. Oxenby moved quickly, darting a hand out and back under his cape as two excitable Mexicans who reeked of garlic and sweat were making a scene over something, one of them tossing badges around the table and the other grabbing handfuls of the numbered squares. Suitably equipped, Oxenby slunk away to get the lay of the land and plan his strategy.

* * * *

Outside Bisley railway station, a bus waited. Its engine was ticking over and making a dirty cloud of exhaust that lingered in the air, despite the rain. The destination blind read *Special*, though this clearly did not refer to the vehicle itself, which was one of the angular, grey-painted Austerity types, whose hard wooden seats and stiff suspension rendered every journey a form of purgatory. The driver, seated in a little glass cabin to the side of the nose of the engine compartment, had a Union Jack pinned up behind her and a colourful rosette on the lapel of her uniform jacket. She grinned and waved at the approaching group in a friendly manner.

'At least someone's entering into the Olympic spirit!' Vi waved back.

'Thank goodness. You would never know anything is happening here: not a flag, not a strip of bunting, not even a poster on the wall,' remarked Anna, looking around at the dilapidated station, that clearly had not seen a lick of fresh paint since the 1930s.

'Come along, you two: we don't want to keep the lady waiting.' Vignoles walked towards the rear platform of the bus.

The bus rattled and swayed its way along a pretty country lane, that dipped and rose amongst sandy dunes cloaked in flowering heather, the clutch whining and complaining all the way. Twenty minutes later they arrived, had their tickets inspected and stood on the covered terrace of the pavilion, looking down upon long rows of canvas marquees set into a wide and shallow sandy hollow. In the far distance, the rifle ranges faced a steep bank, with hay bales stacked into a long yellow wall, in front of which the targets were arrayed. Away to their left was another clutch of tents, but these were of pale canvas and the sides were open. They could just see the lines of the pistol-shooting galleries illuminated by the soft light permeating the fabric roof. Along the other side of the shallow arena, flags hung limply on a forest of white poles. Paths were demarcated by gravel or sandy tracks, little white posts connected with painted chains, and there was a small village of green-painted wooden huts, variously labelled *Cafeteria*, *Competitors' Registration*, *Press Club*, *Chefs de Mission*, and *Judges and Officials Only*.

'Where can we find Lucy?' asked Anna.

Vignoles was surveying the scene, which was bustling with sombre-looking figures in shiny, wet coats. 'Perhaps in the competitors' waiting area, near the pistol ranges, or we can go to where she'll compete.'

'I think over that way,' suggested John, indicating the pale-roofed canvas arcade.

'Shall I take a gander?' asked Harry , already descending the steps in the centre of the pavilion gallery.

They approached the pistol ranges and joined a large throng of people milling around near the entrance and then made their way towards the narrow side galleries, where a limited number of spectators were able to observe proceedings. They stepped onto straw strewn over the sandy floor and avoided the two cadets throwing handfuls of sawdust onto the wetter areas. Vignoles took a deep breath, inhaling the heady scent of canvas, damp grass and straw, mingled with cordite and wet coats. It reminded him of the summer flower shows in Dunton Bassett he had attended as a young boy, and the shooting range where he and Jack had tried to win goldfish at a halfpenny a shot.

Conversation inside the tent dropped to hushed whispers, and anyone forgetting to do so was soon shushed quiet by unarmed soldiers in dress uniforms standing at either end of the narrow viewing galleries.

'Hope we've not missed her,' whispered Anna, craning her neck to see the competitors.

Vignoles glanced at his wristwatch. 'The women's pistol is not due to start for about another hour.'

The sound of sporting pistols cracked and popped in the air, though surprisingly quiet and muffled. 'I expected it to be louder,' Jane observed.

'I say, look at them!' Anna nudged Vi as they settled on one of the two rows of folding wooden chairs that formed the narrow viewing gallery. Both watched as two tall, slender women walked in their direction, wearing well-cut black trousers with a little tricolour sewn on the left hip pocket, and finely tailored white blouses with the golden cockerels of the French Republic embroidered on one of the two pointed collars.

'Three buttons on each cuff. How decadent!' observed Anna.

'The stingy old British would ask questions in Parliament if we were so profligate,' added Jane, looking down at her specially-cleaned policewoman's uniform, which was over four years old.

'And look at those coats! They must have cost a pretty penny, or Franc.' Vi cast a professional eye over the outfits as the women swanned past, coats flung across their shoulders and small, aluminium pistol cases swinging in their gloved hands.

'They even make smoking a cigarette look elegant,' said John, as the two women paused in front of them and placed Gitanes between their bright red lips as one proffered a lighter.

His wife nudged him in the ribs. 'Eyes front, you!'

'Well, they are right in front.'

'Oh look: it's Lucy!' Jane half stood up and waved to attract her attention. Lucy Lansdowne smiled as she caught sight of her colleagues and walked over.

'Hullo! How are you feeling?' asked Anna in a hushed voice, the others falling silent and leaning forwards to catch her answer.

'My hands are shaking dreadfully.' She made a face and glanced across at the French women. 'When I see who I'm up against, the nerves really kick in!'

'Don't you worry about those two. Nice clothes and a ponytail don't mean they can shoot straight!' Harry reassured her.

'They do look rather chic.' Lucy glanced down at her white dress; pinned to one hip was a small square of paper displaying the number 229. 'What do you think of the beret? Some of the girls are quite up in arms over it.' Violet and Anna were in agreement that it looked very smart.

'At least you know how to wear one correctly,' observed Jane. 'Regulation one inch above the eyebrows, dead level and the badge over the left eye.'

'Aye aye, cap'n!' Lucy laughed and saluted.

A soldier leaned forward to speak softly but firmly. 'Quiet, please.'

'I'm on in about an hour and ten minutes. I'll have to get changed shortly.'

'What's in the box, Lucy?' asked Harry, tapping the lid of a square, white cardboard box she was carrying.

'That's my Olympic lunch!'

'You lucky thing.'

'Hardly!' Lucy rested it upon the wooden rail that separated the viewing public from the shooting range. She lifted the lid. 'One stale Olympic cheese sandwich, one small, sour Olympic green apple and one Olympic boiled egg. That's to last me all day. We've had the same every day,' she sighed. Harry looked mildly disappointed.

'But an egg *every* day? That's more than we can hope for,' observed Jane.

'Not a lot, I agree, but I wouldn't say no,' observed Trinder, 'I'm starving.'

'John, you had a whole plate of real scrambled eggs this morning. We do get them off ration.' Vi put a hand to her mouth. 'Oops, me and my big mouth!'

'Shhhh!' The soldier put a finger to his lips.

Lucy took a deep breath. 'I'm off to get ready, then I'll sit quietly till it's my time. Steel my nerves and all that. And eat my apple.'

'Yes, you must keep your strength up!'

'Good luck!'

'Give it your best shot, girl!'

Lucy's slight figure was soon lost behind a very tall and sun-tanned man with a blond crew cut and a short, more swarthy man in green military fatigues with the Peruvian flag sewn onto the breast pocket.

Vignoles stood up. 'I think I'll take a perambulation around the place and get my bearings. See what's what. On the way back I'll call in at that cafeteria hut and see if I can get a tray of tea and some bottles of Coca-Cola. Anyone care to join me?'

The rain drummed harder upon the canvas roof.

'Not likely!' answered his sergeant. The others laughed in agreement, drawing another stern look of rebuke from the soldier.

Vignoles readjusted his cape and sou'wester, then ducked through the canvas door, squeezing past a balding man with a fringe of hair like Friar Tuck who stared long after him through wet spectacles before following him.

After Vignoles had gone, Anna and the gang did their best to get to grips with the remarkably uninteresting spectator sport of competitive pistol shooting. This appeared to involve a flurry of sharp reports from long-barrelled guns fired by a row of men wearing very large spectacles, followed by a period of dull silence, and then some scurrying to and fro along the range and huddled consultations over paper targets and a lot of chalking of names and numbers on a blackboard. A surprisingly large number of people, whose exact role in the proceedings was unclear, stood around looking intense and severe, until occasionally (and for no obvious reason) there was a ripple of murmured appreciation and a few breathy gasps of excitement as something happened that everyone agreed they had not seen.

As Anna was whispering to Violet about how boring most of it was, she felt the touch of a hand on her forearm and was startled to look up and see Captain Henderson leaning towards her, his hat dripping spots of water onto her sleeve, his eyes alive and restless.

'Why, captain, fancy seeing you here. What a nice surprise.'

'No time, Mrs V. Where's the inspector?'

'Oh, he went for a walk. Why?'

'How long ago?'

'Um, about a quarter-of-an-hour, I suppose.'

'Is anything wrong?' asked John, looking slightly anxious.

'This is Captain Henderson, he's looking for Charles.'

'We must find him before it's too late! If you and your friends help, we might still have a chance.'

'Too late for what? What's this all about?'

The soldier standing guard stepped forward. 'I must ask you all to remain quiet, or leave. The competitors require silence to—'

'Yes, yes.' Henderson waved him away impatiently. 'Follow me, I'll explain as we walk.'

They all stood up, hurriedly grabbing their hats and coats as they started to file along the row of seats. As they did so, John addressed Captain Henderson in urgent tones. 'Look here, I'm the inspector's sergeant, my name's Trinder, you really must tell me what this is about.' Henderson did not reply but led the group away.

As they ducked through the doorway, Anna was surprised to see Staff Sergeant Rose Gretton standing to attention, accompanied by two surly-looking British soldiers. She smiled quickly at Anna, but immediately searched amongst the group filing out behind her.

'He's not here, Gretton!' barked Henderson.

She winced and looked serious.

'We've got the camp circled and men closing in, sir,' reported one of the two soldiers.

'Then find him!'

'He might be at the refreshment hut,' suggested Harry.

'Right, we'll start there. Listen up, all of you. The inspector has someone on his tail, someone who intends to shoot him. And this gunman is a slippery piece of work, to boot.'

'Oh, my God!' Anna exclaimed, as she brought a hand to her mouth.

'Don't you fear, Mrs V; we've got some crack men around the camp. We just need to find Vignoles and keep him in a crowded place. We expect a sniper with a rifle and so, if we keep the inspector away from open spaces — indoors, preferably — it'll give us time to find the assassin.'

'Assassin?' cried Anna. She shuddered with fear and her eyes pricked with tears of anxiety. 'But why, in heaven's name? Why him?' She was trying to walk, speak and look around, all at the same time.

'He's been asking one too many questions about my line of work, and I think he's made a startling connection about someone.'

'Who would that be?' asked John.

'The Director of the Information and Research Department — a man called Oxenby. Turns out the cad is a Soviet spy! This nasty little quisling has been working from inside and right under our noses. Heaven knows how much he's compromised our country!' He charged forward, dodging between the black- or grey-coated figures, lifting the edges of umbrellas to peer at the startled faces beneath.

'Good God!' exclaimed John, keeping up with the captain. 'Is this connected to the case in Italy?'

'The inspector must have rumbled Oxenby — we don't have the details of how, but Oxenby knew it would be only a matter of time before Vignoles blew his cover. Where is that blasted tea room?'

'Over there! That must be the queue!' Anna charged towards a long snake of people sheltering under umbrellas. 'Charles! Charles! Where are you?'

'And how did you know,' asked John, stumbling over a tent peg and guy rope, 'that this Oxenby fellow has it in for the inspector?'

'Got a call from the cypher room last night. They intercepted something odd.' Henderson was looking left and right, his eyes sharp as a hawk's. 'An unusual exchange from Oxenby to an agent not on our books. It was a hell of a risk reading the director's private, coded messages, but we're trained to expect the unexpected. Spent half the night making further checks, and eventually the penny dropped. Turns out he'd been preparing for the past week for some covert operation up in Scotland. Had false papers made up, all the works.'

'But he didn't go to Scotland?' asked Trinder.

'Gave us the bloody runaround, sergeant; but no, he came to Bisley, as a competitor.'

'Of course!' Anna stopped and looked into the captain's face. 'What better place to carry one without attracting suspicion?'

John Trinder looked frantic with worry. 'There must be a hundred or more people here today with a gun — and firing it.'

* * * *

Oxenby was crouched in the corner of the little wooden belfry surmounting the pavilion building. He had a commanding view of the series of ranges and was sheltered from the worst of the rain, able to rest the extra-long barrel of his specially constructed, high-velocity rifle on the thin, black-painted reinforcing bar that tied the wooden supporting pillars of the roof together. He could swivel the gun to take in almost any angle and yet he was virtually invisible. Besides, who was going to be standing around looking up when the rain was slating down in torrents?

Squinting through the gunsight at the badge sewn on the red beret of a soldier, he adjusted the focus until he could read the regiment name. He smiled slyly, like a cat waiting to pounce on a bird, moved the gun, and followed the back of someone's head, then selected a dark hat passing in front, then another. But everyone was dressed so similarly, so he wondered how he could pick out Vignoles. He swung the barrel left and right, impatiently settling on random figures and drawing a bead on their hearts. But he could feel his pulse quicken with his mounting impatience, his heart pumping his veins and making his hands move rhythmically — only slightly — but still enough to twitch the tiny cross as he tried to align it on a target. He needed to relax. He could not afford to miss.

Just one shot was all he had. There would be no time to risk a reload. It must be neat and deadly and pierce the rainwear the inspector was wearing. Perhaps Vignoles might clutch a hand to his heart as he dropped to the ground. Yes, that would be a nice touch.

The rifle had a long silencer on the end and, with the sounds of pistol shots on every side, no one would guess the true cause of Vignoles's demise for a few precious moments. The wound would start to bleed but, as it was concealed beneath the folds of the heavy oilskin, they would first think he'd suffered a heart attack, and they would lie him down, check his breathing and pulse as an excited crowd would gather to look. Only when they had loosened his clothing would they start to realise the truth. By then, Oxenby would be down the stairs and out of the front entrance, hopping on the shuttle bus to the station. A few minutes in the gents there would see the last of the hair shaved off and a wig substituted, the false moustache flushed away with the hair trimmings and a pair of ordinary British spectacles in place. Then a race up to the far north of Scotland and onto the fishing trawler awaiting him. They'd get him out. He'd sent the codes and received the reply confirming his immediate evacuation to safety.

If only he could find that blasted Vignoles! He'd lost sight of him some minutes previously. Oxenby put down the rifle and lifted a small pair of binoculars to his eyes. He scanned the crowds and frowned. Was it his imagination or were there now more troops with guns about? Half the crowd was in some kind of service uniform, but none had been carrying service weapons, so this change seemed ominous. He spied two soldiers as they moved through the crowd, rifles held diagonally across their chests, stopping everyone and peering under their pulled-down hats at their faces. A cold shiver ran down his spine. He had little time left.

He hefted the rifle and practised taking aim again, but now his hands were shaking, and far worse than before. He had imagined the day as sunny, the spectators taking tea in the pleasing surroundings, seated in the open, not hunched miserably beneath umbrellas or hiding deep in the marquees. He had to change tactics: he would reassemble his precision rifle and convert it into a pistol.

✻ ✻ ✻ ✻

Vignoles had decided there was little point being miserable about the rain and was determined to appreciate attending the Olympiad. It occurred, after all, only once every four years, and was held in a different country each time, so he may never get another chance in his lifetime. So, better pull his hat down more firmly on his head, do his best to keep his pipe burning, and take in the spectacle.

He had little interest in these shooting events, other than his WPC's involvement, but was fascinated by the exotic mix of nationalities brought together in such concentrated and close proximity. The Algerian team walked past in their light summer short-sleeves, drenched to the bone and yet smiling, as if rain was a novelty to be enjoyed, not endured. Perhaps it was, if you lived in Algeria.

He walked past the drab marquees and listened to the crack-crack-crack of rifles as he stood for a while at the far edge of the range, watching an official change the targets. Edging the range were some small trees, surrounded by purple-and-white heather that rolled away out of sight. Red flags were flying on tall poles to warn of danger, and three soldiers were standing in a huddle, sharing a smoke and staring at the ground.

Turning away, he headed towards the army hut offering refreshments. The crowd was at its most dense there, which perhaps said something about the draw of shooting events as a spectator sport. Journalists were jockeying to get ahead in the queue, their press badges pinned to a wide variety of international tastes in hat design, some using camera bags and others deploying elbows to jostle their way into the relative warmth and promise of the cafeteria, the windows of which were steamed up with little, distorting rivulets of condensation snaking their way downwards.

Vignoles noticed that two soldiers carrying rifles were pushing through the crowd in the same direction, and wondered at such a show of arms. Their guns seemed very un-Olympian, though they were at a shooting event. He soon lost sight of them as three big umbrellas clashed right in front of him, locking spars and fabric like a confusion of fantastical bats. The owners lifted, prodded and proffered apologies as each sought to disentangle them, and in so doing caused others to collide into each other in a soggy press. Vignoles was close to the cafeteria door and tried to ease his way toward it, but at that moment he heard a commotion nearby and so, like all the others around him, he craned his neck to try to see what was going on.

To his complete surprise, there was the lanky frame of his DS. John Trinder was barging between a group of Afghan competitors, brightly costumed in gorgeously embroidered jackets, and Captain Henderson, who was remonstrating with an angry-looking man who looked easily a match in size and fitness. What the devil were they up to?

There was a sudden surge and Vignoles was pushed backwards, his feet hardly able to touch the ground as the mass of people, perhaps moving away from the disturbance ahead and frustrated with waiting to get inside, shifted out of control. His left shoulder collided with the wooden wall of the hut and he used this as leverage to push away the sodden woollen coat of a large man who was half-crushing him. As the pressure lessened, and he tried to lift an arm to signal to Henderson and Trinder, he felt a sharp object jab into his ribs, sending a burning stab of pain into his side. He winced, twisting awkwardly to try and see what was causing this pain, and met the intent gaze of a man with spectacles, straggling reddish hair and oddly wonky moustache.

'Hullo.' The man lifted his hat and Vignoles saw it was Friar Tuck. 'We meet just like old friends, yes? You will walk with me now, no fuss.'

'Ouch! Perhaps you'd be so good as to move your umbrella. It's hurting my side!'

'It's no umbrella, inspector.' He smiled and the metal object set off another sickening wave of pain as it struck Vignoles's broken rib.

'Look out! Ow! Hang on, don't I know you?'

The man moved unpleasantly close to Vignoles's ear and hissed, the accent now gone. 'It's a gun, Vignoles. Absolutely silent and, of course, deadly. Now we'll go this way, and do not attempt to attract attention.' He put a vice-like grip on Vignoles's upper arm and started to pull him away from the door. The press of people was still intense and Vignoles instantly realised the awfulness of the situation. He was surrounded by people, many of whom may well be prepared to help, whilst his sergeant, Anna, Henderson and goodness knows how many soldiers were just yards or even feet away, and yet if he made a squeak, he would be dead in an instant.

He looked at the strange man. 'All right, I'll come, just as long as no one else is involved.'

'That is very sensible.'

Vignoles was working his way along the cabin wall and threw a quick glance towards where he had last seen John Trinder. What to do? Attract attention and risk instant death? Even if he succeeded, without paying the penalty, would he not be leading Anna into danger? Better play along and see what the gunman wanted.

'Over there! I'm sure I saw him!' John was pointing towards the crush outside the cafeteria entrance.

'Come on,' said Henderson, 'and don't be too polite about getting through!'

'Say, who the heck d'you think you are, wise guy?' A broad hand splayed out on Henderson's chest. The crew cut American's eyes were pale blue and fierce. 'Since when d'you get the right to act like you own the damn place?'

'Not now! I'm in a hurry!' Henderson grabbed the American's wrist and pulled it away.

'Oh! So you do want trouble, eh? Right, boys, we've got a fight on our hands!' He pulled back to let fly a punch as two other men swung around, squaring up to join in.

'Stop! We are police!' The tall, bearded figure of Harry Blencowe was holding his warrant card aloft. 'We have to get through; it's an emergency.' To his surprise the Americans instantly relaxed their pugilistic manner, the wind taken out of their sails, and made a gap for them to pass through. He felt gratified that such fight-hungry Yanks showed respect to the British police.

Anna called aloud for Charles just as the crowd suddenly moved in a great wave, first forwards then backwards, some surging to look at the argument and others recoiling. She pushed forward, with Jane following closely behind, but then a wall of wet coats closed in upon her like a vice, holding her fast. She heard more shouts, grunts and a sharp cry of pain. The crowd gasped and there were a few jeers and cheers. Then John barged past them, thrusting a man aside.

'Are you all right, Mrs V?'

'I think so. I can't move. Can you see Charles?' Anna gasped.

He pushed forwards. 'Try to follow me!' He gave another shove and the crowd parted so that he, Anna and Jane were almost catapulted forwards against the wooden wall, where moments before Vignoles had been standing.

'Look! There he is!' Anna caught a glimpse of Vignoles's sou'wester.

Henderson joined them, breathing hard and with a nasty cut above one of his eyebrows. 'Bloody hot-headed fools!' He took another gulp of air. 'Charles is with someone. Who is it?'

'Couldn't see.' John shook his head.

'You follow him, sergeant. I'll try and swing around in an arc left and cut them off.' The captain left, trying to work his way through the umbrellas.

John moved quickly along the gap that had formed between the wall and the throng, Anna and Jane following, whilst Harry said something about 'going around the back' and was gone. John caught sight of the backs of two figures walking away from the hut and charged forwards, Anna close beside him.

'They're talking.' Anna had also located her husband and his companion. 'It's all right, he's a competitor.' She sounded relieved.

'But they're walking into an open area. We need to keep him amongst this crowd. Open space is perfect for a sniper.'

* * * *

Vignoles eyed the man with the gun. His moustache had started to peel away on one side. 'Well, I'll be damned! Oxenby!'

The gun barrel jabbed his side again. 'Not so loud. Do not force me to use this here. We'll take a little walk near the ranges.'

They stepped away from the noisy throng, Vignoles praying that Trinder and Henderson would not barge in at this delicately balanced moment. 'So, I was right: you were behind the whole operation, right from the very start.'

Oxenby chuckled in a mirthless way, acting as though they were two friends discussing the competition. 'Very good, inspector. I underestimated you.'

'You controlled Shrike, and ordered those soldiers to be killed.'

'I did not specify if they lived or died. But you must expect casualties in such operations. What's a handful of lives set against the tyranny of fascism and capitalism?'

'You're crazy. It's all over for you now. Your cover is blown and there's no escape from here.'

'Oh inspector, if only you had done what you were told, I would have lost interest in you, and left you alone. Oh well, such is life.' He sneered at Vignoles, his moustache barely clinging on at one end, giving his face a comical look, but his eyes were without pity. He steered Vignoles across an open area of soggy grass towards the side of the rifle range.

The rain suddenly intensified, falling in pale curtains of water that reduced visibility dramatically and making a soft sighing sound as it struck the sandy soil. Such a torrent was too much, even for those who had become used to the persistent rain. People began running for cover. A loud drumming noise rose from the canvas roofs around them.

'Keep walking!'

Vignoles pretended to stub his toe as Oxenby pushed him forwards but, in regaining his balance, Vignoles swished his oilskin so that a heavy fold slapped against the gun barrel, moving it away from his stomach. In an instant he had thrown his whole body weight against Oxenby's slight frame and they stumbled sideways, crashing into a telegraph post. Vignoles waited for the bullet to rip into his flesh, whilst clawing for his gun hand, but he did not make a good enough purchase. Was Oxenby able to point the gun at his back? Vignoles pressed his weight against Oxenby to force him against the pole, staring into the rain-speckled spectacles that shattered the image of his eyes into many small beads. He managed to work his forearm up against Oxenby's gun arm, both men now exerting all the force they could muster, locked in a motionless struggle of power, Vignoles feeling searing stabs in his chest as his ribs screamed out in pain. He could not take more than a few seconds of this. Suddenly, Oxenby launched himself forwards from off the pole, having used this to kick against, sending Vignoles flying backwards, arms flailing as he tried to regain balance. He was now falling helplessly onto his back as he watched the polished steel of the gun swing around and point towards him, the dark hole of the silencer steady. It was a strange gun, sleek and polished and looking as though made from a kit of parts. Perhaps it was a competition gun? He took a deep breath and waited for the review of his life that was supposed to flash through his mind in the moment of death, as he felt himself falling in slow motion, almost weightless as he became acutely conscious of all that was happening, of the sound of the rain hissing on the sand, of the weight of the waterproof cape as it enveloped him. He was pleased to see Anna step into the picture, hatless, her thick, dark hair glistening with rain, the collar of her burnt-orange-coloured coat turned up against the wind, a programme in one hand, her nail polish bright against the paper, a furled umbrella in the other.

In this endless moment before death he found he had time to wonder why she was not using the umbrella to shelter from the rain. Still, he should not waste time analysing his vision. The main thing was, he was being given one last chance to gaze lovingly upon his dear, precious wife — the only woman he had ever loved — before he sank into oblivion.

His shoulders met the legs of someone running behind him, and they both crashed to the ground in an untidy muddle. Henderson sprawled face-first over his head and onto the grass, then slid along the slippery surface. But Vignoles could not take his eyes off Anna, who ran boldly up to Oxenby, proffering a programme and calling in her sweetest voice, 'Oh please! May I have your autograph?'

Oxenby was momentarily distracted by this unexpected entrance stage right, turning his head to look with astonishment as Anna rushed forwards, 'Oh do, please!' He started to shape his mouth to speak, shifting his weight, and his gun wavered for a second. Vignoles rolled sideways and watched as Anna mercilessly rammed the spike of her umbrella hard under Oxenby's ribs, causing him to double over as a wad of turf blasted from the ground beside Vignoles's shoulder, the gun making no more sound than a sharp exhalation of air. Anna drove the point home, pushing on the umbrella with all of her might, forcing Oxenby to drop the pistol and clutch in desperation as the weapon impaled him, releasing an agonising cry of pain.

Vignoles got to his knees and picked up the pistol, watching his trusty sergeant rush to Anna's aid and land a left hook to Oxenby's cheek, a punch that sent him reeling, before gently hauling Anna away. Henderson was on his feet.

'Shoot!' Henderson's order was barked out and Vignoles, kneeling in the soaking grass, looked at the pistol in his hands. 'Do it!' Henderson glared at Vignoles, who continued to hesitate. He could not shoot a man in cold blood.

Oxenby was staggering backwards, his moustache had gone, spectacles skewed on his face, his hat trampled on the ground. He looked a pathetic creature, rain-soaked, choking, clawing at his stomach and groaning in pain, his pale cheek already showing a red wheal where Trinder had struck it. Vignoles remembered the three young British soldiers lured to their deaths, and his old friend Jimmy having his strings pulled and twitched by this puppet-master. Oxenby was a traitor, embedded deep inside the British government. How many others had died because of his actions? How many secrets had he sold to the enemy?

Oxenby suddenly lunged forwards. In one swift move he fended John Trinder off with one arm and used the other to reach into his waistband and pull out a miniature pistol. As the man loomed towards him, Vignoles took a sudden breath and squeezed the trigger. Soundlessly, the gun fired. Oxenby hit the ground, and did not stir.

At that moment, Harry Blencowe appeared, accompanied by a clutch of soldiers and Staff Sergeant Rose Gretton. She stood, open-mouthed for a few seconds, staring firstly at Oxenby and then at Vignoles. At last she spoke: 'Good shot, sir!'

* * * *

'A bronze medal! But that is quite the most wonderful thing, Lucy!' Anna gave her a hug.

'I knew you could do it! I am so proud of you!' Jane rushed to join in the congratulations.

'Bravo, our very own Olympian!' Harry was grinning from ear to ear.

'I'm just so sorry we missed seeing you do it.' Anna looked apologetically at the young WPC.

'It rather sounds like you had your hands full!' Lucy's eyes widened as she replied. 'My goodness, what a shocking business! But sir, from what the sarge tells me, you would have fared better than me in the pistol event. A gold medal, for certain.'

Vignoles winced slightly at her gung-ho attitude to such a horrible incident. 'Hardly. It was a thoroughly nasty job and nothing to cheer about. I can't take any credit; I just closed my eyes, pulled, and hoped for the best.'

'You stepped up to the mark when it counted, old boy.' Henderson blew a smoke ring. 'Actually, it may help lift the spirits if I tell you that Oxenby shot himself with that little pistol. You just winged him. You are absolved of all responsibility for his death.'

Vignoles felt huge relief at this news. Taking a human life, regardless of how foul and dastardly the person may have been, would never sit easily on his conscience. 'It does help to know that, but my intent was still there.' He exchanged a glance with Henderson, and they both knew that the other was remembering the security guard in Trieste. 'But let's say no more of this now,' Vignoles continued, 'there will be plenty of time to reflect upon this sorry affair in the days and weeks to come.' Anna watched a dark shadow pass across his face. He stood up and faced Lucy. 'Our heartiest congratulations! You have done us and the country proud! We'll all go into London, and, if we can find any, the champagne is on me!' A chorus of cheers rang out, followed by another round of hugs and handshakes.

'Not that it that matters in the slightest, Lucy, as you are quite the best in our eyes, but who won gold?' Violet asked.

'Mademoiselle Marguerite Chevalier, worse luck! And her charming friend, Claudette Lefebvre won silver. So, perhaps the posh frocks did help, after all.'

~ THE END ~

'The best of the railway detective novels on the market.' *Steam Railway*

'Highly recommended to lovers of steam who don't mind being frozen to the marrow by murder.' *The Oxford Times*

'Amongst the best books I have read in recent years.' *Steve Masters*

'Thoroughly recommended for providing an exciting and captivating read... Each move is meticulously told and there is a pace to the story that keeps one wanting to turn the pages.' *Mainline magazine*

'A real page-turner.' *Daily Mirror*

'An absolutely riveting story that has all the elements of a cracking yarn... A most satisfyingly spectacular, albeit gruesome conclusion.' *British Railway Modelling*

'An intriguing mystery, warm-hearted and evocative.' *Dave Baker*

'Skilfully constructed and features a host of well-observed characters. Bags of wonderful nostalgia and a gripping denouement.' *Tony Boullemier*

'Not just splendidly paced crime thrillers, not just delicious treats for all steam train enthusiasts but really vibrant social portraits... I intend putting them in my Best Read of the Year slot in the run-up to Christmas.' *Ewan Wilson, Waterstones*

'Stephen has originated the new literary genre of Post-war Austerity Gothic.' *Liverpool Daily Post*

For ordering information, please see overleaf

~ The Inspector Vignoles Mysteries Series ~

The Torn Curtain is the third book in the series, which comprises:

Each title is available from UK booksellers, including those online. The GCR bookshop stocks all titles and sales help to support the Great Central Railway.

Books direct from the author

Individual, signed copies of all the books in the series are available at £8.99 plus £2.75 postage (total £11.74). If you missed the other six novels there is a 'catch up bundle' available for just £50, post-free, each one signed by the author. Please send a cheque to Stephen Done, 28a Holland Road, New Brighton CH45 7RB stating clearly which books you require. To pay by Paypal or bank transfer, please email hastings.press@gmail.com or telephone 01424 442142